HIS PRISONER, HIS DESIRE . . .

On orders from his king, the landless knight Damian Stratton arrives in the Scottish Highlands to prevent the wedding that would unite two powerful clans against the English crown. But the intended bride—the wild, headstrong Elissa, Maiden of Misterly—cannot be so easily deterred. Though she's Damian's captive, the proud, defiant, and dangerously alluring lady will never be confined to a convent, nor will she abandon her family or her determined goal of wedding the Gordon laird—leaving Damian little choice but to marry Elissa himself!

. . . HIS BRIDE

The brazen villain will soon learn that he has met his match! Yet Elissa Fraser can't help but be moved by Damian's tenderness and nobility . . . and by a most perilous desire that has no place in her heart. Nothing good can come from uniting with this knight, who first stole her freedom, and now takes her breath away. And though she has brought the dashing enemy warrior to his knees, it is Elissa who now must surrender . . . to her passion and to his love.

"Mason is a master of her craft."
Romantic Times

B.T.

CONNIE MASON

A TOUCH SO WICKED

An Avon Romantic Treasure

AVON BOOKS
An Imprint of HarperCollinsPublishers

This is a work of fiction. Names, characters, places, and incidents are products of the author's imagination or are used fictitiously and are not to be construed as real. Any resemblance to actual events, locales, organizations, or persons, living or dead, is entirely coincidental.

AVON BOOKS
An Imprint of HarperCollins*Publishers*
10 East 53rd Street
New York, New York 10022-5299

First Avon Books paperback printing: February 2002

Avon Trademark Reg. U.S. Pat. Off. and in Other Countries, Marca Registrada, Hecho en U.S.A.
HarperCollins ® is a registered trademark of HarperCollins Publishers Inc.

Printed in the U.S.A.

10 9 8 7 6 5 4 3 2 1

Prologue

❧ ◦◯◦ ❧

London, 1746

Damian Stratton knelt before his monarch, his dark head bent, his broad shoulders rigid. Though still a young man, he had fought bravely for this honor. Damian was proud of the way he had saved his foster father's life at the battle of Culloden when a savage Scotsman had aimed a claymore at Lord Farnsworth's unprotected back, and now he was to be knighted for his courageous deed.

Damian felt the heavy weight of a sword on his shoulder and concentrated on King George's words. The monarch's strongly accented English made understanding extremely difficult, but it mattered not to Damian. He had finally earned knighthood, and he couldn't be more pleased. At the age of seven Damian had been fostered by Lord Farnsworth, and he looked upon the man as a second father.

"Rise, Sir Damian Stratton," the king said in thick, guttural English. "Your country has need of your sword and your courage. Go forth and distinguish yourself for the honor and glory of England. Serve me well and one day you will be rewarded."

Damian rose, bowed deeply, and backed out of the Presence Chamber.

"Sir Damian. Might I have a word with you?"

Damian gave Lord Farnsworth a welcoming smile. "My lord, I am at your service."

"What say you, Sir Damian? Will you go on to greater glory as a captain in the king's army?"

Despite his youth, Damian knew where his destiny lay and did not hesitate to accept the post. "Aye, my lord. I am a landless knight, without family or direction. I am willing and eager to serve my country for as long as it has need of my services."

"King George is not an ungrateful monarch, nor does he easily forget those whose services are vital to our country. Someday you will receive the recognition, honor, and rewards you so richly deserve. You are young yet. In a few years you will be a seasoned soldier and ready to accept greater challenges."

At two and twenty Damian had already survived the bloody battle at Culloden. He was strong and disciplined and ready for more formidable ventures. He would fight for king and country willingly and gladly, and perhaps one day in the not too distant future he'd receive the reward he'd been promised.

Chapter 1

Scotland, 1751

The battle-weary warrior stood on a ridge, his broadly muscled shoulders braced against the wind, his long legs firmly anchored to the gorse covered earth beneath his feet. He pushed his thick, black hair away from his strong, angular face as his silver-gray gaze made a sweeping survey of cliffs, valleys, and mountains.

After the fateful battle at Culloden, Sir Damian Stratton had served in King George's army in Scotland, quelling hotbeds of resistance in the Highlands. The rebellions had been fueled by Highlanders who had been deprived of their lands and routed from their homes with nothing but the clothing on their backs. Those defeated Jacobites still held out hope of placing Bonny Prince Charlie on the English throne.

After five years Damian was thoroughly disgusted with the militant Highlanders who continued to plot and connive for a hopeless cause. Nevertheless, he'd done whatever was required of him by his country as he worked his way up to the rank of captain. He'd looted, plundered, and killed for England; he'd never forgotten that his father had been slain by Highlanders.

Over the years Damian had lost all hope of gaining land of his own, a small piece of England where he could take a wife and raise children. Despite having distinguished himself many times over in England's defense, Damian had yet to receive a reward greater than recognition as a fearless warrior and king's champion.

The Demon Knight, the name Damian had justly earned for his relentless courage in battle, mounted his faithful steed, Cosmo, and returned to his barracks at the military outpost of Inverness.

A young soldier ran up to take the reins as Damian dismounted. Damian could tell by the boy's eager expression that something important had happened in his absence.

"What's amiss, Private?"

"A messenger from the king, Captain," Davey sang out excitedly. "He's awaiting you in your quarters."

Deep in thought, Damian entered his cramped room, wondering where he and his men were needed next in the cursed Highlands. He was weary of his post in Scotland and wished the country would drop off the face of the earth. At seven and twenty he had naught but a modest war chest, an exaggerated reputation, and a trail of women he had tumbled and forgotten.

The king's messenger jumped to his feet. "Captain Stratton?"

Damian eyed the rolled up parchment the messenger held in his hand with wary curiosity. "Aye."

"A message from London, sir. I'm to wait while you read it."

"Very well," Damian said crisply as he broke the royal seal and unrolled the parchment. Where was he to be sent now?

A puzzled expression crossed Damian's handsome features as he quickly read the message. "The king wishes me to attend him?"

"That is my understanding," the messenger said.

"Who are you, sir?"

"I am Lieutenant Ralph Thornsdale of the king's Black Watch."

"Do you have any idea what this is about, Lieutenant?"

"I do not, Captain, though I was instructed to tell you to make all possible haste to London."

" 'Tis late," Damian sighed tiredly. "I'll leave at first light tomorrow."

"Nay, sir, you must leave now, within the hour. I was told that every minute counts."

"But the men under my command . . ."

"They will be transferred to another command."

Though Damian had little respect for the Hanover king who spoke little English, he was a staunch defender of England. When king and country called, he obeyed.

London, 1752

King George reposed in a chair in his Privy Chamber, watching avidly as his Prime Minister, Lord Pelham, spoke to Damian.

" 'Tis the king's wish," Lord Pelham intoned dryly, "that Sir Damian Stratton be rewarded for his faithful service in England's defense."

Damian cocked a dark, sardonic brow. "Has His Majesty finally recalled the promise made to a young knight?"

"Ja, ja, we did not forget," the king said, nodding vigorously. "You have fulfilled the promise of youth and have become a man we can trust. Now we wish to reward your loyalty."

"Over the years you have proven your courage and fealty," Lord Pelham said. "England has need of a man with your experience and strength. Intelligence has uncovered a plot to unite two Highland clans. The united clans have the potential to become a powerful force in Scotland and a threat to England."

Damian's attention sharpened. "Does His Majesty wish me to destroy the rebellious clans?"

"Nay, there is more to it than that," Pelham said, waving his hand imperiously. "We do not wish to start another war. Given the remoteness of the land in question, we paid scant heed to it in the past. But suddenly the situation has the capability of exploding. We learned that a marriage between the Gordon laird and Maiden of Misterly is to take place at Misterly fortress. It's located near the village of Torridon, on Loch Torridon.

"Until recently we've had little reason to suspect anything was amiss there. The deceased Lord of Misterly, the great Alpin Fraser, and his male heirs fell at Culloden, and since we had little use for a fortress situated on the edges of nowhere, we paid it little heed. But should the Gordons and Frasers unite, our hold in the Highlands could be threatened. All those loyal to the Frasers and Gordons will rush to join forces against England."

"Lord Pelham," Damian interrupted, "how does this involve me?"

"Tell him, tell him," the king urged gruffly.

The Prime Minister bowed graciously to the king and continued. "You have served the king and England faithfully, Captain. For your years of devoted service, His Majesty wishes to reward you with Misterly Castle and all the lands that accompany the holding, including the village of Torridon and those serfs and freemen tilling the soil."

Damian went still, his silver eyes narrowing in disbelief. He was to be given land and a fortress in the remote regions of Scotland? He wanted land, but he'd hoped, nay, prayed, it would be on English soil. He had little liking for Scotland and those savage Highlanders. To refuse, however, would be foolish as well as dangerous.

"In addition," Lord Pelham continued when Damian remained silent, "you will be rewarded with a title and the small estate of Clarendon in Cornwall. However," the minister cautioned, "His Majesty expects you to reside permanently at Misterly and maintain order in that remote area of the Highlands. What say you, Damian Stratton, Earl of Clarendon, Lord of Misterly?"

An earl! He was being given a title and land in England! For years the most he'd hoped for was a small piece of land to call his own; he'd had no reason to hope for a title. Now he owned a title, immense lands, a village in Scotland, and an English estate. Perhaps one day, when order was restored to the Highlands, he could retire to his English estate and let a steward manage his holdings in Scotland. In truth, he wanted naught from his Highland estate save its rents and tithes.

Damian's attention sharpened on Lord Pelham as the Prime Minister pointed out what was demanded of him. "His Majesty is depending upon you, Lord Clarendon, to prevent the Maiden of Misterly from marrying the Highland laird Tavis Gordon. A strong man is needed to control the warlike Gordon clan. They are rebels and outlaws. The king is giving you temporary command of twenty of his own Black Watch to escort you to Misterly, but he expects you to hire your own mercenaries for the permanent protection of your holdings. Just remember, England stands to lose valuable lands once considered firmly under our clutches if an alliance is formed between the Gordons and the Frasers."

"I understand," Damian said gravely. "Neither the Gordons nor the Frasers will cause England trouble so long as I am Lord of Misterly."

"We trust you, Lord Clarendon," King George said. "The Demon Knight has earned our respect as well as the title and lands we have bestowed upon him."

Damian was elated, though somewhat disappointed that he must remain in the Highlands in order to collect his title and lands. Suddenly a thought occurred to him.

"What are your wishes concerning the Maiden of Misterly, Sire? Shall I have the Black Watch escort her to London?"

"Ah, the Lady Elissa," the king said. He gestured at the Prime Minister. "Tell him, Lord Pelham."

"Our sources tell us that Lady Elissa resides at Misterly with her mother, Alpin Fraser's widow.

Both her brothers fell at Culloden. His Majesty has decided to send both mother and daughter to St. Mary by the Sea Convent, a day's journey north of Misterly. The convent has already been notified of their arrival and will comply with His Majesty's wishes. Under no circumstances are you to allow Lady Elissa and the Gordon laird to marry or even communicate with one another."

"I understand," Damian said. "Your Majesty's generosity overwhelms me."

The king beamed his approval.

"One more thing, my lord," Lord Pelham said. "You will need heirs. The king intends to search for a proper heiress for you. Misterly must have a mistress."

"I'm to be given a bride? An heiress?" Damian repeated. He wasn't sure he approved of taking a wife sight unseen, but he wasn't going to quibble. It mattered not whom he married; everyone knew a man took a wife to bear his heirs and looked elsewhere for sexual gratification. He bowed deeply. "I am most appreciative, Your Majesty."

"So you should be," Lord Pelham replied. "Do not fail England, Lord Clarendon. If a marriage between Misterly's maiden and the Gordon laird takes place before you can stop it, all will be lost, including your lands and title."

Damian understood perfectly, and he wasn't about to lose everything he'd ever yearned for. Damian executed a courtly bow. "I shan't fail you, Sire."

The king waved him off. "Then be gone, my lord. I will look for the return of the Black Watch once you have everything in hand."

After that surprising interview, Damian headed over to the Cock and Bull, where out of work knights and mercenaries were known to congregate. Though it would deplete his war chest, he had need of loyal men to help maintain order at Misterly once the soldiers departed.

The smoke-filled common room stank of stale ale and unwashed bodies. Damian spotted a close acquaintance seated at a table and cut a path through the crowd to join him.

Sir Richard Fletcher saw Damian and waved him over. "Damian! 'Tis good to see you again. Come join me. What brings you to London? Last I heard you were posted in Scotland."

Damian greeted Richard enthusiastically and seated himself across the table from his friend. A barmaid appeared and he ordered two mugs of ale. The busty woman left and returned with two foaming tankards. Damian flipped her a coin, gave her a pat on her broad bottom, and eyed the enticing sway of her hips as she strolled away.

"Forget the barmaid, Damian," Richard drawled, "you can wench later. You look pleased about something. Tell me your news."

Damian returned his reluctant attention to Richard, who, if his ruddy face and slurred speech were any indication, was already deep in his cups.

Damian had met Fletcher years ago and they had remained friends. During the intervening years they had lost track of one another.

"You are looking at the new Earl of Clarendon and Lord of Misterly," Damian boasted.

"An earl!" Richard repeated, clearly impressed.

"If anyone deserves it, 'tis you. Where the hell is Misterly?"

"Ah, Dickon," Damian gushed, using Richard's nickname, " 'tis a grand fortress deep in the Scottish Highlands. I'll have vast lands of my own and a village filled with people to till the soil and harvest the crops."

"I thought you hated Highlanders," Dickon said. "Did they not kill your father?"

Damian scowled. "Aye, Dickon, but there are also a title and English lands thrown in."

"Ah, so Clarendon is an English title."

"My lands are in Cornwall, but they are inconsequential compared to my Scottish holdings. And though I care little for hostile Highlanders, I must reside at Misterly in order to keep my English title and lands."

" 'Tis about time the Demon Knight received recognition for his efforts on behalf of England," Dickon lauded. "What does the Crown demand in return for so rich a reward?"

Damian shrugged. "I must prevent the Maiden of Misterly from marrying a rebel Highland laird and maintain order."

"Surely you don't intend to go to Misterly without an army at your back," Dickon said.

"I am to have temporary use of twenty soldiers of the Black Watch. I also intend to hire mercenaries to defend my lands and protect my lady wife."

"Your lady wife?" Dickon repeated. "When were you wed? 'Tis news to me."

"The king promised me an heiress to become mistress of Misterly."

"I hope she isn't overly stout," Dickon guffawed. "All joking aside, I'm at loose ends right now and would be pleased to join your service. Mayhap I'll find a feisty Highland lass to warm my bed."

"Don't count on it. She's more like to stick a knife in your heart," Damian jeered. "Have you forgotten that Highlanders hate our guts?"

"Nay. Have you forgotten that I am a great lover?" Dickon bragged.

"You may be a handsome devil, Dickon, and a favorite with the ladies, but it will take more than fancy words to win a Highland lass's heart."

"I don't want her heart," Dickon protested. "I'm more interested in what's between her legs."

Damian loosed a shout of laughter. "Ah, Dickon, I look forward to having you with me, for I suspect I will have need of your lighthearted spirit."

"When do we leave?

"Very soon."

"Then I'd best get back to my lodging and pack."

After Dickon left, Damian glanced about the room for likely candidates willing to hire themselves into his service. His gaze found several battle-scarred soldiers scattered about the room.

Two hours later, Damian had hired twenty mercenaries grateful for the opportunity to serve the Demon Knight. He took an immediate liking to Sir Brody Clements, a grizzled knight who claimed neither land nor wife and had seen more than his share of battles. When he learned that Sir Brody could read and write, Damian appointed him Misterly's steward. Sir Brody eagerly accepted the position.

Two days later Damian rode north, accompanied by Sir Richard, his own hirelings, and twenty soldiers. Damian's thoughts were bleak despite the honor given him. Becoming overlord to people who hated him was not the life he had pictured for himself whenever he'd dared to dream of possessing his own lands. Despite his misgivings, Damian's face hardened with purpose. Misterly was his by order of the king, and if the Gordons and Frasers rebelled, he would do whatever was necessary to bring them to heel.

It was with good reason that Damian Stratton was called the Demon Knight.

Chapter 2

Lady Elissa Fraser stared into the pier glass without really seeing her image. A wealth of coppery curls tamed into a coronet atop her head; startling green eyes and slender curves were blurred by the dire predictions her old nursemaid whispered into her ear.

"Ye willna wed the Gordon laird, lass," old Nan hissed. "He isna meant for ye."

"Oh, Nan, why must you be such a skeptic?" Elissa chided. "You know Tavis was my father's choice of husband for me. He will protect us should England's king remember that my father led a Highland regiment at Culloden moor and decide to punish us. Thanks to the remoteness of Misterly we've been fortunate to have escaped his notice, but we need Tavis and his clansmen should the English suddenly recall that we exist."

"Ye willna wed the Gordon laird," Nan repeated.

"He is an outlaw and will bring trouble to our kinsmen."

Elissa turned away from the mirror. "Donna be foolish, Nan. I *will* wed Tavis. He and his clansmen have already arrived at the village kirk. Lachlan and Dermot Fraser are waiting below to escort me to my wedding. 'Tis time to leave. Are you coming with me?"

"Ye willna leave the castle," Nan said mulishly.

Elissa gave an unladylike snort. "You sorely try me, Nan. Though I love you dearly, you canna stop what is meant to be. I donna know Tavis well, but I'm sure I will come to love him. We both hate Englishmen and are staunch defenders of Bonny Prince Charlie. We have much in common."

"Mayhap not all Englishmen are bad," Nan said cryptically.

"Ha! Tell that to someone who will believe you. All Englishmen are butchers."

"Go, then," Nan muttered dismissively, "but mark my words, lass, ye willna marry the Gordon laird. My 'voices' speak of another man. Yer fate lies in another direction."

"You may *think* you hear voices, but I put no faith in such things," Elissa scoffed. "Nor do I believe in fairies or sprites or witches."

"Ye always were a stubborn child," Nan complained. "How did ye think I found ye those times ye wandered away from the castle on yer own? 'Twas my voices, I tell ye, but never ye mind. One day ye'll learn to trust me."

"I trust you, Nan," Elissa wheedled, "but not your fanciful predictions. I admit you've been right about many things, but this time you're wrong."

"Donna say I dinna warn ye, lass."

Elissa sighed as she picked up a bouquet of freshly cut flowers and turned once again to look into the pier glass. She had chosen to wear the Fraser plaid for her wedding and knew the gray, green, and white became her, though she was a mite pale. She pinched her smooth cheeks to force color into them and turned away from the mirror. Her delicate features set in determined lines, she marched out the door without waiting to see if Nan followed. She was going to marry the Gordon laird just as her father had intended, and nothing, not even her old nursemaid's vivid imagination, was going to stop her.

Damian called a halt at Misterly's outer portal. The gatehouse was deserted and the gate itself was raised. No guards patrolled the walls or were visible within the courtyard.

Damian's first view of Misterly had been impressive. The majestic towers and parapets had been visible from a great distance, rising above swirling mist and darkening sky. The promise of rain hung in the air, thick and oppressive, and Damian wondered if it were a portent of trouble.

Pushing his gloomy thoughts aside, Damian and his men proceeded through the gate and into the courtyard. Damian's shoulders were tense, his hand hovering above his sword. The alarm should have been given before now and their presence challenged. Where was everyone?

The fortress had survived the ages with grace and dignity, Damian reflected. The stark gray stone walls were softened by centuries of wind and rain and sun upon its imposing ivy-covered facade. Damian made note of the fact that sometime during the last century, glass windows had been installed.

Sir Richard Fletcher rode up to join Damian as they approached the front entrance.

"The keep appears deserted, Damian. What do you suppose happened to everyone?"

"We'll find out soon enough, Dickon. Alert the men about unexpected trouble."

Dickon turned and rode back through the ranks, relaying Damian's message in a hushed voice.

The fortress wasn't as deserted as Damian had supposed. Besides the Maiden of Misterly and old Nan, Dermot and Lachlan, both trusted kinsmen, were in the great hall waiting to escort the bride-to-be to the kirk, where the Frasers and Gordons were gathered to witness the joining of their clans.

Lachlan, whose ears were sharper than Dermot's, was the first to realize something was amiss.

He rose abruptly from the chair in which he'd been lounging and strode to the window. "Visitors," he warned.

Dermot, the oldest living Frasier, rose and limped to the window. "Wedding guests?"

Lachlan frowned. "Nay. They fly the English pennant."

Dermot loosed a string of curses. "The bastards have finally set their sights on Misterly. We all feared this would happen one day. What do ye suppose they want?"

"Misterly," Lachlan said dryly. "I fear there willna be a wedding this day. I'd best warn the Gordons and send them on their way. Tavis Gordon is an outlaw, a fugitive from the gallows."

"Aye, there has been too much bloodletting," Dermot agreed. "Use the secret passage. Persuade the Gordons to make haste back to their stronghold."

Lachlan quickly disappeared into the dark reaches of the keep.

Dermot threw open the carved oak door guarding the entrance and stood on the top step to await the English.

"Look," Dickon pointed out. "There's someone on the front steps. The fortress isn't deserted after all."

Damian left his men behind in the courtyard as he reined his horse toward the keep. He dismounted and climbed the stairs to confront the old graybeard.

"Are ye wedding guests?" the aged Scotsman asked, eyeing Damian with hostility.

"There's to be a wedding today?" Damian asked, silently thanking his good fortune for getting him to Misterly in time. Or *was* he in time?

Damian fixed the old man with a daunting look. "Has the wedding already taken place? The truth, man, I have little tolerance for lies."

"Stop it! How dare you threaten my kinsman. He's a feeble old man and canna defend himself against one such as you."

Damian's gaze went beyond the old man to a woman, nay, a young maiden whose startling green eyes glittered with outrage.

"Who are you and what do you want?" the maiden asked.

Damian drew himself up to his full impressive height. "I am Damian Stratton, Earl of Clarendon and Lord of Misterly."

"The Lord of Misterly is dead."

"I am very much alive, my lady, and eager to inspect my holdings."

Damian eyed the maiden with blatant interest. Was this the Maiden of Misterly, then? The girl was clearly dressed for a wedding. Her coppery hair, braided and twisted atop her head into a regal crown, had begun to unravel, sending unruly tendrils trailing down her slender neck. The sprinkling of freckles across the bridge of her pert nose and high cheekbones distracted naught from her vibrant beauty. And her lips! Bloody hell! Her lips were soft and full and lush. A healthy dose of pure animal lust raced straight to his loins. He hadn't expected the Maiden of Misterly to be so lovely—or so shapely. His gaze lingered briefly on her breasts before he brought his wayward thoughts under control.

"Misterly belongs to the Frasers," the girl said with asperity.

Damian's bold perusal traveled the curvaceous length of her and back. "Who are you, lady?"

Elissa stiffened her shoulders and raised her chin proudly. "I am Lady Elissa Fraser, daughter of the great Alpin Fraser, Lord of Misterly. Move aside, Englishman, today is my wedding day and I am expected at the kirk."

Damian's expression remained inscrutable despite his lustful thoughts. He hadn't expected to feel desire for the lady he'd been sent to evict from her home. But lust aside, her fate had already been decided by the Crown and he could not change that decision even had he wanted to.

"There will be no wedding today, or ever, lady," Damian said harshly. "The king has forbidden an al-

liance between the outlaw Gordon clan and the
Frasers."

"Your king canna tell me what to do," Elissa spat.
"I am a Highlander, not an English subject."

"Your kinsmen were defeated at Culloden, lady.
Your father led a regiment into battle. Had you remained in your fortress and not brought attention
upon yourself by aligning your clan with the rebellious Gordons, King George would most likely have
left you in peace. But I do thank you, lady, for your
decision to wed the Gordon chieftain has brought
me rich lands and a title."

"English butcher!" Elissa hissed. "You canna take
my home from me. I willna allow it."

Dermot, who had been listening to this exchange,
chose that moment to interfere. "Did ye say yer
name was Damian Stratton, me lord?"

Damian dragged his gaze from the volatile Elissa
to the old man. "Aye, I am Damian Stratton."

"Are ye the man they call the Demon Knight?"
Dermot asked, paling.

Damian cocked a dark brow. Was it possible that
his reputation had preceded him to this remote area?

"You've heard of me?"

"Aye, we've heard. How many of our kinsmen
did ye slay at Culloden?" Dermot spat.

"Which of your kinsmen killed my father?"
Damian returned with remarkable restraint.

"So you're the Demon Knight," Elissa said, her
eyes shimmering with hatred. Her gaze slid away
from Damian to his small army filling the courtyard.
"Do you intend to slay us, my lord?"

"Nay, no matter what you've heard about me, I
am no cold-blooded killer. I need your kinsmen to

till the soil, tend my sheep, harvest the crops and serve in the keep. Nothing will change. Things will go on as before, except that the new Lord of Misterly is an Englishman."

Elissa squared her shoulders. "What's to become of me and my family, my lord?"

Damian strode past Dermot and Elissa, forcing them to follow him into the hall. "Sit down, lady."

"Nay, I will stand. Has my fate already been decided?"

Just then Dickon came striding into the hall. "Damian, I cornered a young lad in the stables. He said the Frasers and Gordons were gathered at the village kirk, waiting for the bride to arrive."

"Ride to the kirk, Dickon. Take half the men with you in case of trouble, but avoid bloodshed if you can. To show that I intend be a just overlord, allow the Gordons to return to their stronghold and escort the Frasers back to Misterly to meet their new master."

"My clansmen are neither serfs nor slaves," Elissa snapped. "They live in the village, tend the fields and sheep, and work at Misterly because they wish to. Misterly is their home."

Damian settled his silver gaze on Elissa, admiring her spunk and the fact that she was not intimidated by him. She also possessed a formidable temper. He wondered how she would react when she learned she was to spend the rest of her life behind the cloistered walls of a convent.

He scowled. It would make things easier for everyone were she to accept her fate gracefully. Damian didn't relish having antagonistic people serving him in his new role as Lord of Misterly. If Elissa left Misterly without argument, her kinsmen might be less inclined to reject him. Unfortunately, it hadn't taken Damian long to realize that Elissa was a staunch Jacobite with a healthy hatred for Englishmen. The Highlanders had been defeated soundly at Culloden five years ago, but Elissa still fought that battle. The king was right in sending her to the convent, Damian concluded.

Staring at the too handsome, arrogant Englishman who had come to steal her home, Elissa felt naught but rage. Englishmen had taken her beloved father and brothers from her, now they wanted to claim her home.

Elissa had indeed heard of the Demon Knight. Who hadn't? Rumors held him to be a blackguard butcher without a conscience, a man who had distinguished himself at Culloden while still a lad, a man who had cut a swath of death and destruction throughout the Highlands in the name of English justice.

Without being told, Elissa knew that the English king and his Demon Knight had plans for her she wasn't going to like. Her chin firmed. She had a family to protect; she'd fight tooth and nail to make sure they weren't going to be mistreated by the man who had come to destroy her world.

If only he weren't so handsome, Elissa thought despite herself. When he looked at her with those compelling silver-gray eyes she nearly forgot to breathe. In black doublet and tight breeches, he cut a dashing figure. He was tall, muscular, and lethal, a man whose strong, handsome features had been hardened by countless battles.

Damian took a threatening step forward, but Elissa held her ground. He could glare at her all he liked; she wasn't going to give an inch.

"I understand your mother currently resides at Misterly," Damian said.

Elissa's heart pounded with dread. "My mother is ill, she canna be disturbed."

Elissa hated the way the Demon Knight cocked his dark brow, as if questioning her veracity.

"Ill or not, you will both be escorted to St. Mary by the Sea Convent within the hour. You may take your personal belongings but naught else. The keep and everything within it belongs to me."

Elissa folded her arms across her chest, her expression defiant. "Did you not hear me? My mother is in fragile health. She canna be disturbed."

Unmoved, Damian said, "I will be the judge of that. I will see her after I speak to your kinsmen."

"What of my little sister, my lord? She is recovering from a serious lung infection. Would you send her to a damp, cell-like cubicle to die? The good sisters long ago took a vow of poverty. They eat sparsely and live without the small comforts we are accustomed to. I understand they donna allow fires in their sleeping quarters. My mother and sister canna survive under such harsh conditions."

"A sister? You have a mother *and* a sister?"

"Dinna I just say so? Are you addled, my lord?"

"More like stunned. I knew naught about a sister. Nor was I informed of sickness at Misterly. How old is your sister?"

"Lora was born shortly after Father was slain at Culloden. She's just five. Mama never recovered after the deaths of my father and three brothers and rarely leaves her room. She is verra frail."

"Bloody hell! I had no idea. Nevertheless, their fate is for me to decide."

Tension thickened between them as they stared at one another. Elissa felt shaken clear down to her bones. This impossible Englishman, her enemy, was affecting her in ways that were difficult to understand. Her anger was meager protection against the sensations swirling inside her. Intuitively she knew that once she let her guard down Damian Stratton would win. She had yet to discover what he would win but she feared it was more than she was willing to part with.

A commotion beyond the heavy oak door brought Elissa's thoughts back to the problems at hand. She watched anxiously as her kinsmen filed inside the hall, followed by a small army of armed Englishmen.

"The Gordons were gone when we arrived at the church, Damian," Dickon said. "We've brought the Frasers and their clansmen here as you directed."

"Someone must have alerted the Gordons," Damian said darkly.

Lachlan Fraser stepped forward. "I warned them."

"Who are you?"

"Who are ye?" Lachlan asked curtly.

Ignoring the man's insolence, Damian said, "Damian Stratton, Earl of Clarendon and the new Lord of Misterly, at your service."

"I am Lachlan Fraser, yer lordship," Lachlan said proudly. "One of the few men to survive Culloden."

Damian admired the man's honesty. "Why did you warn the Gordons?"

"I feared bloodshed, yer lordship," Lachlan replied, "and thought it prudent to diffuse the potentially dangerous situation. I advised the Gordons to leave before yer men arrived. Tavis was reluctant at first, but decided to heed my warning when I told him ye had come with an army."

"You were wise, Lachlan Fraser. Spilling blood is not the way to preserve peace. As the new Lord of Misterly, I intend to maintain peace in this remote corner of Scotland. Pray God there will be no need for bloodshed."

Lachlan's gaze shifted to Elissa. "What will become of Lady Elissa, Lady Fraser, and little Lora? They were much loved by our laird. Mayhap I should escort them to Glenmoor, to reside with their Macdonald kinsmen. Christy Macdonald was wed to an Englishman as a child and mayhap would offer shelter to her kinswomen. Christy and Elissa are verra fond of each other."

"The king has made his wishes clear concerning Alpin Fraser's widow and daughters," Damian said. "They will be sent to St. Mary by the Sea Convent. I can make no other arrangements without the Crown's approval."

"Lord Alpin's widow and youngest daughter are ill, yer lordship," Lachlan protested.

" 'Tis unfortunate, but I cannot gainsay the king."

"Heartless wretch!" Elissa spat. "Slayer of women and children!"

Had Elissa known how close Damian was to locking her in the tower and throwing away the key, she would have been more prudent.

"I have never harmed a woman or child," he rasped through clenched teeth. "However, I'm tempted to make an exception with you."

Old Dermot quickly came to Elissa's defense. "Donna touch the lass, me lord, lest ye wish to rile our kinsmen. If 'tis peace ye want, yer going about it the wrong way."

Angry shouts of agreement followed Dermot's words, and Damian feared he'd have a rebellion on his hands if he didn't soften his stand. He needed the clan's cooperation if he was to succeed at Misterly.

"Your lady is in no danger from me," he vowed. "Misterly is your home; I need your full cooperation and loyalty for things to run smoothly. You'll find me a generous landlord. Tithes will not be raised nor taxes increased.

"I hope to maintain peace without the use of force. But make no mistake," he warned, searching the sullen faces staring back at him, "as the Lord of Misterly, I demand your respect. If I uncover signs of rebellion, I will not hesitate to retaliate accordingly."

A spate of grumbling followed his words, but Damian was quick to note grudging approval for his pledge not to raise taxes and tithes.

"All I require is your cooperation and loyalty," Damian continued.

"How can ye ask that of us when yer sending away Alpin Fraser's widow and daughters?" Dermot argued.

"Hear me, good people," Damian said, growing alarmingly short of patience. "I will tolerate no dissension. I am your lord and demand fealty. In return, you will be treated fairly."

He waited a moment for that to sink in before announcing, "There will be no alliance between the Gordons and Frasers. The Maiden of Misterly, her mother, and her sister will make their permanent home at St. Mary by the Sea Convent. Return to your homes; I've said all that needs to be said."

The assembly slowly, reluctantly, returned to their homes or duties amid much whispering and fearful glances at the Demon Knight. Damian stopped Lachlan before he could join the exodus.

"A word with you, Lachlan Fraser."

Lachlan stopped dead in his tracks. "Aye, yer lordship?"

"Obviously you and your clansmen don't agree with my acquisition of Misterly and your kinswomen's fate."

"Aye, ye have the right of it."

" 'Tis not my decision, Lachlan," Damian explained. "Tavis Gordon is an outlaw and a rebel. He wants to renew a war that was lost long ago. The Crown is justifiably opposed to an alliance between the Gordons and Frasers. 'Twould be disastrous to the tenuous peace that prevails in the Highlands. Lady Elissa cannot be allowed to wed Tavis Gordon. The only way to prevent such an alliance is to send her where she is out of Gordon's reach."

"I can understand England's concern," Lachlan admitted. "Highlanders have ever been vocal about their hatred for yer countrymen. Can ye blame them? But why should Alpin Fraser's widow and daughters be punished?"

"They are *not* being punished," Damian maintained. "They are merely being sent to a safe haven. I must obey my king in this. You have my word that no harm will befall them."

"The Frasers will hold ye to yer word, yer lordship."

Damian dismissed Lachlan with a nod of his head.

Elissa had heard enough. Nothing the Demon Knight had said was the truth. The English king wanted to punish the Frasers for their beliefs and had sent the Demon Knight to accomplish the deed.

"You lie!" Elissa charged. "The Demon Knight isna known for his mercy. Sending Mother and Lora to the convent is . . . is inhuman."

"They will not suffer," Damian argued.

Elissa stiffened her spine. She had naught to depend upon but her own wits. Sparring with Lord Damian was a frightening prospect, yet strangely exhilarating.

"What now, my lord? Will you rouse my mother and sister from their sickbeds to send them away?"

Damian's black scowl sent a shiver down Elissa's back. The new Lord of Misterly appeared short on patience. How far could she push this hard, ruthless man before he retaliated? she wondered.

"I will make my decision after I've seen your mother and sister, lady. I know enough of sickness to distinguish between a life threatening illness and an imagined one. Lead the way, lady. I will speak to your mother now."

"Nay! She couldna survive the shock."

"Follow me, me lord, I will take ye to Lady Marianne."

"Nan! How could you?" Elissa exclaimed.

Damian looked down his nose at the old hag hovering at Elissa's elbow. "Who are you?"

"Nan is my nursemaid," Elissa explained. "She lives in the keep and tends the hurts and illnesses of our kinsmen."

Damian made a thorough inspection of the diminutive old woman while her keenly intelligent blue eyes studied him in return.

"Very well, Nan, take me to Lady Marianne."

"Nan! No! Can you not see that he means us harm?"

"Nay, lass, the dark lord will nae harm yer mam. Dinna I tell ye there would be no wedding? Mayhap next time ye'll heed me. The Englishman will judge fairly after he sees for himself how ill yer mam and sister are. Follow me, yer lordship."

Elissa cringed as Damian grasped her arm and pulled her along with him. "At least someone is showing good sense," he muttered.

They climbed a circular stone staircase to the solar. Nan stopped before a closed door, then gave Damian a piercing look. "Elissa should prepare her mam before ye barge in."

Damian hesitated a moment, then nodded. "Lady Elissa may have a few moments alone with her mother."

Elissa jerked free of Damian's grasp, opened the door, and slipped inside the chamber.

Lady Marianne Fraser lay propped up in bed against several pillows, her paleness relieved by two red spots beneath her cheekbones and the brilliance of her green eyes. She lifted a frail hand in greeting.

"Elissa, my love, how fetching you look. Where is your bridegroom? Have the festivities begun? Ah, how I wish I could attend the celebration."

Elissa took her mother's fragile hand in hers and knelt beside the bed. "How are you feeling, Mama?"

Marianne searched her daughter's expressive face. "Something is amiss. What is it?"

"Oh, Mama, so much has happened since I looked in on you early this morning. I fear it will upset you."

Marianne's perceptive green eyes did not stray from Elissa's face. "I am not as ill as you think, Elissa. In fact, I'm growing stronger every day. Tell me what's wrong so that I may help you."

Elissa feared her mother was being overly optimistic about her state of health. Marianne had been sick for years with a vague illness that seemed to be sapping her strength. Nan said Marianne had lost the will to live and Elissa feared it was true.

"Has Tavis Gordon done something to upset you? I told your father I dinna like the man. He wasna right for you. The marriage hasna been consummated, we will ask for an annulment."

"Oh, Mama," Elissa said, choking down the lump in her throat, "if only it were that simple. There was no wedding. An English lord arrived this morning with a small army. Misterly has a new lord. Our home is lost to us."

"Why now?" Marianne asked in a tremulous voice. " 'Tis been five years. I had hoped the English had forgotten us."

"Those bastards have long memories. They left us in peace because our holdings were of little value to England. But that changed once they learned I was to marry Tavis Gordon. The English fear that uniting the Gordons and Frasers will disrupt peace in the Highlands."

" 'Tis Tavis Gordon's fault," Marianne said bitterly. "He's been plotting ever since Culloden. The English are right to fear the consequences should Tavis Gordon recruit large numbers of Highlanders, including our own clansmen, to his cause. I donna condone what the English did to us, but neither do I want more bloodshed. I'm sick unto death with war."

Marianne wrung her hands. "What are we to do? Lora isna well enough to travel. Her poor lungs are still weak. Does the English lord intend to turn us out of our home?"

"The English lord will do whatever is necessary to keep peace," Damian said from the doorway.

Chapter 3

Damian walked into the chamber, searching Lady Marianne Fraser's face for signs of illness, and found them. The lady was indeed ill, which made his task all the more difficult. Her lively green eyes were huge in her pale face, and her frail body barely made a swell beneath the bedcovers.

Damian was somewhat surprised to learn that Lady Fraser appeared younger than he had assumed her to be, despite her illness . . . no older than thirty-five or -six, if he was any judge. She must have married young to have a daughter Elissa's age, and Elissa looked to be somewhere between eighteen and twenty.

"Elissa tells me you've been ill, madam," Damian said.

"I'm getting better," Marianne replied. "I understand you're the new Lord of Misterly."

"Aye, madam."

"What's to become of me and my daughters, my lord?"

"The Demon Knight is sending us to a convent, Mama," Elissa spat, sending Damian a hate-filled look.

A small gasp escaped Marianne's throat. "You are the Demon Knight, my lord?"

Damian slanted Elissa a quelling look. "You have naught to fear from me, madam. You and your daughters will be safe at St. Mary by the Sea."

"Nay! Can you not see that my mother is too ill to travel?" Elissa cried. "Have you no heart? No compassion?"

Damian's face hardened. "I cannot afford maudlin sentiments, lady. I have not the necessary wealth to be ruled by my emotions. I've fought hard for everything I've earned in my life, and I'm not going to lose Misterly because I failed the king."

"Of course you must obey your king," Marianne conceded with fatalistic calm, "but I fear neither Lora nor myself is able to sit a horse. If you would be so kind as to prepare a litter, I will be most grateful."

"Nay!" Elissa protested. "We need at least a week to prepare for a journey. Only a heartless monster would force a sick woman from her bed."

Unaccustomed compassion softened Damian's inflexible stance. He couldn't in good conscience send a woman in Marianne's condition from her home, and he hadn't even seen the child yet. This wasn't good. Not good at all. There had to be some way to circumvent the king's orders without sacrificing Misterly and the culmination of all his dreams.

The idea came to him while Elissa was berating

his cruelty and implacable nature. Since Elissa was the one the king wanted out of the way, Damian saw no need to punish her sick mother and sister.

"Still your poisonous tongue, lady," Damian warned harshly. "I will accede to your wishes concerning your mother and sister if you will agree to my terms."

Elissa stared at him, her green eyes narrowing suspiciously. "Terms, my lord? What terms would those be?"

"Merely this. Your mother and sister may remain at Misterly under Nan's care if you go to the convent peaceably, without rousing your kinsmen to open defiance."

"How do I know you willna hurt my mother and sister once I am gone?" Elissa challenged.

Damian hung onto his temper by a slim thread. "My word is my honor. Your family will be cared for as long as I am Lord of Misterly. I will not send them to the convent until both are fully recovered."

"Verra well, then, I'll go." The lie came easily to her lips. She'd promise anything if it helped her loved ones.

"How wise of you," Damian said sarcastically. "You may have today to bid your family good-bye, but I expect you to be ready for travel at first light tomorrow."

Though Elissa nodded her acquiescence, Damian could tell by her belligerent stance that she wasn't happy about it. Truth to tell, he wasn't all that pleased himself. This entire situation was becoming burdensome. He hadn't anticipated the situation into which he'd been thrust, nor expected to find Lady Elissa so tempting. Were it not for the king, he'd take the lady to his bed and keep her until he tired of her . . . or the king found him a wife.

Damian found it difficult to remain indifferent to Elissa's plight with burgeoning lust raging through him. She would be a virgin, of course. He'd never had a virgin—his tastes usually ran toward more experienced women—but with Elissa he would make an exception. She'd be small, but if he was careful, she could probably accommodate him. He stifled the groan rising unbidden from his chest. No matter how much he wanted her, he would never know her carnally; all he could do was wonder if she possessed a passion to match his own.

"Duty calls," Damian said, nodding briefly at Marianne. "Say your farewells now, lady, while there is still time."

Turning abruptly, he exited the chamber. As he strode down the hallway toward the stairs, he heard violent coughing coming from behind a partially open door. He paused, briefly debated with himself, then pushed the door open. His gaze settled on old Nan as she bent over a child lying in a bed much too large for her.

"Take yer medicine, sweeting," the old woman crooned. "I'll have ye out of this bed in no time at all, if ye do as I say."

"It doesna taste good, Nan," came a plaintive reply.

"Drink up," Nan urged. "Yer going to need yer strength for what's to come."

"What's happening below stairs?" the child asked. "Has the wedding party returned? I wish I could have attended."

"Look out the window, lassie. 'Tis raining. The dampness isna good for yer wee lungs."

"Is the Gordon laird going to live at Misterly?"

"Nay, Lora, the wedding dinna take place. A new Lord of Misterly arrived today. An Englishman. He wouldna allow the wedding to take place."

"An Englishman!" A brief spate of coughing followed the child's outburst. "Are we to be sent away, then? Where will we go?"

Damian knew little about children, and had never spoken to one if memory served, but he felt compelled to speak to Elissa's little sister, if only to ease her mind.

He stepped into the chamber and cleared his throat. The child's eyes widened and she clung to Nan with a tenacity that brought a scowl to Damian's face. Was he that fearful to behold?

"You must be Lora, Lady Elissa's sister," he said, summoning forth a smile. The child was much like Elissa, Damian thought. Wide green eyes and burnished hair just a shade lighter than her sister's wreathed a small flushed face that betrayed her illness.

"Are you the new Lord of Misterly?" Lora asked in a tiny voice. "Please donna kill us, my lord."

Damian scowled. Wherever did the child get that idea? Before he could answer, Nan said, "Lord Clarendon is a great knight, lass, he wouldna hurt ye." Her fierce expression dared Damian to challenge her.

"You are safe here, child. You and your mother will remain at Misterly under Nan's care."

Lora's relieved look was quickly replaced by one of concern. "What of Lissa, my lord? Ye dinna mention her."

Damian was at a loss for words. He didn't know

how to speak to children, especially when it came to conveying unwelcome news. "Perhaps your nurse had better explain. I have duties to attend and business to conduct." He nodded curtly and made a hasty exit.

"What did the English lord mean?" Lora asked, staring at Damian's departing back.

"Donna trouble yerself, dearling," Nan soothed. "When all is said and done, Elissa will have the happiness she deserves. Demons can be tamed, and yer sister has a will nearly as fierce as the new lord's. They will have a long road with many pitfalls to travel, but 'twill be worth it."

"I donna understand," Lora complained. "Should I be frightened? I know your 'voices' tell you things. What do they say?"

"I canna explain, for sometimes my 'voices' are confusing, lassie, but I promise ye will come to nae harm."

Irritation rode Damian when he returned to the great hall and found Highlanders and Englishmen in open confrontation, separated by an invisible wall of animosity. Damian strode into their midst, hands on hips, a scowl darkening his brow.

"I will countenance no hostility in my home," he roared over the spate of angry outbursts between his English retainers and the Highlanders. "I expect everyone to treat each other with respect. I have appointed Sir Brody my steward. Take your complaints to him and he will convey them to me if they warrant my attention." He motioned Sir Brody forward so the Frasers could identify him.

"Life at Misterly will change little," he continued.

"We must all work together to maintain a peaceful existence. Who has charge of the stores?"

Lachlan Fraser stepped forward. "That be me, yer lordship."

"Very good. I want a complete inventory of food-stuffs, materials, and tools. I need to know whether the grain bins are full or empty, and what you expect the yield and condition of this year's crops to be."

Lachlan gave Damian a sullen look but nodded his compliance.

"Who is in charge of arms?"

"We have nae weapons," Dermot said.

"We do now," Damian retorted. "Thomas, come forward." One of Damian's mercenaries pushed through the throng. "You will act as master of arms. I'm sure there's an armory somewhere in the fortress. Sir Richard, you're in charge of security and billeting. I want guards posted in the gatehouse and on the walls at all times.

"One more thing," Damian said before dismissing everyone. "My table will be open to everyone, Frasers and Englishmen alike. Those who take meals in the keep will be expected to do so without dis-sention. There *will* be peace at Misterly."

Once the hall cleared, Damian strode to the kitchen in search of the cook. A rotund woman of middle years looked up from the pot she was stirring when he entered, a startled expression on her face.

"Are you the cook?"

"Aye, I be Winifred." She pointed a spoon at an-other woman standing beside a bleached wooden table. "And this be Vera, me helper."

Damian nodded in curt acknowledgment. "You are to go about your duties as before. Just remember that you will be cooking for larger numbers now. Tell my steward your needs when they arise and he will take care of them."

Later that day, Damian rode out to speak to the shepherds. He was pleasantly surprised at the size of the flocks dotting the nearby hills and valleys. Misterly would not want for fresh meat during the winter months. And judging by the look of the fields, there would also be sufficient grain to feed hungry Frasers as well as his own men. With the fresh game his hunters would bag, he didn't expect a shortage of food in the near future.

While Damian was engaged elsewhere, Elissa knelt at her mother's bedside, their voices hushed as they spoke together.

"I canna bear a separation," Lady Marianne bemoaned. "You and Lora are all I have left. I donna care about Misterly, 'tis you and your sister I worry about. What will become of you, dear one? 'Tis cruel, so verra cruel."

"I'm not going to the convent, Mama," Elissa whispered. "He canna make me go."

Concern darkened Marianne's eyes. " 'Tis dangerous to thwart the Englishman. He looks to be a hard man. I donna want to see you hurt."

"I'll be careful, Mama. When everyone is sleeping, I'm gong to leave the keep through the tunnel and make my way to Tavis's stronghold. I canna bear the thought of being cloistered within the walls of St. Mary's. Tavis is right, Mama. We must band together and fight English oppression."

"Nay, daughter. We have seen too much bloodshed already. Did Culloden teach you naught? Our loved ones have been taken from us forever."

Elissa hardened her heart against her mother's pleas. She had to escape. She'd be of no help to anyone in a convent. With Tavis's support, mayhap she could return Misterly to the Frasers and send the Demon Knight fleeing back to England.

"My mind is made up, Mama. I'm leaving tonight. I'll try to send word when I reach the Gordon stronghold."

"Promise you'll bid your sister good-bye before you leave," Marianne begged. "Lora will miss you dreadfully."

"I promise," Elissa said. Tears blurred her eyes as she kissed her mother on the forehead and quietly retreated.

A few moments later she entered Lora's chamber and closed the door behind her.

"Lissa! I'm so glad you're here. Nan said there was no wedding. I'm ever so sorry."

" 'Tis all right, sweeting," Elissa said. "You must concentrate on getting well. I have to leave, but Nan will take good care of you while I'm gone."

"You're leaving?" Lora cried. "Donna go, Lissa. I'll be lost without you. Who will protect me from the dark lord?"

"I have to go, Lora, but donna worry. Lord Clarendon has promised to care for you and Mama and I . . . believe him." Elissa prayed she wasn't placing trust where she shouldn't.

"When are you leaving?" Lora asked on a sob.

"Tonight, after everyone is asleep. Be brave, sweeting. I willna abandon you forever."

Unable to withstand Lora's pitiful sobbing, she kissed her sister and quickly left.

Elissa decided not to take the evening meal in the hall and asked Nan to bring a tray to her chamber. She was packing a small knapsack for her flight when someone rapped sharply on the door.

"Is that you, Nan? Come in."

The door opened. "Nay, 'tis Maggie. Lord Damian requests yer presence in the hall."

Maggie was one of Elissa's kinswomen from the village who served in the keep. Elissa closed the knapsack and slid it out of sight under the bed. "Tell him I'm not hungry."

"He said he willna take no for an answer."

Rather than arouse Lord Damian's suspicion, Elissa decided to honor the request. She saw him sitting at the head of the table when she entered the hall, his silver eyes fastened on her with brooding intensity. Head held high, she deliberately made her way to one of the long trestle tables and slid in beside Dermot. She paid scant heed to the Demon Knight's sour look as she placed food on her plate and made a pretense of eating.

From the corner of her eye she saw Lord Damian rise and stride purposely toward her. Her heart began to pound when he stopped behind her and placed his hands on her shoulders.

"Your place is at the head of the table," he said.

She swiveled her head around to glare at him. "My place is with my kinsmen."

"You made me a promise," he reminded her. "Do as I say and your loved ones will remain safe."

"Donna threaten me before my kinsmen, my lord."

Damian's expression hardened. He grasped her

arm, pulled her up, and hissed into her ear, "Your kinsmen must believe that you accept your fate."

"That would be a stretch of the imagination, my lord," Elissa returned sarcastically.

Rather than cause a ruckus, Elissa let Damian usher her to the head table.

"Have you made your farewells to your mother and sister?" Damian asked.

"Aye," Elissa answered sullenly.

"You will be given a proper escort for your journey," Damian allowed.

Elissa picked at her food and sipped ale sparingly. Sitting beside the dangerous dark lord was unnerving. Power emanated from his pores, and his blatant sexuality flustered her. Dimly she wondered how many women he had tupped, and whether there was a special woman in his life.

"Are you married, my lord?" The question came unbidden, startling her. She hadn't the slightest interest in the ruthless Englishman sent by his king to destroy her life.

If her question surprised him, he did not show it. "Nay, lady, I have no wife, but the king has promised me an heiress."

Elissa said nothing as she pushed her food around her plate. In a fit of pique, she fervently prayed that Lord Damian's heiress had pendulous breasts, protruding teeth, and a lumpy figure. It would serve him right, she thought, smiling with self-righteous pleasure.

"Has something amused you?" Damian asked. "Perhaps you'd like to share it."

" 'Tis naught, my lord. I'm not hungry. If you'll excuse me, I'd like to retire to my chamber."

"I will escort you," Damian said, rising gallantly.

"Donna bother, I know the way."

" 'Tis no bother." He picked up a brace of candles from the table. "After you, lady."

Elissa rose stiffly and stalked toward the spiral staircase. "Do my kinsmen know I am to be sent away tomorrow?"

"They've been told. Be careful, lady, the stairs are treacherous."

"I've climbed these same steps every day since I learned to walk," came her scathing reply. "You needn't proceed any further if you're afraid of falling."

Her words earned a growl that began deep in Damian's broad chest as he prodded her up the stairs. Elissa paused at the top landing and turned abruptly, placing a small hand on Damian's chest. " 'Tis far enough, my lord."

Damian looked beyond her. "Which chamber is yours?"

Elissa had no intention of answering his impertinent question. "Good night, my lord."

She turned with a swiftness that startled them both and consequently lost her balance. Damian had the presence of mind to anticipate disaster and reached for her. Elissa made a desperate grab for the closest support, which happened to be Damian. He was ready. He had already blown out the candles and dropped them, holder and all.

Damian's large hands sought purchase on Elissa's slim waist, preventing her headlong plunge down the stairs. A tremor went through him as he took the full length of her soft body, breast to chest, thigh to thigh. He felt her tremble. He groaned in response, and without conscious thought, shifted his hands downward to the taut mounds of her buttocks. He pulled her close, inserting his knee between her legs in a purely instinctive move.

She raised her face to him, her eyes luminous in the darkened passage. His reaction was spontaneous as his lips descended to devour hers. She looked so innocently shocked, tasted so sweet, that he lost all semblance of control. He plundered her mouth ruthlessly, his tongue battering against her lips until they opened to him.

Damian could tell she'd never been kissed before and he exulted in that knowledge. It would be a shame to confine her in a convent before she experienced passion at least once. And the vixen was passionate, whether she realized it or not. Her mouth had softened beneath his and her sweet tongue met his with a shy eagerness that brought him to throbbing erection.

Clasping her tightly against him, he lifted her and walked down the passageway. "Your chamber. Which one?"

"The one beyond Lora's," she gasped. "Please put me down. I can find my own way."

"Not bloody likely," Damian growled.

He found the chamber, opened the door with one hand, and carried her inside. He slammed the door shut with his boot heel and scanned the dimly lit room for the bed. He was so aroused he didn't feel her hands drumming against his chest, or realize that the gurgling noises rumbling from her throat were protests. It wasn't until he released her mouth and shoved her backward onto the bed that he realized things had gotten out of hand.

"Don't, please. Would you send me to the convent with my innocence ripped from me?"

He stepped back, utterly astounded. "Bloody hell! What have you done to me?"

Her breathing was erratic but her voice was strong. " 'Tis you who attacked me. I've done naught, my lord."

"Naught but entice me, vixen," Damian said harshly. He backed away from the bed, his staff a painful throbbing within the tight confines of his breeches. "Be ready to leave at first light."

Damian stormed from the chamber, his swollen sex reminding him that he needed a woman. Any woman would do. But when he searched the hall for a likely young maid, none had the vibrant red hair and glittering green eyes of the vixen he'd just left in her chaste bed. With a snort of disgust, he decided it was a good thing the Maiden of Misterly was leaving the next day, for if he had his way she wouldn't remain a maiden for long.

Elissa lay where Damian had left her, her chest rising and falling with each rapid heartbeat. What had just happened? she wondered dismally. What had she done to the Demon Knight to turn him into a rapacious animal? She touched her lips. They still tingled from his kisses, and she felt wet and swollen in private places she rarely thought about.

The new Lord of Misterly was far too attractive, too experienced for a maiden who had never been kissed. Thank God she was leaving, for nothing good could come of what happened tonight.

Elissa was still shaking when she rose and pulled her knapsack from beneath the bed. She placed a few more articles of clothing inside and snapped it shut. Then she donned a woolen dress, flannel petticoat, and warm hooded cloak. Finally, she located some sulfur matches and placed them in her pocket.

Elissa waited until the darkest part of night. When all was quiet, she opened her door and peered down the darkened hallway, breathing a sigh of relief when the only sound drifting up from the great hall was that of muted snoring.

Holding her knapsack against her chest, Elissa crept down the stairs, grateful for her dark cloak that blended with the shadows. She had tread these same stairs so many times in the past she had no need of a light to guide her. When she reached the bottom, instead of picking her way around sleeping men to reach the front door, she slipped into the dark void beneath the solar stairs. It took but a moment to locate the tunnel exit. Opening the door noiselessly, she slipped through. Fumbling in the dark, Elissa found the lamp hanging from a hook embedded in the solid rock wall and stuck a match to the wick. Guided by the lamp's mellow glow, Elissa continued down the dank passage. Mice scurried out of her way but she tried to ignore them and any other creepy creatures that inhabited the little used tunnel.

It seemed to Elissa that she had walked forever before she arrived at the exit. A few wooden steps led to a trapdoor that opened inside a shabby hut in the forest beyond Misterly. Lord Alpin had ordered it built many years ago to conceal the tunnel exit. He had also kept the passageway clear of debris should a hasty escape be needed.

The trapdoor opened with little difficulty. Elissa doused the lamp and left it on the step before leaving the tunnel and closing the trapdoor behind her. She exited the hut a few moments later and soon disappeared into the dark forest.

Damian paced his room, his mind and body too restless to sleep. He was a fighting man, one who had survived by relying on his instincts, and instinct told him all was not as it should be, even though he hadn't sought the chamber he had taken for himself in the north tower until the keep had settled down for the night. Could something be amiss with Lady Fraser and her small daughter? Sleep was impossible until he learned what had set his nerves on edge. Holding a candlestick to light his way, he left his chamber.

When he arrived in the great hall, he encountered the overflow of men who hadn't found beds in the barracks, sleeping on mats near the glowing hearth, but nothing appeared out of the ordinary. Damian glanced toward the solar, deciding to check on the ailing Lady Marianne and Lora before returning to his bed. He mounted the stairs and found naught amiss. His instincts had failed him, he decided, as he turned to retrace his steps to his own chamber. Suddenly someone stepped out of Lora's room, startling him. He recognized Elissa's kinswoman but didn't recall her name. When she saw Damien, she nearly dropped the candlestick she carried.

"My lord! You frightened me."

"Who are you? What are you doing up so late?"

"I'm Maggie Fraser. I often stay with Lora when she has a bad night."

"What seems to be the trouble?"

"She's coughing something fierce. I was on my way to ask Nan for a potion to ease her."

"Then you'd best hurry, mistress. Unless my ears deceive me, the child is still coughing."

Maggie scurried off. Since Damian was already awake, he decided to sit with the child until Maggie returned. He stepped into the chamber and approached the bed. Lora was stirring restlessly after a fit of coughing, her small face flushed. She saw Damian standing over her and her eyes widened with fear.

"Nay, child, you have naught to fear from me. Rest easy. Mistress Maggie has gone for Nan."

"I donna like you," Lora said. "I want Lissa."

"I'll get her for you."

Lora shook her head. " 'Tis too late. She's already gone."

"Nay, she's just . . ." Damian went still as a prickling sensation crawled up the back of his neck. "What are you saying? Why wouldn't Elissa be in her chamber?"

Apparently Lora realized she had spoken out of turn, for she clapped her palm to her mouth. Damian gently removed her small hand.

"Tell me, Lora, 'tis all right. If your sister is not in the keep, she could be in trouble."

Lora said naught; she merely stared at Damian through luminous eyes.

"Donna frighten the lass, me lord."

Damian spun on his heel, surprised to see Nan standing behind him. "I didn't hear you enter." Nan leaned over the bed and touched Lora's forehead. "I wasn't trying to frighten the child, Nan.

I'm concerned about her health. Will she be all right?"

"Aye. She's getting better, but sometimes her cough becomes worse during the night. I'll handle it."

"Administer to her, then. I'll wait in the passage. I would have a word with you."

Turning on his heel, he left the chamber. But instead of pacing outside the door, he rapped on Elissa's door and burst inside when no answer was forthcoming. He was angry but not surprised to find the bed empty and Elissa missing. Muttering a curse, he turned abruptly, almost knocking Nan down.

"What do you know of this?" Damian roared.

"Naught."

"You're lying. You're not helping your mistress by withholding the truth. Did she leave the keep? How did she get past the guards? A young maiden wandering the countryside on her own is an invitation to disaster."

"She willna come to harm, me lord," Nan said with utter confidence.

Damian gave her a strange look. "What makes you so certain?"

"I know many things," she said cryptically. "Ye'd best hurry if ye want to catch her before trouble finds her."

Damian realized there was more to the old crone than met the eye. "I'll leave immediately. Can you tell me in which direction to look? Does she seek Tavis Gordon?"

Nan shrugged. "Mayhap. His stronghold is deep in the mountains, me lord, but ye'll find Elissa in the forest."

Damian's eyes narrowed suspiciously. "Are you

telling me the truth? I thought all Frasers considered me the enemy."

"There are many definitions for enemy, me lord. Neither Elissa nor Misterly will find peace with the Gordons. Elissa doesna believe me but she canna stop the hand of destiny."

Damian shook his head in dismay. He already knew his own fate and it didn't include the Maiden of Misterly. The heiress promised to him by the king was his future.

Chapter 4

Elissa plunged deep into the forest, ignoring the brambles snagging the hem of her petticoat and tree branches snatching at her cloak. The rain that had fallen earlier had turned the earth mushy beneath her sturdy boots but the sky had miraculously cleared and the moon had suddenly appeared to guide Elissa to her destination. She didn't know exactly where to find Tavis's stronghold, but she was convinced that if she didn't find him, he'd find her.

Tavis had once held vast lands south of Misterly, but he had been forced into hiding after Culloden and his lands had been given to an English lord. Tavis and the surviving clansmen had fled into the mountains, where they lived in crude huts and caves. Though they were considered outlaws, they had lived in relative freedom ever since. Then word reached the king that Tavis Gordon was planning insurrection and intended to unite his clan with the Frasers.

Following a little used path through the forest, Elissa was making good time until a bank of rain-swollen clouds scudded across the moon, pitching the forest into blackness. Then a heavy mist rose up and swallowed her.

Elissa soon lost her way amid the towering trees. She knew that to go on without light to guide her was dangerous. But some good would come of the weather that had suddenly turned against her, she reflected. It would hinder searchers, should Lord Damian decide to look for her.

Elissa shivered as the first drops of rain hit her face. She stopped beneath a broad-leafed tree and slid down its trunk to the ground. Resting her head against her knapsack, she decided the best thing to do was to rest while she could and continue her journey at sunup.

She hadn't intended to sleep, but her eyes were so heavy she couldn't hold them open. Despite her best intentions, she huddled miserably beneath her cloak and drifted off.

Damian was wet, cold, hungry, and furious. The chilling rain did nothing to improve his foul mood. He'd been tramping through the forest for hours. When the moon had scudded beneath a bank of clouds and rain began to fall, Damian cursed his rotten luck. He was somewhat consoled, however, by the knowledge that Elissa had to be as uncomfortable as he was.

As rain poured down upon his head, his temper notched upward several degrees. By the time a murky dawn arrived, Damian was in a murderous mood. Didn't the red-haired vixen realize the dangers an unprotected maiden might encounter in these turbulent times? Brigands and four-footed predators roamed these forests in search of prey, and Elissa was a tasty morsel.

Damian reined his horse through the forest, his keen eyes searching for clues. He wasn't about to give up, for to do so would be admitting defeat at the hands of a woman. In all his years as a soldier, he'd never lost a battle or given up. If Elissa eluded him now, he stood to lose the future he'd always dreamed of. Nay, he decided, his face hardening with resolve. Elissa would *not* escape him. There was too much at stake.

Suddenly Damian spied something caught on a thorn and reined Cosmo to a halt. He reached out and plucked a small piece of material from the bush. Turning it over in his fingers, he recognized it as a scrap of flannel. Was this a piece of Elissa's petticoat? His lips curved into a smile. Had Elissa seen that smile, she would have been terrified.

A short time later, Damian found a small footprint in the soft earth and another piece of cloth. Grimly determined, he pushed forward. Caught up in the thrill of the chase, rain, cold and hunger were forgotten as he became a hunter running down his prey.

Elissa awoke with a start, dismayed to find the murky light of a dismal dawn greeting her. She picked herself up from the ground and stretched. Her bones protested the exercise as well as the chill that had stiffened them. Her stomach rumbled but she ignored it; she had no time for hunger. It was her own fault she'd forgotten to provide food for her journey and had eaten very little the day before.

She picked up her knapsack and quickly found the path she had abandoned during the night. Shortly thereafter she heard a rustling noise behind her and froze. Was an animal stalking her? There were plenty of them in the forest. Mayhap brigands. Or poachers. Pray, Lord, not the Demon Knight. 'Twas unlikely he'd find her so soon; her absence wouldn't have been noticed yet. The sound grew closer, louder. Someone was definitely behind her. When she heard a horse blowing through his nostrils, she dropped her knapsack and fled, her heart bouncing erratically against her ribcage.

Elissa ran as fast as her legs could carry her but the pounding hooves came closer, closer still, until she feared she'd be run down. She dared a glance over her shoulder and saw a sight so frightening it caused her to stumble. A dark rider perched high upon a black stallion, his cloak billowing out behind him and his powerful thighs girding his mount, came pounding after her. That one brief glimpse hadn't revealed her stalker's face, and Elissa was sure she was better off not seeing it.

Abruptly she was lifted off her feet. She felt the strength and determination in the brawny arm clasped around her middle and gasped out a painful breath. She was a scant moment away from expiring from lack of air when the horse skidded to a halt and she was dragged up roughly into the saddle before her captor.

The man holding her between his strong thighs said nothing, as if waiting for her to speak. Though she was frightened by this dark devil, her fury overcame prudence.

"How dare you!" Elissa rounded on her captor. "Do you know who I am?"

When an ominous silence ensued, Elissa raised her eyes to her captor's face and fear renewed its hold on her.

"You!"

"Were you expecting someone else?" he mocked. "Tavis Gordon, mayhap?"

"How did you . . . who told you? I shouldn't have been missed yet."

"I should have placed a guard at your door," Damian growled in a threatening voice. "What a fool I've been! I didn't realize how desperate you were to reach Tavis Gordon. Perhaps I've misjudged you. Perhaps you know Tavis Gordon more intimately than I assumed. Are you lovers?"

Elissa raised her arm to strike Damian, but he grasped her wrist and held it behind her.

"Don't ever do that again," he warned.

"Donna insult me again," Elissa shot back.

Elissa ground her teeth in frustration when Damian reined his horse back toward Misterly. "Where are you taking me?"

"Home. How did you leave the keep without being seen? The gate was closed. Is there a way in and out of the fortress that I don't know about?"

Elissa glared at him, her lips clamped tightly together.

"Not talking?" Damian mocked. "Never mind, if a secret exit exists, I'll find it."

She made a sound of derision deep in her throat. "Your guards aren't as vigilant as you think. There is no secret exit. I'm warning you, Lord Damian, there are no walls high enough to keep me where I donna wish to be. Send me to the convent if you wish, but I'll not stay there."

Her words created a firestorm in Damian's brain. He hadn't counted on the Maid of Misterly's rebellious nature. Would the convent walls contain her? he wondered. He knew precisely what would happen if she escaped. Her people would follow her to the Gordon stronghold and that which he'd hoped to prevent would happen.

There had to be some practical way to keep Elissa from finding her way to Tavis Gordon. The problem seemed insurmountable, but Damian considered himself up to the task. He pondered the situation all the way back to the fortress.

Sir Richard met them. "You found her," he said, slanting Elissa a quelling look.

"Aye, Dickon, soaked through but apparently unhurt. Have a tub and hot water sent up to my chamber."

"Will she be traveling to the convent today?"

"Nay, Dickon, I'm not sure sending her away is the best solution."

"What! Are you daft, Damian? The woman is a troublemaker. Send her away before she causes more problems. How did she escape without being seen?"

"If you think I'm trouble now, wait until they have me in the convent," Elissa charged. "They'll rue the day."

" 'Tis exactly what I'm afraid of," Damian muttered darkly. "See to the tub, Dickon."

"As you will, but don't say I didn't warn you."

"What *do* you plan to do with me, my lord?" Elissa asked.

"I haven't decided. Until I do, you'll remain locked in the tower."

Damian saw her shiver and realized she was as

cold and probably as hungry as he was. Grasping her arm, he ushered her through the hall to the winding staircase that led to his tower chamber.

"I demand to be returned to the solar."

Damian gritted his teeth. "You have no right to demand anything. Your fate lies entirely with me. I don't think the king cares whether you're in a convent or . . ." His words ended in an ominous silence.

Elissa's small chin notched upward. "Go ahead, finish your sentence. Nay, let me do it for you. I would be less of a problem to your country if I were dead."

"Don't put words in my mouth, lady. Right now I'm not too kindly disposed toward you. I'm soaked to the bone and in need of food."

"And I'm not?"

Elissa's prickly bravado amused Damian. She appeared fearless, but he knew she wasn't as brave as she pretended, for her lips were trembling and her hands were clasped so tightly her knuckles were white.

When they reached the stairs, Elissa dug in her heels. Rather than argue, Damian swept her into his arms and carried her up the stone staircase as if she were weightless.

Damian's chamber was the only one in that particular tower. His door stood open and he carried her inside, slamming it shut behind him. The moment he set her on her feet, Elissa whirled to confront him.

"Why have you brought me here? Don't you dare touch me."

"Fear not, lady. As thorny as you are, I fear I'd bleed to death from a thousand puncture wounds."

"I wish to see my mother and sister."

"I'm afraid that's impossible. You're to see no one

until I've decided what's to be done with you."

"I thought that had already been decided."

"I'm not sure the convent's the wisest choice. I need time to mull over the options where you're concerned. As you so kindly pointed out, convent walls are not secure enough to keep you from escaping and running to Gordon. Perhaps I should wash my hands of you and send you to London for the king to deal with."

Elissa recoiled in horror. "Nay! You'd be sending me to my death."

"Not necessarily. Perhaps the king will find an English husband for you. Someone who would beat you into submission."

The fiery sparks in her green eyes all but singed him. "I willna go to London and I willna marry an Englishman!"

Damian's answer was forestalled by a discreet knock on the door. He strode forward, flung it open, and stood aside as servants rolled a large tin tub into the chamber and placed it before the hearth. While Damian looked on, the tub was filled with buckets of hot and cold water. The lass, Maggie, remained behind, casting anxious glances at Elissa.

"You may go," Damian said dismissively.

"Nay, stay," Elissa said. "The Demon Knight means me harm."

Damian swung around to face Elissa, one dark brow winging upward. "Your lies are beginning to annoy me. No harm will come to you at my hands." He turned back to Maggie. "You have my word on it, mistress. Kindly shut the door behind you."

"Donna believe him, Maggie! He means to ravish me."

"Out!" Damian shouted.

"What's amiss?" Sir Richard asked, poking his head into the chamber. "I could hear you shouting all the way down to the hall."

"Mistress Maggie has duties elsewhere, Dickon," Damian bit out. "She's not needed here."

"Damian . . ."

"Nay, Dickon, I know what I'm doing. Escort Mistress Maggie from my chamber and close the door behind you."

Dickon looked as if he wanted to object but apparently thought better of it. Grasping Maggie's arm, he drew her out into the passageway. Damian turned the iron key in the lock and placed it in a pouch he carried on his belt.

"Get in the tub," Damian ordered. "You'll catch your death in those wet clothes."

Elissa glanced longingly at the tub and shook her head. "Not until you leave."

He cast her a dark look. "Shall I undress you? I'm quickly losing patience, lady. I intend to use the tub after you and I don't enjoy bathing in cold water."

He took a menacing step forward.

"Nay! I . . . I'll do it myself. Turn your head."

Damian stared at her, then turned his back and walked to the window. "You needn't worry. Your dubious charms hold little interest for me."

He nearly choked on the lie. When Elissa sat between his thighs on Cosmo's back, he'd been painfully aware of every tempting curve beneath her wet dress. Not even his anger could make him forget the kisses they had shared, or the way her rounded bottom filled his hands. He remembered her soft, supple body and firm, tempting breasts. He'd wanted her then and he wanted her now.

Damian heard the rustle of clothing and felt a tightening in his groin. She was undressing. Blood swelled his loins. A splash of water was followed by a contented sigh. Torment rode him as he visualized his hands sliding over her slick flesh. Suddenly the window and the scenery beyond held little appeal for him and he whipped around. His gaze found her.

Her eyes were closed, her head resting against the rim, the upper curves of her rounded breasts visible above the water line. Because the tub wasn't large enough to accommodate her length, her legs were bent, revealing dimpled knees. Damian's heartbeat accelerated. What in bloody hell was wrong with him? He'd seen more than his share of naked women in his lifetime, so why should this insignificant woman affect him?

As if aware that he was watching her, Elissa opened her eyes and met his heated gaze. She gasped and pulled her knees up to her chest, denying him a view that pleased him greatly.

Her voice rose on a note of panic. "What are you doing? Turn around."

Damian's silver eyes darkened with ill-concealed desire, but he forced himself to remain motionless. Had he succumbed to his body's dictates, he would have swept Elissa from the blasted tub and carried her to his bed for a night of unbridled passion. This wouldn't do. He had to find a willing woman soon or go crazy.

"Enjoy your bath," Damian grunted as he strode away. "I'll take my bath elsewhere."

He fished for the key and unlocked the door.

"Wait! I need fresh clothing. Those I was wearing are soaking wet. I canna leave without clothes."

"I'll see that your chest with your personal items are brought to you. As for leaving this chamber, ah, well, that's another story. I don't trust you, lady. You're willful, stubborn, and untrustworthy. 'Tis becoming increasingly apparent that the convent won't detain you."

Elissa blanched. "Then what . . . ?"

Damian didn't offer an answer as he left her and turned the key in the lock.

Truth be known, he didn't have an answer.

Damian returned to the hall. He stopped to draw himself a mug of ale from a nearby keg, then wearily sank down in a chair before the hearth. Dickon joined him a short time later.

"What are your orders concerning the Fraser wench?"

Damian stared thoughtfully into his mug. "I'm not sure sending her to the convent is a good idea. The lady is as resourceful as she is beautiful. I'm beginning to think there is no clear answer where Elissa is concerned. 'Tis obvious the convent won't hold her for long. Look how easily she found her way out of the keep. She'll escape the convent within a week of her arrival and flee to the Gordon laird."

"You have to obey the king, Damian."

"The Crown is interested only in keeping Elissa and Gordon from marrying."

"That's why she's being sent to the convent," Dickon pointed out. "Did she tell you how she managed to leave the keep?"

"Nay, but I'll find out. I'm inclined to believe there's a secret exit."

"Of course," Dickon exclaimed. "That's how she did it. Shall I help you search?"

"Nay, I'll find it."

"What are you going to do? Perhaps you should send her to London and let the king decide her fate."

Damian scowled. "I might be sending her to her death. I don't want that on my conscience."

"Bloody hell, Damian, there must be something you can do. I say send her to the convent and let the nuns worry about her. You can't be blamed for her actions once you've carried out the king's orders."

"Ah, but I *could* be blamed, Dickon. I'm supposed to prevent a marriage. Should that marriage take place, I stand to lose my lands and my title."

"I'm glad I'm not in your boots. What will you do with the troublesome baggage in the meantime?"

"Lock her in my chamber where I can watch her and throw away the key."

Dickon's eyebrows shot upward.

" 'Tis not what you think, Dickon, though I admit I find the lady beyond tempting. My only concern, however, is isolating her from those who might be inclined to release her. I've inspected every chamber in the fortress and mine is the only one decently furnished besides those in the solar."

Dickon sent him a skeptical look. "Where will you sleep?"

"I haven't decided," Damian said cryptically.

"Good luck," Dickon said, rising.

Damian sat brooding over his ale until his damp clothing reminded him that he was in desperate need of a hot bath and food. Hailing a maid passing through the hall, he asked that a tub and food be sent to the barracks and issued orders concerning Elissa's immediate needs.

* * *

Elissa heard the key turning in the lock and looked up expectantly. The door swung open and two men entered with her trunk balanced between them. Maggie hurried in after them, carrying a tray of what Elissa hoped was food.

Elissa huddled beneath the blanket she'd worn since her bath, watching as the men set her trunk down and retreated, leaving her alone with Maggie.

"I brought food," Maggie said, arranging the tray on a nearby table.

"Have you spoken to Lord Damian?" Elissa asked as she nibbled on a hunk of cheese. "Did he reveal his plans for me?"

"Nay. He but instructed me to bring food to ye and fetch yer clothing. Oh, Elissa, what has he done to ye? Does he want ye for his mistress? Does he intend to ravish ye?"

"He's done naught . . . yet, but I donna trust him," Elissa said thoughtfully as she stuffed a piece of bread into her mouth.

Elissa was wary of Lord Damian but chose not to unburden herself to Maggie. She'd seen the look in the dark lord's eyes; she could still feel the pressure of his kiss upon her lips and his hands upon her body. She might be a virgin but she wasn't stupid. Damian wanted her. Wanted her in the same way a virile man wants a woman.

"What can I do to help?"

"Who has access to this chamber?"

"Just me. Everyone has been warned away. The Demon has even posted a guard outside the door. He doesna trust ye, Elissa."

"The bastard," Elissa bit out. "Dinna worry, Maggie, I'll think of something. He canna keep me under lock and key forever."

"What if he . . . you know . . . wants ye in his bed?"

She chewed on her bottom lip. Maggie was too close to the truth. "He wouldna dare. I wouldna let him even if he did."

"Let me help you dress," Maggie said, removing items of clothing from Elissa's chest.

"Aye, I'd prefer to be dressed when the Demon returns." Placing temptation in his path was the last thing Elissa wanted.

To Elissa's relief, the Demon Knight didn't return. She had no idea where he made his bed and didn't care as long as he stayed out of hers. Though she professed not to care, when Maggie appeared with her breakfast the following morning, she casually asked her kinswoman if she knew where and with whom Damian had slept last night.

"Dermot said Lord Damian spent the night in the barracks," Maggie informed her. "I donna believe any of our kinswomen would have accommodated him had he demanded a woman, but some of the village girls have been . . . frolicking with the English soldiers since they arrived at Misterly. Mayhap Lord Damian invited one of them to his bed."

"Perhaps," Elissa said sourly. She had no idea why the thought of Damian bedding a woman of easy virtue should bother her, but it did.

"Speak of the devil," Maggie hissed as the door opened and Damian stepped inside.

"Be gone, mistress," Damian said, holding the door open for Maggie.

Maggie sent a pitying look at Elissa and scurried out.

"I've come for my personal belongings," Damian said.

"When may I leave this chamber?"

"Perhaps never," Damian returned curtly.

Elissa became immediately defensive. "You canna keep me under lock and key forever!"

"I am the master here, I can do whatever pleases me, and it pleases me to keep you confined."

"I'd prefer the convent."

"I'm sure you would. I've decided, however, that confining you in a convent isn't satisfactory. I considered sending you to London for the king to deal with, but after careful consideration I decided he'd deal more harshly with you than I would. I don't wish you harm, Elissa."

"I willna be your mistress," Elissa asserted. "I know how men like you treat women and I willna allow you to corrupt me."

"Saving yourself for Tavis Gordon?" Damian mocked.

"He's a better man than you are."

"That remains to be seen."

"I'll die cooped up like this."

Damian cocked his head to one side and stared at her. "Aye, perhaps I'm being unreasonable. I'll instruct your guard to escort you outside for a stroll each morning and afternoon."

He placed some personal items inside his clothes chest and turned to leave.

"Wait! I donna wish to turn you out of your chamber. If I'm to be confined, why not lock me in my own room?"

"The tower is easily guarded," Damian explained. "Too many people come and go to the solar during the course of a day. You'll stay here until I decide otherwise."

"Where will you sleep?" The moment the words were out she wished them back.

A slow smile stretched Damian's lips. "Do you care?"

Elissa turned her back on him. "Nay. You can sleep with the hogs for all I care."

Suddenly she felt him behind her. Close. Too close. The heat of his body scorched her clear through the layers of her clothing. He touched her shoulder and she stiffened. A cry of alarm left her lips when he spun her around and forced her against him.

"Are you as innocent as you pretend, lady? I wonder . . ."

"Wonder no longer, my lord," Elissa bit out. "No man has ever touched me."

"I am a man, my lady, and I have touched you."

"Without my permission. Let me go."

"You enjoyed my kiss, Elissa, I know you did."

"I endured it."

"Can you endure another?"

"Nay. You have no right to torment me like this."

Damian dropped his arms and backed away. "You're correct. I have no right. Please excuse my behavior. Someone will come for my chest." Then he was gone.

Elissa let out a shaky sigh. Her knees were quaking and her hands trembling. What was wrong with her? Damian had but to touch her and her wits scattered.

What would have happened had he kissed her again? Sweet Mother, just thinking about the arrogant Lord of Misterly kissing her, touching her, made her heart pound and her blood heat. She had to be mad.

After that uncomfortable confrontation, Elissa was escorted from her prison chamber for an hour twice a day to stretch her legs in the courtyard. She knew her clansmen weren't happy with the situation for Maggie had told her there was mutiny afoot. She worried excessively about her mother and sister, until Maggie revealed that Lord Damian visited them regularly to inquire about their health and needs. Was there a side to the dark lord Elissa hadn't discovered yet?

Late one afternoon Elissa was sitting in the courtyard with her eyes closed, her face tilted up to the waning sun, when she heard a familiar voice say, "You're looking well, lady. Do you have everything you need?"

Her eyes flew open. "I need my freedom, my lord. And I want to visit my mother and sister. 'Tis cruel of you to keep me apart from my family."

Damian gave her a long, thoughtful look. "Perhaps you're right." He offered his arm. "Allow me to escort you to the solar so you may see for yourself how well your family is being treated."

Joy suffused Elissa's face as she rose and placed her fingers on Damian's arm. Dark looks followed them as they progressed through the hall and ascended the steps to the solar.

"Your kinsmen appear displeased with me," Damian said, scowling. "I had hoped for acceptance."

"You canna blame them for disliking you. Everything has changed for them. Their future is uncertain and they donna approve of the way I'm being treated."

"I've done nothing to you."

"I'm your prisoner."

"Hardly," Damian scoffed.

They reached the top landing. "Who would you like to visit first, your mother or sister?"

"Mother, please."

Damian knocked on Lady Marianne's door and waited for a reply.

"Come in, my lord."

Elissa sent him a startled look. "How does she know 'tis you?"

"I usually visit this time of day. Shall we go in?"

Elissa was stunned. Did the Demon Knight have a heart after all? It appeared he had compassion for everyone except her. Her thoughts fled when she saw her mother, still pale, still frail, but looking much better than the last time she'd seen her.

Marianne's eyes lit up and she stretched out her arms. "Elissa! My dear one. Thank you, my lord, for bringing her to me."

"I'll wait outside," Damian said, closing the door behind him.

"Are you all right, Mama?" Elissa asked, kissing her mother's pale cheek. "You look better. Has Nan concocted a new elixir for you? Lord Damian hasn't mistreated you, has he?"

"I do feel better, dearling," Marianne said. "Mayhap 'tis due to Nan's medications and mayhap 'tis because I've decided life is worth living. And nay, Lord Damian has been verra kind. We've had some long talks. He made me realize that giving up isna fair to you and Lora."

Stunned, Elissa could do little more than stare at her mother. "The Demon Knight said that?"

"Aye, and more. You havena been harmed, have you? I donna like to think Lord Damian would hurt you but I'd rather hear it from your own lips."

"I'm fine, Mama. I've not been harmed in any way. I hate being locked up, and not knowing what's to become of me is unnerving, but somehow I'll find a way to get us to Tavis Gordon," she vowed. "You're getting better. One day very soon, you, me and Lora will leave Misterly together."

"Take care, daughter," Marianne warned. "What you wish for may not be the best thing for you."

Suddenly the door opened and Lora flew inside. Damian followed in her wake. Lora's cheeks were flushed but she appeared to be well on the road to re-covery. Elissa opened her arms and Lora rushed into them.

"Lissa! I've missed you."

Elissa sent Damian a sour look over Lora's head. "I'd have come to see you sooner had it been al-lowed. What are you doing out of bed?"

"I donna have to stay in bed," Lora replied, beam-ing. "Nan said I'm almost well. I hardly cough any-more. Damian promised to take me on his horse as soon as Nan says it's all right."

"You call his lordship 'Damian'?" Elissa gasped.

"Donna scold me, Lissa, Damian said I could." She skipped over to Damian and grasped his hand. "Will you tell me a story before I go to sleep tonight, Damian?"

Elissa's mind refused to believe what she was hearing. What was going on? She met Damian's amused gaze over Lora's head and felt the shock of it clear down to her toes.

Chapter 5

Once she had returned to Damian's chamber, Elissa sat in the windowseat and let her mind wander. It was difficult to reconcile the ruthless man she knew with the gentle demeanor that Damian presented to her mother and sister. Was she the one who brought out the worst in him?

It was growing dark. Elissa gazed out the narrow window at the mountains rising in the distance. How she wished she were free. She should be with Tavis right now instead of a prisoner of the Demon Knight.

A whisper of sound brought Elissa's head around. The door opened and Maggie entered the chamber.

"I've brought yer supper, Elissa. Come and eat."

Elissa sighed. "Set it down, Maggie, I'll eat later. I'm not hungry right now."

Maggie set the tray down, glanced furtively at Elissa, then whispered, "There's trouble brewing."

"What kind of trouble?"

"Our kinsmen are angry with his lordship for treating you badly."

"Sweet Mother," Elissa said on a shaky breath. "I want no bloodshed on my account. You must tell our people that I have not been mistreated, that I am well and coping."

"I will tell them," Maggie said in a hushed voice.

The conversation drew to a quick conclusion when Sir Richard knocked on the door, then poked his head inside. "Ah, there you are, Mistress Maggie. You're wanted below."

"I'll try to return later," Maggie hissed.

Elissa paced restlessly, her supper forgotten. There had been enough blood spilled at Culloden to last a lifetime and she hoped her kinsmen realized they had neither arms nor men to launch a rebellion. She wanted none of her kinsmen hurt on her account.

When Maggie failed to return to her chamber that night, Elissa sought her bed, but sleep was hard won.

Damian awoke at dawn and threw aside his blanket, shivering in the morning chill. Why was the barracks so cold, he wondered, thinking fondly of the comfortable room he'd given up to his provocative prisoner.

Banishing thoughts of Elissa, Damian stared at the cold hearth, a small frown drawing his brows together. Usually one of the servants came early and laid a fire in the grate, but for some reason no one had performed that duty today. He'd learned to heed his instincts and they told him now that something was amiss.

Dressing quickly, Damian left the barracks to correct any problems that might have arisen. He entered the hall, his gaze skipping over the empty chamber and settling on the cold hearth. Where was the cheery fire that usually warmed the cavernous room? Where was the sound of voices usually heard this time of morning?

The air carried no cooking odors, no sounds of pots and pans banging in the kitchen. An ominous silence prevailed. Curious, Damian strode down the passageway to the kitchen. It was deserted. No food was being prepared for the hungry men who would soon crowd around the trestle tables to break their fast. Damian spun around and returned to the hall, his boot heels echoing hollowly on the flagstone floor. Men were gathering in the hall for food and ale now, and Damian wondered how in bloody hell these men were going to be fed.

Damian spied Dickon and intercepted him.

"What's amiss, Damian?"

"I wish I knew. Have you seen any Frasers about this morning?"

"Nay, but I'll check the kitchen."

"I already did. No one's there. The whole bloody fortress is deserted. If Elissa is behind this I'll wring her beautiful neck." The words had scarcely left his mouth as he whirled on his heel and marched resolutely toward the tower staircase.

He halted abruptly when he spied Dermot hobbling into the hall.

"Where is everyone?" Damian asked harshly. "There's no food on the table nor fires in the grates."

"Nor will there be if ye continue to keep Elissa imprisoned in the tower," he charged. "We donna like what yer doing to our lass, me lord."

"I've done nothing," Damian defended. "Ask Mistress Maggie, if you don't believe me."

" 'Tis not good enough, me lord. Our lass shouldna be locked away from her kinsmen. If ye donna release our lass from the tower, no one will cook yer meals or till yer fields or harvest yer crops. The shepherds will let yer sheep go astray. Yer fortress will fall down around yer ears without the villagers who come in each day to serve ye. Release the Maiden of Misterly, yer lordship, and the people will return to their duties."

Rage seethed through Damian. He was Lord of Misterly; how dared they dictate to him?

From the corner of his eye, Damian spied Sir Richard standing nearby. "Dickon! Assign three men to the kitchen until I put an end to this blatant act of rebellion."

Dickon sent him a skeptical look. "I doubt there's a cook among the ranks."

"I know that," Damian said curtly. Then he turned and strode away, his anger escalating as he climbed the spiral staircase to the tower. He dismissed the guard with a nod of his head, turned the key in the lock and burst inside without knocking. The first thing he noticed was the warmth of the room and the flames that spit and crackled merrily in the hearth. That made his mood even darker. He started violently when he saw Elissa standing beside the washstand in her shift. The light was behind her, rendering her fine linen transparent. His breath hitched. Heat spiraled through him as he feasted unashamedly upon lush curves and seductive shadows.

Her breasts were exquisite; full and round with delicious cherry red nipples. His passionate gaze skimmed over slim waist and curvy hips, pausing at the shadowy patch at the apex of her thighs. Would it be the same dark fire as the hair on her head? he wondered as his gaze locked on that enticing part of her anatomy. His arousal was instantaneous and he fought hard to ignore it. He forced himself to concentrate on his reason for being here, not on the seductive Highland vixen who had somehow managed to incite a rebellion while locked away in the tower.

Elissa stood frozen in place. "What are you doing here?" she gasped. "Go away!"

Stalking her, Damian backed her against the washstand and grasped her shoulders, his fingers digging into her soft flesh. The heat of her struck him with shattering force and he struggled to retain some semblance of control.

"What have you done?" Her eyes widened and he felt her shoulders stiffen beneath his hands.

"I've done naught!"

"Don't play innocent with me. You know bloody well what you did. You encouraged your kinsmen to flout my authority. The fortress has been abandoned. My men are hungry and the hearths are cold."

His gaze strayed deliberately to the hearth, and the fire blazing within. His lips curled with derision. "Yours, however, seems to be well tended."

"Donna blame me for my kinsmen's behavior," Elissa braved. "They donna like Englishmen any more than I do."

Damian stared at her lips and suddenly felt adrift. His nerve endings tingled with awareness and he felt himself harden inside his tight breeches. He tried to concentrate on what she was saying when what he really wanted to do was to stop her words with a kiss.

He dragged her against him. "I've done nothing to harm you. I've never laid a hand on you, but I know what I'd like to do to you."

Elissa stared pointedly to where his fingers were curled around her shoulders. "You're laying a hand on me now, my lord."

Her words seemed to have little effect on him as he pulled her closer, until his mouth was scant inches from hers. She felt his swollen manhood stirring against her belly and tried to arch away, to no avail.

"The truth, lady," he growled against her lips. "Did you advise your kinsmen to abandon the fortress?"

Elissa's knees were quaking as his arms tightened around her. She could feel his brute strength, thinly restrained, and she braced herself against the washstand, gripping it so hard her fingers turned white. "I told you, I donna know what you're talking about. I've spoken with no one but Maggie."

His silver gaze slipped to her mouth and she shivered beneath the sudden impact of his fierce desire. She gulped back a surge of fear. She didn't want his desire; she wanted him gone.

"Being locked in a room is obviously an uncomfortable situation for you," Damian allowed, "but I have sufficient reason for confining you. You're disrupting my entire household."

"If my kinsmen have abandoned the keep, you have no one but yourself to blame. I had nothing to do with it."

He released the painful grip on her shoulders and

slid his arms down her back, caressing her and molding her more closely to him. Elissa shuddered. He was staring at her mouth as if he wanted to devour it. His eyes probed deeply into hers. She inhaled sharply and leaned backward in a vain attempt to escape his mouth as it came down hard over hers. Forcing her lips apart with his tongue, he forged deep inside her mouth. Trembling with a strange mixture of fear and awakening desire, she wrenched her head away and braced her hands against his chest.

"Why do you resist? I could take you now and no one would gainsay me." He cupped the back of her head and kissed her again.

Elissa felt herself spinning and clutched at him to keep from falling. She thought she heard him groan, but the taste of him rendered her incapable of coherent thought. He ravished her mouth with possessive hunger. Flames touched her skin, kindling a burgeoning passion she'd never experienced before. She knew she was wicked to allow this but she couldn't seem to help herself.

He rubbed himself against her thinly clad form. She felt the solid ridge of his sex prodding boldly between her thighs and warning bells went off in her head. *This is madness!* That thought turned into raw panic as Damian swept her off her feet and strode toward the bed. She was utterly defenseless; there was no one to protect her virtue. The Demon Knight would have his way, with or without her compliance. What truly frightened her was the fact that Damian made her feel things inappropriate for a maiden promised to another man.

Elissa hit the mattress and tried to scoot away

from Damian's weight, but he caught her about the hips and rolled her beneath him. She gave an involuntary cry when he slid her shift upward with a sweep of his strong hands.

"You mustna do this! Send me away, but donna dishonor me."

She felt his muscles tense, then his mouth swooped down on hers again, as if he hadn't heard her. Slowly, purposefully, his hands explored her quaking body—her breasts, the slope of her back, the curve of her waist, the shape of her thighs. Elissa feared her ravishment was just moments away when a small voice called to her from outside the closed door.

"Lissa, Lissa, can I come in? Tell the bad man to let me inside."

"Lora!"

Damian jerked backward, his face a mask of bewilderment as he stared down at Elissa. "Bloody hell! I must be mad."

His thoughts coincided exactly with Elissa's.

"Get off me!" She shoved against his chest and he sprang to his feet. Elissa was off the bed in an instant. She quickly donned her gown, then rushed to the door and flung it open.

A man-at-arms held Lora by her thin arm. "I caught her sneaking up the stairs, my lord."

"Release her!" Damian barked.

"Damian!" Lora squealed, flinging herself at Damian the moment she found herself free. After a quick hug, she launched herself at Elissa.

Elissa searched her sister's upturned face then gathered her in her arms. "What are you doing here, sweeting?"

"I wanted to see you."

Damian's grin appeared genuine as he touched Lora's bright head. "Are you all right, little one? Should you be out of bed?" Lora nodded to both questions. "That's good news indeed. Now all we need to do is get your mother well."

Lora fingered the fine plaid of her gown and slid Damian a shy smile. "Well, mayhap I told a tiny lie. I still cough, but not as much as I did. Nan said it won't be long before I can run and play again."

Her words were followed by a fit of coughing.

"Perhaps I should carry you back to bed," Damian offered, holding out his arms to the child.

"Nay, *I* will carry my sister to bed," Elissa declared. She had no idea why Lora was so enamored of the Demon Knight, for she found him arrogant and offensive. He would have taken her virginity with little remorse had Lora not appeared at a propitious time.

"I should like Lissa to carry me back to my chamber," Lora said, sending Damian an apologetic look. "I miss her. Why don't you play with me like you used to, Lissa?"

Elissa shot Damian an aggrieved look. "You must ask Lord Damian that question, sweeting."

Lora stared up at Damian with all the innocence of a five-year-old. "Why donna you want Lissa to visit me?"

Damian looked decidedly uncomfortable. "There are things you don't understand, little one."

Lora's next question threw Elissa off balance. Judging from Damian's expression, he was as stunned as she was. "What are you doing in Lissa's bedchamber, Damian? Mama said a man and woman shouldna be alone unless they are wed. Are you and Lissa married?"

Elissa blanched. "Nay, Lora! You know I am promised to Tavis Gordon."

"Your sister is mistaken, Lora," Damian said with authority. "Elissa and the Gordon chieftain will never marry." He turned his intimidating gaze on Elissa. "Take your sister to bed, lady. We will finish this discussion later."

Elissa scurried off before Damian could change his mind. Even this small concession was welcome. She spent two enjoyable hours playing with Lora in her chamber. Then she tucked her sister in bed to rest and hastened to her mother's chamber. Marianne was still pale but appeared somewhat stronger. At lunchtime, Nan arrived with a tray laden with enough food for the three of them to share.

"Maggie carried a tray to Lora," Nan said. "The lassie ate her fill and fell asleep." She grinned at Elissa. "Ye tired her out, lass, but yer visit did her a world of good. She'll soon be well and scampering about as if she was never ill."

"Elissa, love, have you been let out of the tower for good?" Marianne asked hopefully. "Lord Damian is a good man, I knew he'd realize how senseless it was to confine you."

"Lord Damian a good man?" Elissa choked. She could tell her mother a thing or two about the Demon Knight but didn't want to upset her.

"Aye," Nan agreed. " 'Tis only Elissa who gets his dander up." She chuckled. "Ye both are stubborn as mules."

Elissa bristled. "What's that supposed to mean?"

"Figure it out for yerself, lass. Eat yer food. I had

the devil's own time smuggling it out of the kitchen without having it snatched away by a hungry Englishman."

Elissa bit into a bannock and chewed thoughtfully. "What's going on, Nan? Lord Damian accused me of instigating a rebellion. Where is everyone?"

"Ah, well, they willna cook for nor serve the English lord while yer imprisoned in the tower."

Elissa smiled despite herself. Though the situation was grave, she'd never been prouder of her kinsmen. "Are there no cooks among the Englishmen?"

"Nay, they've no skill in the kitchen. No one can prepare mutton like Winifred, or bake bread like Vera." She cackled gleefully. "Mark my words, the Demon Knight will relent when his stomach hits his backbone."

"I pray Nan is right," Marianne said.

Marianne began to doze. Nan gathered up the dishes and carried the tray away, leaving Elissa alone with her sleeping mother. Reluctant to leave and return to the tower, she sat with her mother while she slept. Not too long ago Elissa feared she was going to lose her only parent, but now Marianne appeared to be rallying. Had Damian wrought this miracle?

Lost in thought, Elissa didn't hear the door open. A whisper of sound brought her head whipping around. She glanced at the bed, then rose abruptly, meeting Damian before he could disturb her sleeping mother. Compressing his lips, Damian motioned to her with an impatient gesture and waited for Elissa to follow him.

"What do you want?" Elissa hissed.

"This has gone far enough. My men are hungry. Order your kinsmen back to the keep."

Elissa couldn't keep the gleeful note from her voice. "Are you bargaining with me, my lord?"

"Nay, I do not bargain with women. I'm telling you how it will be and I expect you to obey."

He grasped her arm and pulled her into the passageway. "Will you release me from the tower?" Elissa challenged.

"That depends. I need your kinsmen and only you can bring them back. Swear fealty to me and I'll allow you to occupy your former chamber and move freely about the castle." His eyes narrowed dangerously. "Do not take this as an invitation to escape. You are but one small woman. There are ways you may not enjoy to keep you inside the fortress and away from Gordon."

Elissa bit back a scathing retort. Had he discovered the secret tunnel? Surely not, or he would have said something.

"I wouldna dream of escaping, my lord," Elissa replied, her words dripping with sarcasm, "since I find your company so fascinating."

"Keep in mind," Damian warned, ignoring her gibe, "that your mother and sister are entirely at my mercy. Their welfare depends on your obedience."

"Arrogant bastard," Elissa hissed.

His smile was far from reassuring. "That is one title I cannot claim, lady. My parents were happily married. Will you or will you not guarantee your kinsmen's loyalty?"

Elissa's eyes fixed on his hard face. "I canna vouch for my people, my lord."

"Then I cannot guarantee your family's safety."

His harsh words brought her gaze up to meet his. Her breath caught in her throat as something insidious and mesmerizing flared between them. She looked away before her expression revealed something she didn't want discovered. Elissa had no idea what was happening, but when her gaze involuntarily fastened on his mouth, she couldn't help remembering how those full lips felt on hers, how utterly transfixed she had been when he'd kissed her.

She shook her head to clear away her disturbing thoughts and concentrated on what was important: getting herself, her mother, and her sister away from the Demon Knight and to the Gordon stronghold. Lora was nearly well, and even Marianne appeared stronger. She'd bide her time and do as Damian asked, she decided, but only until she deemed her family able to travel.

"Well," Damian said, tapping his foot impatiently. "What is your decision, Elissa?"

"I dinna give you leave to use my name," Elissa said disdainfully.

"I do not need your permission, *Elissa*. Answer my question."

"Verra well, I'll talk to my kinsmen, but I canna promise their compliance."

"Would you prefer that I banished your kinsmen from Misterly and bring families of good, sturdy English stock to till Fraser soil? I will give them the land that belonged to your ancestors. Is that what you want?"

The thought of Englishmen living on the lands that rightfully belonged to Frasers was reprehensible. "Nay, you know 'tisna what I want. I donna want *you* here, either. Why canna you leave Misterly in peace? We were bothering no one."

"If you wanted to preserve Misterly for your kinsmen, you shouldn't have conspired with Tavis Gordon. The Crown is simply trying to prevent another uprising in Scotland."

"You exaggerate, my lord. Tavis Gordon isna planning a rebellion."

Damian cocked Elissa a skeptical look. "Is he not?"

Elissa flushed and looked away. In truth, she knew Tavis was planning some sort of mischief, and that he needed her kinsmen's cooperation to succeed.

"You can move back into your chamber as soon as your kinsmen return to their duties in the keep and elsewhere," Damian continued.

"Am I free to go to the village and speak with them?"

"Nay, you will remain within the castle walls. Furthermore, I've decided that keeping you occupied will prevent you from wreaking havoc. A fortress this large can always use extra help. Henceforth, you will work in the kitchen and serve meals."

"I'm to be a servant?" Elissa gasped.

"Aye, did you not understand me?"

"What if I refuse?"

"Then you'll remain locked in the tower until you accept my terms."

"How long am I to be a prisoner in my own home, my lord?" Elissa shot back.

Blowing out a breath of exasperation, he said, "That's for you to decide. King George is searching for an heiress for me to wed. When she arrives, serve her well and you may remain a part of this household."

Elissa's lips flattened. "An heiress. How wonderful for you."

"Aye. Finally I'll have everything I've ever dreamed of."

"I donna suppose it matters who you step on to get what you want," Elissa muttered, turning her back on him.

Damian glowered at her stiff back. Bloody hell. What was wrong with him? Elissa made him feel as if his world were tilting on edge. His steely control wavered dangerously whenever he was alone with her. He wanted her; that much was clear to him. Even the rigid line of her back appealed to him. His eyes narrowed. Perhaps he should slake his thirst for the little vixen before his intended bride arrived.

He touched her shoulder. She jerked as if he burned her and shied away from him. "Don't touch me."

"Are you afraid of me?"

"Should I be?"

"I've never deliberately hurt a woman."

She whirled to face him. "I donna like that look on your face."

"What look?"

"As if you . . . want to kiss me."

He scowled darkly. Was he that transparent? "Would kissing me be so terrible?"

" 'Tisna decent! A *gentleman* wouldna take advantage of my position."

"I thought you'd have realized by now that I am no gentleman. I am a skilled soldier and ruthless defender of England. They call me the Demon Knight; that should tell you something about me."

"You *are* trying to frighten me."

"Perhaps." He reached for her, bringing her hard against him. "You must know I want you."

"I know you enjoy tormenting me. What have I ever done to you?"

"You entice me, lady. You tantalize and seduce me with your tempting body and sultry green eyes. I won't have it, do you hear me? I refuse to be beguiled."

"I do nothing of the sort!" Elissa defended.

Damian knew he was being unreasonable, but Elissa seemed to affect him in ways that drove him crazy. She tempted him, enticed him, provoked him. He wanted to toss her on her back and drive himself to a thundering climax inside her. What in the hell was wrong with him?

Damian had always prided himself on his control. Even when he'd been without a woman for a long time he could direct his passion as he saw fit. He stared at her lips for a long, tense moment before he turned away.

"Dermot and Lachlan can carry my terms for your freedom to the village. Meanwhile, go down to the kitchen and see what you can do about feeding my men. We brought no cooks with us from London and the culinary attempts of my men are inedible."

"How do you know I willna poison them?" Elissa charged.

His eyes turned hard, uncompromising. "Because you value the lives of your mother and sister." Then he spun on his heel and walked away.

Damian muttered dark imprecations as he descended the stairs. He wasn't supposed to be attracted to the Maiden of Misterly. He wasn't supposed to feel compassion for members of her family. He should have obeyed the king and sent them all to the convent, and his conscience be damned. The Demon Knight wasn't supposed to have a conscience. What in bloody hell was he going to do now that he'd found one?

Sir Richard hailed Damian as he entered the hall. "Why the dour look, Damian?"

"I'm glad you're here, Dickon," Damian said as he sat down at the table and filled a tankard of ale from a pitcher. "Would you fetch Dermot and Lachlan for me?"

"They're not in the castle."

"Find them," Damian growled.

"Of course, I'll leave immediately. Do you want to tell me what this is all about?"

"I've promised to release Lady Elissa from the tower if her kinsmen return to their duties. I need Dermot and Lachlan to spread the word to the villagers. Elissa's fate is in their hands. 'Tis up to them to decide what is important."

"What are your plans for Lady Elissa's future?"

"I truthfully don't know," Damian said, scowling into his ale. "For the time being, she's to help out in the kitchen."

"In the kitchen! You're really asking for trouble, aren't you? I've said this before. Rid yourself of the problem. Send her to London."

Damian's frown deepened. "I can't, Dickon. My way is better. She's where I can keep an eye on her."

"What makes you think she won't cause further trouble?"

"Two reasons. Her mother and sister."

"Two good reasons, I suppose, but don't say I didn't warn you. The Maiden of Misterly is no ordinary woman. What do you suppose will happen when your bride arrives?"

"I'll work it out," Damian said grimly. "No woman is going to defeat me." He lowered his voice. "I've found the secret tunnel. The entrance is cleverly disguised by stonework beneath the solar staircase. You're the only one I've confided in thus far. As you know, I've been searching for just such an escape route since Elissa disappeared. One day, knowledge of an alternate route in or out of the keep may come in handy."

Dickon grinned. "Good work! Don't worry, I'll keep your secret. I'm off now to find Dermot and Lachlan. Mayhap I'll encounter mistress Maggie. She's a winsome lass I'd like to get to know better."

Damian laughed. "You're an irredeemable rogue, Dickon. Leave the virgins alone."

Dickon took himself off just as Elissa entered the hall. Damian's appreciative gaze followed her until she disappeared into the kitchen. He drained his cup and slammed it down on the table.

This was madness!

He rose abruptly and followed her.

Elissa was up to her elbows in dishwater when Damian arrived in the kitchen. He took one look at the mess the soldiers had left and spat out a curse. Elissa dropped the pan she was scrubbing and whirled to face him.

"What are you doing here? Have you come to help?"

"Leave that for the servants," Damian barked.

"I *am* a servant."

"Aye, but not a scullery maid. Leave it, I say."

Elissa sent him a scathing look and turned back to

her pots and pans. Damian took exception and spun her about. Her eyes rose up to meet his, the challenge in them unmistakable.

"Make up your mind, my lord. I am but following your orders."

Confusion rode Damian ruthlessly. Watching Elissa perform physical labor bothered him. His gaze sought her lips, remembering how soft they had felt, how sweetly they had clung to his.

Before he could call back his words, he said, "I like it when you follow orders. What if I ordered you to kiss me?"

She glared at him. "I would refuse."

"What if I ordered you to come to my bedchamber tonight?"

Indignation stiffened her shoulders. "That, my lord, will never happen."

Damian merely smiled as he turned and strode away.

Chapter 6

Damian prowled the hall, his patience wearing thin as he waited for Elissa's kinsmen to appear. If they refused to return to the fortress, he might have to force them to it, but he didn't really want that. To his relief, people began drifting through the door. Within an hour, villagers were clustered together in the great hall, waiting for Damian to address them.

Damian motioned for silence. "Who is your spokesman?" he asked.

Dermot pushed through the crowd. "I speak for the Frasers, me lord. Ye asked us to come, and here we are. What is it ye wish to say?"

"Only this. I need you, all of you." He made a sweeping gesture with his hand. "I've asked you here to offer a compromise to this impasse."

"All we want is for ye to free our lass," Dermot challenged.

" 'Tis exactly what I intend to do," Damian allowed. "Return to your duties in the keep and fields, and Lady Elissa will be given her freedom."

Hands on hips, Maggie shoved past Dermot. "Freedom to come and go as she pleases, my lord?"

Damian frowned. "I cannot allow her full amnesty. I must obey the king's wishes. What I meant was freedom within the castle and inside the walls surrounding Misterly. No harm will befall your lady at my hands."

"Where is our lass?" Lachlan called out.

"I am here," Elissa exclaimed from behind Damian.

Damian remained watchful as she strode toward him. What she said to her kinsmen would be vital to his tenure as Lord of Misterly.

"Are ye well, Elissa?" Dermot asked anxiously.

"I am fine, Dermot."

"Tell us what to do," Lachlan said. "Shall we cooperate with his lordship? Ye have but to say, lass."

"I donna like being locked in the tower," Elissa replied, sending Damian an acerbic look.

"As I've explained, you have but to return to your duties to win Lady Elissa her freedom."

"What about Lady Marianne and little Lora?" Winifred, the cook, ventured.

"I will do everything in my power to return them to health," Damian promised. "Lady Elissa can verify that they have prospered under my care."

All eyes turned to Elissa.

"He speaks the truth," Elissa admitted with obvious reluctance.

Damian let out the breath he hadn't realized he'd been holding. "You heard the lady. As Lord of Misterly, I vow to deal with you fairly and maintain peace for future generations."

"For *yer* heirs, not ours," Dermot grumbled.

"There will always be Frasers at Misterly," Damian maintained. "I give you my word."

"The word of an Englishman," Elissa muttered beneath her breath. Fortunately, no one heard but Damian.

"What will become of our lass?" Lachlan demanded.

Damian had no ready reply, for he didn't know the answer himself. He could only repeat, "I mean her no harm. She will work here among her kinsmen and serve me and my future bride."

"Work!" Winifred huffed. "As a servant? 'Tisna right."

"I will work," Elissa said, sending Winifred a warning glance. "Haven't I always pitched in where I was needed? 'Twill be no different now."

"Are ye sure, lass?" Dermot asked.

Elissa nodded slowly and Damian allowed himself to hope that harmony would be restored.

"Verra sure. Cooperate with Lord Damian until I find a way to return Misterly to the Frasers."

Damian didn't like the sound of that. What the devil did she mean?

Dermot's shaggy brows arched upward, as if he understood perfectly what she had tried to convey. Then he winked at her. None of this was lost on Damian.

"Ye win, me lord," Dermot allowed. "We will work with ye, but harm one hair on our lass's head and ye'll answer to us."

"I dislike threats, Dermot," Damian said, "but you

force me to issue one of my own. Don't even think about allying yourselves with rebels and their causes. I have men and arms to retaliate. Now back to your duties, all of you."

Unseen by Damian, Elissa gave an imperceptible nod. After a moment of indecision, the hall cleared, leaving Damian, Elissa, Sir Richard, and the cadre of soldiers Sir Richard had brought in case trouble ensued.

"That was close, Damian," Sir Richard said.

Damian gave Elissa a cursory glance. "Lady Elissa was wise to avoid trouble. Send the soldiers back to their duties, Dickon, they won't be needed today."

Dickon nodded and strode away.

"You've had your way, my lord," Elissa said. "I hope you are pleased."

"Peace pleases me. I'm sick of war, tired of killing. Believe me or not, Elissa, I've known naught but war and bloodshed for more years than I care to remember. The only home I've known since Culloden has been an army tent. A knight's life is a hard one. I had no land to call my own, nothing but my skill and cunning to rely upon. I want Misterly more than I've ever wanted anything in my life."

After telling Elissa more than he'd intended, he clamped his lips together and turned away. What was wrong with him? He was telling Elissa things she had no business knowing. Suddenly he felt open and vulnerable, a sensation utterly foreign to him. The Demon Knight wasn't a man known for baring his soul. When he'd gained control of himself, he turned back to confront Elissa, but she had slipped away.

* * *

Elissa returned to the kitchen with new insight into the harsh reality of the Demon Knight's mind. When he'd mentioned his former life he'd sounded lonely. But how could it be? Men of Damian's ilk were never lonely. He was a handsome man, she knew without being told that he did not lack for female companionship. And with friends like Sir Richard, Damian was luckier than most.

Could his lack of land be the driving force behind him? Elissa wondered. All men wanted land of their own. But why did it have to be her land? Once Damian's bride arrived, an Englishwoman would become mistress of Misterly. It would be a stretch of the imagination to believe Damian's bride would want Elissa and her family to remain.

Damian lounged against the ornately carved back of his chair, his silver gaze following Elissa as she moved about the tables distributing trays of food. Except for an occasional smile for one of her kinsmen, she blatantly ignored him, though she had to be aware of his intense scrutiny.

She looked tired, he thought, and wondered why he cared. The answer didn't surprise him: he cared because he wanted her in his bed. He was convinced that having her one time would cure him of the obsessive attraction that existed between them. She could deny it till doomsday, but Damian could tell when a woman was ripe for the taking. Elissa wasn't immune to him; her mouth had tasted sweetly of surrender each time he'd kissed her.

Damian shifted in his seat. Carrying around a permanent erection was ridiculous. Nothing was preventing him from taking Elissa, so why didn't he?

Bedding the lass would cure him of the uncomfortable itch that plagued him. Mayhap even rid him of the need she inspired in him. He should concentrate on Misterly, and harboring erotic thoughts about the vixen challenged his sanity.

Damian saw Elissa moving around the tables serving ale and lifted his tankard for her to fill. She did as he bade, but when she turned to leave, he grasped her arm, preventing her from moving away.

"Let go of me," she hissed.

"Not yet."

"What do you want of me?"

"I thought it was obvious," Damian drawled. "I want you in my bed."

"Donna shame me before my kinsmen."

"What they don't know won't hurt them," Damian defended.

Elissa's shoulders stiffened. "You canna demand that of me. I am promised to another."

A hush settled around them as everyone stopped eating to watch the byplay between Elissa and Damian. Damian didn't want to publicly embarrass Elissa, but neither did he intend for her to refuse him. He was the Lord of Misterly; his word was law. Taking Elissa would harm no one. He would be gentle with her, and make sure she gained pleasure from their mating.

"I do demand it," Damian insisted. "Go to my chamber and prepare yourself for me."

Dermot, Lachlan, and several other Frasers glared belligerently at Damian. Damian's men-at-arms became instantly alert. Damian felt the tension building and realized he had inadvertently created a potentially explosive situation.

"If you wish to avoid trouble," he whispered in an aside to Elissa, "you'd be wise to obey me."

"Verra well, my lord," Elissa said, awarding him with a beguiling smile. She was still grinning when she upended the pitcher of ale in his lap.

"Devil take you!" Damian yelled, jumping to his feet. He reached for her; she skittered away.

Damian started to follow but Dickon grasped his sleeve. "Let her go, Damian. Don't make an ass of yourself before her kinsmen. I heard you order her to your bed. That wasn't well done of you. Are you sure 'tis what you want?"

"I'm not sure of anything where the Maiden of Misterly is concerned," Damian growled. "Just one time, Dickon, 'tis all I ask. She's not immune to me, and I'll make it good for her."

"Take care, my friend. She'll not make it easy for you. Just look around you. Her kinsmen will defend her should you dishonor her."

"Elissa is too smart to seek help from her kinsmen. She doesn't want bloodshed anymore than I do. Her kinsmen are ill prepared for a confrontation with professional soldiers."

"I wouldn't discount the lady's intelligence. I don't envy you, Damian. Take another woman to your bed, but as a favor to me, don't set your sights on Maggie."

Damian's eyes widened. "So that's how it is. Maggie, eh, well, you could do worse. She's a comely lass. Is she interested?"

"Not in becoming my mistress," Dickon lamented. "But she'll come around."

Damian chuckled. "Ever the optimist, eh Dickon?

I wish you luck." He glanced toward the kitchen and wondered what Elissa was up to, but forced himself to finish his meal. It was difficult to swallow when his thoughts were elsewhere and certain parts of his body were hard as stone.

He imagined Elissa in his bed, her naked body revealed to him beneath the luminescent glow of candlelight. He would be gentle but insistent, bringing her to climax despite her inexperience. After one night of bliss in her arms, Damian was convinced that his inexplicable lust for Elissa would trouble him no more.

Elissa cornered Nan in the kitchen. "I need your help," she whispered.

Nan regarded Elissa through intelligent blue eyes. "So the Demon Knight has finally succumbed to his need for ye."

Elissa went still. "You know?"

Nan chuckled. "Aye, I dinna know when, but I knew 'twas coming. 'Tis obvious Lord Damian wants ye in his bed."

" 'Tis not what I want, Nan."

Nan's gnarled fingers stroked Elissa's cheek. "Ah, lass, are ye sure?"

"Of course I'm sure," Elissa said indignantly. "Lord Damian merely wants me in his bed until his bride arrives. I willna be used like that. Why doesna he send me to the convent?"

"Ye know the answer to that. He canna trust ye to stay there and canna afford to let ye run to Tavis Gordon. Failure to comply with the king's wishes could cost him Misterly."

"What am I going to do, Nan?" Elissa wailed. "He expects me in his bed this very night. I fear if I donna comply, he'll come and get me."

"Do ye wish Lord Damian's death?" Nan asked craftily. "Mayhap I can help ye achieve it. I could give ye a potion . . ."

Damian's death? "Oh, nay, nay, I donna want his death on my soul! I . . . I couldna bear it."

It was true. There was much she resented about Damian, but she didn't wish him dead.

"There must be another way to stop him from . . . ravishing me."

"I could give ye a sleeping potion to put in his wine. It willna kill him," Nan added when Elissa started to protest, "merely put him to sleep."

Elissa's mind raced. "If he drinks enough wine, will he go to sleep before he . . . he can hurt me?"

Nan searched Elissa's face. "If that's what ye want, lass."

"Of course it's what I want. How soon can you have it ready?"

"Everything I need is in my chamber. Bring along a pitcher of the good French wine and I'll doctor it for ye."

Elissa went immediately to the larder and filled an ewer with the wine used only on special occasions. Then she joined Nan in her small chamber behind the kitchen. Elissa had been in Nan's room before and knew what to expect. The air was fragrant with the odor of herbs. Bunches of them were suspended from the rafters to dry and others lay on a flat table, waiting to be crushed into various mixtures and potions.

Nan had learned her healing skills from her

mother, who had been a highly respected herbalist. Some called Nan a white witch, but no one feared her, for her skills were used with good intention.

Elissa found Nan at her narrow worktable. "Here ye be, lass," she said, holding up a vial of white powder. "Valerian. It makes one tranquil. Enough of it will induce deep sleep."

"I hope you're right," Elissa said on a fervent sigh.

Nan poured a small amount into the pitcher and gently stirred it with a wooden spoon to mix the flavors. "This will take care of his lordship tonight, but what about tomorrow? Ye canna drug him every night. He wants ye, lass, and he's not one to give up."

"I'll think of something," Elissa said with false bravado. "Right now, I canna think beyond tonight."

"Then go, lass. He grows impatient."

Elissa nodded jerkily and hurried off. Cradling the pitcher against her lest she spill it, she darted toward the tower. Her heart was thundering in her ears as she negotiated the narrow staircase. *This has to work*, she thought, mindful of the sloshing liquid in the pitcher. She needed every precious drop if she were to escape Damian's attentions.

Elissa reached the top landing and paused before Damian's closed door. She dragged in a fortifying breath, lifted her hand to knock but hastily withdrew it when the door opened abruptly. She gazed up into Damian's face and took a step backwards. Candlelight illuminated his hard expression and a frisson of fear raced down her spine.

"What kept you?" he said, stepping back to allow her to enter. "I was about to come after you."

She scooted past him and carefully set the pitcher

of wine on his desk. "I thought you might be thirsty and went to the larder for a flagon of wine."

Damian regarded her with suspicion. "I suppose you've laced it liberally with poison."

Had he guessed? "Why would I do anything that stupid while you hold my mother and sister hostage?"

"Hmmm," Damian said, eyeing the wine with distrust. "Am I to assume, then, that you want this as badly as I do?"

Elissa bristled. "Assume anything you like."

Damian poured wine into two goblets and handed one to Elissa. "You'll join me, of course."

"Of course," Elissa said, taking the first sip . . . a tiny one. She tasted nothing unusual, and relaxed.

Damian watched her a long moment, then drank deeply from his own goblet. He rolled the wine on his tongue and let it slide down his throat.

"Excellent. French, I believe. Your father had good taste." His next swallow emptied the glass and he set it down on the desk. Then he reached for her. Elissa set her glass down and backed away. "I canna do this, my lord. You are forcing me to do something I donna want."

"I can make you want it," Damian said with a conviction that made her legs tremble.

The hard, set look on his face made Elissa all too aware of her vulnerability.

"I won't hurt you, Elissa. I promise you'll find pleasure in my arms."

"I donna want pleasure from you."

"You don't hate me, I can sense it."

Elissa tossed her head. "I canna like an Englishman. 'Tis against everything I hold dear."

"Give me your hand, Elissa."

When she refused, Damian grasped her arm and pulled her toward the bed. "I'll be gentle. There's no hurry, we have all night."

Elissa became aware of two things; the snakelike hiss of coals in the hearth, and the distant rumble of thunder. And something else: the naked hunger in Damian's eyes.

"Shall I undress you, Elissa?"

Her mind raced furiously. "Nay! I . . . my wine! I dinna drink it."

"Drink up," he said as he snatched up her glass and handed it to her.

"Wait! I donna like to drink alone. Drink with me."

Damian gave her a hard stare, then refilled his goblet. "If it pleases you, but if you're hoping I'll get drunk, forget it. I rarely drink to excess, especially on momentous occasions like this."

He placed her glass in her hands and she took another tiny sip, pleased to note that he had emptied his goblet in one long gulp. Fearing to drink more than what she'd already imbibed, Elissa deliberately let the glass slip from her hands. It shattered, just as she'd intended, leaving a blood-red stain on the carpet.

Damian slanted Elissa an impatient look. Did he suspect?

"Shall I pour you another? It will only prolong the inevitable, you know."

"I've had enough, thank you," Elissa murmured. She watched him closely, waiting for the drugged wine to take effect. She prayed he had gotten enough of the drug, for she doubted she could get more wine down him.

Damian turned her around and began unfastening ties and buttons. Her gown fell away and she tried to grab it, but Damian would have none of it. He pulled her hands away and it pooled at her feet. He made no move to remove her knee-length shift as he lifted her out of the gown and brought her into his arms.

"You can't begin to know how much I want you."

"I know naught of what you're talking about. You were the first man to kiss me."

Damian looked properly abashed. "You mean Tavis Gordon never . . . I can't believe it. You're a lovely woman, Elissa, 'tis hard to believe no man ever tried to kiss you."

Damian thought she was lovely, Elissa thought with pleasure. But the pleasure quickly vanished when she realized a smooth-tongued rake like the Demon Knight would say anything to get what he wanted. Fortunately she knew better than to believe his flattery. There wasn't an Englishman alive who could measure up to a braw Highland laddie.

His lips hovered scant inches from hers; she smelled wine on his breath, and something else: his own special scent she would recognize anywhere. He was going to kiss her. Oh, God, she couldn't bear it. Why was he still standing? He was supposed to be unconscious . . . or at the very least, groggy. She stifled a smile when he staggered.

Then his lips swooped down on hers and her thoughts scattered. She was aware of nothing but the taste and feel of him, of his hands roaming freely over her, of his hard body pressing urgently against hers. Her eyes drifted shut, and when she opened them, she found him watching her with hooded intensity. Her breath caught. She couldn't breathe, couldn't move. She called forth her strength and tried to push him away, but her resistance was half-hearted, a fact of which she was all too aware.

"You'll not escape me," Damian murmured against her lips. "I've been ready for you since the day we met."

He grasped her hand and placed it on his groin. "That's what a man in need feels like, Elissa. How much do you know about what takes place between a man and a woman in bed?"

"Enough to understand 'tis wrong outside the bounds of marriage," she snapped.

"I'm talking about the physical aspect. Do you know what's going to happen tonight?"

"Nothing is going to happen."

"You're wrong, sweeting. I can't possibly let you leave now."

Before she could form a coherent thought, he scooped her up and placed her in the center of the bed. Her breath hitched painfully. It didn't take an experienced woman to know he was a man in rut, fully charged and eager to take what he wanted.

She stared up at him, mesmerized by his taut expression. There was a sleepy look about his eyes, and a lazy, sinfully sensuous slant to his smile. Why was he still able to function? Had Nan failed her? Then she took a closer look. His pupils were dilated and his smile drooped a little. Pray God he passed out soon.

He didn't. His knowing smile increased her panic and she raised up on her elbows. His gaze dropped to her parted lips, then moved slowly downward, lingering on her linen-clad breasts and the sweep of her bare legs. When he dropped down on his haunches beside her and whispered in a low, driven tone precisely what he intended to do to her, Elissa lost the ability to breathe.

She swallowed convulsively as he covered her body with his and his mouth found hers again. His kiss sent spirals of heat charging through her body, and she hated herself for it. This was an Englishman kissing her, a man who looted and stole from Highlanders, and, aye, killed them.

Guilt rode her relentlessly, and she renewed her efforts to resist him, but his superior strength overwhelmed her. And then something strange and frightening happened: she started kissing him back. Her hands crept around his neck, pulling him closer, and her lips softened and molded to his. She heard him laugh, a dark and seductive sound deep in his throat, and she knew the misbegotten blackguard had won.

"Let me take off my clothes first," Damian panted into her ear. He tore off his clothing and tossed it aside.

Had Elissa been in control of her mind, she would have leapt from the bed and fled. Yet she could do nothing but stare at him with mouth agape. She looked her fill at his broad, sculptured chest, bulging biceps, and thickly muscled legs. Though she tried to avoid it, her gaze was drawn to his thick manhood. A gasp left her lips. She never imagined a man in full rut would be so huge. He would kill her.

Fear pummeled her. But before she could flee, he grasped the hem of her shift and stripped it up and off. One dark hand held her in place while, with the other, he reached down and touched her between her thighs.

"Nay!" She trembled, shaken by violent stirrings of arousal. Devil take her, she liked that too well.

"Shh." He dropped down beside her then shook his head, as if bewildered by something.

"What is it?" Elissa asked, hoping, praying that the drugged wine was finally working.

He shook his head again. "That's odd."

"What's odd? Would you like some more wine?"

"Nay, I want my wits about me when I make love to you. Spread your legs, sweeting," he whispered.

He pulled her beneath him and settled between her thighs. His lips brushed her breast and he drew the tender nipple into his mouth. Elissa moaned and arched against him as he began to suckle her. Then she felt something warm and hard and thick probing against her center and waited fearfully for the pain. She knew so little about how this was accomplished and had hoped to wait for her wedding day to find out. Now a despised Englishman would despoil her and for some strange reason the only thing she regretted was allowing herself to be seduced by the enemy. What kind of woman was she to betray her principles for a moment of pleasure?

Guilt rode her mercilessly.

"Elissa, look at me."

Damian's voice sounded strangely slurred. She looked up at him and noted that his eyes were glazing over. His eyebrows were together, producing one dark slash across his forehead.

"This is how I want you. Beneath me, gazing up

at me with those . . . magnificent . . . green eyes.
Devil . . . take it! What's . . . wrong with . . . me? I . . .
can't seem to . . . think."

Finally, Elissa thought with relief. The drugged
wine was working. Twinges of conscience still
plagued her, however, for finding pleasure in
Damian's kisses and enjoying his touch far too
much.

Elissa blew out a sigh when Damian slumped
against her. She started to ease out from under him
when he lifted his head and stared at her with a clarity that belied his drugged state.

"Damn you! What . . . did you do . . . to me?"
Then his eyes rolled back in his head and he went
limp.

Elissa pushed him away and eased off the mattress, scrambling out of reach. But she needn't have
worried. He wasn't going to move for a very long
time. The longer she stared at him the more she worried that the drug had killed him, and that's not
what she wanted. She dressed hurriedly, her gaze
never straying from Damian's face.

Inhaling a steadying breath, Elissa cautiously approached the bed. When Damian made no threatening move, she leaned closer and placed a hand on his
chest, relieved to feel the steady cadence of his heart
beneath her palm. Suddenly he stirred, and she drew
back sharply, but he gave no sign of awakening.
Then she turned and fled. It wasn't until she was
safely in her own chamber that she allowed herself
to relax.

"Did the drug work, lass?"

Elissa spun on her heel, startled to find Nan
standing behind her.

"Aye, thank you, Nan. But it took longer than I expected."

"Lord Damian isna a wee man. I should have told you it wouldna work immediately." She gave Elissa a shrewd look. "Are ye all right?"

Elissa flushed and looked away. "Aye, he dinna . . . well, he passed out before . . . the deed was done."

"I donna need to tell ye he's going to be furious when he awakens. If I were ye, lass, I'd stay out of his way until his anger cools."

"I intend to."

Nan grunted. "So will I, but I fear 'tis ye who will suffer his temper. I shouldna have helped ye. 'Twill only postpone what fate has already decreed."

Elissa's head snapped up. "Nan! What are you saying? You're hinting that Damian and I . . . that we'll . . ."

"Aye, lass, 'tis bound to happen."

"Naught is going to happen between Damian and me. I willna let it."

"Are ye saying the demon's touch disgusted ye? I canna believe it."

"You donna understand, Nan," Elissa cried. "Damian's touch dinna disgust me, just the opposite. I enjoyed his kisses, welcomed his hands on me, and I hated myself for it. I felt like a traitor. If the drug hadna worked, I would have allowed him to take me like a . . . trollop."

Sobs shook Elissa. Nan patted her shoulder, making comforting sounds. Guilt was a powerful emotion and Elissa was suffering a double dose.

"Donna fret, lass. Ye were experiencing passion for the first time."

"But I wanted to experience passion with Tavis

Gordon, not with an accursed Englishman," Elissa wailed. "Does wanting someone make me a wanton, Nan?"

"Nay, lass. Ye are a woman attracted by a man ye want to hate. Ye should have listened when I said ye wouldna wed Tavis Gordon."

She regarded the old woman with dread. "Am I to remain a spinster all my life?"

Nan cackled. "A spinster? Ye will present yer first child to yer husband within the year."

Elissa recoiled in dismay. "You're mad! Leave me, your nonsense is making my head ache." Deliberately she turned her back on her old nurse.

"Verra well, lass, but donna waste yer time looking for a husband; he abides beneath yer verra nose."

When Elissa whirled to deliver a scathing retort, Nan had already let herself out the door.

Chapter 7

Damian cranked his eyes open, aware of several things at once: his head throbbed, his mouth tasted foul, and sunlight was slanting through the window. It wasn't like him to sleep past dawn. His brows drew together in painful concentration as he tried to recall the night past.

Memory returned in fits and starts.

Elissa . . .

Gingerly he shifted his body and reached across the bed. The place beside him was empty, and suddenly he remembered. Despite his rattled brain, he recalled the wine he'd imbibed at Elissa's insistence, and anger exploded through him. She'd drugged him! Rage brought him surging out of bed. The moment his feet hit the floor he swayed dizzily and grasped the bedpost to keep from falling.

The deceitful vixen! This was the first time a woman had made a fool of him and he vowed it would be the last. He'd be the laughingstock if anyone got wind of this. He tottered over to the washbowl, filled it with water from the pitcher, and plunged his head into the bowl. After two dunkings, his wits returned, and he forced his mind back to the events of the previous night.

He'd been suspicious of the wine from the beginning. It wasn't like Elissa to be so obliging. He should have gone with his gut feeling, but he was so damn aroused he could think of nothing but being inside Elissa. And like a besotted fool he'd watched her sip the wine and believed it safe.

Aye. A bloody fool he'd been.

Bitterness welled up inside him. Did she intend to kill him? He discarded that thought immediately. Had she wanted to, she could have plunged a knife into his heart while he lay unconscious. Elissa wasn't a killer; she was a conniver. He'd have to watch her carefully, be on his guard for her next trick. But whether she liked it or not, he *would* have her. And soon.

Damian found Elissa in the courtyard with Lora. She'd managed to avoid him the entire morning, but he wasn't about to let her escape his wrath so easily. Lora spied him first.

"Damian! Would you like to see the rag doll Lissa made for me?" She held Elissa's creation up for Damian's inspection.

Damian smiled at Lora, then slanted a dark glance at Elissa, pleased to note the flicker of fear in her green eyes. She had good reason to fear him.

"You're looking well, little one," he said, returning his attention to the child.

"I'm verra well, thank you. Nan said I'm well enough to be up and about now."

"That is good news," Damian said, genuinely pleased.

Just then two children skipped up and grasped Lora's hand. "Come to the stables with us, Lora. Patches had her kittens."

Damian had seen the children about before but didn't know who they belonged to.

"Is it all right, Lissa?" Lora asked hopefully.

"Nay, I donna think . . ."

"Run along, Lora," Damian said in a voice that brooked no argument. "I would like a private word with your sister."

Lora and her friends skipped off. "Who are they?" Damian asked. "I've seen those children around but don't know who they belong to."

"They're Lachlan's grandchildren," Elissa said. "Their father died at Culloden and Lachlan's been supporting them since they were just wee bairns. Now if you'll excuse me . . ."

"Not so fast. Walk with me," he said, grasping her arm to keep her from fleeing.

Elissa dragged her feet but Damian would have none of it. He pulled her along with him until they reached a place where they couldn't be overheard. He stopped so abruptly she bounced against him. Then he rounded on her, his face ripe with accusation.

"You tried to kill me! Did you think to escape Sir Richard's wrath had you succeeded? You would have been put to death."

Elissa blanched. Kill him? How could he think that of her? "Nay, I did no such thing."

"What drug did you use?"

"A sleeping potion. It did you no harm."

"Treachery! Do you despise me so much?"

"You're an Englishman," she said, as if that explained everything. "I belong to Tavis Gordon."

He grasped her shoulders and dragged her against him, his expression fiercely determined. "You belong to me. Accept it. Your fate is in my hands. You *will* come to my bed, Elissa, without coercion on my part. I swear it!"

"Never! The verra fact that you're an Englishman makes that unlikely."

His inflexible stance should have warned her. Silent tension stretched between them. She knew she should say something to break the taut silence but the words died in her throat when she realized he was going to kiss her. Though it was the last thing Elissa wanted, her face tilted upward and she moistened her parted lips with the tip of her tongue.

"Vixen," he said in a low, driven voice. "While you batter me with words, your body bids me welcome. Do you enjoy teasing me?"

Elissa blinked. Why did she let him do this to her? He seemed to take great pleasure in leading her down the path of betrayal. She had to be more vigilant in the future. The darkly seductive Demon Knight mustn't be allowed to destroy her pride, her very honor.

Shaking her head to clear it of Damian's tantalizing scent, Elissa fought to free herself. "Go away!"

Damian laughed as his arms closed tightly around her. "Not yet," he growled.

She closed her eyes as his mouth took hers. His lips were soft but the rest of his body was stiff and unyielding. Clutching awkwardly at his shoulders, she fought his desire as well as her own. It shouldn't

be like this. She couldn't . . . shouldn't want him.
She'd spent most of her life hating Englishmen.
What made this man different?

Abruptly Damian broke off the kiss and stepped
away, his expression strangely tender. But his voice
held a hard edge as he said, "We'll see who can hold
out longer, my lady. Compared to me, you're a
novice at this game."

Elissa regarded him with derision. "I'm playing
no game, my lord."

"Women always play games. 'Tis their nature."
His grin unnerved her. "My chamber door will always be open to you. Come to me when you wish to
learn more about the pleasure I promised."

She turned her head away. "I will never come to
you."

Then a strange thing happened. From the corner
of her eye Elissa noticed a man who seemed oddly
familiar enter the courtyard with a group of tradesmen. He wore Fraser plaid and a bonnet pulled low
over his forehead. But for one spellbinding moment,
the man raised his head and looked directly at her
and Damian.

Recognition shuddered through her and she felt
the warmth drain from her face.

Tavis Gordon!

"What's wrong?" Damian asked sharply. "Are
you ill?"

Did Damian suspect the reason for her distraction? "Naught is wrong. 'Tis time I found Lora and
returned to the keep to begin her lessons."

Damian released her instantly. "Lora's a bright
child, she'll do well at lessons. Will you teach her
yourself?"

Elissa nodded. "If you have no objections."

"Nay, 'twill keep you out of trouble."

Elissa hurried off. She'd never understand Damian. He was a hardened soldier, an unrelenting adversary and ruthless in many ways, but he seemed genuinely concerned about Lora and Marianne. It was almost as if he were two different men, and the face he showed her was not the same one he presented to her mother and sister. But Elissa had other things to worry about. What was Tavis Gordon doing at Misterly?

Tavis appeared from nowhere as she rounded the corner on her way to the stables to find Lora. He grasped her arm and roughly dragged her into the shadowy interior of the building.

"Tavis, you shouldna be here."

"I had to see you. Are you all right? What has the English bastard done to you?"

Elissa wondered if Tavis had seen Damian kiss her. "He's done naught. I was supposed to be sent to the convent but Lord Damian dinna think that was a good idea. I may yet be sent to London for the Hanover to deal with me. The English donna want us to wed and unite our clans."

"They canna stop us," Tavis said fiercely.

"What can you do? 'Tis dangerous for you to be here."

" 'Tisna safe to talk here," Tavis hissed. "Meet me in the stables tonight, after the evening meal. Donna let anyone see you. I'll explain everything then."

They heard voices and Tavis stepped deeper into the shadows. "Tonight, lass, donna fail me."

He disappeared around the corner just as Lora and her friends appeared.

"Lissa, you should see the kittens! They're adorable."

"Some other time, sweeting," Elissa said. " 'Tis time to resume your lessons. Shall we go up to the schoolroom and begin?"

"If you say so," Lora said without enthusiasm. "Can I come back out and play later?"

"We'll see how you feel," Elissa hedged.

The day passed slowly for Elissa. She spent two hours teaching Lora her letters and visited a few minutes with Marianne. Afterward, she went to the kitchen to assist with the midday meal. Many hours remained before she was to meet Tavis, and she wondered where he had hidden himself. Had he come to take her away? She wouldn't leave without her mother and sister. Though Damian treated them well, that could change in a heartbeat should she leave them at his mercy. Had Marianne been well enough to travel, she would have attempted to take her away through the secret tunnel long ago. Dimly she wondered if Damian had found the escape route or if he was still looking.

Damian watched Elissa through shuttered eyes. She appeared distracted and he knew she must be up to something. And it couldn't be good. She refused to meet his gaze, though she had to be aware of his scrutiny. He knew she wasn't worried about her family for he'd checked on them earlier and they were fine. Lady Marianne's spirits had seemed good, and that had pleased him. He had been shocked to find Sir Brody in her chamber and moreso to discover that it wasn't the first time the grizzled old knight had visited with Marianne. Was something going on that he should know about? Or was his imagination running away with him?

Damian waited until the hall emptied after the evening meal before confronting Elissa. He intercepted her as she headed toward the solar to seek her bed.

"I'd like a word with you, Elissa."

"Your words weary me, my lord. I'd like to retire."

"In a moment. Is something amiss?"

Elissa regarded him from beneath hooded lids. He thought her deliberately evasive and was convinced that she was hiding something from him.

"I'm a prisoner, my lord. What could be more amiss than that?"

His probing gaze lingered on her for a long moment. "If it is treachery you're planning, forget it. You can't win. Go seek your bed, lady. Should you wish my company, you have but to climb the tower stairs." Then he turned and strode away.

Elissa stared after him, admiring things about him she had no business noticing. She had seen him naked; she knew what lay beneath his clothing. How could she not remember the knotted muscles beneath skin marred only by battle scars? It was difficult to believe a man existed who was more physically attractive than the Demon Knight.

The memory of the long, thick lance between his thighs called forth the shimmering pleasure his kisses and caresses had brought her. She gave an angry toss of her head. Lurid thoughts about her enemy were wicked; she had to stop this nonsense.

Elissa reached the top landing and decided to bid her mother good night before seeking her own chamber and preparing for her meeting with Tavis. She was stunned to find Sir Brody sitting in a chair beside her mother's bed. He rose immediately.

"Lady Elissa."

"Sir Brody. How kind of you to keep my mother company. I know she gets lonely confined to her bed so much of the time."

"Sir Brody seeks my opinion often about the daily workings at Misterly. He is doing a good job as steward, but . . ."

"I couldn't do it without Lady Marianne's advice," Sir Brody was quick to add. "If you'll excuse me, I'll bid you both good night."

Elissa was dismayed to note the way Marianne's gaze followed Sir Brody's substantial form.

"He seems like a nice man . . . for an Englishman," Elissa ventured. "He appeared comfortable here with you."

"As I said before, we confer on castle business. I was mistress here for many years and know everything there is to know about managing an estate this size."

"Just so his visits donna tire you, Mama."

"Is there something you wanted to discuss with me, dear one?"

I want to tell you about Tavis. "Nay. I wanted to make sure you have everything you need for the night."

"Nan and Maggie take good care of me."

"Then I'll bid you good night."

Marianne grasped her hand. "Wait! You appear troubled."

"Is it so obvious?"

"To me it is. Is it Lord Damian? Does he mistreat you?"

Elissa looked away. "Nay, not exactly. 'Tis just . . . oh, Mama, please donna tell anyone."

"Tell them what? You can say anything to me, daughter, and I will understand."

Elissa had to talk to someone and her mother was the logical choice. She dragged in a sustaining breath. "I saw Tavis. He's at Misterly."

Marianne sat up a little straighter. "Tavis? Here? It canna be. Is the man daft? Did you speak with him? What does he want?"

"I donna know what he wants. I'm to meet him tonight in the stables."

"Oh, Elissa, donna do it. No good can come of it."

"I have to, Mama. He's my betrothed. Tavis can help us escape. If we band together, the Gordons and Frasers can drive the English devils from Misterly."

Marianne gave a shaky sigh. "I lost as much, if not more, at Culloden than anyone, but even I know 'tis time to give up the fight. The Highlanders were defeated and severely punished. The English now control our lands. Conspiring with Tavis Gordon could wipe out our clan, and I know you donna want that. We've already lost too many loved ones."

Elissa's tortured words came from deep within her soul. "I want my home back; I want to live free of cursed Englishmen. I want the Demon Knight to disappear from my life."

"Accept that which canna be changed," Marianne advised. "Donna listen to Tavis, he's a rabble rouser. Neither Nan nor I believe he's right for you."

"What *is* right for me? The life of a nun? Imprisonment? Death?"

A tear slipped from Marianne's eye and Elissa

was immediately contrite. "Forgive me, Mama, I dinna mean to burden you." She leaned forward and kissed Marianne's forehead. "You're tired, I'll leave you now."

"Promise you willna do anything foolish," Marianne pleaded. "Think about what's best for our kinsmen. Lord Damian isna so bad. Sir Brody says Misterly is prospering under his guidance."

"I promise, Mama," Elissa said guardedly.

Elissa hurried to her chamber and donned a dark, hooded cloak. Glancing out the narrow window, she saw the moon slip behind a bank of clouds. She smiled. It was time. Damian should be in his chamber and the soldiers in their barracks.

There was a guard in the hall but Elissa was able to duck past him and into the passageway leading to the kitchen. Dimly Elissa wondered if the guard had been posted because Damian had found the tunnel. But right now she had other things on her mind.

The kitchen fires were banked and no one was about. She opened the back door and slipped outside, stumbling through the kitchen garden to the stables. She entered the shadowed building, redolent with the soothing scent of horses and leather, and paused to get her bearings. A surprised gasp left her lips when a strong arm snagged her around the waist.

"What kept you?"

"Tavis, you scared the daylights out of me."

He pulled her to the darkest reaches of the stables before speaking.

"Did anyone see you?"

"Nay. What are you doing at Misterly? What do you want of me?"

"I would think 'tis obvious," Tavis murmured against her ear. "You're my betrothed."

"I . . . I'd hoped you still thought of me as your betrothed. Oh, Tavis, so much has happened since the day we were to wed."

"Naught good, I suspect. There's a way we can be together, lass, like your father intended."

Elissa was doubtful but willing to listen. She needed to get away from Damian's none too subtle seduction as soon as possible. "Have you come to take me away with you?"

"Not just yet, lass. There's something verra important you can do for me and for our kinsmen who lost their lives at Culloden."

"What can I do, Tavis? I'm not free to come and go as I please. Someone is always watching me."

"Aye, the Demon Knight is watching you." His voice dripped with malice. "I saw you with him today. He's hot for you, lass. We can turn his lust for you against him if you follow my orders."

Elissa's smooth brow furrowed. "How so?"

Though she could not see Tavis's face, she could sense the venom festering inside him.

"By giving yourself to him, then killing him when he's most vulnerable. We'll take care of the others. I've dedicated my life to killing Englishmen and chasing the survivors back to English soil. The Gordons and Frasers and their allies are in a position to become a major force in the Highlands again. Once Damian Stratton is dead and Misterly mine, I'll make the fortress impregnable to English attack."

Elissa found it difficult to catch her breath. How could Taviss suggest such a plan . . . and such a role for her in it? Was so much killing and death necessary? She wanted Misterly back, but not at the expense of her kinsmen's lives . . . or Damian's.

"The Demon Knight fancies you," Tavis continued. "I've seen it with my own eyes. Has he had you yet?"

"Tavis!"

"Forgive me, lass, but you are the only one who can maneuver the Englishman into a vulnerable position, and 'tis best accomplished in his bedchamber."

Elissa went still. She felt numb, betrayed. Her own betrothed wanted her to bed the enemy.

"You want me to slay Damian? In cold blood?"

"Aye. Do whatever it takes, for no Highlander will judge you harshly."

"You want me to let him bed me," she repeated, wanting desperately to understand, "and then kill him?"

He grasped her arms, his desperation palpable. "Heed me, lass, 'tis the only way. The Demon is a wily and skilled soldier, he'll kill too many of us before he's brought down. You are the only one who can get close enough to kill him."

"Nay!"

"Have you forgotten that your father and brothers lie rotting in their graves? Or that Gordons and Frasers and their brave kinsmen were slain at Culloden?

"Now think about the man who calls himself Lord of Misterly. He was at Culloden; mayhap he killed your kinsmen. He might have dealt the fatal blow to one of your loved ones. You have to do it, lass. For your clan, for your honor."

Elissa mentally retreated. Her relationship with Damian might be volatile, but she couldn't kill him. "I canna."

"Here, take this knife. Hide it in your clothing.

The deed must be done soon. Tonight and each night afterward, I will be watching from the forest for your signal."

"What signal?"

"Has the Demon taken the north tower for his own?"

"Aye."

"Verra good. After you kill him, hold a lighted candle before the open window. That's the signal for us to remove ourselves to the unguarded postern gate and wait for you to let us in. You're smart, lass, you should have no trouble sneaking from the keep to open the gate for us. Once inside, we'll spread out and kill the guards and sleeping soldiers. Finding the enemy within the keep and their lord dead will create a confusion that will defeat them in the end. We will slay them before they can arm themselves."

Numb with disbelief, Elissa closed her eyes and whispered. "I canna do it."

"You must! Here," he thrust the knife into her hand, "take the knife. I will be waiting for your signal."

Despite her reluctance, Elissa's hand curled around the handle. Her eyes flew open. "Nay, I willna have their blood on my hands." But when she tried to give the blade back to Tavis, he had disappeared.

Elissa shuddered. She couldn't do it. She wouldn't. Tavis was mad to demand such a thing of her. She wanted Englishmen on Scottish soil no more than he did, but what Tavis asked of her was murder and beyond her capability. Disturbed by the startling turn of events, Elissa returned to the keep in a daze. When she reached the kitchen door, she entered as stealthily as she had exited and made her way to her bedchamber.

Elissa collapsed on the bed, her mind in turmoil.

A long time elapsed before she found the energy to rise and remove her cloak. With mounting horror, she realized she still clung tightly to the knife Tavis had thrust into her hand.

Uttering a cry of dismay, she flung the knife away. It landed on the floor with a metallic clunk. The sound seemed to snap her out of her confused state. She retrieved the knife and looked about for a place to hide it. In desperation, she thrust it beneath her mattress.

Elissa tried not to think about Tavis Gordon the following day. She went about her duties and refused to answer her mother's questions about her meeting with Tavis. Another day passed. Then another. And each day she tried to avoid Damian lest he grow suspicious of her distraction.

Elissa was sharing lunch with her mother when Marianne said, "You seem distraught, daughter. Does it have anything to do with Tavis Gordon? What did he want with you? I hoped you'd tell me about your meeting with him without my asking."

"Tavis merely wanted to . . . to ask how we were faring."

Marianne rolled her fine green eyes. "I donna believe you. Is Lord Damian troubling you, then?" She searched Elissa's face. "Has he done something to offend you?"

"His being here offends me," Elissa said fiercely. Her voice gentled. "Donna fret, Mama. Naught is wrong. I am fine. I'm merely anxious for you to get well enough to leave before Lord Damian discovers the tunnel. He's been actively searching for it."

"Do you really want to leave, dearling?"

Elissa would do anything to escape Damian's sensual allure. "Aye, 'tis what I want."

"Then I shall endeavor to rise from this bed and get strong enough to flee with you and Lora."

Elissa's eyes lit up. "Oh, Mama, I want you well for myself and Lora, as well as for your own sake, for I willna leave Misterly without you."

"Tomorrow I shall ask Maggie to help me walk about a bit so that I may strengthen my legs."

"I love you, Mama," Elissa said, giving her mother a quick hug.

Suddenly the door opened and Lora burst through. "Mama! Damian let me ride his horse! Did you know Cosmo carried Damian in battle?" She cast a glance behind her. "Tell Mama how brave I was, Damian."

Elissa froze as Damian appeared in the doorway. "I hope I'm not intruding, Lady Marianne."

"Not at all, my lord. Please come in and tell me about my daughter's adventure."

Damian smiled at Lora. "Lora was very brave, indeed, and Cosmo acted like a perfect gentleman. I sat her before me and we took a turn about the courtyard."

Elissa looked down when Damian's silver gaze found her. Did her guilty expression give her away?

"Lady Elissa," Damian said in a commanding voice. "A word with you in private, if you please."

"Go, daughter," Marianne said, "Lora and I will be fine here. You canna imagine how pleased I am to see her health improving. Thank you, Lord Damian, for your good care of her."

" 'Tis no trouble, my lady," Damian said. "Now if you'll excuse us, I would speak with Elissa."

He guided Elissa out the door and down the corridor to her chamber. He opened the door and ushered her inside. He followed and shut the door firmly behind him.

"We shouldna be in here alone," Elissa said, backing away.

"A private word is all I want." His eyes darkened. "Though in truth I'd like much more from you."

'Tis best accomplished in your bedchamber, Tavis had told her. *Kill him. No one will blame you.* She couldn't. Not Damian. He was so vibrantly alive. Let someone else wield the knife, for she couldn't . . . wouldn't.

"What do you wish to say to me, my lord?"

Damian sighed audibly. "Still stubborn, I see. Ah, well, in that case, I'll state my business as succinctly as possible. 'Tis about your mother. She seems to be gaining strength. Do you not agree?"

Elissa was immediately suspicious. "Perhaps. Why do you ask? Do you still intend to send Mama and my sister to the convent?"

" 'Tis what the king wishes, but I'm willing to delay the journey until Lady Marianne's strength is fully restored. She seems to be much improved, for which I am grateful. I want no woman's death on my conscience. I have grown fond of your sister and mother and believe they will be safe in the convent. The king's arm is long, I want them where no harm will come to them."

"What about me, my lord? Donna you wish me safe?"

A slow smile stretched his lips. "I can keep you safe, Elissa. Come to my bed and I will protect you from the king with my life."

"I must refuse your offer, my lord. We both know the king will have his way whether you make me

your mistress or not. Send me to the convent with
Mama and Lora."

Damian's expression hardened. "So you can escape and wed Tavis? Nay."

"Then we have nothing more to discuss, my lord."

"We have a great deal to discuss. The least of
which is the way you respond to my kisses. Why are
you fighting the inevitable?"

Why indeed? Elissa wondered. Tavis wanted her to
bed Damian, but for a reason she couldn't countenance. Did her refusal make her a traitor? She did not
like the sound of that. She was a loyal Highlander.
Killing a hated Englishman, the usurper of her home
and lands, should not be a difficult task, so why did
she balk when so many people depended on her?

"If you are finished, my lord, you may leave,"
Elissa invited. His presence in her room was dangerous . . . and far too daunting.

A growl began deep in Damian's throat as he
grasped her waist and pulled her against him. She
opened her mouth to protest at the same time
Damian's mouth slammed down on hers. His kiss
was not gentle, but neither was it brutal. It was hot
and hard and needy. And arousing. Her lips had just
begun to soften beneath his when he broke away, a
satisfied smile curving his mouth.

"You know where to find me if you want more, my
lady," he said with an arrogance that made Elissa's
teeth clench. He left her standing with her lips
clamped together and rage seething through her. In-
sufficient rage, however, to convince her to kill him.

Later that day Elissa was walking through the
great hall when Dermot intercepted her. He glanced

about to see if anyone was listening, then whispered, "I have a message for ye, lass."

"A message? From whom?"

He leaned close. "I saw Tavis Gordon in the village today. He told me to tell ye that time was running out. It has to be tonight. What did he mean, lass?"

"I donna know."

"Yer lying, lass. I can see it in yer eyes. What is Gordon up to?"

She drew Dermot aside and whispered, "Tavis wants me to kill Lord Damian but I canna do it."

"Thank God," Dermot said fervently. "Yer not a killer, lass. How were ye expected to do the deed when the only time his lordship is vulnerable is when he is abed?"

Dermot's eyes widened when the answer came to him. "If what I'm thinking is right, Tavis is demented for asking ye to compromise yerself."

"Tavis is counting on me," Elissa whispered.

Dermot searched her face, his own softening with compassion. "This has to be yer own decision, lass. I realize having an Englishman take what is yers is difficult, but ye are not the only Highlander to suffer such a fate. I willna be unhappy to see the last of the English soldiers at Misterly, but I donna wish to see another Culloden in my lifetime."

"Nor do I," Elissa said, "but neither do I want Englishmen on Fraser land."

Her expression hardened. Could she do it? Could she go to Damian tonight and avenge her kinsmen?

Chapter 8

The great hall emptied quickly after the evening meal. Sprawled on a bench before the hearth, Damian stared morosely into his freshly drawn pint of ale. Sir Richard sat across from him in silent camaraderie. Despite Damian's distraction, he could tell Dickon had something on his mind.

"Is something bothering you, Dickon?"

Dickon cleared his throat. "Have you thought about returning the soldiers of the Black Watch to London? They are unhappy in the Highlands and wish to return to their former posts."

"I have come to the same conclusion, Dickon. Things are well in hand here. We have seen neither hide nor hair of the Gordon clan and probably won't. We can defend Misterly without outside help."

"Things are certainly going your way," Dickon allowed. "According to Maggie, Lady Marianne is recovering and young Lora's health has already been restored. You must be looking forward to sending them to the convent."

Damian wasn't so sure. He'd miss Lora's friendly chatter. And unlike Elissa, Lady Marianne didn't hold him personally responsible for Culloden.

"Lady Marianne and Lora are not the problems in this household," Damian muttered. "Lady Elissa could take lessons from them."

Dickon grinned. "I take that to mean your seduction of her isn't working."

"Take it any way you please. The little vixen just won't give up. How are you faring with your Maggie? Is she still resisting? 'Tisn't like you to spend so much time on an unwilling wench, Dickon."

"I could say the same for you, Damian. Mayhap I should try my luck in the village. Women are the same the world over—some are willing, others are not."

Just then Maggie crossed the hall on some errand or other and nodded a greeting at the two men. Damian watched with amusement when Dickon leapt to his feet and ran after her. So much for Dickon's plans to find a willing wench in the village.

The hour was growing late. Damian uncoiled his long form from the bench and sought his bed.

Freshly bathed and wearing a linen nightdress and robe, Elissa stared out the window. Was Tavis waiting for her signal? No matter how much he was counting on her, she couldn't kill Damian. Could she? Did she have it in her? Hands behind her back, she began to pace.

Elissa doubted Tavis had come this far to give up. There was bound to be a bloody battle whether

Damian was dead or alive. She wracked her brain for a plan short of murder that would aid Tavis. There was none. Tonight she would go to Damian's chamber and let him have his way with her. Once he fell asleep . . . God help her.

Englishmen or no, Elissa objected to the murder of men in their beds. A bloodless coup was more to her liking but she knew of no way to make that happen.

Elissa drew the pins from her hair and ran her fingers through the fiery mass until it fell in thick, long waves down her back. In a dreamlike state she picked up a candlestick and left her chamber.

Her tread was light as she descended the winding staircase and across the deserted hall. Her heart was pounding erratically and her blood pumping furiously as she climbed the tower stairs. Her hand was trembling as she lifted it and rapped lightly on the door.

Damian didn't answer immediately and she turned away, more relieved than she cared to admit. Then abruptly the panel opened. Larger than life and twice as threatening, Damian loomed in the doorway, his tall form barely covered by a robe tied loosely at the waist.

Damian's startled gaze roamed leisurely over Elissa's scantily clad body. He was scarcely able to believe his eyes, and surprise rendered him momentarily speechless. Elissa had come to him in her nightdress, her glorious hair down and her attitude meekly submissive. Submissive? Ha! He didn't believe *that* for a minute. Everything Elissa did was suspect.

He leaned against the doorjamb, his arms crossed over his bare chest. "To what do I owe this pleasure?"

He swore when he saw a flash of anger in her eyes despite her calm voice and composed features. "If you donna want me, my lord, I can leave."

Not want her? He'd have to be insane to let her leave now. He held the door open and stepped aside. She swept past him with regal grace, the scent of violets trailing behind her. Damian shut the door and leaned against it.

"Dare I hope you've suddenly found me irresistible?"

"You may hope whatever you please. I'm here. What more do you need to know?"

He reached for her and gathered her into his embrace. "No games this time, Elissa. There will be no pulling back, no maidenly protests. What we do in this room tonight will happen because 'tis what you want."

He saw her eyes widen and sought to allay her fears. " 'Tis what I want too, sweeting, have wanted for a very long time. The pleasure we share tonight is just the beginning. There will be many more nights like this one."

He kissed her then, holding her head steady with one hand while his other curled around her hip, bringing her hard against the burgeoning thrust of his manhood. Her lips were moist and sweet, but he could taste her fear. Was he that frightening? Or was it something else? Once again suspicion rose like a dark specter between them.

"Relax, sweeting," he whispered against her lips. "You do want this, don't you?"

"Aye, I am here, am I not?"

He released the tie holding her robe together and waited for her reaction. It was nearly imperceptible, but he still felt the tiny quiver she tried to suppress. He peeled the robe down her arms and tossed it aside. Her nightdress was so voluminous she could have been shapeless beneath it, but Damian knew better.

She was staring at him, her green eyes translucent in the flickering candlelight. He returned her gaze, knowing his raw need shown in it. "Elissa, you *do* know how much I want you, don't you?"

She nodded mutely.

"Then give yourself over to me. Let me lead you where you've never gone before."

She relaxed in his arms, and he heaved a sigh of gratitude.

"Take me where you will, Damian. I'm ready to follow wherever this night leads."

She sounded sincere, but Damian wasn't the fool she thought him. Did she carry a weapon? Did she intend to kill him this time? She'd brought no drugged wine, so there would be no repeat of the last time she'd come to his bedchamber.

He dropped his arms and stepped away. "Take off your nightdress, Elissa, I want to look my fill at you."

She hesitated so long, Damian drawled, "Shall I do it for you?"

Her head rose sharply. "Nay, I'll do it."

Damian literally shook with impatience. His sex rose thick and rampant between his thighs. She had barely lifted the hem of her nightdress when his patience snapped. Grasping yards of material in his hands, he pulled her nightdress over her head and off. Her hands flew up to cover her breasts but he grasped her wrists and anchored them at her sides. Then his heated gaze trekked leisurely over her tempting curves.

When he'd looked his fill, his gaze returned to her face. Her eyes were closed, her face was pale. He released her wrists, loosened the belt on his robe, and shrugged out of it.

"Open your eyes, Elissa."

Her lids slowly opened. Her startled gasp reverberated loudly in the waiting silence.

"Aye, neither of us have anything to hide now. You've seen my body before. Does it please you?"

Please her? Elissa couldn't begin to explain how his body affected her . . . how *he* affected her. Her mouth went dry. She couldn't look away. She shouldn't feel like this. She felt like a traitor to her people.

"Elissa, I asked you a question. Does my body please you? Yours pleases me."

"Your body is . . . very fine, my lord," she murmured, averting her gaze from his groin.

"So formal, Elissa? My name is Damian. I would like to hear the sound of my name on your lips." He reached out and caressed her breast, his fingers lingering on the tip, which had suddenly become swollen and aching. "I think your body is very fine, too. I can't wait to discover all its secrets."

Circling his arms around her, he crushed her against him as his mouth tasted hers, lightly at first, then with growing ardor. He urged her lips apart and his tongue swept in to taste her more deeply. Heat shimmered through her in wild, intoxicating waves that made her yearn for more. Then came despair. She enjoyed his kisses too much. She liked the hot, delicious feel of his skin against hers, and the heady pleasure it brought her.

He cradled her between his legs, holding her fast with the long, thick muscles of his thighs. She felt the hard wall of his chest against her breasts and heard the accelerated pounding of his heart. His mouth was hard but his lips felt soft. A compelling combination. The thick ridge straining against her belly was daunting, and more than a little frightening. There was no way she could take him inside her.

Elissa knew exactly what to expect. The eve before she was to marry Tavis, her mother had told her what would happen on her wedding night. Marianne had told her not to fear it, and that in time she might even enjoy it. Instinctively Elissa knew she would enjoy it with Damian, and that thought angered her. She didn't want to enjoy anything with the Demon Knight.

His kiss went on and on, until she hadn't a breath left in her lungs. Her hand curled around his neck; she felt a vein pulsing strongly along his throat. The heat of his desire scorched a burning path to her throbbing center. Then suddenly she was floating, caught up in Damian's strong arms. She felt the coolness of the counterpane beneath her back and Damian's solid weight as he came down over her.

Air spilled from Elissa's lungs at the first touch of Damian's mouth upon her breast. He suckled her, flicking his tongue over her swollen nipple before paying her other breast the same rapt attention. She moved restlessly, stretching, arching beneath his stroking hands. He caressed her from her breasts to her waist, then cupped her bottom in both his large hands.

Threads of tension pulled her taut as his mouth left her breasts and traveled downward. Then his head dipped down and he kissed her *there*, that moist, aching place between her thighs. Pleasure she'd tried to withhold burst inside her. Her head tilted back, a cry vibrated in her throat.

"Damian, nay! 'Tis wicked."

He lifted his head. "Aye, sweeting, wicked and wonderful. But perhaps you're right. We'll save that pleasure for another time. I need to be inside you."

He settled between her legs, pushing them wide with his knees. His hips twisted; he ground himself against her core. A flush began beneath her skin, heating her flesh from the inside out. Her breath stilled as she waited for the pain of his entry. It was a pain she welcomed, for it was little enough punishment for allowing Damian to seduce her. She'd feel far less guilt if she didn't enjoy what he was doing to her.

"Relax," Damian whispered against her temple. "The pain will only last a moment, then the pleasure I promised will begin."

His hand slid between them. She felt it low on her stomach, then drifting through the downy thatch below. He touched her; she let out a hiss of breath as his fingers slid over wet, swollen flesh.

"Sweet, sweet vixen," he murmured. "My fingers are wet with your honey. Let me in, Elissa."

His erotic words swept away her shame and guilt like a ship before a strong wind. Raw need inhabited her mind; urgency to experience this ultimate act with Damian, only Damian, controlled her body. She

clutched his shoulders, her legs falling open. He settled deeper into the cradle of her thighs, flexed his
hips, and thrust past every point of resistance.

Her eyes flew open. She screamed and tried to
push him away. The pain of his entry had startled
her, even though she expected it.

"Lie still," Damian said in a strangled voice. "Let
yourself adjust to my size."

"You're too big . . . you're killing me."

"The pain will subside if you let yourself relax." He
pulled out slightly, then pushed himself back inside.

Elissa squirmed, trying to escape the agony.
"Stop, Damian, please."

"Ask anything of me but that. Remember what I
told you about bringing you pleasure? I didn't lie,
sweeting."

He moved again, a subtle in and out that caused
Elissa's breath to hitch. He pulled out again, then
thrust deeper. Elissa's breathing calmed, and she experienced a feeling of fullness, of stretching, as her
body adjusted to accommodate him. Little by little
she began to relax; she felt herself soften around him
even as he grew harder, thicker. Then she felt a tiny
beginning of something else that made her gaze up
at him, a question in her eyes.

"There are better things to come," he said. Then
he proceeded to show her.

He came up on his knees, putting his strong
hands under her hips and pulling her up to meet his
sure, hard strokes. She couldn't help herself; she
cried out with every drive of his hips. Then it began:
the slow, spiraling heat, the heady pulsing where
they were joined, spreading outward throughout her
body. When he dropped his head and suckled her

breast, it was like adding kindling to flame. With the next thrust of his hips, shards of pleasure exploded through her and she screamed.

Her body convulsed, tautened. He pushed himself to the hilt, held himself suspended inside her for a breathless moment, then came in a rush of liquid heat.

Elissa struggled to catch her breath, stunned by what she'd just experienced. Her surrender was supposed to be a sacrifice, but Damian had made the act memorable, something to be treasured forever. Her entire body trembled as waves of pleasure undulated through her. She was scarcely aware when he pulled out of her and eased down beside her.

Elissa turned her head away. She couldn't look at him, knowing what she was going to do as soon as he fell asleep. She was going to betray him in the worst possible way.

Damian turned and gathered her into his arms. "Was that so bad, sweeting? Are you sorry you let me love you?"

"It was . . . I never dreamed . . . sweet Mother! You're an Englishman."

Damian grinned. "I never presumed to be anything else. Deny it all you want, but I *did* give you pleasure. You're too inexperienced to pretend."

Elissa looked away. "Aye, to my everlasting shame, I did find pleasure in your arms."

Damian went still. "You found that shameful? Is that how you'd describe what we did?" His expression hardened. "If I remember correctly, you came to me tonight. Is there a hidden reason behind your capitulation? An agenda I'm not aware of?"

Elissa's heart fluttered. *He mustn't become suspi-*

cious. "Oh, nay, nay!" she denied. "I came to your
chamber because I wanted you. I wanted to know
pleasure, and I wanted you to give it to me."

The reality behind her words gave her momen-
tary pause. Was it true? Had she secretly *wanted*
Damian to make love to her? No wonder she was
consumed with guilt.

"Why don't I believe you?" Damian murmured,
nuzzling her neck. "You're here, however, no matter
what your motive, and the night is still young."

Elissa's eyes widened. "You mean . . . again? Is
that possible?"

"Trust me."

He rose and padded barefoot to the washstand.
She watched warily as he poured water into a bowl,
wet a cloth, and returned to bed.

"Relax, I'm not going to hurt you," Damian said.

Gently spreading her legs, he wiped away all
traces of blood and seed. Then he returned the soiled
cloth to the washstand and joined her in bed. Elissa
was too embarrassed to look at him.

"Look at me, sweeting."

The plea in his voice was irresistible. Her chin
notched upward as she stared into the glowing
depths of his silver eyes. His blatant desire overwhelmed her. She started violently when he cupped
her between the legs and pressed the heel of his palm
lightly, insistently, against her core, his fingers
stroking over silken inner folds.

"Soft," Damian whispered, "so soft. I knew you'd
be responsive. There's a fire in you that pushes me
over the edge. I burn for you, Elissa. Only you can
quench the yearning within me."

A voice inside Elissa cautioned against taking

Damian's pretty words to heart, for they meant nothing. They were enemies, and always would be. Then her thoughts scattered as Damian rolled with her in his arms and brought her over him.

"Take me inside you, Elissa," he muttered thickly. Then he thrust upward, impaling her.

She felt dizzy, aching, as he brought her to the brink and held her suspended. Moments later she tumbled into paradise, her body pulsing with rapture. She felt him convulse violently, then go limp.

Elissa must have dozed, for when she awakened Damian was sleeping soundly, his breathing steady, his brow smooth and untroubled. A lock of dark hair clung to his damp forehead and she had the sudden urge to push it away, but she feared to, lest he awaken.

Easing herself from the warm bed, Elissa shivered, overcome by a chill that had nothing to do with the cool night air. She scrambled for her robe and pulled it on. Then she glanced out the window. The night was as dark as the inside of a tomb; a night designed for treachery. The moment of truth was at hand. Tavis had demanded that she kill Damian and signal him when the deed was done.

The knife! She had forgotten it in her chamber. With a start Elissa realized that killing Damian had never been her intention. She could still do as the Gordon chieftain directed and unlock the postern gate. But could she stand by and let Gordons kill Damian because she'd been too weak to do it herself? Who should she betray? Her clansmen or Damian? Could she live with herself if she didn't align her loyalty with Tavis Gordon and his cause?

Indecision rode her mercilessly as she picked up

the candlestick. She glanced at Damian. He was still sleeping. She took a step toward the window. So much depended on her. To betray Damian, all she had to do was show a light in the window and slip away to unlock the postern gate.

Bloodshed would ensue. Men would be slain in their sleep. Her own kinsmen could suffer. Was her honor worth the terrible loss of lives?

To whom did she owe her loyalty? To Highlanders who had been sadly abused by the English, or to the man who had just made love to her as if he truly cared for her? In her heart Elissa knew there was far more between her and Damian than simple attraction. She had succumbed to his seduction eagerly, had responded with a passion that had both appalled and thrilled her. She'd never known making love could be so rewarding for a woman, and she suspected she wouldn't have enjoyed it had Tavis been the man loving her.

Nay, she wanted only Damian, her avowed enemy.

Her grip on the candlestick tightened. Her hand shook. Flayed by indecision, she couldn't seem to take that final step to the window. The candlestick grew too burdensome to lift.

You're a traitor to your people. The words reverberated in her brain. *Only a whore would make love to a man, then heartlessly betray him.*

Somewhere in the deep recesses of her mind, Elissa heard Tavis's words reminding her of her father and brothers who had fallen at Culloden. Could Damian have wielded the blade that had slain them?

Her legs were leaden as she took another step toward the window.

Torn.

Oh God, she was torn; wrenched between loyalty to her kinsmen and the newly discovered empathy for the man who was her enemy. Her choices were woefully slim; none of them pleased her. Damned if she did and damned if she didn't.

She took another small step forward, then stopped, a silent cry of denial building in her throat. She couldn't go through with it. Her heart demanded that she awaken Damian and tell him about Tavis's plan and her part in it. She whirled to do just that and hit a solid wall of human flesh.

"So lovely yet so deceitful," Damian hissed. "I knew better than to trust you, lady." He grasped the candlestick from her hand and extinguished the flame. "Who were you going to signal, lady?"

"No one!" A sob caught in her throat. "I couldn't do it. Tavis wanted me to . . ."

"To do what? Kill me?"

"Aye . . . nay . . . I brought no weapon, Damian."

His voice rang with mockery. "You tried to poison me once and failed."

"I merely put you to sleep."

His hands tightened on her shoulders; she cringed, but her gaze did not waver from his. She was frightened, but somehow she knew he wouldn't hurt her, though he had good reason to.

He gave her a rough shake. "What treachery did you and Tavis hatch?"

Her mouth went dry. She shook her head.

His expression turned murderous, his voice low and threatening. "Tell me. No more lies. You've too much to lose."

Elissa knew exactly to what Damian was referring. He could do anything he wanted to her mother and sister with the king's blessing, and it would be all her fault.

"Tavis entered the gates with a group of tradesmen a few days ago," she blurted. "He found me alone and presented his plan."

Damian's eyes narrowed. "Aye, go on."

"He gave me a knife and asked me to kill you. He suggested that I come to your chamber and let you bed me, then I was to kill you while you slept. After the deed was done I was supposed to signal with the candle. Then I was to open the postern gate so the Gordons could slay your men while they slept."

"Are they still waiting for the signal?"

"I suppose. But I wasna going to do it, Damian. I couldna."

"Where is the knife Gordon gave you?"

"I forgot it, but even if I had the blade, I could never kill you, Damian."

Why wouldn't he believe her? She stiffened as his large hands slid over her body, searching for the knife.

"I'm surprised you didn't use my own sword to kill me. 'Tis sitting in the corner. Did Tavis tell you to seduce me?"

She looked away. His sword was indeed sitting against the wall, but using it hadn't even entered her mind. "Tavis suggested I do whatever was necessary. But that's not the reason I came to you tonight. I wanted you, Damian. I . . . wanted you to love me."

He shoved her away, a feral growl on his lips. She stumbled backward and tumbled onto the bed.

"Liar. I didn't trust you when you came to my chamber all sweetness and seduction, and I don't trust you now."

"Damian, please, I'm not capable of killing in cold blood."

"Not even your enemy?"

She regarded him solemnly, her eyes misty. "*Are* we enemies, Damian? Truly?"

"I was never your enemy, Elissa. You're the one who chose that relationship for us."

He pulled on his breeches and shirt and snatched his sword and scabbard from the corner. He buckled it around his hips and headed out the door.

"Where are you going?"

He didn't turn around. "Be here when I return, or you'll be very sorry."

Then he was gone, the hollow sound of his boot heels echoing loudly through the charged silence. She heard a commotion in the hall, then nothing more. When she dared to open the door, a guard stepped forward.

"Is there something you require, my lady?"

"N . . . no, thank you."

She closed the door and leaned against it. A noise in the courtyard brought her rushing to the window. A cry caught in her throat when she saw Damian and a company of castle guards ride out from the fortress. Darkness closed in behind them and she saw nothing more.

Elissa had no idea how many men had rallied to Tavis's cause, or if they were still waiting in the forest for her signal. What she did know was that should they engage in battle, Damian could be killed, and that would destroy her. She started to tremble, fearing the consequences this night had wrought.

* * *

Damian led the charge into the forest. As he thrashed through the thick underbrush, he spared a thought for Elissa and what she'd almost accomplished. Fortunately he was a light sleeper. He made a sound of disgust deep in his throat. Did she have the courage to kill in cold blood? He doubted it. Had she the instincts of a killer, he would already be dead. What really hurt was the knowledge that she came to him with one purpose in mind, to betray him, not because she wanted him, while he . . . well, 'twas best he didn't delve too deeply into his heart for the answer.

Why did Elissa insist on making him her enemy? He certainly hadn't harmed her . . . yet. It was unfortunate that she couldn't see past Culloden and look to the future.

Damian's thoughts scattered when he spied a number of dark shadowy figures fleeing through the forest. It appeared that Gordon had succeeded in mobilizing enough men to risk an assault upon Misterly. Fortunately Damian had nipped the plan in the bud, but it still rankled that Elissa would have opened the fortress gate to Gordon's savage horde.

"After them!" Damian yelled, as he plunged deeper into the woods. But even as he said it he knew it was a fruitless pursuit. The Highlanders knew this land like the back of their hands and could disappear at will.

Nevertheless, Damian continued the search till dawn. Then, tired and hungry, he ordered his men back to the keep. Preparations were under way to serve the morning meal when Damian entered the great hall. Ignoring the food, he drew himself a tankard of ale and stared moodily into the hearth.

His fury at Elissa hadn't abated. When he thought of all the good Englishmen who would have been slain in their sleep had she opened the gate to Gordon, he wanted to . . . what? Shake her until her teeth rattled? Or love her until his name trembled from her lips?

"How did you know the Gordons were hiding in the forest?" Sir Richard asked, when he joined Damian a few minutes later.

Damian said nothing.

"I suspect Elissa is somehow involved," Dickon guessed. "You haven't . . ."

"I haven't harmed her . . . yet. Excuse me, Dickon."

Surging to his feet, he strode away, his face intent with purpose.

Chapter 9

$\sim\!\!\infty\!\!\infty\!\!\sim$

Elissa steeled herself to face Damian's wrath as the bedchamber door opened. She nearly collapsed with relief when Nan, not Damian, entered the room.

"What have ye done, lass?"

Nothing in Nan's expression offered comfort. Elissa saw only pity and concern.

"I did naught, Nan. Tavis wanted me to kill Damian and unlock the postern gate, but I couldna. I dinna even bring the knife Tavis gave me to Damian's bedchamber."

"Why dinna my 'voices' warn me?" Nan moaned. "I knew something was afoot, but the tension between ye and Lord Damian was so thick I couldna get through to the heart of things. I should have been more wary."

"There's naught you could have done, Nan. Tavis entered the courtyard disguised as a tradesman and waited until I was alone to approach me. He gave me a knife and said I was to kill Damian, signal him when the deed was done, and unlatch the postern gate."

"Ye couldna kill Lord Damian," Nan surmised.

"You're right. Nor could I give the signal once Damian had fallen asleep. I donna want Damian to die. No matter what he did at Culloden."

"What's to become of ye, lass?" Nan asked anxiously.

"Nothing pleasant, I suspect."

Nan stared at her, her keen blue eyes intent upon something only she could see. When she finally spoke, her voice sounded reedy and hollow, as if she had peered into the future and feared the consequences.

"Ah, lass, yer headed for difficult times."

"They canna be more difficult than they are now," Elissa scoffed.

"I fear for ye," Nan said, searching Elissa's face. "But ye are strong, ye will survive. Yer son will bring peace to Misterly and the Frasers."

Elissa went still. "My son and Tavis's?"

Nan chuckled. But when she would have explained, the door burst open and Damian stepped into the chamber.

"Out, woman!" he roared, gesturing wildly at Nan.

Nan sidled past him. "Donna hurt her, me lord," she warned, "lest ye destroy yer future."

"Babbling old woman," Damian muttered, slamming the door behind her. He spun around, his gaze narrowing on Elissa.

Elissa sucked in a calming breath, but it did little to still the erratic pounding of her heart.

"They got away," Damian bit out. "Every bloody one of them. My instincts tell me to attack their stronghold, but my heart knows another Culloden isn't in England's best interest."

Elissa said nothing, gauging Damian's anger. She waited with baited breath for him to unleash his formidable temper as he paced before her like an enraged bull. She didn't have long to wait.

"Everything that passed between us last night was a lie!" he charged. "Your beloved Tavis would have slain me in my bed while you cheered him on."

Elissa recoiled beneath his fury. "Nay! I was going to warn you, not kill you."

His sarcasm bit deeply into her soul. "Of course you were. You let me make love to you while you planned my death. Why didn't you let Gordon in through the secret tunnel?"

Elissa blanched. "You found it?"

Damian gave her a smug look. "Of course. I told you I would. 'Tis beneath the solar stairs."

"Despite what you think, I never wanted your death. I'd never tell Tavis about the tunnel. 'Tis a family secret."

Damian didn't look at all convinced. "Where is the knife Gordon gave you?"

"Still in my room. I had no intention of using it."

"What was your intention when you came to my chamber?"

She bit the soft underside of her lip. "I'm not sure."

"You're lying," Damian charged. "I believe you intended to kill me and let Gordon into the keep. For your information, the attack would never have succeeded. Gordon was a fool to think Misterly could be taken so easily. Even had you succeeded, Dickon would have avenged my death and successfully defended the keep." His voice was harsh with condemnation. "Your life, sweet vixen, would have been forfeited. And I can't even guess what would become of your mother and sister had I been dispatched by your knife."

"I swear, my lord, I donna want your death."

He gave her an angry shake and shoved her away. "What . . . what are you going to do?"

"I know what I *should* do, but then I'd have a rebellion on my hands. I don't want to make enemies of the Frasers, so I will think of a punishment they will accept. Meanwhile, you will be confined in my chamber, denied visitors but for myself."

"How long am I to be confined?"

"Forever, if I have anything to say about it."

"You canna!"

"I can do anything I please."

Spinning on his heel, Damian stormed from the chamber.

Damian felt as if his life was unraveling. How could Elissa have done this to him? She was fiery temptation and primal torment. He was still stunned by the knowledge that making love to Elissa had been the singularly most satisfying experience of his life. One he wasn't sure he wished to terminate. Elissa had betrayed him, however, and that deed could not go unpunished.

Needing time alone to think, Damian went to the stables and ordered his horse saddled. He had no idea where he was going, he just knew he had to get away. He was well away from the fortress when he heard someone pounding after him. Glancing behind him, he saw Dickon hard on his heels. He halted to let Cosmo drink from a burn as he waited for his friend to catch up with him.

"What are you going to do about her?" Dickon asked without preamble when he reined in beside Damian.

"I wish I knew," Damian said dully. "Elissa's continued defiance baffles me. I thought I knew women, but she is an enigma."

"A profound statement, given your experience with women," Dickon chuckled. "You might consider sending her to London."

"This is no joking matter, Dickon," Damian argued. "I can't send her to London. It could mean her death, given the state of the king's mind where Jacobites are concerned."

"There is one solution you haven't considered."

Damian made a dismissive sound in his throat. "I've considered every reasonable solution."

"How about this one? Marry the lady to one of your knights. Preferably to someone who can keep her in line. After a babe or two, I predict she'll cause no further mischief."

Damian stared at Dickon as if his friend had blasphemed. The idea was outrageous. Marry Elissa to someone else? Let another man take her to his bed and make love to her?

"You have to admit the idea has merit," Dickon continued blithely.

He raised one dark brow. "Do you have someone in mind?"

"Aye," Dickon said, nodding vigorously. "Wed her to someone she can't wind around her finger. A strong man capable of putting an end to her shenanigans. I believe Sir Brody is such a man. He's a battle-scarred knight known for his short temper and heavy hand. Let him deal with her."

Damian gave a bark of laughter. "Haven't you noticed that Sir Brody's affections lean more toward the mother than the daughter?"

Dickon gave an elaborate shrug. "It makes little difference where his affections lay. Sir Brody will do as you say."

Damian discarded Dickon's suggestion out of hand. The idea wasn't at all feasible. He suspected that beneath Sir Brody's crusty exterior lay a soft heart. If Elissa were to wed an Englishman, it should be to a man who would deal harshly with her without breaking her spirit. A man like . . . himself?

A violent shake of his head cleared his mind of that ridiculous notion. Soon he would have a bride who would bring riches to his coffer, one chosen specifically for him by the king. What he didn't need was a woman who hated him, a vixen who bore watching like a hawk lest she slay him in his sleep.

"I'll consider your suggestion, Dickon," Damian hedged. "But Sir Brody isn't the right man for Elissa."

"You will give it serious thought, won't you, Damian?"

"Aye. Shall we continue our ride?"

Damian and Dickon returned to the keep in time for the noon meal. Damian plopped down in his chair, a thoughtful expression on his face. He served himself from a platter of meat and chewed thoughtfully. But after the first bite his appetite for food abruptly vanished.

His hunger for Elissa, however, was still potent and inescapable. He recalled every nuance of their lovemaking the night before, every little sigh he'd wrenched from her, each moan, and the final scream at the height of her climax. Had she been pretending? It seemed unlikely, given her inexperience. No matter, real or pretense, he knew Elissa would betray him again and yet again, given the chance.

"Fix a tray for Lady Elissa," he growled to a passing servant. "I'll take it up to her myself."

Damian returned his attention to his food but was interrupted when Lora skipped into the hall with Nan following in her wake. "Am I late, Damian?"

Despite his dark mood, Damian smiled at the fetching child. "You're just in time, Lora." He scraped back his chair. "Here, take my place."

Lora scooted into Damian's chair, then looked about her, as if searching for someone. "Where is Lissa?"

"Your sister won't be coming to the table today," Damian proclaimed in a voice loud enough to carry throughout the hall. "She's been confined to the tower."

"Again?" Lora wailed. "What has she done now?"

"You're a child, you wouldn't understand," Damian said, more harshly than he intended.

Maggie appeared with a cloth-covered tray in her hands. Damian took it from her, nodded his thanks, and strode off. "We'll talk later, Lora," he called over his shoulder.

Elissa heard footsteps approaching and marshaled her courage. Hands clenched at her sides, she was prepared when the door opened and Damian stepped inside. His expression was cold and unrelenting, devoid of all emotion. She watched warily as he set the tray down on a nearby table.

"I thought you might be hungry."

"Thank you."

He regarded her with such cold hostility that Elissa blurted out, "Go ahead, do your worst, my lord."

"My worst? I fear you wouldn't like my worst."

He stalked toward her, until they were standing toe to toe. Elissa refused to give an inch.

"Why did you do it, Elissa? I've done nothing to harm you. You came to me and I gave you pleasure. Was it all a sham, an act to throw me off guard? Do you hate me so much?"

Hate Damian? Nay. She didn't hate him, she . . . "I dinna hate you, Damian. My response to you was genuine. I wanted you. I admit I was undecided about my intentions when I entered your chamber, but there was never any doubt in my mind about killing you. I couldna, I wouldna."

His brows drew together in a thick, black slash. "Am I supposed to believe you? You said you wanted me. Do you still want me? Will you respond to me just as you did last night if I make love to you now?"

She gave him a startled glance. "Surely you donna mean . . . you donna intend to . . . now?"

"Aye, Elissa, now."

He crowded her against the bed, leaning forward until she was forced to bend under his weight. She fell onto the mattress and stared into his face. His expression was unreadable, but his eyes were glinting like newly minted coins. She watched with mounting alarm as he slowly began to undress. How could he want her when he was so coldly furious? Was this, then, her punishment—to suffer his attentions knowing there was no warmth in the act? How could she bear it after last night?

Her thoughts scattered when she felt the mattress dip beneath Damian's weight. He was naked, a flesh and blood man of magnificent proportions. The heat of his body assaulted her through the layers of her clothing. She couldn't help herself; her body sought his of its own volition. She heard Damian chuckle, but there was little mirth in his laughter.

"Keep moving like that, sweeting, and this will end before you find pleasure."

His hands moved over her, undressing her with a swiftness that took her breath away.

"Damian, nay . . ."

Her plea fell on deaf ears. She sensed the passion building within him, felt his hands shaking, and knew he wasn't as unmoved as he pretended. The realization that he wouldn't hurt her came in a brilliant flash of insight. She stopped struggling and let desire for this impossible Englishman sweep her away.

She felt his lips against her throat, and the pulse of her own heartbeat in the pounding of her blood. The tip of his tongue teased her flesh, searing a path between her breasts, a slow, sensuous trail that ultimately centered on the peak of her nipple. The brush of his tongue, the graze of his teeth, brought the knowledge that he was taking his time to arouse her instead of using her with ruthless disregard for her feelings.

The liquid heat of his mouth ignited flames deep in her being. She stirred against him, murmuring senseless words, aware of the fire that burned in him, of the pulse of life within him. She should press him away; she pulled him against her instead, her fingers stroking over him.

His tongue laved her navel as the hard heel of his palm slid over her mound and his fingers slid into slick, swollen flesh. His thumb found a sensitive spot, stroking, caressing. Gasping, she rocked against him. Then his mouth was there, his tongue teasing, penetrating. A wail left her lips and she tautened like a bowstring.

Incredible, erotic heat sheared through her. "Damian, you canna . . ."

He lifted his head and smiled. "Aye, I can. Lie back and enjoy it." Then his head dipped and his mouth returned to its succulent feast.

She arched and writhed against him, her protest a dim memory as the wet lash of his tongue sent shards of lightning streaking through her. Her hands clutched convulsively in his hair as she surrendered to a rapturous climax.

Dimly she became aware that Damian was on top of her, parting her legs, sinking deeply inside her. She closed her eyes, unwilling to reveal the depth of her feelings, but Damian would not allow it.

"Open your eyes, Elissa."

Her lids opened slowly and she stared into his eyes. She saw confusion and wondered what he was thinking.

"Are you a sorceress?" he whispered hoarsely. "Have you placed a spell on me? You must have, for you enchant me."

"I am no witch. I know naught about enchantment. This isna right. It shouldna be happening."

Damian rolled his eyes. " 'Tis right, sweeting, more than right."

He thrust forward, burying himself deeply. She sighed, aware of his heat, his hunger, and the fullness of his sex within her. The pulse of his heart matched her own. She felt his strength, the texture of his skin, the rasp of his flesh against hers. Every detail of the man was hers to savor. Nothing mattered but the pleasure of their merging, and the inexplicable need for something deeper.

With a cry of surrender, she climaxed. Thunder filled the chamber, fire consumed her; a blaze centered where they were joined and she felt herself receding from reality. Moments later she felt his liquid heat seep into her, heard him gasp out her name.

Elissa's wits returned slowly. She stretched her limbs and realized that Damian's weight had been lifted from her. She turned her head and regarded him solemnly. He was lying on his back, one arm covering his eyes, his breathing harsh and untamed. She was startled from her contemplation when Damian reared up and said, "You are a sorceress. 'Tis the only explanation." He surged to his feet. "Nothing good will come of this. What if I gave you a child?"

"A man of your experience should know how to prevent such an occurrence," Elissa charged.

He pulled on his breeches. "I have no control where you're concerned. You keep me in a constant turmoil. I'm torn between wanting to strangle you and wanting to make love to you. When I'm inside you, there's no pulling back."

Elissa touched her stomach. "We've only done this twice. Perhaps I should ask Nan for a potion to expel your seed should it take root in my womb. I donna want to bring a bastard into the world."

Damian whirled, his face dark with fury. He placed his hands on her shoulders, pinning her to the bed. "Nay! I forbid it! You will kill no child of mine."

Elissa breathed a sigh of relief. It was a sin to kill an innocent bairn. Sometimes a village woman asked Nan for a potion to rid herself of an unwanted bairn, but Nan always refused, advising them instead to practice abstinence.

" 'Tis highly unlikely you have conceived," Damian said, as if to convince himself. "Rest assured this will never happen again. Meanwhile, you're to remain under lock and key until I decide your fate. Harsh punishment isn't the answer, for it will serve only to anger your clansmen. But I vow you'll never have the chance to betray me again."

Damian's words lingered in the charged air long after he left her chamber.

The day passed slowly. Elissa missed her mother and sister. She was surprised when Maggie arrived later with clean clothing and a pitcher of water. Had Damian changed his mind about allowing visitors?

In the time allotted her, Maggie related the latest gossip. Elissa learned that patrols had been doubled, but Damian still intended to send the Black Watch back to London. Elissa thought Maggie had something more on her mind, but unfortunately the guard summoned her kinswoman from the chamber before Elissa could question her. Maggie sent Elissa a sympathetic look over her shoulder as the door closed behind her.

Elissa spent the day in supreme boredom, with nothing to do but gaze out the window. She was more than a little surprised when Damian himself arrived with her evening meal.

She sent him a wary look. "Where is Maggie?"

"Taking the air with Sir Richard."

"I should have known."

"Do you have any objection?"

Elissa shrugged. "What good would it do? You Englishmen will have your way."

Damian placed the tray on the table and stood over her as she pulled up a chair and picked delicately at the slices of venison and green vegetables. Her fork paused halfway to her mouth when she realized Damian had removed his jacket and shirt.

"What are you doing?"

"Getting ready for bed."

"You're sleeping here?"

"This *is* my chamber."

"But I thought you said we wouldn't . . . be together anymore."

"We won't. I'm testing myself. I'd like to think I'm not so lacking in will that I can't control myself around you. What happened earlier won't happen again because from now on I'll be on guard against your wiles."

Elissa threw the fork down. "My wiles! How dare you. You're the one who attacked me."

Damian scowled. "Eat, lady, the hour grows late and I am weary."

He sat on the edge of the bed and pulled off his boots and breeches. Elissa pointedly ignored him as he stretched out atop the covers. The food tasted like straw but she forced herself to eat and drink in an ef-

fort to prove her contempt for the man many called
the Demon Knight.

When she'd eaten her fill, she pushed the plate
aside and asked, "Where am I to sleep?"

"You may share the bed, if you like."

"No, thank you. The hearth rug will do. May I
have a pillow and blanket?"

"Of course," Damian said. "You'll find what you
need in the chest at the foot of the bed. Good night."

Elissa found the bedding and laid it out before the
hearth. Then she lay down fully clothed and pulled
the blanket up to her neck. She didn't allow herself
to relax until she heard the even cadence of
Damian's breathing. But when she tried to sleep, the
memory of making love with Damian intruded.

Never would Elissa have believed she could crave
a man's touch like she did Damian's. She was
cursed. Wanting her enemy was the worst kind of
betrayal. The thought of wedding Tavis and being
intimate with him, however, was repulsive. Uniting
the Gordon and Fraser clans had been her father's
wish, and she had assumed she would go to her
bridegroom a virgin.

Elissa's respect for Tavis had plummeted when
he'd suggested that she seduce Damian in order to
kill him. But truth to tell, she had made love with
Damian because it was what she wanted, not because Tavis had demanded it of her. But she was well
aware that she couldn't have Damian. He was her
sworn enemy, and what they had done together
made her a traitor to her clan. Besides, Damian was
promised a wealthy bride and Elissa had no idea
what the future held for her, except that it didn't include an Englishman.

* * *

Throughout the endless days of Elissa's imprisonment, Damian steadfastly returned each night to his bedchamber, which didn't make Elissa's life any easier. By now she knew when to expect him and made sure she was curled before the hearth with her face turned away from him when he arrived. Though he rarely spoke to her while he prepared for bed, she sensed his gaze on her and wondered how long would it be before lust destroyed his good intentions?

Damian felt as if he were balancing on the edge of an abyss. One wrong step would send him to perdition, and the way he felt now, he'd welcome it. Anything was better than this wanting, this perverse, aching need that kept him sleeping in the same chamber with Elissa when he knew he couldn't have her. What was wrong with him? He didn't believe in spells or witchcraft, but there was no other explanation for his obsessive longing for the Scottish vixen.

One day Damian was in the courtyard watching his men at swordplay when a messenger bearing the king's pennant rode through the gate. As Damian waited for the messenger to dismount, he grew tense with apprehension.

"Greetings. I am Sir Lowell. I bear a message to Lord Damian from the king."

"Welcome, Sir Lowell. I am Lord Damian. You must be exhausted after your long journey. Ale and food await you within."

"Thank you, Lord Damian, I must admit my mouth is parched."

Damian led the way into the keep, wondering what the king wanted of him this time. He sat down at the table and invited Sir Lowell to do the same. A maidservant approached with two foaming mugs of ale. Sir Lowell drank deeply, then sat back with a satisfied sigh.

"The message is verbal, my lord," Sir Lowell began. "I left London two days before your intended bride and her entourage. They should arrive within a few days."

"My bride?" Damian repeated, choking on the words.

"Lady Kimbra Lancaster, an heiress of outstanding beauty and social standing among the *ton*. King George sends his greetings and wishes you to know he hadn't forgotten you. He hopes you approve of his choice of bride."

When Damian remained silent, Sir Lowell said, "Would that I were in your shoes, my lord. Lady Kimbra is a favorite of the court. I envy you."

Damian finally found his voice. "The king does me great honor. Everything will be in readiness for Lady Kimbra's arrival. If you'll excuse me, I must confer with my steward. Chambers must be prepared for our guests. Will you abide with us long?"

"Just this night," Sir Lowell said. "I'm to return forthwith and give a report on conditions at Misterly. The Council instructed me to stress the importance of keeping Misterly in English hands."

"Everything is as it should be," Damian maintained.

Damian left Sir Lowell to his ale and went in search of Sir Richard. He found his friend in the courtyard, matching swords with a man-at-arms.

"A word with you, Dickon," Damian said, interrupting the play.

Dickon lowered his sword. "What is it, Damian? I saw the messenger. Is it bad news?"

"Nay, the news is good," Damian said with forced joviality. "King George is sending me an heiress. She's on her way as we speak."

"Congratulations!" Dickon crowed, slapping Damian on the back. "I hope for your sake she's a great beauty."

"I must prepare for her arrival," Damian said. "You're the first to know."

"Damian, wait! What about Lady Elissa?"

Damian frowned. "What about her?"

"Your bride is bound to hear the talk. Keeping Elissa confined to your bedchamber wasn't the wisest move. Everyone knows of your sleeping arrangements. 'Tis a forgone conclusion that you've already had her. What do you suppose your bride will say? You should send her away, Damian. I'm telling you this for your own good."

Damian stiffened. He was well aware of his shortcomings without Dickon spelling them out. He'd heard the gossip concerning his relationship with Elissa and had ignored it without considering the consequences. Until the messenger had arrived, he'd relegated all thought of his bride to the remote future . . . long after he'd had his fill of Elissa.

But now his bride had become a reality, and he was no closer to deciding Elissa's fate than he'd ever been. Suddenly his ache for Elissa turned sharp, cutting, born of frustration and unrequited need. It was that need that turned his steps toward the tower.

Elissa watched the new arrival from the tower window and wondered what it meant. Nothing good for the Frasers, she supposed. She placed her hands behind her back and stretched; the gnawing ache reminded her of the uncomfortable nights she'd spent tossing and turning on the floor before the hearth. How long would Damian keep her confined? What was to become of her?

She was still ruminating on her fate when Maggie entered the chamber. She set a fresh pitcher of water on the table and fussed with its placement, refusing to meet Elissa's gaze. Elissa immediately became wary.

"Maggie, what is it? Has something happened?"

Maggie finally raised her head, her eyes glistening with compassion. "Aye, Elissa, I fear the news is not good."

"Tell me."

"A messenger arrived. Lord Damian's intended bride is on her way to Misterly."

Elissa felt as if a giant hand had squeezed her heart.

"His lordship is preparing for her arrival. The south tower is being made ready for her and her entourage."

"What of my family, Maggie? What's to become of them?"

Maggie shrugged. "His lordship hasna said. But . . . there's something ye should know."

Elissa searched Maggie's face and didn't like what she saw. "You can tell me, Maggie. Whatever it is, I can take it."

"Our kinsmen are saying . . . forgive me, Elissa, that ye are the Demon Knight's mistress."

Elissa recoiled as if struck. How could she explain her dalliance with Damian? She couldn't, so she maintained her silence.

" 'Tis true, then," Maggie whispered. "He *has* dishonored ye. Yer a brave woman, Elissa. Do ye think Tavis will still want ye?"

Elissa gave a snort of disgust. "Donna mention that man's name to me. He wouldna care if I became Damian's mistress as long as he thought it would help his cause."

"Oh, Elissa, surely not."

Damian chose that moment to storm into the chamber. He pointed to Maggie and said with little patience, "Out."

Maggie turned and fled as if the devil was nipping at her heels. Damian slammed the door behind her and leaned against it, arms folded across his broad chest.

"What did she tell you?"

"She said your intended bride is on her way. I hope she pleases you, Damian. I have but one question. What will happen to me and my family?"

She could tell by his expression that he hadn't the slightest idea how to handle the situation, and for some reason that frightened her.

Chapter 10

Damian's fierce expression spoke eloquently of his indecision. His responsibility toward Lady Marianne, Lora, and Elissa shouldn't concern Lady Kimbra, but odds were she would object to their presence in her home. Therefore, Damian decided that he and Elissa should no longer share his bedchamber, even if there was nothing going on between them.

"Lady Kimbra's arrival will change naught," Damian said.

Elissa sent him a disgruntled look. "Unless your intended bride is dimwitted, I doubt she'll accept the fact that I am a prisoner in your bedchamber."

Damian's frown deepened. "Aye. That will have to change. I've decided to end your confinement. But rest assured you'll be kept under constant surveillance. You're free to return to your chamber in the solar, but you're not to leave the keep unless accompanied by one of my men. If you try to contact Gordon again, I'll find a place of isolation where you'll not see the light of day. Do I make myself clear?"

"Perfectly," Elissa snapped. "May I leave now?"

"Soon." His gaze shifted away from hers. "But first, there's something you should be aware of."

Elissa glared at him. "I know everyone is saying I'm your mistress."

"You've heard? I should have known."

Elissa's cheeks reddened. " 'Tis true I went willingly to your bed, but . . ."—she squared her shoulders—"that doesna mean I've become your mistress."

She looked so defenseless, so guilt stricken, that Damian felt an unaccustomed pang of compassion. What was happening to him? He was far too dedicated a sinner to change in a matter of weeks, but the feelings were there nonetheless.

He felt himself being drawn to her, his body suddenly reacting to her nearness in a way that made it impossible to turn away from her. He wanted her, aye, but he knew that taking her would lead them further down the path to disaster.

Unfortunately his body refused his mind's edicts as he reached for her and brought her into his embrace. Initially she stiffened, then she swayed against him. It was all the encouragement Damian needed. His arms tightened around her.

"You're a threat to my position at Misterly, not to mention my sanity," he whispered against the silken softness of her hair. It smelled like a field of flowers, making him giddy with desire. A desire he knew could lead to unwelcome repercussions in the future.

She murmured something against his shoulder that sounded like a protest.

"I shouldn't want you like I do," Damian muttered.

"Nor I you." As if realizing what she'd just said, she pushed away from him, her face red with embarrassment. "I dinna mean that."

"Too late, for both of us, I fear."

"Nay! Your bride is on her way. She will share your bed and bear your children. I am your enemy."

"I am not yours." Framing her face in his large hands, he stared at her lips. Then he lowered his head to taste her mouth for what he thought would most likely be the last time. Her tiny gasp fueled his need to intensify the kiss. His tongue delved deep as his hands molded her, caressed her arms, her ribs, her breasts, memorizing every curve and indentation of her responsive body.

He unbuttoned the yoke of her gown; his lips burned a path between her breasts as his fingers bunched up her skirts and his hand cupped between her thighs. She kissed him back, her legs parting in welcome. Then, as if realizing what was happening, she broke free and pushed herself away.

"Nay, Damian, I willna be your mistress. Submitting to you now would but confirm what my people believe of me. I am a Jacobite and you are an Englishman. Nothing will ever change that."

Damian's hands dropped away. His voice turned hard, implacable. "You're right, of course. Thank you for reminding me of our positions, lady. If we can't be lovers, then enemies it shall be."

He turned to leave, then spun back around to confront her. "I suggest you get along with my bride when she arrives if the well-being of your mother and sister mean anything to you."

Elissa stared at the closed door for several long minutes after Damian left. Get along with his intended bride? That hardly seemed likely, given what had happened between her and Damian. She could take care of herself; it was her mother and Lora she worried about. She knew intuitively that Lady Kimbra wouldn't welcome them in her home. Why was Damian so adamant about keeping her at Misterly? What reason could he have for wanting her underfoot? Nothing made sense where Damian was concerned.

Elissa left the tower a short time later. There was no guard at the door, but she could feel eyes following her as she crossed the hall and climbed the stairs to the solar. Damian hadn't lied. She may have been released from the tower but she was still a prisoner.

Happy to be in her own chamber again, Elissa bathed and changed and went to visit her mother. She was pleased to find Lora with Marianne, snuggled next to her on the bed reading a book.

"Lissa!" Lora greeted as Elissa entered the chamber. "I'm so glad Damian let you out of the tower. I told him he was being mean for keeping you there."

Elissa gave her sister a quick hug. "I agree with you, sweeting."

Marianne held out a fragile hand and Elissa grasped it. "How are you, Mama?"

Marianne gave her a reassuring smile. "Much better. I'm up and walking a bit now. Thanks to Lord

Damian, I've come to realize that life goes on. I have much to live for. My husband and sons are gone, but I still have my precious daughters."

"I hope you're not becoming too fond of Damian, Mama," Elissa chided. "He's our enemy. He's taken our home and our lands from us. Mayhap he wielded the weapon that killed our men."

Marianne sighed. "I know, sweeting, but our men chose to go to war. They fought for Prince Charles and his right to rule, and they lost. I deeply regret the carnage, but 'tis over and done with. We still have our pride and our courage, no one can take that from us. I will miss your father and brothers till the day I die, but I have you and Lora. If living in peace means accepting Lord Damian as Lord of Misterly, then so be it."

"I'm sorry, Mama, but I canna repress my hatred for the English tyrants."

"Why donna you like Damian?" Lora asked.

"Lora, love," Marianne interrupted, "run down to the kitchen and ask Winifred for a treat to tide you over till dinner. Dinna you just say you were hungry?"

"I hope she made fresh gingerbread," Lora said hopefully.

"Why donna you ask her?"

"Verra well. Will you finish the book later, Mama?"

"Aye, love. Off with you, now."

"You *are* better, aren't you, Mama?" Elissa asked after Lora scooted off.

"Verra much so, daughter. I'm even eating more in order to get my strength back."

"Oh, Mama, I'm so glad. Once you're strong

enough, perhaps I can convince Damian to let us go to cousin Christy at Glenmoor."

Marianne searched Elissa's face. "Are you sure you want to leave, Elissa?"

Elissa recalled her recent conversation with Damian in his chamber and touched her lips, recalling his kiss and how she'd been ready to succumb to him again. He threatened her sanity and her loyalty; she had to get away.

"We *must* leave, Mama. Damian's intended bride will arrive soon. She willna like us living here. 'Tis her right to insist that Damian sends us away."

"Do you still wish to wed Tavis Gordon? Do you love him, daughter?"

Elissa hesitated. "I donna love Tavis. He is one of us, but there are things about him I donna respect."

"I suspect you're right about Damian's bride not wanting us at Misterly, but I believe his lordship will have something to say about sending us away." Her hand tightened on Elissa's. "I would ask you a question, daughter."

Elissa knew what was coming and steeled herself.

"Is it true that you've become Lord Damian's mistress?"

"Nay, I am not the Demon Knight's mistress."

"Has he dishonored you?"

Elissa looked away. "Donna ask, Mama. 'Tis complicated."

"Elissa . . ."

"Nay, Mama, please. Whatever exists between Damian and me is personal. I canna talk about it."

Lady Marianne touched her daughter's face. "I pray that you donna harbor feelings for Lord

Damian. He's going to wed an heiress. Naught can change that."

"I said I donna wish to speak of it," Elissa repeated. She rose abruptly. "I have to go. We'll visit later."

"Elissa . . . do you wish me to speak to Lord Damian about it?"

Elissa frowned. "About what?"

"About his lordship taking advantage of your innocence."

Elissa debated with herself long and hard before answering. "Damian did nothing I dinna want."

Her words hung in the air like autumn smoke as she made a hasty exit.

During the following days Elissa kept herself busy from dawn till dusk, taking great care to avoid Damian. It irked her no end that she couldn't leave the keep without an escort, but since she didn't want to be isolated again, she suffered Damian's guards.

What hurt worse was the way she'd been regarded since her release from the tower. No one actually came out and asked if she was Damian's mistress, but she could tell they were thinking it.

Elissa had heard nothing more from Tavis and wondered if he had abandoned his plans to drive Damian from Misterly. The more Elissa thought about Tavis the less she wanted to become his wife. She couldn't forget how he'd used her. Nor could she wed a man who had urged her into another man's bed for a cause that had already been lost.

Elissa was giving Winifred a hand in the kitchen one day when an excited Maggie burst through the door.

"She's here! Lord Damian's bride! Her entourage just rode into the courtyard."

Elissa's heart lurched. Though she'd been expecting the lady's arrival, she hadn't been prepared for any kind of emotional response.

"What does she look like?" Winifred asked.

"I dinna see her, but I heard she's a great beauty."

Elissa tried to convince herself that Lady Kimbra's beauty or lack of it was no concern of hers. That didn't stop her from being curious about Damian's bride, however. Would the lady be a sweet, demure miss who doted on Damian? she wondered. Lord help the poor woman if she fell in love with the scoundrel. Damian would never give his heart to a woman, for he guarded it too closely.

Elissa heard a commotion in the great hall and the devil inside her made her slip away for a peek at the new arrivals. Hovering near the kitchen door, she peered over bobbing heads at Damian's heiress.

Elissa's heart plummeted. Lady Kimbra was indeed a beauty—a typical English rose with golden blond hair, peaches and cream complexion, and doll-like features almost too perfect to be real. Small and petite, her womanly figure was rounded in all the right places. Oh, aye, the lady was indeed lovely, and smiling up at Damian as if she wanted to devour him.

Elissa crept closer. She saw Damian bring Lady Kimbra's dainty white hand up to his lips and buried her own reddened hands beneath her apron. With sudden insight, Elissa realized that while Damian might not love his bride, he surely would appreciate her beauty.

"Welcome to your new home, my lady," she heard

Damian say. "I hope you learn to love Misterly as much as I do."

Elissa noted Lady Kimbra's disdainful look and realized something that Damian did not. *Damian's bride hated Misterly.*

"I suppose it will do for short visits," she said with bored indifference, "but my lord, surely you don't intend for us to languish in this savage land during the Season, do you? Why I would simply perish without balls and fêtes and parties to attend."

Elissa saw the tiny frown gathering between Damian's eyes and waited anxiously for his reply.

"We're both here at the king's command, my lady," Damian reminded her with more gentleness than Elissa would have credited him. "I'm sure you'll grow accustomed to the beauty of Misterly and learn to enjoy the peacefulness."

"You expect me to find peace in a place inhabited by Jacobite traitors?" Lady Kimbra spouted. "I think not, Lord Damian." She waved her fan languidly before her face. "I am fatigued, my lord. Perhaps one of the servants can show me to my chamber."

Damian lowered his voice; Elissa sidled closer to hear. "I thought we should discuss our wedding, my lady. Did His Majesty set a date for the nuptials?"

A man dressed in severe black stepped forward. "I am the Reverend Trilby, my lord. It will be my pleasure to perform the nuptials. Our gracious sovereign left it up to you to decide the date for the wedding ceremony."

"Welcome to Misterly, Reverend," Damian said. "I hope you enjoy your stay."

Elissa held her breath as Damian considered his

next words. " 'Twould seem proper that Lady Kimbra and I get to know one another before wedding."

"I agree, my lord," Reverend Trilby said amicably. "Not many men would be as understanding of a woman's feelings as you."

Kimbra lowered her head demurely. "Whatever you say, my lord." Her throaty purr held a hint of promise. "I am, of course, at your disposal." She placed a dainty hand on Damian's chest. "I'm not displeased with the king's choice of husband, Lord Damian, and I look forward to . . ." her brows lifted for emphasis, "becoming better acquainted."

Elissa decided she'd heard enough when Damian's gaze found hers. She tried to appear inconspicuous and cringed when he motioned for her to approach.

Her steps dragged as she made her way to his side. "Elissa, please show Lady Kimbra and her maid to the south tower. Her trunks have already been delivered to her chamber."

Elissa nodded but said nothing, suffering Kimbra's insolent gaze.

"Are all the servants as flamboyant as this one?" Kimbra asked.

Damian's brows lifted. "Flamboyant? How so, my lady?"

"All that flaming red hair. 'Tis indecent. Who is she, my lord?"

"I am Elissa Fraser," Elissa said proudly. "Misterly is my home."

"Elissa," Damian warned.

"A Jacobite," Kimbra sneered. "What is she doing here, Lord Damian? 'Twas my understanding that Lord Alpin's daughter had been exiled."

"We will discuss this later, my lady," Damian said. "Chambers have been prepared for you and your maid in the south tower. I'm sure you will enjoy the view. If you'll excuse me, I'll make arrangements for the Reverend Trilby and your escort."

"If you please, my lady," Elissa said coolly, indicating that Kimbra should follow her.

"Come along, Daisy," Lady Kimbra said, speaking to the mousy little maid hovering behind her.

Elissa was aware that Damian had ordered the south tower prepared especially for Lady Kimbra. The keep had been ransacked of all the best furniture to furnish the future countess's chamber. Elissa had given up the walnut desk that had belonged to her grandmother and Marianne had lost the delicate chaise that once sat beneath her window. Elissa hoped Lady Kimbra appreciated it.

"Your suite has a lovely view of the mountains, and there's a small chamber close by for your maid," Elissa said as Kimbra, followed by her maid, swept past her.

"The hillsides are wondrously pleasing when the heather is in bloom," Elissa continued.

Kimbra stopped so fast her maid bumped into her, her nose wrinkling in obvious disgust. " 'Tis hardly up to my standards," she sniffed derisively. "Is this the best the keep has to offer? I'm accustomed to much better."

Elissa's mouth flattened. "Lord Damian had it prepared especially for you."

"Ah, Lord Damian. I didn't expect him to be so . . . handsome. He's rather fearsome, too, but I like that in a man." Her eyes glittered. "He'll be all the rage in London."

"London, my lady? Lord Damian doesna like London. Misterly is his home. He doesna plan to leave."

Kimbra's eyes narrowed on Elissa. "How can you presume to know what Lord Damian is thinking? What are you to him?"

"I am nothing to Lord Damian. Less than nothing. Shall I help your maid unpack your trunks?"

"Nay, Daisy is quite capable. Inform Lord Damian that I wish to dine in my chamber tonight. I'll send Daisy down for a tray."

"As you wish," Elissa said, eager to part company with Damian's haughty bride.

"Wait!"

"Aye?"

"Inform Lord Damian that I expect a visit from him before he retires. We have much to discuss."

Indeed, Elissa thought as she took her leave. She could well imagine what would take place in this chamber once Kimbra got Damian alone.

Damian had already left the hall, so Elissa headed for the kitchen. Maggie intercepted her.

"Lady Kimbra will find few friends at Misterly," Maggie said. "She may be a great beauty, but she has no respect for our land or our people. It doesna bode well for Lord Damian."

"It doesna concern me," Elissa said with a shrug. She lowered her voice. "I canna remain at Misterly."

"How will ye escape? Yer too well guarded."

"I donna know yet."

Maggie squeezed her arm. "Good luck to ye."

Maggie turned away and walked into the solid wall of Sir Richard's chest. Elissa watched with interest as Dickon's arms came around Maggie to steady her.

"Sir Richard, is there something ye wanted?" Maggie asked, pushing herself away from him.

"Aye." His eyes glittered suggestively and his voice lowered, but Elissa could still hear him. "You know what I want, Maggie girl."

Elissa regarded the couple with speculation. Dickon was a handsome man, but too sure of himself where Maggie was concerned.

"I'm not that kind of a girl, Sir Richard," Maggie replied.

Richard laughed cynically. "Don't tell me you're the kind of woman who is saving herself for marriage."

Maggie stiffened. "What's wrong with that?"

"As long as there are willing women around, I've no need to marry."

"I suggest you find one of those willing women."

"Perhaps I will." Whirling on his heel, he strode away.

Damian returned to the hall in time to watch the interplay between Dickon and Maggie. From the look of things, his friend was making little progress with the stubborn lass. Ah well, he had his own problems to deal with. His intended bride had arrived and his marriage was at hand.

Damian spied Elissa filling a pitcher with ale and followed her with his eyes. There was much to admire about Elissa besides her beauty, but stubbornness wasn't among her finer qualities. His expression turned grim when he recalled how she'd come to his bed, then lied about her motive.

Damian caught Elissa's attention and beckoned to her.

"More ale, my lord?" she asked coolly.

"Nay. Has Lady Kimbra settled in?"

Elissa gave a derisive laugh. "Hardly. Surely you realize Lady Kimbra despises Misterly. She says it isn't up to her standards. The Highlands isna London, and well she knows it."

"She'll learn to like it," Damian said with more conviction than he felt.

"Your lady asked me to convey a message," Elissa informed him. "She will await upon you in her chamber tonight."

Damian nodded. For some reason he didn't relish the meeting. He was grateful for the king's beneficence in this arranged marriage, but he feared the cost to his peace of mind would exceed the benefits to his livelihood. What little he saw of Lady Kimbra did not impress him, but he was willing to give her the benefit of the doubt. Not one to make snap decisions, Damian decided to withhold judgment until he knew his intended bride better. It was unfair to compare Kimbra to Elissa on such short acquaintance.

After the evening meal, Damian conferred with Sir Brody concerning billeting arrangements and provisions for the extra guests. Sir Brody assured him that their guests would not stretch Misterly's budget.

"May I make a suggestion, my lord?" Sir Brody said.

"By all means," Damian replied, his curiosity piqued.

"Lady Marianne has made a remarkable recovery. I think it would benefit both her and her kinsmen if she took her evening meals in the hall. The Frasers need to see how well their lady is prospering under your care."

Damian searched Sir Brody's face. "There's more to it than that, isn't there?"

Sir Brody nodded. "Lady Marianne feels she has been isolated too long and misses contact with her kinsmen. She asked me to convey her request to you."

Damian pondered Lady Marianne's request. He had no objection and told Sir Brody as much. The width of Sir Brody's smile told Damian that the lady and his steward had gotten even closer than he had suspected.

Aware of the passing of time, Damian rose and ascended the stairs to Lady Kimbra's chamber. Kimbra's timid little maid answered his knock, her smile wavering when Damian strode past her before she had time to announce his presence.

"You may leave, Daisy," Kimbra said, waving the girl away. Daisy scooted off with remarkable haste.

Damian's steps faltered when he saw Kimbra draped across the bed in daring dishabille, her generous bosom all but exposed by her low cut dressing gown and one shapely leg bared nearly to her thigh. Dimly Damian wondered why the sight of her lush curves failed to stir him.

"Thank you for coming," Kimbra purred. "I thought perhaps your fiery little mistress would fail to give you my message."

"If you're referring to Elissa, who by the way is *not* my mistress, she did deliver your message. What is it you wish to discuss?"

Kimbra patted the bed beside her, her eyes bright with invitation. "Come sit beside me, my lord. As you said, we should begin immediately to get to know one another."

Damian perched gingerly on the edge of the bed. This woman was to be his wife, his life's mate. Why did he feel so uncomfortable around her?

"Now then," Kimbra began, "shall we discuss our living arrangements? How long must we remain in this savage land," she asked with a delicate shudder that sent the sleeve of her dressing gown tumbling downward, "before we can take up permanent residence in London?"

Damian's gaze dropped to her breasts, wondering how many men had been privileged to gaze upon them as he did now. Was he getting an innocent? He wouldn't be surprised if she cuckolded him before the ink was dry on their marriage papers. He shook his head to dispel his doubts and vowed to be more tolerant of her flirtation. Born and raised in London, she was probably conducting herself according to the behavior she'd learned at court.

"You haven't answered my question, my lord," Kimbra said archly.

"I have no intention of taking up permanent residence in London," Damian replied. "Misterly is now my home."

Kimbra pouted, then reached for him, running her hands down his chest in a suggestive manner. "I have been known to change men's minds."

Damian pulled away. What was wrong with him? Kimbra was a beautiful, sensual woman, he should be quivering with desire instead of shrinking away from her. "You'll find I'm not easily swayed."

"I refuse to be stuck away in this godforsaken place after our marriage," Kimbra proclaimed petulantly. "These people are strange to me. They hate me. My bath water was tepid, the food was disgusting, and your mistress was disrespectful."

Damian gritted his teeth in frustration. "I repeat. Elissa is not my mistress."

Kimbra glared at him, her displeasure palpable. "Why is the woman still here if she isn't your mistress?"

Damian flew to Elissa's defense. "Leave Elissa out of this, my lady. She has nothing to do with our marriage. I'm sure we will deal well with one another as husband and wife after we get to know one another."

"That doesn't answer my question, my lord," Kimbra persisted.

"Your question is irrelevant, though I suppose I should tell you about Elissa before someone else does. Her father and brothers were slain at Culloden. She and her family were allowed to live at Misterly because of its remoteness and uselessness to the Crown. Then London received word of the intended marriage between Elissa and the outlaw Tavis Gordon.

"I was called to London and given Misterly with the understanding that I would prevent the marriage and hold the land for England. Elissa is but a pawn in a nasty game to unite the clans for another attempt at rebellion."

"Why is she still here?" Kimbra demanded. "She is a traitor. Send her to London and let the Crown deal with her. 'Tis a fitting end for the Jacobite witch."

The venom in her voice stunned Damian. He said coldly, "I don't want Elissa's death on my conscience. The lady will remain at Misterly until I say otherwise."

"*Lady?* You call that traitor 'lady'? As your wife,

my lord, I have the right to say who stays at Misterly and who goes, and Elissa Fraser will definitely go."

Damian stood abruptly. He had to leave before he lost his temper along with his wits and ordered Kimbra back to London, which would be a mistake. The king would never stand for that kind of disobedience.

Kimbra must have realized she was treading too close to the edge of Damian's anger for she sent him a beguiling smile and grasped his arm.

"Don't be upset with me, my lord. Once we wed you will have no need for a mistress. I will even plead with the king to let us take up residence in London. I am his ward, he has affection for me."

"We shall see, my lady," Damian said, pulling free and affecting a negligent bow. "I bid you good night. Breakfast is served early in the country."

"I rarely rise before noon," Kimbra exclaimed with mock horror. "I'll send my maid to the kitchen for chocolate and a sweet bun when I arise."

"Good luck," Damian muttered beneath his breath. She was lucky to get weak tea and oatcakes. But that was something his very spoiled, very demanding bride-to-be would soon learn for herself.

Damian strode from the chamber, his opinion of Lady Kimbra quickly eroding. He'd been willing to give her a chance, but despite her great beauty he was not impressed with her. Unfortunately there was little he could do about it. In four weeks he would wed and bed Lady Kimbra and welcome the heirs she bore him.

That gave him pause for thought. For some unexplained reason he had pictured his children with vibrant red hair and green eyes.

Chapter 11

Damian made himself scarce the following day. He joined his men at sword practice, met with Sir Brody, and went hunting with Dickon. When he returned to the keep he found a disturbance in the hall that had gotten out of hand. Kimbra and Elissa were squared off against one another, arguing like fishwives. Damian plowed through a crowd of onlookers and stepped between them.

"What in bloody hell is going on?"

Kimbra whirled on him, fury darkening her blue eyes. "Please do not curse in my presence, my lord."

"My pardon, my lady," Damian bit out sarcastically. "Perhaps you'd be kind enough to tell me the meaning of this unladylike behavior."

"With pleasure," Kimbra said, shooting Elissa a spiteful look. "The Jacobite wench insulted me."

Damian raised a brow in Elissa's direction. "Elissa . . . ?"

"I merely suggested that since Misterly was to be Lady Kimbra's home, she should try harder to get along. Your future bride came storming into the kitchen screaming insults. Then, without provocation, she poured a cup of tea on Winifred's head, insisting that her orders had been deliberately ignored. She'd sent her maid down for a cup of chocolate and Winifred sent tea instead. Winifred explained to Lady Kimbra that there was no chocolate available. I merely attempted to explain that we had few luxuries at Misterly."

"I bring great wealth to this marriage, my lord," Kimbra asserted, "and should be granted whatever I wish."

Damian stifled a groan. "Make your wishes known to Sir Brody and he will do his best to meet your needs within a reasonable time."

Kimbra stamped her foot. "I want chocolate now!"

Damian raised his eyes heavenward and prayed for patience. "Do we have any chocolate, Elissa?"

"Nay, my lord. 'Tis just as I said. Chocolate is a luxury the Frasers havena been able to afford. Even if we had any, after this outburst, Winifred would bury it in the garden before serving it to your lady."

Damian stifled a smile. "There you have it, Lady Kimbra. We shall certainly endeavor to obtain your favored drink in the future."

Kimbra pointed a finger at Elissa. "I demand that you punish her for her disrespectful behavior."

"What do you suggest?" Damian asked in a deceptively calm voice.

Kimbra sent him an engaging smile. "A good beating should put her in her place. You need to set an example for the other Jacobites, my lord."

Damian's temper dangled by a fragile thread. "I'm endeavoring to get along with Elissa's kinsmen and you're not helping. I need them to make Misterly prosper. Not even your wealth will help if there is no one to work the fields, reap the crops, and tend the sheep. You must learn to get along with these people, for they are now your people."

Kimbra reeled back as if struck. "My people? Hardly, my lord. These peasants are beneath me."

Damian reacted spontaneously. Grasping her arm, he pulled her away into an alcove where they could be seen but not heard.

"Am *I* beneath you, my lady? Do you consider me inferior to your London swains? I am master here. You will not tell me what to do."

Damian saw her eyes widen, heard the breath catch in her throat, and felt her fingers dig into his shoulder. But instead of pushing him away, she pulled him closer. He gave a snort of disgust, suddenly aware that she was aroused. He had stirred her to passion when he'd hoped for anger, or at least fear.

"Damian, Damian!" she panted. "Oh, God, you're so masterful. I love strong men. Take me to your bedchamber and make me yours. Now, please, my lord."

Before Damian could respond, she pulled his head down and pressed her lips against his. Curious, Damian let her kiss him, wondering if her kiss would affect him in the same way Elissa's did. He'd tupped countless women, shared numerous passionate kisses, but only Elissa made him yearn for something deeper.

Oddly detached, Damian felt nothing but mild disinterest for Kimbra's kisses. His first thought was that she knew more about kissing than a virgin ought to. Her wicked little tongue probed his mouth as if she knew exactly what she was about. Despite her best efforts, Damian remained unmoved. He broke off the kiss and stepped away.

"Damian, please," Kimbra pleaded, "don't you want me? We'll be married soon, what does it matter?"

"I am but protecting your good name," Damian hedged. "My wife must be above reproach."

That seemed to mollify Kimbra, for she favored him with a sultry smile. "Four weeks seems like a long time, but perhaps it will be worth it."

"Shall we discuss your behavior today?" Damian asked, adroitly changing the subject. "Making enemies of the Frasers will hardly endear you to them."

"Perhaps I would be more inclined toward tolerance if you sent Elissa away."

"I will think on it," Damian replied in an effort to placate her. "Meanwhile, perhaps you'd like to inspect the keep. 'Tis quite impressive despite its great age. I'll explain the improvements I intend to make as we tour the various chambers."

Kimbra wrinkled her pert nose. "Some other time, perhaps. If your cook can prepare something to tempt my delicate appetite, I should like to eat. I'll send Daisy to the kitchen to instruct your staff as to my likes and dislikes."

"I'm sure they'll do their best to accommodate you," Damian said, backing away. "If you'll excuse me, my lady, I have accounts to go over with my steward."

Elissa couldn't hear what Damian and Kimbra were discussing, but she and everyone else had seen what had taken place in the alcove. The kiss Kimbra and

Damian had shared spoke volumes. The passion behind the kiss had been so potent Elissa half expected Damian to drag Kimbra posthaste to his bedchamber. The lady had certainly looked willing enough.

Elissa was more than a little surprised when Damian abruptly broke off the kiss and strode away, leaving Kimbra looking bemused and smugly satisfied. Elissa braced herself when Kimbra sauntered up to her, a condescending smile on her lips.

"I'm hungry," Kimbra said. "A light lunch will do. Poached fish, vegetables seasoned with a hint of rosemary, and freshly baked bread. Honey instead of butter. See to it at once."

Elissa was tempted to tell Kimbra to go to hell, but wisely held her tongue. Trouble now bore a new name. Lady Kimbra Lancaster.

The hall buzzed with activity as Damian took his place at the head table that evening. Word had circulated that Lady Marianne would make an appearance in the hall and her kinsmen were eager to see for themselves how their former chieftain's lady was faring under Damian's care.

Then Lady Kimbra strolled into the hall and conversation halted. Suddenly she became the center of attention. The elaborate court gown she had chosen for her first meal in the hall was cut low over her breasts and richly adorned with lace and ruffles. Damian thought the ostentatious display far too elaborate for the occasion and vowed to school Kimbra about proper country attire. It was unconscionable to flout one's wealth when these people had been stripped of everything but their pride.

Damian stood courteously when Kimbra appeared; then he stepped forward, offered his arm, and seated her on his left.

"I hope the food tonight is better than what I've been offered so far," Kimbra commented. "I had to make do with smoked salmon and those dreadful oatcakes for lunch. I fear my delicate stomach won't tolerate such heavy fare."

"I've found the cooks at Misterly quite satisfactory," Damian defended. "Take your likes and dislikes up with Sir Brody."

"Hiring a French chef will be my first appointment once I'm Mistress of Misterly," Kimbra purred.

Damian felt the beginning of a headache. "I think not, my lady. I'm perfectly satisfied with Winifred and her helpers."

Kimbra opened her mouth to reply and left it hanging open when Sir Brody entered the hall carrying a fragile but beaming Lady Marianne. Little Lora skipped behind them, dragging the doll Elissa had made for her from rags and straw.

Damian stood. "Welcome, Lady Marianne. We're pleased to have you join us tonight."

Lora let loose a shriek and threw herself at Damian. He lifted her high in the air, then seated her on his right.

"Who are these people?" Kimbra asked disdainfully.

Damian ignored her as he bade Sir Brody to seat Marianne next to her daughter.

"That child is too young to eat with adults," Kimbra complained. "Who are they, and what are they doing at the high table?"

Damian waited until Marianne was seated before offering an introduction.

"Lady Marianne, allow me to present Lady Kimbra, my intended bride. Kimbra, this is Lady Marianne Fraser and her daughter Lora."

Lady Marianne nodded her head graciously, which Kimbra chose to ignore.

"Since this is to be my home, please explain why these people are taking advantage of my hospitality."

"Lady Marianne and Lora are Lady Elissa's mother and sister. This is their home."

"Why are they still here? 'Twas my understanding that the traitor's family had been properly disposed of."

"Look around you, my lady. You're surrounded by Frasers."

"But to harbor the wife and children of a known traitor is a treasonous act in itself. Whatever would the king say?"

"Let me worry about the king, Lady Kimbra. Lady Marianne and Lora are recovering from grave illnesses. Getting them well is my prime concern."

"Why should you care?" Kimbra challenged.

"Be careful what you say, my lady," Damian warned.

Kimbra assumed a repentant look as she directed her gaze to her plate and folded her hands in her lap, but Damian was not fooled. It was apparent that his volatile bride-to-be was fuming inside. Then he spied Elissa and a devil inside him prodded him to say, "Elissa, there's an empty seat beside your mother. I think she'd be pleased to have you join us."

Elissa was startled by Damian's invitation. Didn't he know his sudden interest in her would infuriate Lady Kimbra? She considered refusing, then changed her mind. After a moment's hesitation, she calmly seated herself in the chair Damian had indicated. The food was delicious; Elissa thought Winifred had outdone herself. Those partaking of the meal quickly devoured the first course, consisting of saddle of mutton and sirloin of beef.

A fricassee of chickens and pigeons and spinach followed. The third course consisted of poached salmon, fried sole and sweetbreads, and an assortment of green vegetables. Custards and pies concluded the meal. The great feast had been ordered by Damian to honor Lady Kimbra's arrival. The lady appeared not at all impressed.

Elissa's temper ignited as she watched Kimbra push her food around her plate with her fork. Elissa had helped in the kitchen earlier and knew how hard Winifred and her helpers had worked to provide the feast Damian had requested. She wanted to berate Kimbra soundly, but Damian beat her to it.

"Is the food not to your liking, Lady Kimbra?" Damian asked curtly.

"The beef was too well done and the mutton raw. I prefer my sole poached and I do not like salmon at all. The custard lacked sufficient vanilla and was runny," she added, pushing her plate away for emphasis. "I require perfection in my kitchen."

"I should like to retire," Marianne said, forestalling Damian's reply to Kimbra's complaints. " 'Tis been wonderful sharing a meal with my kinsmen, but in the future, Lora and I will dine in my chamber. I donna wish to cause dissention in your household, my lord."

Damian rose, waving Sir Brody aside as the steward moved to convey Marianne to her chamber. "I will carry Lady Marianne to her room," he said. "Come along, Lora."

He lifted Marianne into his arms and strode off as if she weighed nothing. Sir Brody hesitated a moment, then trailed behind Damian. Lora followed in their wake.

"You should follow your mother's example," Kimbra said in an aside to Elissa. " 'Twas a most uncomfortable situation. I shall ask Lord Damian to remove all three of you from my home. The king will be displeased to learn that Lord Damian is harboring a traitor's family beneath his roof."

"Remaining at Misterly is not my choice," Elissa explained. "I've begged Lord Damian to let me leave, but he refuses."

"Mayhap I can be of some assistance," Kimbra whispered slyly. "Let me think on your dilemma."

Damian returned to the hall and slid into his chair.

"Is Mama well?" Elissa asked anxiously.

"A bit tired, but joining us tonight has been good for her. I told her she is welcome to take her meals with us whenever she feels up to it."

"Really, my lord," Kimbra exclaimed, "you are too generous. Harboring political prisoners isn't in your best interest. Send them away."

"I will take your advice under advisement," Damian said in a tone that should have warned Kimbra that she was treading on dangerous ground.

Elissa turned away in disgust when Kimbra smiled at Damian and asked, "Will you escort me to my chamber, my lord?"

Damian rose and offered his arm. "Of course, my lady."

Kimbra latched possessively onto Damian's arm and swept from the hall, tossing Elissa a smug look over her shoulder.

Elissa stared moodily into her empty plate, unaware that Dermot had joined her until he spoke.

"That woman is trouble, lass."

Elissa smiled up at him. "Aye, Dermot, but there's naught we can do about it. She's Damian's woman."

"His lordship will have another Fraser rebellion on his hands if things donna change."

"That wouldna be wise, Dermot. At one time I wouldna have hesitated to foster a rebellion, but I no longer believe 'tis for the best. Besides, I donna believe Damian will allow his bride to run roughshod over him or us."

"Mayhap yer right, lass, but I canna predict how long our kinsmen will stand for Lady Kimbra's insults. Winifred is ready to quit the kitchen."

"I'll speak to Lord Damian. He must be made to realize what's happening in his own home."

Dermot took his leave. Her thoughts tumbled one upon another as Elissa climbed the stairs to the solar. Dimly she wondered what Kimbra had meant when she'd said she'd help Elissa leave Misterly. Her short acquaintance with Damian's English bride-to-be had shown Kimbra to be spoiled, vain, and ruthless. She seemed quite taken with Damian, however, and he with her. How else would one explain Damian's indulgence for his intended bride? He had never treated *her* with the same patience or consideration, but then, she made no secret of her loathing for Englishmen and their Hanover king.

Once inside her chamber, Elissa sat in the window seat and stared out over the grounds. She had decisions to make and plans to formulate. She needed to decide where she would go after she left Misterly. Fleeing to her cousin Christy at Glenmoor was always an option, but since Christy had been wed as a child to an Englishman, she worried that she'd cause trouble for her kinswoman. As close as she and Christy had been as children, there was a difference in their situations. Christy felt no affection for her absent husband while she loved Damian. Elissa's heart told her she couldn't remain at Misterly once Damian and Kimbra were wed. Her strong feelings for Damian were becoming more of a problem with each passing day.

Why did her heart pound and her body burn when he touched her?

Why did she obsess about him?

Why did she hate the idea of Damian marrying Lady Kimbra . . . or anyone?

Elissa's thoughts skidded to a halt when she heard the whisper of approaching footsteps. Her head snapped around. "Nan, you startled me. I dinna hear you enter."

"Ye were lost in thought, lass." She searched Elissa's face. "Do ye want to tell me about it?"

Elissa studied her folded fingers. "There's naught to tell."

"Donna do it, lass."

Elissa's head shot up. "Whatever are you talking about?"

"Donna believe anything Lady Kimbra tells ye. She's a sly one."

Elissa's eyes widened. "What do you know of Lady Kimbra?"

"My 'voices' warn me of her," Nan said. "Heed me, lass. Donna endanger yer bairn."

"You're daft, Nan," Elissa scolded. "I am not with child."

Nan gave her an enigmatic smile. "Will ye be able to say that tomorrow with the same confidence?"

"Nonsense!" Elissa jeered. "Take your bizarre statements elsewhere, I have no patience for them."

"Verra well, lass, but donna forget my words. Sleep well."

The way she said, "sleep well," sent chills down Elissa's spine. Nan's premonitions were often vague and sometimes frightening, but this time they made no sense.

Still pondering what Nan had said, Elissa undressed and readied herself for bed. Sighing wearily, she turned the lamp low, slid under the covers, and closed her eyes, trying not to think about what was going on in Kimbra's bedchamber. Damian was a virile man and Kimbra a seductively lovely woman. Their marriage was a foregone conclusion; they had every right to indulge themselves in any way they wished.

Elissa was flirting with sleep when a creaking of the door hinges warned her that she wasn't alone. Had Nan returned to spout more nonsense? Was something wrong with her mother? She sat up and struck a match to a candle.

It was Damian. He was leaning against the closed door, a dark shadow of a man she'd recognize anywhere. Blades of diffused light slashed across his face, concealing more than they revealed. His expression was guarded, his eyes were unreadable.

"What do you want?" Elissa asked over the thunderous beating of her heart.

Damian pushed himself away from the door. "I couldn't sleep. I tried to engage Sir Richard in conversation or a game of cards, but he preferred Maggie's company. Sir Brody had already retired, and there was no one else about."

Elissa pulled the covers up to her neck. "Go away. How dare you enter my chamber without my permission? Have you tired of Lady Kimbra's company already?"

Damian approached the bed with catlike grace. "This is my home. I go where I wish. As for Lady Kimbra, I've had all I can take of her for one night."

"I hope you realize your lady's behavior will lead to trouble if she isn't curbed."

"Forget Kimbra. There is something I wish to discuss with you."

"Can't it wait until tomorrow?"

He settled on the edge of the bed, ignoring Elissa's murmur of protest. "We will talk now."

"Verra well. What is it?"

"I want you to know that neither you nor your family will be sent away because Lady Kimbra wishes it. No message she dispatches to the king concerning you or your family will reach London."

"Why would you do that? I would think you'd wish to please Lady Kimbra."

"Aye, well—the lady doesn't please *me*. I will wed her because I must, but I don't have to like it."

Elissa blinked up at him. "I thought she pleased you very well. Lady Kimbra is a great beauty. You seemed to enjoy kissing her."

"She kissed *me*," Damian whispered in a voice suddenly grown hoarse. "Her hair is blond and there isn't a freckle to be found on her aristocratic nose."

Elissa touched her nose, well aware of the smattering of freckles she'd tried to bleach with lemon when she was a child. Her gaze locked with Damian's. His took on a seductive glint that irresistibly drew her into their glittering promise.

"Damian, nay . . ." She whispered the words so softly they scarcely stirred the air. She knew what he wanted for she wanted the same thing. But she couldn't . . . wouldn't . . .

"I haven't asked you for anything . . . yet."

"Then go, before . . ."

"Before your desire becomes as great as mine?"

"Aye . . . nay . . . I donna know. I canna think straight when you look at me like that."

"Then why not admit you want me?"

" 'Tis not . . . wise. You're going to wed Lady Kimbra. She despises me. You should let me leave before the Hanover learns I havena been disposed of according to his wishes."

"You want me to let you go so you can run to the Gordon chieftain?"

"Nay, I will go somewhere . . . anywhere but to Tavis. He lost my regard when he asked me to . . . never mind, 'tis over and done with."

Damian was silent a long time, then he said, "I will consider your request."

"When can I leave?"

"When I decide the time is right."

He grasped her shoulders and pulled her against him. His voice held a desperate note. "You don't understand, do you, sweeting?"

"What am I supposed to understand?"

His voice was taut, as if stretched to the limit. "That no matter how hard I try to stay away from you, I find myself being drawn ever closer. Lust is a strange emotion. I've been smitten before, but never like this. I've always prided myself on my self-control, until you came along. What happened to me, Elissa? Has your old nurse put a spell on me?"

"There is no such thing," Elissa scoffed.

He shifted, melding their bodies together. "Can you feel how much I want you?"

Her breath hitched; desire pounded through her. He was already swollen and hard. Her resolve melted as she fell headlong into his passion, letting it fill her until there was nothing but raw need throbbing through her.

"You shouldna be here," she whispered tremulously.

He gave her a wolfish grin, then captured her lips, moving his mouth passionately over hers. Elissa tried to tell herself she didn't want this, but the lie stung her tongue. Dimly she recalled Nan's words earlier tonight, after she'd denied that she carried Damian's bairn.

Will ye be able to say that tomorrow with the same confidence?

Not if Damian had his way tonight, a small voice cautioned. The warning was like chaff in the wind as Damian's mouth and hands made a mockery of her resolve. She wanted to feel him close to her, wanted to savor every dazzling, exciting moment while she could, before reality intruded. Her mouth clung to his; her arms crept around his neck, needing more than mere kisses.

She responded eagerly, holding nothing of herself back. The urgent pressure of his body against hers made her feel gloriously alive. His kiss deepened; she responded with a moan of surrender. She wanted him inside her . . . now.

Damian ended the kiss; she clung to his lips,

breathless, dazed. He regarded her solemnly, his voice raw with feeling. "There's no place I would rather be at this moment."

"I'll never forgive you for doing this to me."

He bunched her nightdress in his fists and raised it slowly upward. "Doing what?"

Her heart slammed against her ribs. "Making me want you."

She raised her eyes to his and saw naught but his raw need. There was no pretense in his steady gaze, only a dark and heady intensity that hung heavy in the air. It was effortless seduction, and she was his willing partner.

His hand found her. She felt her wetness flow over his fingers, felt hot and damp and swollen as he slid his fingers inside to tease and arouse. His fingers reached deeply. She uttered a raw cry and climaxed violently, arching up against him.

She returned to reality slowly, dimly aware that they were both naked, and that Damian was stroking her breasts, his silver eyes aglow with anticipation. He kissed her open mouth, drawing in her small panting breaths as his clever hands began arousing her again.

" 'Tis my turn, sweeting," he murmured brokenly.

He settled himself into a comfortable position against the headboard and suspended her over his rigid arousal. Elissa felt the engorged tip nudge her opening and guided him inside.

Damian's lashes drifted downward as Elissa's tight sheath closed around him. Intense pleasure overwhelmed him as he thrust upward. He groaned. Paradise could never be as sweet, as perfect as this moment. His thoughts scattered as she melted around him, and suddenly he was desperately frantic, wildly rampant, for he felt like a cannon ready to explode.

"Hurry, sweeting," he gasped harshly. "I don't know how much longer I can wait."

He opened his mouth and took one turgid nipple into his mouth, suckling her. He heard her breath quicken and felt his control slipping. He thrust upward, at the same time bringing her hips forcefully downward. She writhed and thrashed in a fierce fury and clung to him more tightly each time his engorged erection lunged inside her.

When he felt her stiffen and vibrate around him, he allowed his own climax to burst upon him. He continued to pump vigorously until he was utterly drained, totally spent. Then he slid down onto the mattress and held himself inside her. Elissa stirred and settled into his arms. He held her close while she slept, his mind churning restlessly.

What had just taken place between him and Elissa was an eruption of raw, unbridled desire. His hunger for Elissa was a wild, uncontrollable thing that shook him to the core. He'd always been a man who depended on his wits to survive. He'd been a loner most of his life, a ruthless soldier with neither kith nor kin. He had friends like Dickon, but not since he'd lost his father at Culloden and his mother years before that had anyone really cared about his welfare. Misterly gave him a sense of belonging, of finding the peace that had been lacking in his life.

As for Elissa, she made him human, changing him from the Demon Knight to a man. Lust was part of it, but what he felt for Elissa was more than that, and not nearly as simple to define. For his own preservation, he vowed to keep that elusive emotion at bay lest he lose everything he'd struggled so hard to achieve.

He couldn't bear to lose Misterly. He already loved the land, and he'd even come to appreciate the dour, hardworking Highlanders. Lady Marianne was an exceptional woman who had survived the loss of loved ones, and little Lora was an adorable urchin who seemed to like him for himself. There were few people he could say that about.

He pulled Elissa closer and placed a kiss on her damp forehead. He admired her for so many things: her strength, her tenacity, her courage. He felt a stab of unaccustomed guilt for seducing her, but he didn't regret it. Even though she had come to him, his seduction of her had begun the day he'd arrived at Misterly. He couldn't remember a time when he hadn't wanted her.

His rationalization faltered when he realized her eyes were open and she was staring at him. He wanted to ask what she was thinking but lacked the courage. Lady Kimbra stood between them like a solid rock wall. Instead, he kissed and caressed and slowly aroused her again. When he slid atop her, she opened her legs in welcome.

Damian left Elissa's bed soon after they'd made love a second time. She'd been half-asleep when he kissed her lightly on the lips and left the chamber. When he returned to the hall he was surprised to find Sir Brody, Dickon, Dermot, and Lachlan seated on benches before the hearth, talking in muted tones.

Dermot rose and hailed him. "A word with ye before ye seek yer bed, yer lordship."

A prickling sensation crawled up Damian's spine as he joined the men. Someone shoved a tankard of ale into his hand as he dropped down beside Dickon.

"What keeps you up so late?" Damian asked.

"We could ask ye the same thing," Dermot replied. "What were ye doing in the solar at this hour?"

"I owe you no explanation, Dermot Fraser."

" 'Tis true, then," Lachlan spat. "Ye've made the Maiden of Misterly yer mistress."

"You wrong the lady," Damian said harshly. "Elissa has never consented to become my mistress."

"Yer intended bride sleeps in yonder tower," Dermot pointed out. "Ye have no right to cast yer eyes upon our lass. She is promised to the Gordon chieftain."

"No marriage between them will ever take place," Damian maintained. "If any of your kinsmen are thinking of fleeing to the Gordon stronghold, I strongly advise against it. I prefer peace, but if need be, I'll take action to destroy the Gordon clan if they become troublesome."

"We Frasers are sick of war," Dermot said, looking at Lachlan for confirmation. "But if ye continue to dishonor our lass, we will do what is best for our clan."

"Aye," Lachlan agreed. "We were willing to give ye a chance to better our lot, but we willna stand by while Elissa is being mistreated. Nor will we allow Lady Kimbra to disparage our home or our kinsmen. Think about it, yer lordship."

On that note of warning, Lachlan and Dermot rose and strode away.

"They're right, you know," Dickon ventured.

"You, too, Dickon?"

"You're setting yourself up for trouble, Damian. If you value Misterly and wish to keep it, leave Elissa alone."

Damian noticed Sir Brody's disapproving look and raised an eyebrow in his direction.

"Far be it from me to tell you what to do, my lord," Sir Brody said, "but Lady Marianne is distressed about the situation beween you and her daughter."

Damian's hands balled into fists at his sides. "Don't you think I know that? I can't help myself, dammit! Something strange is happening. I don't know what the hell is wrong with me."

"I have a suggestion," Sir Brody ventured.

"So do I," Dickon said.

Damian heaved an impatient sigh. "Very well, you first, Dickon."

"Send Lady Elissa to London and the rest of her family to the convent. You need to concentrate on your bride. Whether you approve of her or not, Lady Kimbra brings considerable wealth to your coffers. Your new title and holdings are guaranteed only if you wed the king's choice of bride."

"That solution is not acceptable to me, Dickon. Lady Marianne might be accepting of the convent, but little Lora's spirit would be broken behind convent walls. As for Elissa, sending her to London is not an option. The Crown has little sympathy for Jacobites."

He turned to the grizzled knight. "I hope your suggestion is more acceptable, Sir Brody."

Sir Brody cleared his throat, then faced Damian squarely. "Wed the lass, my lord."

Chapter 12

*W*ed Elissa.

Sir Brody's words thrummed through Damian's head like the blast of a trumpet long after he'd returned to his chamber. Instead of seeking his bed, he slumped in a chair, a snifter of brandy in his hand and his legs stretched toward the hearth.

Wed Elissa.

Utterly preposterous.

The king would never allow it.

He tossed the brandy to the back of his throat and swallowed noisily. Then he poured himself another. He was astounded that he even let himself consider such a ridiculous idea. His mind mired in indecision, he stared into the flickering flames until his head dropped forward and sleep finally claimed him. He awakened when the snifter dropped from his hand and shattered on the flagstone floor. Then he rose and fell fully dressed onto his bed.

* * *

The following days sped by much too quickly for Damian's peace of mind. In a few days he and Kimbra would join in marriage before an assembly of Englishmen and Highlanders. As the appointed day approached, the more demanding Kimbra became. Nothing pleased her. She carped constantly about the food, the lack of simple luxuries, the remoteness of Misterly from London, and Damian's lack of control over the servants.

Damian was losing patience with the woman he was expected to wed, bed, and get heirs upon. Her spitefulness was uncalled for and her boldness disgusted him. She sought him out like a bitch in heat, determined to seduce him. It wasn't difficult for Damian to resist, for he knew her purpose, aside from the sexual aspect, was to persuade him to send Elissa and her family away.

For the past week Kimbra had been excessively demanding, ordering special food for the wedding feast, becoming loudly vocal about the decorations she favored, and declaring how she wished the wedding ceremony to proceed. Every available servant was cleaning and scrubbing and polishing, until the hall sparkled. And it was blatantly obvious that Kimbra took special delight in giving the most difficult chores to Elissa.

Because he wished for a peaceful coexistence with Kimbra, Damian tried not to interfere, but it was difficult to watch Elissa struggle with the chores Kimbra had assigned to her. A time or two he felt obliged to intercede and asked one of the men to take over Elissa's duties when he found her on her knees scrubbing the solar stairs.

Damian's nerves were stretched to the limit. The day before the wedding, he escorted Kimbra to her chamber for a private word. The moment the door closed behind them, Kimbra flung herself into his arms.

"I knew you'd change your mind, Damian." Her fingers worked frantically at the buttons on his coat. "You want me and can't wait to make me yours."

Damian removed her busy hands from his person and held her at bay. "You're wrong, Kimbra. I merely want to set you straight on a few things before we wed."

Her lips turned downward into a pout. "Whatever do you mean? Don't you want me?"

"I want Misterly," Damian replied. "Since you're included in the deal, I am obliged to wed you. You've sorely tested my temper these past weeks, Kimbra. Lord knows I've been more patient with you than you deserve. But heed me well, my lady, your behavior is unacceptable and I will not stand for it."

Kimbra's mouth dropped and her eyes rounded.

"I am master here," Damian continued. "You will cease to destroy the peace I'm trying to preserve in my home. Your complaints are unfounded and your harsh treatment of Elissa and her kinsmen is intentionally cruel and unjust."

Kimbra reared back as if struck. "How dare you! The king shall hear of this. You owe your loyalty to me, not to Jacobite traitors. When the king told me I was to become your countess, I was willing to come to this wilderness for the wedding, but I had no intention of removing myself from London society for good, or making my home in this savage country. 'Tis best that we settle this here and now."

'Tis best if we don't marry, Damian thought but did not say, for he had to wed Kimbra, whether or not he liked it.

"I must have an heir," Damian said, grimacing at the thought of bedding the spoiled witch. "You will remain at Misterly until you give me one."

Kimbra gave him a blinding smile, her avid gaze lingering on his massive chest, then sliding downward to his groin. "I will have no problem making love with you, Damian. Strong, forceful men excite me."

"Are you a maiden, Kimbra?"

Kimbra flushed and looked away. "Of course, my lord, why would you think otherwise?"

Damian didn't believe her for a minute, but time would tell. "I'll make a deal with you, Kimbra. One that should satisfy both of us."

"A deal, Damian?"

"Yes. After you give me a son, you can go your own way, live wherever you want, do as you please. But the child will remain with me."

"Will you keep your mistress with you at Misterly?" Kimbra challenged contemptuously. "Do you think I'm blind? I know you're bedding Elissa. That's why you don't want me."

"You delude yourself, Kimbra. Since you've been here, you've done nothing but complain. You find fault with everything and are quite vocal about your contempt for Misterly and its people."

"Misterly is not London," she sniffed.

"My deal, Kimbra. Do you accept?"

She gave him a sly smile. "Only if you promise to send Elissa and her family away."

Damian turned to leave. "I had hoped we'd find common ground, but I see I was mistaken."

"Do you love Elissa?" Kimbra challenged, stopping Damian in his tracks. His silence was damning. "How can you? You fought Jacobites at Culloden; you lost your father there."

Damian whirled to face her. "The battle was fought and won long ago. I hold no grudges. Lord Cumberland has decimated the Highlanders' ranks; only a few lucky souls remain to carry on their tradition, and most of them are in hiding. I was given Misterly to hold for England and to maintain peace in this remote corner of Scotland. I'd hoped you'd be a helpmate to me."

"I will be your countess and share your passion, but I simply refuse to spend my life at Misterly." She looked away. "Leave me. There's much to be done before our wedding tomorrow."

Had Kimbra not turned her back, she would have seen Damian's expression harden before he stormed from the chamber, slamming the door behind him. How in bloody hell was he going to survive this marriage?

Fate intervened.

The Gordons appeared at Misterly the following day. Damian was awakened at dawn with the news that a man bearing a white flag was approaching the gate. Damian dressed and hurried down to the gate to meet the messenger.

Dermot had gotten there before him. " 'Tis the Gordon chieftain," he said.

Damian studied Tavis Gordon with avid curiosity.

The man was handsome, he grudgingly allowed. Tall and rugged, he held himself proudly beneath the forbidden clan tartan thrown carelessly over his shoulder. Damian could understand Elissa's fascination with the man.

Tavis Gordon rode to within shouting distance, then stopped.

"What do you want, Gordon?" Damian demanded.

"My intended bride," Gordon shouted. "Send her out and we'll leave peacefully.

"You know I can't do that," Damian returned.

"Elissa was promised to me by her father. Release her. If ye donna send Elissa out to me now, we will attack. We have enough strength on our side to win."

"You're welcome to try, Gordon," Damian challenged, "but you won't succeed."

"More than a hundred Highlanders are camped in the forest, Englishman. What say ye to that?"

"Go to hell."

Gordon stared at Damian for a long moment, then he wheeled his mount and rode off into the dense forest beyond Misterly.

"Does Gordon speak the truth, Dermot?" Damian inquired of the old man. "Could he have rallied that many Highlanders to his cause?"

"There be outlaw clans living in exile in the mountains," Dermot said. "It wouldna take much to persuade them to retaliate against the English butchers who killed their kinsmen and seized their homes and lands. It wouldna surprise me if Gordon had enlisted a hundred or more men to join him."

"He knows he cannot win," Damian said.

"Highlanders are a curious lot," Dermot mused.

"Their strength lies in their tenacity and their unshakable belief in themselves. Gordon believes Elissa is his and that Misterly should belong to him by right of marriage to Alpin Fraser's daughter."

Sir Richard appeared at Damian's side. "I alerted the soldiers while you negotiated with Gordon. They're waiting for your orders."

"I can always count on you, Dickon," Damian said, slapping the knight on the back. "I want around the clock guards and double patrols on the bulwarks. For now we'll wait and watch."

"What about the villagers? Are they in danger?"

"I doubt it. The villagers are mostly farmers and shepherds. It seems unlikely that Gordon would attack Elissa's kinsmen."

"Can you trust the villagers not to join Gordon and take up arms against you?"

"I don't know, Dickon. I can only hope they will realize I can do more for them than the Gordon chieftain."

Another voice joined the conversation. "Tavis Gordon will do whatever it takes to punish you."

Damian spun around. "Elissa! I didn't see you approach. How much did you hear?"

"Enough to know Tavis willna leave unless you send me out to him."

"Forget it," Damian said tersely. He turned to Sir Richard. "You have your orders, Dickon." Dickon saluted smartly and left. Dermot followed in his wake.

Damian grasped Elissa's arm and steered her away from the gate. "Why should I give in to Gordon's demands?"

" 'Twould make sense. You donna know how many men Tavis has rallied to his cause."

"Are you that anxious to go to him, Elissa?"

"Nay. 'Tis true I want my home back, but not if it means your death. I've changed my mind about . . . many things. Tavis is one of them."

"Do I take that to mean you no longer hate me?"

"I hate what you stand for and what your countrymen have done to my homeland. I hate the devastation wrought by the Hanover and his butcher. And I hate being held prisoner in my own home."

"But you don't hate *me*."

She faced him squarely, her face rigid. "I hate you."

"Liar."

"Your bride awaits you, go to her."

Bloody hell! He'd forgotten that today was his wedding day. Pulling Elissa along with him, he returned to the keep. The Reverend Trilby met him at the door.

"What's amiss, my lord? There seems to be confusion in the hall."

"We are under siege, Reverend. There will be no wedding this day. Please inform Lady Kimbra."

"Aye, my lord. I understand perfectly. It wouldn't be seemly to celebrate a wedding when the enemy is at our door. I'm sure Lady Kimbra will understand."

"What will I understand?" Kimbra asked as she joined them.

"There will be no wedding today, my lady," Trilby explained.

Kimbra's delicate brows lifted as she stared at Damian's hand resting upon Elissa's arm. "Kindly explain why you are postponing our nuptials, Lord Damian."

"In case you haven't heard, my lady, the fortress is

under siege. 'Tis not the best time to hold a wedding."

Kimbra stamped her foot in a childish show of temper. "I won't have it! Who dares to attack you?"

"Tavis Gordon and his clansmen," Damian said tersely.

"Why?"

"They want Lord Damian to release me," Elissa explained.

Kimbra shot Elissa a venomous look. "Then by all means, Damian, give them what they want and let us get on with the wedding."

"Heed Lady Kimbra, my lord," Elissa advised. "Once I walk out the gate, Tavis will leave Misterly in peace."

"You're naive if you believe that, Elissa. You're not going anywhere. Gordon doesn't stand a chance against my seasoned soldiers."

"Have you considered that Tavis's men outnumber yours? Misterly has never been under attack. Its safety lay in its remoteness. Father was the great Alpin Fraser, Laird of Misterly; no hostile clan dared to invade his lands."

Damian considered Elissa's words. It was true Misterly had its shortcomings, but the soldiers under his command were more than able to defeat Gordon and his ill-trained band of savages. He would not send Elissa to the Gordon chieftain.

"Nay, Elissa, you will stay here. Lady Marianne and Lora must be wondering what is going on. Perhaps you should go to them. Tell them not to worry, that I will protect them."

Elissa stared at him a moment, then spun on her heel and marched off.

"I don't like it, Damian. Why are you so protective of Elissa?" Kimbra demanded to know. "Deliver her to Gordon and forget about her."

"I agree with Lady Kimbra, my lord," Reverend Trilby ventured. "If the Gordon chieftain meant her harm, I could understand your reluctance. But she is his kind; 'tis doubtful he'll hurt her."

"I appreciate your concern, Reverend," Damian said with waning patience. "His Majesty has forbidden a marriage between Elissa and Tavis Gordon, and I but carry out his orders. Now if you'll both excuse me, my men have need of me."

The Gordons' first attack came an hour later, with an attempt to scale the walls. A shower of arrows preceded the attack, but Damian's men drove them back and they retreated to the relative safety of the forest. But Elissa knew Tavis hadn't given up. She also believed that Tavis wouldn't have risked an attack if he hadn't sufficient men and arms to warrant success. She wished now that Damian hadn't sent the Black Watch back to London.

Elissa huddled with Lady Marianne and Lora while the battle raged below, but her mind was with Damian. She had to know what was happening. He could be hurt. Or, God forbid, dead.

"I can't sit here any longer, Mama," Elissa said. "I'm going below to help Nan with the wounded. As much as I dislike Englishmen, I hate to see anyone suffer."

"Be careful," Marianne warned, as Elissa let herself out.

Lady Kimbra accosted Elissa at the foot of the

stairs. "Why aren't you in your chamber?" Elissa asked.

"I was looking for you. Where can we talk in private?"

"Can't it wait? I'm needed to help with the wounded."

"This is important. I have an idea that should please you."

Elissa didn't think anything Kimbra had to say would please her, but she decided to listen anyway. "We can talk right here, no one is around to hear us. What is it you wish to say?"

"Your home is as inhospitable as these lands. After Damian and I are wed, I will convince him to take me to London. I'm confident I can persuade the king to let us take up residence in town."

"Why are you telling me this?"

"I want to help you escape so my wedding can proceed as planned."

"Damian will never agree to leave Misterly permanently."

Kimbra gave her a conspiratorial smile. "I'd risk the king's wrath for Damian. I'm sure you're aware that Damian's lovemaking is exceptional." She preened for Elissa's benefit. "He pleases me, and I him. I didn't want to consummate our vows before the ceremony, but you know how persistent Damian can be. You are a distraction he doesn't need. Therefore, I've decided to help you join your intended bridegroom."

Pain sliced through Elissa. She'd suspected that Damian and Kimbra had been intimate, but hearing the truth from Kimbra's lips made the hurt even more unbearable. Armed with that knowledge, Elissa knew she couldn't . . . wouldn't refuse Kimbra's offer. It would mean leaving her mother and Lora behind, but she was convinced that Damian wouldn't harm them. Once she was gone, Kimbra would probably convince him to send her mother and sister to the convent.

Elissa nodded slowly. "Verra well. Tell me how you'll help me."

Since Damian already knew about the secret tunnel and had stationed a guard near its entrance, Elissa was willing to listen to Kimbra's plan. She was convinced that joining Tavis was the only way to end the siege.

"Listen," Kimbra said, lowering her voice. "Here's what we'll do."

The Gordons retreated into the forest under cover of darkness; their campfires could be seen from the bulwarks. A hot meal was being served to those men within the keep not on guard duty. Once they had eaten, they hunkered down before the hearth to catch whatever sleep they could before the Gordons' likely attempt to storm the keep at dawn. The wounded had been treated and no deaths had been reported. After dining, Damian joined Dickon on the bulwarks.

Dressed in her father's shirt, baggy britches held in place by a wide leather belt, and a too large jacket, Elissa slipped out the kitchen door. Pulling her father's old bonnet low on her forehead, she hugged the shadows as she skirted around the keep to the front gate. It wasn't as dark as she would have liked, for a pale moon hung low in the sky. Elissa prayed that Kimbra would uphold her part of the bargain, for without Kimbra's help her escape was doomed to failure.

Elissa had explained the plan to her mother, and why she thought it necessary to place herself in Tavis's hands. Lady Marianne had been adamantly opposed but failed to dissuade her.

Elissa breathed a sigh of relief when Kimbra sidled out from the shadows. "Reverend Trilby promised to distract the guard," Kimbra whispered. "He agreed with me that your leaving was best for everyone inside the keep.

"Listen carefully," Kimbra continued. "When we reach the gatehouse, distract the gatekeeper so he won't see me sneaking up behind him. Once I render him unconscious, I'll help you raise the gate. From there you're on your own. No one will suspect me of helping you, and 'tis unlikely you'll be missed until tomorrow." She gave Elissa a shove. "Hurry."

Elissa glanced at her home one last time before creeping toward the gate. Kimbra's plan wasn't perfect but it could work if everything went as planned, Elissa thought. She spied the night guard and the Reverend Trilby speaking together in low tones and circled around them.

Her heart pounding erratically as she neared the gatehouse, Elissa sensed the moment Kimbra was no longer behind her. Shoulders slumped, chin tucked low, she approached the gatekeeper and was immediately challenged.

"Who goes there?"

"The kitchen lad, sir," Elissa said in a thick brogue.

"What are you doing here, lad? You'd best return to the keep."

"The kitchen was hot, I needed some air." She stepped past the gatekeeper and peered through the gate's narrow iron slats, pretending interest in something beyond the walls. "What is that?" she asked excitedly.

The gatekeeper pushed her aside. "I see nothing, lad. Are you sure . . ." His sentence ended in a sigh as Kimbra struck him from behind with a rock.

"Help me," Kimbra said, struggling with the apparatus operating the gate.

Together they managed to lift the gate high enough for Elissa to slip through. The gate lowered behind Elissa and she hugged the wall a moment to catch her breath. When no alarm sounded, she blew out a sigh of relief and moved out from the shadow of the wall.

The guard who had been conversing with Reverend Trilby must have heard something suspicious, for he advised the Reverend to return to the keep before sprinting toward the gatehouse. Once he was gone, Kimbra emerged from the shadows.

Damian leaned against bulwarks, gazing at the numerous campfires visible through the trees.

"Do you think they'll attack tonight?" Dickon asked.

"Nay, they appear to be settling down for the night. I look for a dawn attack."

Suddenly a scream rent the air. Damian peered over the bulwarks to the courtyard below.

"I can't see what's going on," Damian stated as he turned and sprinted toward the stairs, "but I'm going to find out." Dickon followed him down the stone steps to the courtyard.

Damian braced his body as Kimbra launched herself at him. He tried to disentangle her arms from his neck but she clung to him like a vine.

"Calm down, Kimbra," Damian bit out. "What are you doing out here? Was that you screaming? What happened?"

"Spies, Damian. Gordon spies. I heard them planning treason. They spoke of raising the gate and letting the Gordons inside. I followed them outside but became frightened and decided to return to the keep to warn you. Then someone shouted and I didn't know what to do, so I screamed."

"Go back inside, I'll take care of this."

Men-at-arms spilled from the keep, following close behind Damian as he raced to the front gate. Kimbra followed at a discreet distance though Damian had forbade it.

"Over here," a voice shouted.

Someone held a lantern aloft. The circle of light revealed two men, one propped against the wall and the other bending over him. To Damian's relief, the gate was down.

"What happened, Betts?" Damian asked.

"I was conversing nearby with the Reverend Trilby when I heard a suspicious noise. I ran to the gatehouse and found Corbin unconscious," Betts said, "but he seems to be coming out of it."

"Move aside," Damian ordered, "I wish to question him." He dropped to his knees. "What happened, Corbin? Did you see your assailant?"

" 'Twas a lad, my lord," Corbin said groggily. "But

he wasn't the one who hit me. Another attacked me from behind while we were talking. The lad must have had an accomplice."

Kimbra pushed her way to Damian's side. "I told you there was treason afoot. They must have let themselves out the gate."

"Aye," Betts concurred. " 'Twas the sound of the gate opening and closing that alerted me. When I arrived, I found Corbin unconscious."

"You have to stop them, Damian," Kimbra said urgently. "No telling what the traitors have planned. They mustn't reach Gordon's camp."

"I'll take a patrol out," Dickon volunteered.

Damian's lips thinned. He wanted Gordon's spies alive. "Can you describe the men, Corbin?"

"The one I spoke with claimed to be a kitchen lad," Corbin recalled. " 'Tis all I can tell you. 'Twas too dark to see clearly."

"What are your orders, Damian?" Dickon asked.

"I'm going after the spies alone," Damian decided. "One man is less likely to draw attention."

"I'm coming with you," Dickon insisted. "Shall I send someone for the horses?"

"Nay, we go afoot. Betts, open the gate."

"Kill them, Damian," Kimbra hissed. "They're traitors."

Damian slanted Kimbra an exasperated look. "Go back to the keep, my lady."

As the gate cranked open, Damian and Dickon ducked through. "Open the gate to no one until we return," Damian instructed. "Everyone else, return to your posts."

"Keep to the shadows," Damian whispered. "The spies couldn't have gone far. Had they crossed open ground, the guards on the bulwarks would have seen them."

Damian scanned the narrow open area between the fortress walls and the forest beyond. Nothing stirred. Campfires still flickered in the distance and the mournful wail of a forbidden bagpipe floated through the air.

"Something moved up ahead," Dickon hissed. "Close to the wall."   •

Damian peered intently through the darkness. At first he saw nothing, then a small form emerged from the shadows. Probably the kitchen lad Corbin had described, Damian decided. He watched intently as the boy pushed away from the wall and crept toward the forest. Blessing the moonlit night, he removed his pistol from his belt and took careful aim. He didn't want to kill the lad, but the distance was too great to guarantee he wouldn't.

Damian squeezed the trigger at the same moment a gust of wind blew down from the mountains, stirring the dirt around his feet and ruffling his hair. As the bullet blasted from his pistol, the wind lifted the spy's bonnet from his head. A terrible premonition shot through Damian as a wealth of red hair tumbled down the spy's back. He cursed violently when the lad hit the ground and lay still, then he took off at a run.

"You got him!" Dickon crowed.

Damian skidded to his knees before the lad and turned him over on his back. A cry gathered in his throat.

"What have I done?" The beautiful face limned in moonlight belonged to Elissa.

When she didn't stir, Damian scooped her into his

arms and raced back to the fortress. He had no idea how badly she was wounded, but he felt her blood soaking his arm.

"Who is it?" Dickon asked.

"Elissa," Damian cried as he ran past a startled Dickon, who turned to follow him.

Clutching Elissa to his chest, he sprinted to the gate. "Open up!" he cried.

The gate cranked open. Damian sped toward the keep with a lifeless Elissa in his arms. "Dickon, fetch Nan!" he called over his shoulder.

Kimbra was waiting at the door for Damian, but he paid her little heed. "Is she dead?"

Had Damian not been out of his mind with worry, he would have thought it strange that Kimbra knew immediately who had been wounded.

Nan came bustling down the stairs from the solar. She shoved Kimbra aside to reach Damian.

"Ye've gone and done it now, yer lordship," the old woman charged. "Take her to her chamber while I fetch my herbs and medicines. I should have stopped ye before this happened, but I dinna think Elissa would act so soon."

A flash of anger darkened Damian's eyes. "You knew what Elissa intended and didn't tell me?"

"Aye, I suspected, but there was no time to warn ye."

"I swear I didn't know it was Elissa out there. I wouldn't have shot her had I known."

"There's one here who knew," Nan said, pointing a bony finger at Kimbra. "Look to yer intended for answers before ye place blame."

Before Damian could ask Nan to explain, she turned and hurried off.

"The woman is mad," Kimbra charged. "Don't listen to anything she tells you."

"I don't have time for this now, Kimbra," Damian said, shoving past her, "but rest assured, I'll demand answers later. Find Maggie and send her up to Elissa's chamber. Nan might have need of her."

Damian took the narrow steps two at a time. Elissa was still unconscious when he laid her on the bed. Her pale face was bathed in blood and she was as still as death. He stroked her face and murmured soothing words until Nan arrived a few minutes later.

"Will she live?" Damian asked anxiously.

"Move aside, my lord. I need to examine her before I can tell ye anything."

"Bloody hell! I had no idea I was shooting at Elissa," Damian defended. "Why did she do it? Who was her accomplice?"

"My lass was betrayed," Nan spat. "She placed her trust in the wrong person."

"How badly is she hurt?" He shuddered. "There's so much blood."

"Yer bullet plowed a furrow in Elissa's scalp. She'll recover, but she'll bear the scar for the rest of her life."

Damian heaved a grateful sigh. "Are you sure that's all?"

Nan sent him an inscrutable look. "Donna fret, yer lordship, Elissa willna die. She will live to bear yer bairn."

Damian thought he must have misunderstood Nan and let it pass. He had more important things on his mind.

Someone wanted Elissa dead.

Chapter 13

Damian had intended to sit with Elissa until she regained consciousness, but duty intervened when Dickon came forward with the startling news that the Gordons had set fire to the village and that the villagers were at the gate, begging entrance.

"Open the gate," Damian ordered. His expression turned grim. "The Gordons have gone too far this time. We'll attack at dawn."

Damian climbed to the bulwarks and stared at a sky turned blood red from the flames. Wishing Gordon to hell, he returned to the hall to address the villagers, who had been routed from their beds in the middle of the night. Father Hugh, the village priest, informed Damian that no lives had been lost to the fires.

"Do what you can to comfort your flock, Father," Damian directed. "Tell them I will personally see the rebuilding of those cottages damaged by fire."

The priest, a middle-aged man with thinning hair and kindly face, regarded Damian with new respect. "Thank ye on behalf of my people, my lord. The majority of Highlanders are Catholic, ye know. Their faith is an important part of their lives. As we speak, God has answered our prayers. Do ye hear it? 'Tis raining. A sign that God is on our side."

Damian heard the splash of raindrops against the windows followed by a clap of thunder, and rejoiced along with the priest. "God is indeed looking after you and yours, Father. Are Lady Elissa and her mother of the Catholic faith?"

"Aye, did ye not know?"

"Nay. Lady Elissa has been sorely hurt. Would you offer her comfort?"

Father Hugh gave Damian a startled look. "Hurt, ye say? Aye, my son, I will go to her as soon as I see to my parishioners."

"Thank you, Father."

After Father Hugh left, Damian sought out Lachlan. "What think you of the Gordon chieftain now?" he asked harshly.

Lachlan shook his head. "I canna believe a man in his right mind would attack his own allies. He doesna deserve to wed our lass. How is Elissa? I understand she was hurt attempting to leave Misterly."

"Aye. 'Tis a story better left for later. There are unused chambers in the keep. Sir Brody will help find beds for the women and children. The men can bed down in the hall."

They parted company. Damian returned to the solar to check on Elissa. Maggie met him in the hallway, her brow creased with concern.

"Lady Marianne is distraught," Maggie revealed.

"She knew about Elissa's attempt to escape and warned her against it, but Elissa wouldna listen. I told Lady Marianne that Elissa wasna seriously hurt but she is upset nevertheless."

"I'll speak to her," Damian said.

Damian entered Marianne's chamber and found her every bit as distressed as Maggie claimed.

"Lord Damian, thank God. Please tell me the truth. How is my daughter?"

"Nan says she'll be fine and I have no reason to doubt her. I didn't aim to kill and my bullet only grazed her. I had no idea I was shooting at Elissa until a gust of wind tore her bonnet from her head and her hair tumbled down her back. But it was too late. What can you tell me about her decision to leave now? Who helped her?"

"I canna say why she chose to leave now, but I can tell you who helped her. 'Twas Lady Kimbra."

An unassailable rage shook Damian. "Are you sure?"

"Oh, aye, Elissa explained everything before she left. I warned her not to trust your lady, but you know Elissa. She was that determined. Something or someone upset her."

Damian took a deep breath and asked, "Does she love Gordon? Is that why she was so anxious to go to him?"

" 'Twas not a love match," Marianne explained. "Elissa's father wanted the marriage and Elissa is a dutiful daughter."

"Thank you for telling me this, my lady. I will settle with Lady Kimbra when I'm done with the Gordons."

"What do you intend to do?"

"Drive the Gordons from my land," Damian bit out. Then he bid Lady Marianne good night and took his leave.

Before seeking his bed, Damian returned to Elissa's chamber to check on her. He found Nan dozing in a chair beside the bed. She lifted her head and beckoned him inside.

"How is she?" Damian asked. "Has she said anything?"

"The lass hasna stirred since ye left," Nan replied. "Ye should find yer own bed, yer lordship. Dawn will arrive sooner than ye wish. I know ye go to meet the Gordons, for my voices speak of yer victory. Ye are an Englishman and I shouldna wish ye well, but Tavis Gordon showed his true colors when he torched the village. And 'tis my belief that Misterly will prosper with ye as its lord."

"Thank you, Nan," Damian acknowledged. "Take care of Elissa, I'm going to follow your advice and get some rest."

"What about Lady Kimbra?" Nan asked.

Damian smiled grimly. "I will deal with her in my own good time."

Sleep eluded Damian. The knowledge that he could have killed Elissa weighed heavily on him. But for an errant wind and a quirk of fate, Elissa might be dead now. He was an excellent shot; he hadn't aimed to kill but one never knew. He wouldn't have been able to live with himself had he slain the woman he cared for.

And he did care for Elissa. No woman of his acquaintance had ever affected him like the redheaded vixen. Though other women might be more conventionally beautiful and refined, Elissa had a special quality that made her unique.

As dawn approached, Damian rose and readied himself for battle. He strapped on his sword, placed his pistol in his belt, and descended the stairs to the hall. Servants were moving about the tables, setting bowls of porridge and platters of fried ham before his men, and from the corner of his eyes he saw Dickon and Maggie in a shadowed corner, conversing in hushed voices. He watched as Dickon touched Maggie's face in a tender farewell.

"Maggie arranged to have an early breakfast served," Dickon explained when he pulled up a chair beside Damian. "Our mounts are waiting in the courtyard for us."

Damian clasped Dickon's shoulder. "You're a good man to have around, Dickon. Shall we break our fast?"

A soggy dawn that promised more rain crept over the gray horizon when Damian rose and signaled the end of the meal.

" 'Tis time, men," he said. "The enemy awaits us."

The Gordons were just stirring from sleep when Damian and his men burst into their campsite. Staggering from their bedrolls, the Highlanders quickly rallied under their battle cry and engaged the attacking Englishmen in hand to hand combat. The forest resounded with the sound of battle. Damian's forces were outnumbered but the Highlanders' weapons were crude and their warriors lacked the fighting skills of trained and seasoned knights.

The fighting was fierce and bloody, but Damian had the weight of countless battles and as many victories on his side. He was a canny strategist and soon devised a plan to surround and divide the Highlanders into small groups.

Too many men had fallen, Damian decided, as he deflected a sword thrust aimed at his heart. Spying Tavis Gordon, he fought his way toward the chieftain.

"Surrender, Gordon," he demanded.

"Never," the man snarled, immediately engaging Damian in swordplay. "We outnumber ye."

Damian turned aside Gordon's sword and thrust beneath his guard, smiling in satisfaction when he drew blood.

"You can't win," Damian asserted. "Look around you. Your men are falling. Despite your numbers, our superior weapons and skill will win the day."

His face a mask of rage, Gordon raised his sword with both hands and slashed downward. Damian danced aside to avoid the sharp edge of the blade but the tip caught his arm, cutting a shallow groove from shoulder to elbow. Ignoring the wound, Damian became the aggressor, driving Gordon back.

"English butcher!" Gordon snarled. "A Gordon! A Gordon!"

His battle cry went unanswered. Apparently he realized the futility of continuing, for he abruptly broke contact with Damian. Raising his voice, he gave the cry for retreat.

"Ye havena seen the last of me, Englishman," Gordon hissed as he turned and fled into the dim reaches of the forest.

Dickon appeared at Damian's side, his sword dripping blood. "Shall we give chase, Damian?"

"Nay. What's the point? This is their land; we'll never find them. Let's hope they learned a lesson."

Dickon nodded. "I'll arrange for the wounded and dead to be conveyed back to the fortress."

Damian returned to the keep, his mind churning with the problems now facing him. The first thing he had to do was provide for the villagers. Since their cottages were constructed of stone and thatch, he assumed that the damage would be confined mostly to the roofs and furnishings. Last night's rain had been a godsend. It had contained the fire and kept the damage to a minimum. He hoped to have the cottages inspected yet today and arrange for repairs.

Then he would deal with Lady Kimbra.

Damian strode into the hall, stopping short when a tense silence ensued, every nerve ending he possessed alert and on edge. What was amiss? He sensed hostility. For him? For Gordon? Were the Frasers willing to forgive Gordon his vile attack upon their village simply because they hated Englishmen?

"The Gordons have been routed and driven back to their stronghold," Damian announced to the hushed crowd.

No one spoke. The silence was deafening. Then a voice rose up from the sea of faces.

"We thank ye, Lord Damian. 'Tisn't right what the Gordon did."

A few "ayes" followed; then suddenly the hall rang with cheers. Stunned, Damian stared at the villagers in confusion.

"What about our homes?" a woman asked in a timid voice.

"Every cottage will be repaired," Damian promised, finally finding his voice. "Whatever you lost in the fire will be replaced." He turned to the priest. "Father Hugh, appoint some men to inspect each cottage and list the repairs needed. I'll expect a full report tomorrow."

"Can we return to our homes before the repairs are made?" someone asked.

" 'Tis entirely up to you. Most of you are anxious to see how badly your homes were damaged, so I won't stop you from returning, if that is your wish. Keep in mind, however, that whatever assistance you need will be made available. Food and staples will be provided from Misterly's stores."

"God bless ye, yer lordship," a woman sobbed. "Yer a good man, for an Englishman."

Damian stifled a smile, wishing that a certain red-headed vixen agreed. Then he turned his mind to a more pressing matter: Lady Kimbra. He was moving away to confront Kimbra in her chamber when Maggie tugged at his sleeve.

"Yer lordship, yer wounded. Let me fetch Nan."

Damian glanced at his arm and shrugged. " 'Tis nothing, Maggie."

" 'Tis indeed something," Maggie scolded. "Sit down, it willna take a minute for Nan to bring her herbs and poultices." She paused, then asked shyly, "Have ye seen Sir Richard? He's not among the wounded, is he?"

"Sir Richard is unscathed," Damian assured her. Maggie nodded and hurried off.

Damian was surprised at Maggie's concern for his welfare and wondered if the Frasers were finally beginning to trust him. Nothing would please him more.

Nan arrived posthaste with her basket of herbs and medicines. "Are there many wounded besides yerself?" she asked as she set her basket on the table and pushed Damian's shirtsleeve up to inspect his wound.

"A few. Both sides suffered casualties. You'll find the wounded in the infirmary. They will be grateful for your attention."

"I'll tend them after I see to yer wound. Yer lucky, yer lordship. 'Tis but a shallow cut. You'll be good as new once 'tis cleaned and bandaged."

"How is Elissa?" Damian asked as Nan worked over him.

"She's awake and in control of her senses. She doesna know 'twas ye who hurt her, but she does know that Tavis Gordon set fire to the village. Will ye go to her now?"

"Later," Damian replied distractedly.

"Aye," Nan nodded. "Ye know in yer heart what must be done. 'Tis our lass ye must think of now. There ye be, yer lordship," she said, tying off the bandage.

"Thank you, Nan." He rose. "I know what must be done no matter how unpleasant it is."

His body taut with determination, Damian marched up the stone staircase to Kimbra's chamber. He paused a moment on the top landing to bring his rampaging temper under control, then knocked on the door.

No answer.

"Kimbra! Open up. I know you're in there."

Still no answer.

Damian cursed aloud and turned the knob. The door was locked. He was considering breaking down the door when it swung open. The Reverend Trilby's stocky figure blocked the doorway.

"Where is she?" Damian demanded, pushing Trilby aside. He spied Kimbra cowering in a corner and ordered Trilby to leave the room.

"No, stay!" Kimbra pleaded.

Damian sent the reverend a quelling look. "Leave now, or I'll throw you out."

"Reverend Trilby, please," Kimbra whispered in a quavering voice.

Apparently Trilby took Damian's threat to heart, for he sent Kimbra an apologetic look and backed toward the door. "You must promise not to hurt her, my lord."

"No matter how much I might be tempted, Lady Kimbra will suffer no physical harm at my hands."

Trilby nodded and made a hasty exit. Damian slammed the door behind him, then rounded on Kimbra.

"Beneath your beauty, you're a ruthless bitch. Admit it. You deliberately planned Elissa's death."

Kimbra's chin notched upward. "If Elissa told you that, she's lying. I am innocent."

"Tell that to someone who will believe you. What did you hit Corbin with? You could have killed him."

"I didn't hit him hard enough to hurt him!" Kimbra cried. Suddenly her eyes rounded and her mouth clamped shut, as if realizing what she had just admitted.

Fury blazed from the depths of Damian's eyes. "What did you expect to gain by Elissa's death?"

"She didn't die."

"No thanks to you. 'Twas a miracle my bullet didn't hit something vital."

Kimbra sidled up to Damian and wound her arms

around his neck. Her voice lowered to a sultry whisper. "Can we not forget what happened? I can make you happy, I swear it. I want to be your wife."

Damian removed her arms and pushed her away. "That's not going to happen. I'm sending you, the Reverend Trilby, and your escort back to London."

Kimbra's eyes narrowed. "You can't send me away. The king personally chose me for your bride. He will be swift to punish you for your disobedience."

"I'll take that chance," Damian replied. "I intend to send a letter of explanation to the king with one of my own men. The letter should reach London before you do."

"I'm sure we can work this out to our mutual satisfaction," Kimbra wheedled. "Don't let a Jacobite traitor come between us."

Damian's contempt was palpable. "There is no *us*, Kimbra. There never was. Pack your belongings. Your escort will be waiting after you break your fast in the morning."

Kimbra's gasp of outrage went unheeded as Damian slammed out the door. Sending Kimbra away would probably lose him both his title and Misterly, but nothing could convince him to wed Kimbra. She wasn't the kind of wife he wanted. He had no intention of living in London, or taking a wife who craved only the excitement city life offered.

An outrageous thought suddenly occurred to Damian and he nearly laughed aloud when he paused to ponder the ramifications. It would mean openly defying the king, but at this point it no longer mattered. In fact, the more Damian thought about it, the less outrageous the idea became.

Still smiling, Damian took the solar steps two at a time, rapped on Elissa's door, and entered. He found her sitting on the edge of the bed, reaching for her robe.

"How are you feeling?" he asked.

Elissa slanted him a defiant look. "Do you really care? How did you find out I'd left the keep?"

"Kimbra raised the alarm. You should have known better than to trust her," he said bluntly. "Are you in pain?"

What a fool she'd been to believe Kimbra, Elissa thought regretfully. She touched her injured head. "I've felt better."

"You were lucky. The bullet just grazed you. I was led to believe you were a Gordon spy." He regarded her thoughtfully. "Why did you leave?"

She blinked up at him. "You and Kimbra were to speak your vows. I wasna willing to live at Misterly as your mistress. Kimbra hates me; life would have been unbearable had I remained."

Her gaze wavered. "I decided to flee to Glenmoor, to my kinswoman, Christy Macdonald."

"You weren't fleeing to Tavis Gordon?" Damian asked with surprise.

"Nay. I'm done with Tavis."

"There's no need for you to go anywhere now," Damian said. "There will be no wedding. I'm sending Kimbra and her entourage back to London tomorrow."

Elissa's eyes rounded and her mouth fell open. "Why? You have to wed Kimbra in order to keep Misterly."

Damian's determination did not waver. "I'm hoping the king will understand once he reads my letter explaining the misalliance between me and Kimbra. I can protect Misterly without Kimbra as my wife."

Elissa leaned back against the pillows and studied Damian through narrowed lids. She tried to imagine what Damian's decision meant for her family . . . and for her. She acknowledged his desire to keep his newly acquired lands, but not his stubborn compulsion to defy his king.

She was about to ask Damian to let her go to Glenmoor when Maggie opened the door and peered into the chamber. "Yer mother and sister wish to visit ye, Elissa."

Lady Marianne entered the chamber behind Maggie. She was walking slowly, but Elissa was thrilled at the progress her mother was making.

"Mother, is it wise for you to be exerting yourself?"

"Aye, daughter, I'm determined to regain my strength."

Suddenly Lora shot past Marianne. "Lissa! Are you all right? Mama said you were hurt. I wasna allowed to leave the solar these past two days, but I knew something was amiss." Her gaze turned to Damian. "You dinna hurt Elissa, did you?"

Before Damian could answer, Elissa said, " 'Twas an accident, Lora." She patted the side of the bed. "Sit down beside me, both of you. How long have you been up and about, Mama?"

Lady Marianne perched on the side of the bed while Lora climbed into Elissa's lap. "For some time now, though I havena left the solar or attempted the stairs." She sent a meaningful look at Damian. "I need to be strong for my family. Lady Kimbra wishes us ill. 'Tis why I've kept Lora close since the arrival of Lord Damian's bride."

"You need worry no longer, my lady," Damian assured her. "Kimbra is returning to London."

A faint smile curved Marianne's lips as her gaze moved from Damian to Elissa. "God moves in mysterious ways. How are you feeling, daughter? I've been worried despite Nan's assurance that you suffered no serious harm."

"As you can see," Elissa said, "I'm fine."

"What about the villagers, my lord? Are they being provided for? Were my husband alive, he would see to their needs."

"The villagers are my responsibility now," Damian said. "The cottages are being inspected for damage and the necessary repairs made. I'm providing food and whatever else they need to make them comfortable. We should fare well this winter. Ripened fruit is fairly falling off the trees, wheat is golden in the fields, and vegetable gardens are thriving. We've lost some sheep to reivers, but I foresee no shortage of food in the near future."

Marianna appeared pleased. " 'Tis as it should be. Misterly has always provided for its own."

"Can you play with me, Elissa?" Lora piped up, apparently weary of grown-up talk.

"Nay," Damian said, before Elissa could answer. "Your sister needs to rest today."

"We'll start lessons again tomorrow," Elissa promised when she noted Lora's disappointment.

"Come, Lora," Marianne said, rising. " 'Tis time we left. Lord Damian said the danger is over so you can play in the courtyard with the other children today."

"Aye," Damian concurred. "Misterly is safe now; you may move about as you please."

"Is there anything else you require, Elissa?" Maggie asked before she followed Marianne and Lora out the door

"Nay, thank you, Maggie. I should be up and about tomorrow."

"You should be exactly where you are," Damian said sternly. "I'll leave so you can rest."

Elissa was startled when Damian bent and kissed her fully on the lips. It was a strange kiss. It tasted of carefully controlled passion, of possessiveness, and something else. When he finally released her mouth, Elissa couldn't help wondering if he'd kissed Kimbra in the same manner. Then he was gone, leaving Elissa longing for something a loyal Highlander shouldn't want.

Elissa was almost asleep when she realized someone was standing beside the bed. She opened her eyes, startled to see Kimbra standing over her.

"You haven't won yet," Kimbra hissed venomously. "The king will be told how you used your wiles to turn Damian against me. Damian is mine. You can't have him." She touched her stomach, a sly smile curving her lips. "I'm almost certain I'm carrying his child."

A cry of dimay shot past Elissa's lips. Kimbra was carrying Damian's bairn? "Nay, how can that be? 'Tis too soon to tell."

"A woman knows her own body," Kimbra replied. "Even you must be aware that a child usually results when two people couple. I will insist that the king punish you harshly for your deceitful ways."

"I've done naught!" Elissa protested. "You've brought this on yourself."

Kimbra made a derisive sound in her throat and

whirled on her heel. "Enjoy your freedom while it lasts," she threw over her shoulder.

Elissa remained in her chamber the following morning until Kimbra and her party had left for London. She watched from the window as they rode off, then made her way below to the hall. Her legs were still wobbly but her head didn't hurt nearly as badly as it had the day before.

Elissa saw Damian speaking with a group of men and slipped past him to break her fast in the kitchen with people she knew and loved. For some reason she was hungrier than usual this morning and ate with gusto. When she left the kitchen, she walked headlong into the hard wall of Damian's chest.

"Were you trying to avoid me?" he asked with amusement.

Elissa's cheeks reddened beneath his disarming smile. Suddenly recalling the startling news Kimbra had revealed to her last night, she pushed herself away and glared up at him.

"Should you be out of bed?" Damian asked.

"I'm fine," she answered coolly.

Damian nodded but didn't look convinced. "I've been looking for you. I thought you'd be pleased to know that the damage to the village was minimal. The rain prevented what could have been a tragedy. Only six cottages lost their roofs and the rest were only slightly damaged. Some furnishings were lost, but nothing that can't be replaced or repaired. At least no lives were lost. Father Hugh said the church had been spared."

"What about the tradesmen? Did their shops survive the fire?"

"Most are intact. I've already sent to Inverness for materials and supplies not readily available at Misterly."

"I'm sure my kinsmen are grateful," Elissa said. "If you'll excuse me, I promised Nan I'd help with the wounded."

"There's something I'd like to discuss with you," Damian said.

"We have nothing to discuss."

Damian sent her a curious look. "What's wrong? You sound angry. I didn't shoot you intentionally, if that's what's bothering you."

Elissa bristled. "That's not it at all. You shouldn't have sent her away."

"Are you referring to Kimbra? I thought you'd be happy to see the last of her."

"That was before . . ."

"Before what?"

"If you donna know, 'tis not my place to tell you." She marched away, head held high, shoulders squared.

"Coward," Damian called after her.

Elissa worked in the infirmary beside Nan until all the wounded had been treated.

"Time to wash up and join our kinsmen for the noon meal," Nan said, as she ushered Elissa to the small chamber separate from the infirmary where fresh water and towels awaited.

"There you are," Damian said as he entered the dimly lit chamber. "How are the wounded faring?"

"Well on the road to recovery, yer lordship," Nan replied.

"Excellent," Damian said. "The noon meal is being served. Are you finished here?"

"Aye, but sit ye down first so I can change yer bandage."

Startled, Elissa's gaze traveled over Damian, looking for an injury. She saw nothing to indicate he'd been hurt.

" 'Tis but an insignificant scratch and nearly healed," Damian maintained.

"I insist, me lord," Nan said, leading him to a bench. "Infection is a danger no matter how slight the wound."

Damian sat down and lifted his arm for Nan's inspection.

"Raise yer shirtsleeve while I fetch my basket from the infirmary," Nan directed.

Elissa gave a small cry as she stared at Damian's arm. A blood-soaked bandage covered a slash from shoulder to elbow. She dropped down beside him and carefully peeled away the soiled bandage.

"I thought you said 'twas nothing."

Damian shrugged. "A minor annoyance. It looks worse than it is."

Nan rejoined them a moment later. " 'Tis a shallow wound, but all wounds have the potential to fester." She smiled approvingly. "Yer wound is clean and healthy, me lord. Elissa can apply salve and a fresh bandage. She is as adept at it as I am."

Elissa sent Nan a fulminating look. Nan returned the look with a knowing grin and hurried off. Elissa returned her attention to Damian; he was staring at her with an intensity that sent shards of awareness coursing through her.

"The bandage, Elissa," he reminded softly.

Elissa blinked and reached for his arm. She felt him shiver and jerked her gaze to his face. "Did I hurt you?"

"Nay, please continue."

Elissa bent to her task, fearing she would melt beneath the blistering heat of his gaze. Merely touching Damian made her forget Kimbra existed, and that Damian was an English rogue who trampled on women's feelings. She and Damian had no future together; she refused to become mistress to a man she despised on every level ... every level but one. When he made love to her, he made her feel as if he truly cared for her.

Elissa could never suffer fools, and she was the worst kind. If Kimbra carried Damian's bairn, of course he must marry her.

Chapter 14

After tying off Damian's bandage, Elissa rose and shook out her skirts. Damian surged to his feet; his eyes were hooded, his thoughts unfathomable. Elissa distrusted this inscrutable side of Damian and retreated a step, then another. He followed, stalking her until she felt the cold wall against her back and the searing heat of his body pressing against her.

Damian's silver eyes darkened to pewter as he grasped her waist with both hands and held her captive, the hard press of his rigid sex prodding relentlessly between her thighs. Mesmerized, she felt her gaze latch onto his mouth, hovering over hers, close, so close she could see the pulse beating at the base of his neck. Why did her breath catch in her throat and her body quiver with need? She chided herself for a witless fool even as she raised her mouth to his.

His kiss destroyed her will. Her resistance shat-

239

tered and she melted into his embrace, her body seeking the pleasure she knew only he could give her. His hands sought her breasts and she moaned into his mouth, sagging against him; the pleasure of his touch made her tremble. Then he was dragging her over to the bench, his caresses growing more demanding as he eased her down upon the hard surface.

Elissa was aware of nothing but the raging need he aroused in her. She felt cool air upon her breasts, dimly aware that Damian had lowered her bodice. A sigh left her throat as he bent to her and took a nipple into his mouth. She arched against him, offering him more of herself for his thrilling caress.

"Elissa," Damian moaned against her skin. "I need this. I need you."

She felt his hand beneath her skirt, sliding between her legs, cupping her. Her heart slammed against her ribs. For a wild, unprincipled moment she wanted him as badly as he wanted her. Her legs fell open, inviting a more intimate touch. He eagerly obliged, whispering endearments against her mouth as his fingers explored her cleft.

"Open for me, sweeting. Kimbra is gone. No one will stop us from taking what we want."

Damian's words had a devastating effect upon Elissa. Kimbra! How could she forget? Damian had the power of a sorcerer. With a single kiss he had wiped the memory of Kimbra's parting words from her mind.

She pushed against his chest. "Nay! Let me up. You canna do this."

Damian reared up, confusion furrowing his brow. "Did I hurt you? Does your head hurt?"

Elissa slid from beneath him, her eyes blazing fury. "How dare you! Donna touch me."

"What have I done?"

Elissa took a deep, steadying breath. "Your treatment of women is abominable. How could you send Lady Kimbra away? She's carrying your bairn. I dinna admire Kimbra, but I wouldna like to be treated with such callous disregard were I carrying your bairn."

"What?"

Damian appeared astounded but Elissa wasn't so easily fooled.

"I never heard such nonsense. If Kimbra is carrying a child, it bloody well isn't mine. I never touched the woman."

Elissa snorted in disbelief. "Liar! Lady Kimbra told me herself that you were her lover. I saw you kissing her. She's very beautiful, my lord, a virile man's dream."

"Not my dream," Damian retorted. "If there was a remote chance that Kimbra carried my child, I would have wed her. If anyone is carrying my child, 'tis you."

Uttering a cry of denial, Elissa whirled away, straightening her clothing and hair as she fled.

"Elissa! Wait! I just remembered something Nan said."

But it was too late. Elissa was gone. Damian followed behind at a slower pace. He needed time to compose himself. His arousal was thick and hard and his need undiminished. He took several deep breaths, trying to make sense out of everything Elissa had said, and the things that were left unsaid.

Damian hadn't been oblivious to the consequences when he released his seed inside Elissa, but he had deliberately ignored his conscience to appease his own selfish pleasure. And only Elissa could tell him the truth.

Once he gained control of himself, he made his way to the hall. The meal was still in progress but Elissa was nowhere in sight. He forced himself to sit down and eat, tasting little of what went into his mouth. He had plans to make and bring to fruition. He realized he was treading on dangerous ground, and that the king could punish him for disobeying orders, but he was determined to forge ahead, even if Elissa refused him.

"You look like a man with something on his mind," Sir Richard said as he slid into the seat beside Damian. "Are you worried that Kimbra will renounce you to the king? Pray that your letter reaches His Majesty before Kimbra gets to him. You advised him that you repelled an attack on Misterly, did you not? That should put you in his good graces."

"One never knows with the king," Damian grumbled.

"Do you intend to make Elissa your mistress now that Kimbra is gone?"

"Nay, I have other plans for Elissa."

"Tell me, I'm all ears."

"You'll learn soon enough. Do you happen to know if Father Hugh has returned to the village?"

"He left with a wagonload of food from our stores to feed those who have returned to their homes. Shall I fetch him for you?"

"Nay. I'll see to it myself."

Dickon sent him a curious look. "What's going on, Damian?"

"What's going on with you and Maggie, Dickon?" Damian replied, deftly skirting Dickon's question. "Have you bedded the wench yet?"

Dickon's handsome face reddened. "Aye, but I had to promise I'd wed her first."

"You promised to wed her?" Damian choked out. "And she believed you? Was she an innocent?"

Dickon's flush deepened. "Aye, I did indeed take her maidenhead."

"Then you shall marry her, my friend. I suggest you set a date."

"Bloody hell, Damian! I've told countless women I'd marry them. 'Tis all part of the game."

"Not to Maggie, it isn't. She's not one of your London doxies. She's Elissa's kinswoman and ignorant of the games men play. I won't allow you to dishonor her."

Dickon half rose from his chair. "Like you dishonored Elissa? We're one of a kind, Damian. Bloody hell, we've even shared women. Elissa is no different from the dozens of other women you've bedded."

"There's a big difference, Dickon. I'm going to make Elissa my wife, so be careful what you say about her."

Dickon fell back into his chair, a stunned expression on his face. "You're marrying Elissa? Are you mad? The king will use your ballocks for target practice. I hope you're prepared to lose Misterly and everything else you've been given."

"Perhaps it won't come to that," Damian ventured. "I want her, Dickon. I've never wanted a woman more than I want Elissa."

"I beg you. Keep her as your mistress but don't defy the king. I've been your friend a long time and I care what happens to you."

"Forget about me and Elissa. Let's talk about you and Maggie. Do you care for her?"

"I'm not ready to let this drop yet," Dickon said bluntly. "Has Elissa agreed to marry you?"

"She will. Enough, Dickon. I've made my decision; there's nothing more to discuss. Now if you'll excuse me, I'm off to the village."

Dickon stared pensively after Damian as he strode away. Why was his friend being so stubborn about this? The king's anger wasn't to be taken lightly. When he saw Maggie enter the hall, his thoughts scattered and he hurried after her.

Elissa prowled her chamber like a restless cat, Damian's parting words still echoing in her brain.

If anyone carries my child, 'tis you.

Could it be true? She pressed a hand against her flat stomach. It was far too soon to tell, but she seriously doubted she carried Damian's bairn, and she intended for it to remain that way. Just because Nan seemed to think she carried a bairn didn't make it so.

Aware that she couldn't hide in her chamber forever, Elissa left her room, and met Sir Brody and her mother in the passageway.

"Elissa," Marianne greeted excitedly. "Sir Brody has arranged for a pony cart to take me to the village. I wanted to see for myself how our clansmen are faring. Would you like to come along?"

"That's a wonderful idea, Mama," Elissa enthused. "Shall we take Lora with us?"

"She's already there. Lachlan invited her to spend the day with his family."

The cart was waiting for them in the courtyard. Sir Brody lifted Marianne onto the seat while Elissa climbed in and took up the reins. "I can drive the cart, Sir Brody," Elissa said. "No need for you to tag along."

"Are you sure, my lady? Lord Damian said . . ."

"I donna care what Lord Damian said. I'm perfectly capable of driving myself and Mama to the village."

"We'll be fine," Marianne concurred.

Though still skeptical, Sir Brody buckled beneath Marianne's sweet smile. He bowed and backed away. "If you have no further need of me, I shall return to my duties."

Elissa had no idea if Damian would approve of her leaving the keep, and she didn't care. She was so happy to see her mother take an interest in life again that she wouldn't miss the chance of an outing for anything.

Elissa handled the cart with ease as she drove along the winding road to the village, elated at her mother's renewed interest in life. Before Damian had arrived at Misterly, Elissa was convinced her mother was on her deathbed. Admittedly, Damian had made a difference since becoming the Lord of Misterly. Even her kinsmen had become energized and more mindful of their responsibilities. Damian might be a hated Englishman, but he had brought stability and purpose to Misterly.

Elissa wondered what would happen to them if
the king stripped Damian of his title and lands.
Damian shouldn't have been so quick to send Kimbra away. From what Elissa had heard about the
Hanover king and those who served him, they were
unforgiving when crossed.

"You're quiet, daughter," Marianne said. "Is your
head hurting?"

"My head is fine, Mama," Elissa assured her. "I
was just wondering what will become of us should
Damian lose Misterly."

Marianne's brow puckered. "Pray that willna
happen. We could get a new lord less agreeable than
Lord Damian."

"There's the village up ahead," Elissa said excitedly. "It seems like forever since I've been there.
Shall we visit the shops first? Damian said most had
survived the fires."

"Nay, take me to the kirk," Marianne said. " 'Tis
been too long since I've prayed in a house of wor-
ship. I have much to be grateful for despite our sad
losses."

Elissa reined the horse down the narrow, cobbled
street that was the main thoroughfare. "Father Hugh
was right," she observed. "Damage to the cottages
and shops is minimal. Nevertheless, I'll never forgive Tavis Gordon. What he did is reprehensible."

"Aye," Marianne concurred. "I strongly objected
to the marriage between you and the Gordon chieftain, but your father was adamant. I dinna like Tavis
then and I donna like him now."

"I donna like him, either," Elissa said. The day
Tavis had demanded that she kill Damian had been

the day she'd lost all regard for her intended bride-groom.

Elissa drew rein before the kirk and scrambled down from the cart to help her mother.

"Isna that Lord Damian's horse?" Marianne asked, indicating the sleekly muscled animal teth-ered to the kirk fence.

Elissa's answer was forestalled when Damian came striding from the kirk with Father Hugh trail-ing in his wake. He saw the cart and stopped abruptly. Elissa met his hard gaze without flinching. She'd done nothing wrong. As Damian forged his way toward her, she wondered if he'd visited the kirk to ask God's forgiveness for his sins.

"Lady Marianne, how good to see you looking so radiant," Damian said courteously. "Next time you decide to leave the keep, however, please inform me so I can provide a proper escort. Sir Brody was wrong to let you venture out on your own."

"Oh, nay, my lord, donna blame Sir Brody. He wanted to accompany us, but Elissa . . . I mean, I told him it wasna necessary."

"Donna apologize to him, Mama," Elissa said, bristling. "No one would dare harm us."

Damian sent Elissa an inscrutable look. "One never knows. Next time, I expect you to ask permis-sion to leave the keep."

Elissa stiffened. "Surely there can be no harm in visiting our clansmen. They've suffered a loss and we merely wished to offer our support."

"As you can see, everything is well in hand."

Father Hugh stepped between the bickering cou-ple. "Lord Damian, perhaps Lady Marianne would like to step inside the kirk while you and Lady Elissa settle your differences. If you intend to go through with what we just discussed, I strongly advise you and Elissa to learn to get along with one another."

"Forgive me, Father," Damian said. "I bow to your better judgment."

Elissa thought Damian looked more fierce than sorry. Something was afoot, something she was sure she wasn't going to like.

"I'd love to sit inside the kirk and meditate for a while," Marianne said. "Would you aid me, my lord?"

Damian lifted Lady Marianne from the cart as if she weighed no more than a bird and set her on her feet.

"I will escort Lady Marianne inside," Father Hugh said, offering Marianne his arm.

Elissa waited until Marianne and Father Hugh disappeared inside the kirk before she returned her attention to Damian. Looking at him was a mistake, she decided. If ever a man deserved to be called the Demon Knight, it was the brooding man standing before her. She'd seen him angry, she'd seen him lost to passion, but she'd never seen the look he now wore on his face.

Intense, aye, smoldering, mayhap, and utterly beguiling. He was the seductive male animal, sure of himself and his power, masterful, arrogant. But there was something else; a look that puzzled her. Could it be vulnerability? That was impossible. An arrogant man like Damian would never expose his vulnerable side to anyone.

A tense silence stretched between them. Finally, Elissa asked, "Did you come to the kirk to pray?"

Damian's brooding visage suddenly lightened. "I've reached a decision about your future, Elissa, and I wished to discuss it with Father Hugh."

Elissa stared at him. Her future? What did Father Hugh have to do with her future? The convent! Of course. Damian was conferring with the priest about the arrangements.

"I knew it would come to this," Elissa retorted. "You were waiting until Mama recovered to send us away. Have you changed your mind about Lady Kimbra? Will you go to London and fetch her?"

Damian's voice was low, harsh, and taut with wary tension. "You misunderstand, Elissa. You and I are going to marry. I came to the kirk to make arrangements with your priest."

Elissa paled. "Marry? You and I? You're mad."

" 'Tis the logical solution."

"The king willna permit it."

"I care not."

"I refuse to wed an English butcher."

Damian scowled. "I'd prefer not to be called a butcher. Your kinsmen have come to respect me. I am slowly gaining their trust. I feel certain they will approve of our marriage."

"You canna abandon the woman who carries your bairn."

Damian's eyes glittered with amusement. "I'm not abandoning her, I'm marrying her."

Elissa glared at him. "You are mistaken, my lord, I am not carrying your bairn. Believe me, I'd be the first to know."

Damian sent her a smug smile. "If you're not with child, you soon will be. You're going to marry me, Elissa, and that's final."

"Why?"

Damian assumed a thoughtful look. "Why? Because I'd rather have you than the woman the king chose for me. Is that so strange? You've always known I wanted you."

"I'm a Jacobite and the daughter of a traitor."

"You're a woman, a beautiful, passionate woman."

"I hate Englishmen."

"The war ended years ago."

"My countrymen are still being oppressed."

"You can't blame me for that. Think about it, Elissa. We both love Misterly. I've made it mine and I won't give it up without a fight. We can join forces and do what's best for your clansmen."

"That's impossible."

"Truthfully, Elissa, do you hate me?"

Elissa bit her lip as she considered Damian's question. The answer was as complex as the man who stood before her. After considerable thought, she knew there was but one answer. "I donna hate you, Damian."

"I've never hated you, sweeting."

"What *do* you feel for me?" Elissa blurted out. "Do you love me?"

Elissa saw the subtle change in Damain's expression and gave way to despair. Only a fool would believe a man like Damian wanted anything from her but her body. He believed their marriage a good political move, one that would unite her clansmen against the Gordons and protect his claim to Misterly. The Demon Knight didn't love, he possessed.

"You're asking for more than I'm prepared to give," Damian muttered. "Love makes a man vulnerable, and I can't afford to become weak. I care for you a great deal and promise to honor our vows. How many men would make that kind of concession?"

Elissa stared at him in blatant disbelief. Damian had just promised to be a faithful husband. Should she believe him? He might honor their vows as long as he remained at Misterly, but would he be able to resist bedding other women when he traveled to London, or Inverness, or any other large town? She'd be stupid to expect him to remain at Misterly and not seek diversion elsewhere from time to time.

"Elissa, did you not hear me? I vowed to remain true to our marriage vows. Can you make the same promise? You're still not infatuated with Tavis Gordon, are you?"

"I want nothing to do with that man," she spat. "He has room for naught but vengeance in his heart. You appear to bear no malice for my kinsmen. And my mother and sister are kindly disposed toward you."

"Then 'tis settled," Damian announced. "We'll speak our vows in five days hence."

"I haven't agreed!" Elissa cried.

Damian's eyes narrowed. "Don't try my temper, my lady. I said we'll marry and so we shall. I warn you, it would be unwise to refuse. I'm sure you know what I mean."

"Must you hold my mother and sister over my head like a sledgehammer that will crush me if I donna do as you wish?"

"If I have to. Would you bring a bastard child into the world?"

Elissa gave a disgusted snort. "How many times must I tell you that I donna carry your bairn?"

"Sooner or later it will happen. I cannot believe you'd prefer to become my mistress. Wouldn't you rather bring legitimate children into the world?"

"This talk of children is senseless, unless you're referring to your children with Kimbra."

"This is the last time I'm going to say this, Elissa. I have never bedded Kimbra. She's an accomplished liar and troublemaker."

"What happens when you tire of me?" Elissa asked. "The Demon Knight's reputation for using women and abandoning them is legend."

Grasping her shoulders, he brought her against him. "Don't believe everything you hear," he said in a low, seductive whisper.

His mouth hovered just inches from hers. She closed her eyes as his full lips slowly descended. She thought she was prepared for his kiss, but she wasn't. Nothing could have prepared her for the powerful emotion that surged through her the moment their lips connected. His potent kiss snatched the breath from her lungs. His mouth moved slowly over hers, his tongue gliding wetly over her lips, then thrusting inside as he devoured the taste and scent of her. Her knees weakened; her mouth molded to his as her body melted against his heat and hardness.

Sweet surrender beckoned . . . until she remembered that Damian had given her no choice. He had simply assumed they would marry without allowing her the courtesy of accepting or refusing. He had arranged their marriage without her knowledge or approval.

Damian abruptly broke off the kiss and she clung to him for support. Why was her head spinning?

Why was Damian smiling at her with that smug look on his face? Why did her heart pound and her body burn?

"Here comes your mother," Damian said, moving slightly away from Elissa as Marianne approached. He searched Elissa's face. "Are you all right? You look dazed."

"I'm ready to return to the keep, my lord," Marianne said, her gaze shifting from Damian to Elissa. "Am I interrupting something?"

"I will explain later," Damian said. He turned to the priest. "We will expect you in five days, Father. Kindly inform your flock that they are invited to the keep to celebrate my marriage to Elissa. I've already spoken to Dermot about hiring musicians. We will have music and dancing and feasting. 'Tisn't every day the Maiden of Misterly takes a husband."

"Father Hugh told me of your plans, my lord," Lady Marianne informed Damian.

"Do you approve, my lady?"

Marianne slid a glance at Elissa before answering. "I want what's best for my daughter and Misterly. I will pray for a happy union."

" 'Tis what I want as well, my lady."

Damian handed Lady Marianne into the cart, then turned to help Elissa, but she climbed onto the seat and took up the reins before Damian could touch her. She snapped the reins and the cart rattled forward.

"Are you upset with Lord Damian's arrangements, daughter?" Marianne asked when Elissa remained quiet.

"He should have asked my approval."

"He may have gone about it the wrong way but I know you no longer wish to wed Tavis." Marianne's fine brow furrowed. "I would have objected had I thought the marriage unwise. There are advantages to such a match."

"Advantages? Have you considered the consequences once the Hanover learns that Damian refused to wed Lady Kimbra?"

"I have, but I think Lord Damian is capable of standing up to the king. If you're worried, ask Nan to consult her voices."

"I donna trust Nan's voices, Mama, and neither should you. She's old and fanciful; she doesna know what she's talking about most of the time."

Marianne sent her a sharp look. "Has Nan said something to upset you?"

She shrugged. "No more than usual. Donna let it bother you. Damian and I will settle this ourselves."

Marianne sighed. "You're right, daughter. This is between you and Damian. I'm too weary from my outing to give the matter proper attention."

The cart clattered to a halt in the courtyard. Damian rode up beside them and dismounted. But before he could lift Marianne from the cart, Sir Brody appeared and shoved Damian aside.

"Allow me to carry Lady Marianne to her chamber, my lord."

"As you will," Damian replied, giving way to the knight's bulky form.

"Your mother has a champion in Sir Brody," Damian observed.

"They do seem to enjoy one another's company."

"As do Sir Richard and Maggie."

Elissa's head shot up. "Has Sir Richard dishonored her? I willna stand for it."

"I wouldn't be surprised to see a wedding besides our own very soon. Mayhap two."

"Are you planning to force others in my family to wed against their will?"

"I do not need to use force."

"Not even on me?" Elissa challenged.

He touched her face, his gaze intent upon her mouth. For a moment she feared he would kiss her despite the fact that they were being watched, but he didn't. He merely smiled in that arrogant way of his that raised her hackles, and escorted her into the keep.

"We're just in time," Damian said. "The table is being set for the evening repast. I want you to sit beside me. No more hiding in your chamber."

Elissa didn't argue when Damian escorted her to the dais and seated her beside him. He would have his way no matter how loud or long she protested.

Elissa had just helped herself from a platter when Nan approached the dais. "Might I speak with ye a moment, yer lordship?"

"Of course, Nan. Is something wrong?"

"Nay. 'Tis about the two wounded Gordons that were carried from the battlefield with yer own wounded. They have recovered from their injuries. What are yer plans for them?"

"I'd almost forgotten," Damian mused. "Invite them to the hall to share our food."

Elissa gasped. "Are you sure, Damian?"

"Very sure. I want to end hostilities with the Gordons once and for all. Do as I say, Nan."

Nan scooted away and returned a short time later accompanied by two men still bearing disfigurements from the bloody battle they'd fought. One had a newly healed scar that ran from chin to the outer edge of his eyebrow and the other wore a bandage on his right arm. Wrapped in the Gordon plaid, they stood stiffly before Damian.

"What are your names?" Damian inquired.

The man with the scarred face came to attention. "I am Hugo Gordon."

"And I am Archie Gordon," the second man declared.

"Find a place at the table," Damian bade them.

"Ye want us to break bread with ye?" Hugo asked in disbelief.

"Aye. We need not be enemies."

"Yer an English butcher, sent by the Hanover to wreak havoc upon our people and lands," Hugo spat.

"I want peace to reign at Misterly. Will you accept my hospitality?"

The two men exchanged uncertain glances. "Tell us our fate first," Archie said. "Is this to be our last meal?"

Damian chuckled. "You are free to go back to your homes. You may fill your bellies at my board or leave hungry, 'tis your choice."

"We're free to leave?" Hugo gasped, clearly shocked.

"Have I not just said so? I have but one request, however, before you leave Misterly."

"Name it," Archie said.

"I want you to deliver a message to the Gordon chieftain."

"A message? Verra well," Hugo agreed. "What is it?"

"Tell your chieftain that he is invited to attend a wedding celebration. In five days, The Maiden of Misterly and Lord Clarendon will wed in the great hall at the hour of noon."

A hush fell over the hall, followed by the clamoring of voices, some raised in disapproval and others openly accepting of Damian's effort to achieve lasting peace for Misterly. Elissa's own feelings were hard to define. She knew Damian's announcement of their marriage had come as a surprise to those present. No one had expected Damian to defy the king openly, and everyone was aware of the consequences of such a rash act. He could lose Misterly.

Furthermore, inviting Tavis Gordon to the wedding was asking for trouble. The man was a bomb waiting to explode. Did Damian think he could promote peace by inviting Tavis to Misterly? Was he willing to overlook the fact that Tavis was an outlaw in order to form a tenuous friendship?

Elissa suddenly became aware that Hugo was staring at her. "Is it true, my lady?" he asked. "Will ye wed the Demon Knight? I thought ye were promised to the Gordon."

"Elissa is to be my bride," Damian insisted, forestalling Elissa's answer. "Will you carry my message to your chieftain?"

Hugo nodded jerkily. "Aye, but 'tis a marriage made in hell. The lass bears no love for Englishmen."

Elissa wanted to say there would be no marriage, but the words stuck in her throat. Damian would have his way.

She would become the Demon Knight's wife whether she wished it or not.

Chapter 15

Elissa stood at the window, gazing at the stars twinkling overhead. How she wished she were still that small child who believed that wishing upon a star would grant everything she desired. If wishes came true, her beloved father and brothers would be alive and Misterly would still belong to the Frasers. But wishing didn't bring miracles.

In five days she would become the Demon Knight's bride, a thought as frightening as it was thrilling. Damian was a unique man, multilayered and complex. Men obeyed him without question and women adored him. He was his own man— courageous enough to defy his king and strong enough to hold what was his.

Damian wanted her, but he didn't love her. He believed that emotional love was a weakness. There was no denying, however, that he excelled at lovemaking, for it took little effort on his part to make her want him.

Elissa frowned as she considered her feelings for Damian. She no longer hated him. She had realized that when she couldn't bring herself to kill him to appease Tavis. She'd allowed Damian to make love to her even though she knew she was betraying her clansmen. She cared for him—nay, she loved him—and the guilt was nearly killing her.

Unable to bear her dark thoughts any longer, Elissa turned from the window and pulled the counterpane from the bed. A knock on the door diverted her. She greeted Maggie warmly and invited her to sit down.

"I canna stay, Elissa. I'm spending the night with my family in the village," Maggie said. "Is there anything ye need before I leave?"

"Thank you, but there is naught I need. Is Lora abed?"

"She's sleeping like a babe," Maggie said. "Yer mother, too."

Maggie fussed with the counterpane, looking as if she wanted to say something but didn't know where to begin. Finally Elissa asked, "Is there something you'd like to tell me, Maggie?"

Maggie flushed and wrung her hands. "I donna know how to begin."

Elissa grasped her hands. "Start at the beginning. I know you and Sir Richard have become close. Is that what this is about?"

"I dinna think anyone noticed," Maggie murmured.

Elissa grinned. "We couldna help but notice."

"Sir Richard is a handsome man . . . for an Englishman," Maggie added hastily.

"Do you love him?"

Maggie dropped her gaze. "Aye. Sir Richard promised to marry me."

"Do you believe him?"

Her head shot up. "Is there a reason I shouldna?"

"Some men will promise anything to lure a woman into his bed."

"What did Lord Damian promise *ye* when he bedded ye?" Maggie returned sharply. Elissa's stricken expression must have shamed Maggie, for she appeared horrified by the words that had just tumbled from her mouth. "Oh, Elissa, forgive me. I know ye had little choice in the matter. But yer going to wed his lordship and that makes everything all right."

Elissa took a deep breath. "I forgive you."

Elissa couldn't bring herself to ask if Maggie had given herself to Sir Richard, for she hadn't the right. "I canna tell you whom to love, Maggie. I just want you to be happy."

Maggie squeezed her hand. "Ye deserve all the best, Elissa. I hope Lord Damian makes ye happy. Do ye love him?"

A long pause. "I think so. But I donna know if I could live with the guilt. He's not the husband my father wanted for me."

"Yer father is dead," Maggie said softly. "Tavis Gordon broke the faith when he torched the village. Lord Damian helped us, even your father would agree were he alive. His lordship has provided food and lodging to those in need. He loves Misterly, and for that he has gained our respect. He sent Lady Kimbra away, which pleased everyone. Ye need not fear that our kinsmen willna accept yer marriage to Lord Damian."

Elissa searched Maggie's face. "Are you sure?"

"Aye. I wouldna lie to ye."

"Damian doesna love me," Elissa said on a sigh.

"Are ye sure?"

"I . . . asked him."

Maggie sent her a pitying look. "I'm sorry, Elissa. I thought, nay, I truly believed his lordship cared for ye. He's marrying ye, is he not?"

"Our marriage is convenient to him. He believes our union will strengthen Misterly."

"Lord Damian may surprise ye," Maggie ventured. "I must leave. Sir Richard is waiting below to escort me to the village."

There was nothing more Elissa could say. Maggie trusted Sir Richard, and Elissa prayed she didn't love in vain, for Elissa knew well the feeling. Marrying an Englishman wasn't what Elissa had dreamed of, but she was willing to make the sacrifice if it brought peace to Misterly.

The keep was a beehive of activity during the days preceding Elissa's wedding day. Even the tapestries had been taken down and cleaned. Food was being prepared in enormous amounts, from main dishes to pastries. Elissa had no idea Winifred was so talented in culinary arts.

Elissa saw little of Damian before the wedding. For reasons of his own, Damian had not come to her in the night or tried to seduce her, and Elissa wasn't sure whether she was relieved or disappointed.

Damian's invitation to Tavis had thus far gone unanswered and Elissa feared the outcome should Tavis decide to attend. It wasn't difficult to imagine the havoc he could wreak. Not for the first time, she wished Damian hadn't been so bold, for no good could come of it.

The day before the wedding, Elissa was summoned to her mother's chambers. She stopped just inside the door, surprised to find the room crowded with chattering women.

"Come in, my dear," Marianne invited.

"What's this all about, Mama?"

"I wanted you to have proper wedding attire so I invited a few of our kinswomen to help fit my own wedding gown to your more voluptuous figure."

Elissa spied the lovely pale blue gown spread out on Marianne's bed and gasped in delight. "Are you sure? 'Tis beautiful," she said, fingering the fine silk.

"Verra sure. Put it on so we can see how it fits."

For the next two hours Elissa stood in the center of the chamber while the best seamstresses of the group altered the gown to her form. There was sufficient material in the seams and hem to make the bust slightly larger and drop the hemline, but the rest needed little or no adjustment.

The sleeves were long and fitted, the waist tightly cinched, and the neckline was modest while showing an enticing hint of cleavage. Shimmering blue silk flowed over her trim hips to the tips of her satin shoes. The final touch was a short veil, held in place by a jeweled cap.

"You look lovely," Marianne sighed. "The color is perfect with your red hair and fair complexion."

The effusive compliments that followed Marianne's words made Elissa actually feel like the cherished bride of a man who loved her.

The rest of the day passed with uncommon haste.

Elissa did not see Damian until the evening meal. She took her place beside him at the table and toyed with the food on her plate. Suddenly she felt Damian looking at her and she returned his gaze.

"Your appetite seems lacking tonight, my lady," he said wryly, his half-smile lavish with charm. "Are you worried about the ceremony tomorrow?"

She flushed but did not look way. "We've hardly spoken these past days, I'd hoped you'd changed your mind."

Damian chuckled. "Did you miss my attention? You'll have all of me you wish after tomorrow."

"I wish none of you."

He stroked her cheek with the back of his hand. "I doubt that. I know for a fact that one part of you wants one part of me."

A heated blush crept up Elissa's neck as she adroitly changed the subject. "Have you heard from Tavis Gordon?"

"Not yet."

Elissa tilted her head thoughtfully. "I donna think he will come to our wedding."

"Oh, he'll come," Damian said with conviction.

"Do you think he'll cause trouble?"

"That remains to be seen. We're prepared for him if he does show up."

"I hope he stays away. He's dangerous."

Damian searched her face. "Are you worried about me, sweeting?"

"Not in the least," Elissa returned. "Are you certain this marriage is wise? What if you fall in love with another woman after we've wed? I donna want to stand in the way of your happiness."

"I told you how I feel about love. Nay, Elissa, we'll

deal well enough with one another if you can learn to put the past behind you."

"And if I canna?"

He leaned close. "Then 'tis your loss, my lady. Think about it. Are you finished eating?"

"Aye."

He rose and offered his hand. "I'll escort you to your chamber."

Elissa placed her hand in his and rose unsteadily to her feet. She saw Dermot beckoning to her and pulled her hand from Damian's. "My kinsman wants a word with me, Damian." Damian released her hand and stepped away so she could converse with her kinsman in private.

"His Lordship asked me to take the place of yer father," Dermot said when he reached her. "I'm to escort ye from yer chamber to the hall tomorrow."

" 'Tis your right as the oldest living Fraser," Elissa acknowledged. "You do me honor."

"We all want ye to be happy, lass."

"Oh, she will," Damian said, his voice exuding confidence.

"Have our clansmen accepted my marriage to Lord Damian?" Elissa asked.

"Aye," Dermot said without hesitation. "No one wants ye to wed the Gordon chieftain. He betrayed our trust."

Elissa's voice was low and fraught with sadness. "As I will betray my father's trust when I wed Damian."

"Enough!" Damian said. Then more gently, " 'Tis time you retired, my lady."

Elissa allowed Damian to escort her from the hall. When they reached her chamber, she feared he would follow her inside, but he stopped just short of entering.

"I don't want to wait until we're wed, but I will," he murmured as he brought her into his arms. "I don't understand my need for you. 'Tis like a sickness for which there is no cure." He frowned. " 'Tis not good for a man to be so afflicted."

"Lust isna a reason for two people to wed," Elissa observed. "Once the attraction fades, there is naught left."

"I doubt that will happen with us," Damian replied as he lifted her chin with his forefinger. "Kiss me, Elissa. 'Tis been too long."

Elissa was tempted. She missed Damian's arms around her, his lips on hers, the thrill of his lovemaking. She turned her face away.

"Elissa, look at me." Reluctantly, she returned her gaze to his.

"Tell me. Do you still believe Kimbra is carrying my child?"

"I . . . nay. I've come to realize that Kimbra is a vicious witch who wanted to hurt me."

"Thank God," Damian breathed. "I don't want Kimbra. I never did. She didn't care whom she hurt so long as it benefitted her own selfish needs. Half the women in London are like her."

"At least we agree on something," Elissa muttered.

Damian's silver eyes held a mischievous glint. "There is more than one thing we agree upon. We want one another."

"Good night, Damian," Elissa said, torn by feelings she shouldn't be having.

"Kiss me good night, Elissa," he repeated. "I won't leave until you do."

Elissa sighed and lifted her face, determined to endure his sensual assault calmly. The moment his lips touched hers, however, her resolve melted like a candle exposed to flame. His kiss deepened. She tasted his need and leaned into him as his tongue nudged her mouth open for a leisurely exploration.

Damian groaned and pulled her closer. She was trembling like a leaf in the autumn wind as he scooped her into his arms and carried her into her chamber, slamming the door behind him. The sound returned Elissa's wits.

"Damian, nay! You said you'd wait."

Elissa sensed the conflicting emotions battering Damian as he fought his conscience. Though she wanted him, she refused to succumb to her own unquenchable need. She still battled with her guilt for wanting an Englishman.

"Do you really want to wait?" Damian asked hoarsely.

"You gave your word. 'Tis a test of whether or not I can trust you in our future dealings."

Damian let her slide down the length of his hard body until her feet touched the floor. "You win, Elissa, but you won't always have your way. I choose to submit to your wishes this time, but once we are wed that could change. Sleep well, my lady. Pleasant dreams."

Damian left the chamber and rested his head against the closed door. He was shaking from head to toe. It had nearly cost him his sanity to leave Elissa untouched. He started violently when Nan materialized from the deep shadows.

"Are ye well, me lord?"

Startled, Damian pushed away from the door. "Aye, why do you ask?"

"Ye look shaken."

"Perhaps I am," Damian admitted. "Elissa would drive a saint insane."

"And ye are no saint, are ye, yer lordship?"

"Hardly," Damian chuckled. "I'm glad for this chance to talk with you, Nan. I can't get out of my mind what you said about Elissa. Does she truly carry my child? She denies it emphatically."

"One denies what one refuses to believe," Nan replied cryptically. "Mayhap Elissa doesna wish to wed a man who doesna love her. Mayhap she wants ye to wed her for herself, not because she carries yer bairn."

"I want to wed Elissa for many reasons," Damian said, defending himself. Suddenly he grinned. "If she doesn't carry my child now, she soon will."

Nan nodded her head in agreement; then her expression abruptly turned to one of concern. "I sought ye out tonight to warn ye, me lord."

Damian became instantly alert. "Is Elissa in danger?"

"Mayhap. My 'voices' say that soon Elissa will face an unknown peril. She must take care. Donna trust the Gordon chieftain, his heart is black with vengeance. He will come for the wedding, but I advise ye to turn him away."

Damain considered Nan's words. "I can't do that, Nan. I invited him to the wedding and can't turn him away."

"Then beware, yer lordship."

She slipped away into the shadows. Alarmed, Damian called her back. "Wait! Tell me more."

She paused and glanced at him over her shoulder, her face obscured by darkness. "My 'voices' are not always as enlightening as I would like them to be, and they donna always come in time to prevent disaster. Good night, Lord Damian."

Damian blinked in dismay when Nan seemed to fade away into the gloom. How much of Nan's warning should he believe? One thing made clear from Nan's words, however, was that he should take steps to ban all weapons in the hall during the wedding ceremony except those carried by his own trusted retainers.

Elissa was awakened early on her wedding day after a restless night plagued by dreams. Maggie arrived early to direct the placement of the round wooden tub before the hearth, followed shortly afterward by Marianne and Nan with Elissa's wedding dress.

" 'Tis time to dress for your wedding, daughter," Marianne said. "Into the tub with you."

Maggie left to fetch Elissa's breakfast while Nan shook the wrinkles from the dress and spread it out on the bed.

"I'll leave you in Nan's good hands," Marianne said, "if you have no objection. I should help Lora dress."

"Should you be exerting yourself, Mama? Are you strong enough?"

Marianne's smile warmed Elissa. "Donna worry, dear one, my health improves every day. This is one wedding I donna intend to miss."

Elissa stepped into the tub, sighing as she sank into the water. This was her wedding day. It wasn't too long ago that she had prepared for another wedding, to another man. A man her beloved father had chosen for her. Tears shimmered in her eyes. What would the great Alpin Fraser think of her now? She knew her mother and sister approved, for against all odds they had grown fond of Damian. Even her kinsmen approved of him.

Damian's many good qualities overshadowed his reputation as a ruthless soldier. The one detriment to their marriage was the fact that Damian didn't love her. Of course Tavis didn't love her either, or she him, but she would have had the satisfaction of fulfilling her father's wish to unite the Gordons and the Frasers had she wed Tavis.

"Out with ye, lass," Nan said, spreading a large drying cloth for Elissa to step into. "Maggie will be here with yer breakfast soon."

There was no way to stop the wedding, Elissa realized as she wrapped herself in the soft linen cloth, so she had no reason to dawdle. Her fate was sealed; Damian would not be dissuaded.

Maggie arrived moments later with a tray and placed it on the table.

"Winifred prepared a feast for ye," Maggie said, whisking off the napkin. "There's eggs and sausage, fried ham, a small round of goat cheese, and a pot of tea. There's even berry jam to spread on fresh bread just out of the oven."

Elissa pulled a chair to the table and stared at the food. Though she was hungry, she had too much on her mind to eat. She took a few bites of egg and ham, picked at the cheese, and drank nearly all the strong, hot tea. Then it was time to dress.

Marianne and Lora returned as Nan was hooking Elissa into her wedding dress. Marianne urged her onto a bench, picked up a brush, and brushed her hair until the glistening strands rivaled last evening's sunset. The jeweled cap and veil were placed atop her head for the crowning touch.

"Oh, Lissa, you look so beautiful," Lora gushed. "Donna you think so, Mama?"

"Indeed," Marianne agreed, fixing her loving gaze on Elissa. "I've never seen a lovelier bride."

"Pinch yer cheeks, lass," Nan advised. "Yer too pale." She stared into Elissa's eyes for a long, tense moment, then whispered, "Beware the Gordon."

Elissa became instantly alert. "What did you say?"

A knock at the door prevented Nan from responding. Maggie opened the door and Dermot stepped inside, dressed in his best finery.

"Is it time already?" Elissa asked in a quavering voice.

"Aye, Father Hugh and yer bridegroom await ye below," Dermot said. He held out his arm. "Come, lass, I'll escort ye to yer wedding."

"Go," Marianne said, giving Elissa a fierce hug. "Lord Damian will make you happy if you give him a chance."

"I . . . oh, Mama, if Damian loved me I'd be the happiest woman alive."

"Are you sure he doesna?"

"Are ye ready, lass?" Dermot asked impatiently. "The guests have arrived and grow restless."

Elissa gave a wobbly smile and placed her arm on Dermot's.

Damian paced restlessly, his gaze returning to the arched doorway again and again. What was keeping her? Was she going to change her mind at the last minute? Bloody hell! She had to marry him. Didn't she realize she had no choice? He hadn't wanted to worry Elissa, but it was possible that once Kimbra reached London and spewed her lies into the king's ear, the monarch would react with typical violence. Elissa needed his protection whether she knew it or not.

"Calm down," Sir Richard said, pacing alongside Damian. "Elissa would be a fool not to marry you." He glanced about the hall, his gaze skimming over the wedding guests who had gathered to celebrate the ceremony. "The Gordon must have decided not to show up. 'Tis a blessing, if you ask me."

"The day isn't over," Damian said grimly. "Have the guests been disarmed as they entered the hall?"

"Aye, just as you ordered, but none of the villagers carried arms."

A ripple of excitement caught his attention and his gaze found Elissa, poised uncertainly in the doorway. His breath caught in his throat. Elissa was the picture of fragile vulnerability, but he knew differently. She was strong, stronger than any woman he'd ever known. And so beautiful he couldn't take his eyes off her. The blue gown was becoming, but paled in comparison to the woman wearing it. Her rich burnished hair flowed beneath her shoulder length veil in rippling waves that reflected the glint of sunlight spilling through the windows.

He grinned at her. Her answering smile was tentative. Then Dermot strode forward, forcing her to follow. Moments later she stood beside him. He took her hand from Dermot's arm and placed it on his own. Father Hugh cleared his throat.

"Are ye ready, my lord?"

Damian shot a glance at Elissa, one eyebrow raised. Her nearly imperceptible nod was all the encouragement he needed. "Aye, begin the ceremony, Father."

The hall was fair bursting with clansmen from the village and from miles around. The hall buzzed with excitement as they crowded close, eager to hear the vows spoken between their lass and the Demon Knight. Father Hugh signaled for silence.

An almost eerie hush preceded an unexpected commotion at the front entrance.

"Tavis," Elissa whispered in a strangled voice that raised the hackles on the back of Damian's neck.

Jealousy reared up like a ravening beast within Damian. He'd known all along that Gordon would show up, but knowing he was actually here made him even more protective of Elissa. His expression turned grim when he saw the color drain from her face and felt her clutching desperately at his arm.

"He's come to cause trouble," Elissa hissed. "I donna want him here."

Relief surged through Damian at Elissa's words. She didn't want Gordon here; she didn't want him at all. Damian had invited the chieftain as a last ditch effort to promote peace at Misterly, but if he were to be honest, he'd admit to a more selfish reason. He wanted Gordon to know that Elissa belonged to him, Damian, and always would.

"What manner of greeting is this?" Tavis Gordon bellowed angrily. "Yer hospitality is woefully lacking. 'Tis inhospitable to confiscate weapons from invited guests. I am here alone, amid enemies and at yer mercy. Are ye going to take advantage of me?"

A path opened up for the Gordon chieftain. Clad

in outlawed tartan, he elbowed his way toward Damian and Elissa. Damian felt Elissa trembling and placed a protective arm around her.

"You're welcome at Misterly, Gordon, as long as you relinquish your weapons. This is a time of joy, not war."

Gordon clutched his sword, his face a mask of fury. "Ye stole my bride, now ye want to steal my weapons!"

"Your weapons will be returned when you leave. 'Tis your choice, Gordon. Set your hostilities aside as I intend to do and join the celebration."

Gordon glowered at Elissa. "Elissa was to be my bride. I still want her, even though 'tis common knowledge she spread her thighs for ye."

Elissa stifled a cry with the back of her hand. Damian wanted to smash Gordon in the mouth for his insult to Elissa but managed to contain his fury. "Why don't we ask Elissa which man she prefers?" he suggested, feigning a calm he didn't feel.

Damian realized he was taking a great risk, but he wanted, nay, needed, to hear Elissa's answer for his own peace of mind. Not that it would make any difference. Elissa would be his wife whether or not she wanted Gordon.

"Verra well," Gordon agreed smugly. "Ask the lass who she wants to wed."

Damian grasped Elissa's shoulders and turned her toward him. "What do you say, sweeting?"

The silence was nearly unbearable as Elissa stared at him, her eyes wide, her mouth tremulous. He sensed the tension that held the wedding guests in thrall and felt as finely drawn as a bowstring.

"Elissa . . ."

"Go ahead, lass, donna be afraid," Gordon prompted.

When her pink tongue darted out nervously to wet her lips, Damian wanted to take her in his arms and kiss her until she gave the answer he sought, but he forced himself to wait.

Elissa opened her mouth to speak; anticipation thickened the air around them.

" 'Twas my father's wish that I wed Tavis Gordon," Elissa began, causing Damian's heart to sink, "but 'tis not what I want." Damian began to breathe again. "Tavis, you've proven you're not the man my father thought, nor the man I hoped you'd be." She reached for Damian's hand. "I choose Damian."

"You've made a wise choice, my lady," Damian whispered on a relieved sigh. He turned back to Gordon. "Give over your weapons if you wish to remain for the ceremony."

Gordon hesitated a long suspenseful moment before he presented his sword and pistol to Sir Richard, who stood nearby, poised to act should Gordon turn belligerent.

"You may continue, Father," Damian said. It was over, and well worth the risk, he thought, to hear Elissa voice her preference for him.

Father Hugh began the ceremony. Damian spoke his vows, watching Gordon from the corner of his eye as Elissa repeated her vows in a low but steady voice. Minutes later they were pronounced husband and wife; Elissa was his. He turned her toward him and lifted her chin. Her eyes had a dazed, misty look as he dipped his head to seal their vows with a kiss. Deliberately he turned Elissa's back to Gordon so he could keep the man in his sights, but the moment his lips touched Elissa's, he closed his eyes to better savor the kiss.

Lost to sensation, Damian was dimly aware that Gordon was speaking, but he blocked out the words. When he opened his eyes he saw only Elissa, her warm body pressed against him. Then, from the corner of his eyes he saw sunlight reflect off something shiny in Gordon's hand. All his senses, every instinct came alive.

Gordon held a knife in his hand—aimed at Elissa's unprotected back!

"If I canna have her, neither can ye," Gordon screamed.

Reacting spontaneously, Damian whirled, taking Elissa with him as he presented his own back for Gordon's blade. He felt the bite of pain and steeled himself against it as he shoved Elissa into Sir Richard's arms. A protective circle immediately formed around them. Waves of shimmering red formed before Damian's eyes as he spun around to confront Gordon.

All Damian saw of Gordon was his back. He was lost amongst the throng of stunned wedding guests pressing forward to get a better view. The confusion and shock that followed the assault had worked to the Gordon chieftain's advantage. He had created a chaotic situation and vanished out the door before Damian's men-at-arms even knew what had happened.

Chapter 16

Damian took a staggering step forward, remembered he carried no weapon, and asked a man-at-arms to fetch them.

Elissa grasped his arm. "Nay, you canna go! You're wounded. Let Nan see to your injury."

"I can't let the bastard get away," Damian said. "I'll chase him to the ends of the earth if I have to."

"Donna be so stubborn, Damian. Let Sir Richard handle it. You're bleeding."

Damian twisted free. "Gordon tried to kill you."

"Is Damian going to be all right?"

Damian glanced down at Lora. She was gazing up at him through luminous eyes, her fear palpable.

"Aye, I'll be fine, little one. You shouldn't be here, though." He summoned Marianne, who was standing nearby, wringing her hands. "Take the child to the solar, my lady, she is frightened."

"Aye, Lord Damian," Marianne agreed. "She's too

young to understand what just happened." She grasped Lora's hand and led her away.

Someone handed Damian his sword and he struggled to buckle it in place. "Damn," he said when his fingers suddenly lost their will to obey.

Elissa grasped him about the waist and he sagged against her. At Nan's command, Lachlan hurried over to help.

"Sit him down and remove his doublet and shirt," Nan ordered as she rushed off to fetch her chest of herbs and salves.

Damian resisted. " 'Tis but a scratch. I've suffered worse."

Elissa paid him little heed as she peeled off his coat and shirt. "Donna be so stubborn, Damian. Sir Richard is perfectly capable of handling the situation. He's searching for Tavis even as we speak, but I doubt he'll be found. The mountains are full of hiding places. Not even Cumberland and his army have succeeded in running him to ground. They finally gave up and pretended he dinna exist."

"Oh, he exists, all right."

Elissa carefully inspected Damian's wound, which was still bleeding profusely. Gordon's dagger had delivered a narrow slash on the upper part of his back, below his right shoulder, but it didn't appear life threatening. She wadded up Damian's shirt and pressed it against his injured flesh.

Suddenly Elissa became aware that the hall was still filled with wedding guests; they milled about, speaking in hushed voices. She had no idea what to say to them, until Damian solved the problem for her.

"Our guests should be celebrating our wedding, not standing around with long faces."

"They donna know what to do, Damian."

Damian cleared his throat and asked for everyone's attention. A profound silence settled over the hall.

"You've come for a celebration, and you shall have one. Tables of food have been set up in the courtyard and musicians are tuning their instruments. My bride and I invite you to eat, drink, dance, and make merry."

"Are ye sure, my lord?" Lachlan asked. "Ye've been gravely wounded."

" 'Tis but a scratch. Nan will work her magic and I'll soon be good as new."

A cheer followed Damian's words and a slow exodus from the hall began. Soon the sounds of music and voices raised in laughter drifted to them from the courtyard.

Nan returned with her medicine chest. She placed it on the table and probed Damian's wound with her index finger. Damian's muscles clenched and he stifled a groan.

"Ah," Nan said with satisfaction. "Just as I thought. Yer shoulder bone deflected the worst of it. Ye saved Elissa's life, me lord. Had Gordon's blade struck its intended victim, Elissa wouldna have been as lucky as ye."

Damian shivered. The thought of the dagger puncturing Elissa's tender flesh made his blood run cold. "Hurry and fix me up, Nan. I must join the search for Gordon."

"Yer not going anywhere, me lord. Yer wound isna life threatening but ye've lost more blood than 'tis good for ye. I doubt ye can mount yer horse and stay on. I'll brew a concoction of herbs to build up yer blood. A day or so in bed will do ye a world of good. Now sit still while I clean ye up and take a stitch or two."

"Bloody hell! I can't sit still while Tavis Gordon is free to wreak havoc on innocent people."

"Damian, please listen to Nan," Elissa advised, wringing her hands. "She knows what's best for you. You donna know these mountains like Tavis. He's been living as an outlaw ever since his home was destroyed and his lands seized."

"He tried to kill you," Damian reminded her. "Do what you have to do, Nan, but a little cut isn't going to stop me."

Nan set about cleaning the wound while Elissa watched from the sidelines, determined to keep Damian from leaving the keep until he was healed. She clamped her teeth together and winced when Nan threaded a needle and took the first stitch in Damian's flesh. Elissa could tell by the set of Damian's jaw that it was painful, but to his credit, he didn't flinch.

"There ye be, yer lordship. All done," Nan said, tying off the knot.

"Good," Damian said, attempting to stand. He managed to gain his feet and take one step before his legs collapsed. He grabbed the table for support and hissed out a curse.

"I told you, Damian," Elissa said with asperity. "You shouldna exert yourself. The loss of blood has weakened you."

"I suppose a short rest won't hurt," Damian grudgingly allowed.

He walked off, his gait slow and uneven. Elissa and Nan exchanged glances over his head, then

Elissa started after him. Hanging onto the wall, Damian negotiated the stairs without Elissa's help. She trailed behind him, Nan following close on their heels. When they reached the top, Nan scooted ahead and held the chamber door open. Damian staggered inside and collapsed on the bed.

"I will brew ye a potion for the pain," Nan said, hurrying off.

"A hell of a way to spend my wedding night," Damian complained. He extended his hand. "Come lie beside me."

Instead of taking his hand, Elissa moved to the foot of the bed, grasped his boot, and pulled it off. His second boot was a little more difficult to dislodge, but it finally slid free.

"Raise up so I can remove your breeches," Elissa said as she reached for the fastenings.

Damian grasped her hand, his voice low and strident. "Touch me there and I'll have you on your back before you can say my name."

The breath flew out of her lungs. "You're wounded."

He brought her hand to his groin. "Not here."

"Be serious," Elissa chided. "You're weak from loss of blood."

His eyes darkened to the color of smoke. "I *am* serious. Tonight is our wedding night. I'm not too weak to make love to my wife."

He grasped her waist and lifted her onto the bed. Then he pulled her beneath him and lowered himself to her. Bending his head, he brushed his lips lightly over hers. Warmed by the tenderness of his kiss, Elissa opened her mouth to taste more of him.

"Elissa," he moaned against her lips. "My wife."

"Tsk, tsk, tsk. None of that, yer lordship."

Elissa's gaze met Nan's over Damian's shoulder. Damian groaned and slowly lifted himself away from Elissa.

"You could have knocked," Damian said crossly.

Nan cackled. "Would ye have bidden me enter?"

He glanced down at Elissa's flushed face. "Nay. Leave us, woman. My wife and I need privacy. If I can't go after Gordon, I can at least have a wedding night."

Nan thrust a cup filled with a pungent smelling liquid beneath his nose. "Drink, Lord Damian. 'Twill ease yer pain."

"My pain is below the belt and I doubt that vile concoction will ease it," he muttered beneath his breath.

Nan sent him an exasperated look while Elissa nearly choked on her laughter.

Damian took the cup Nan offered and set it down on the bedside table. "Not now, Nan. Go away."

"Men," Nan muttered, shaking her head. "Their brains lie betwixt their legs. Verra well, I'll leave, but I'm warning ye, tear out those stitches and I'll not be gentle with ye when I replace them." She left in a huff, slamming the door behind her.

"Nan's right," Elissa allowed. "I'll see to our guests while you're resting."

Damian's arm held her in place. "Don't even try it. I might not be able sit a horse, but I can still ride."

He rose to his haunches and turned her over so he could unhook the back of her dress. "By the way, did I tell you how lovely you look? That gown is perfect for you."

" 'Twas Mama's. She wanted me to look nice for my wedding."

"I'll be sure and thank her."

Lifting her arms, he slid the sleeves down and pushed the bodice to her waist. A moment later the gown lay on the floor, and a moment after that her shift followed. Then he sat back on his heels and stared at her.

"You're beautiful," he said on a groan. "You're my wife now; you belong to me."

Elissa caught her breath as his blunt fingers caressed her breasts. Her body tensed with anticipation. She wanted him to touch her everywhere. She wanted to touch him everywhere. She watched in breathless wonder as he rose and removed his trousers. Her gaze roamed over him, and she forgot to breathe as his sex burst free, thick and rigid and turgid with life. She gulped in a tremulous gasp of air, filling her senses with the heady aroma of clean male flesh and the pungent musk of arousal.

"You shouldna exert yourself," Elissa said. "Your wound . . ."

"My wound be hanged," Damian growled. "A little thing like that isn't going to stop me from making love to my wife on our wedding night."

Elissa forgot that she hadn't wanted this marriage as he held her close and molded her body to his. There was no doubting his desire for her, for she felt the solid proof of it throbbing against her stomach. She sighed as his lips moved against her throat, his tongue tracing an erotic pattern along her skin. Could he feel the pounding of her pulse there? His mind-numbing caresses continued, forging a trail to the valley between her breasts. Her fingers twined themselves in the richness of his dark hair and she urged him on with soft sighs of encouragement.

His mouth covered her nipple, and a melting heat radiated through her, centering in that swollen, aching place between her legs. She arched mindlessly against him, her fingers tightening in his hair as his slow assault upon her senses continued, teeth and tongue laving, touching, arousing. He moved lower, his breath whispering sweet seduction against her navel, her abdomen, lavishly bathing her stomach, hips, thighs, then between them with kisses.

"Damian, please."

"Aye, sweeting, pleasing you is what I intend to do."

His tongue swirled around her heated core. She cried out his name, writhing against him as his lips and mouth worked their magic upon her swollen flesh. She ached; bliss whirled through her, enveloping her, exploding inside her.

Then suddenly he was atop her, his fingers opening her as he filled her, stretched her, took her. She shuddered, wrapping herself around him as he began to move on her. She closed her eyes, her body taking flight as he took her once again to the heights of rapture. And then her world fell apart, shattering her, bringing with it a pleasure that nearly stopped her heart. Lost in the throes of her own climax, she was barely aware when Damian gripped her hips, lifted her, and sank into her again and again, until he cried out her name and filled her with his wet heat.

He stayed inside her until he softened, then he shifted away and lay beside her, bringing her into his arms. She heard him groan and feared he had reopened his wound.

"Are you all right?" Her voice was strained with anxiety.

"Better than all right."

"Be serious. Are you in pain?"

He grinned. "Aye, but it was worth it."

"Roll over so I can take a look."

"Don't fuss, Elissa."

" 'Tis a wife's right. Roll over, Damian."

Reluctantly, he acquiesced, presenting his back for Elissa's inspection. The bandage had a small amount of fresh blood on it but not enough to cause Elissa worry.

"Satisfied?" Damian asked. She nodded and Damian cuddled her against him. "Go to sleep."

Damian hurt like the very devil but it hadn't stopped him from making love to Elissa. And it wasn't going to stop him from mounting his horse and going after Gordon. He held Elissa until she fell asleep, then eased away from her and rose stiffly from bed. Music and laughter drifted to him through the open window from the courtyard below, but he didn't intend to join in the merriment.

Elissa was still sleeping blissfully as Damian pulled on his clothes and snatched up his sword and pistol. The door made a single groan of protest as he opened it and slipped into the passageway. A wave of weakness overwhelmed him and he paused just outside the door, hanging onto the wall for support. When his head had stopped spinning, he descended the curving staircase.

Concentrating on placing one foot in front of the other, Damian finally reached the bottom, but the effort had sapped his strength. His legs were trembling, his vision was impaired, and perspiration beaded his forehead. Wiping away the sweat with the back of his hand, Damian staggered into the hall. His knees suddenly buckled and he grasped the edge of a table for support.

"Damian!"

Elissa burst into the hall, her expression fierce.

"Where do you think you're going?"

"After Gordon."

"Nay! Look at you." She touched his forehead. "You've a fever. You canna mount your horse in your condition."

A wolfish smile stretched his lips. "I mounted you, didn't I?"

"And probably shouldn't have. Come back to bed, Damian. I'll fetch something from Nan to ease your fever."

"Don't coddle me, Elissa." His expression hardened. "Gordon tried to kill you. I'm going to hunt him down like the cowardly dog he is."

Suddenly two Elissas danced before his eyes, both scowling at him. He closed his eyes and opened them again. The two forms melded together into one. Damian shook his head, refusing to accept his weakness. How could an insignificant wound cause so much trouble? As much as he wanted to run Gordon to the ground, he realized he wasn't going anywhere this night.

Ignoring his feeble protest, Elissa placed an arm around Damian's waist and turned him toward the staircase.

"Damn Gordon," Damian muttered. "I hope Dickon finds him."

"No one will find Tavis if he doesna want to be found," Elissa replied with conviction. "Tavis knows the mountains like the back of his hand. He will go underground. He's done it often enough in the past."

"Bloody hell! I feel so useless."

She helped him up the staircase and into their bedchamber, then eased him down on the bed. "Rest while I get something from Nan for your fever."

Damian lay back on the pillow, angry with himself for inviting Gordon to his wedding. He had hoped his invitation would serve to end the hostilities between them, but he should have known better. Scotsmen were born stubborn. Damian realized Gordon would never forgive him for stealing his bride and seizing Misterly.

Elissa returned with a vile-tasting potion that Nan had brewed for him. He grimaced but obeyed when she held the cup to his lips and insisted he drink it all. He gulped it down and gagged.

"Are you trying to poison me, woman?" he gasped, shoving the empty cup away.

"Don't be such a bear, Damian. Go to sleep. Mayhap Tavis's luck will run out and Sir Richard will capture him. Will you hang him?"

A soft snoring sound rumbled from his chest. Elissa undressed both Damian and herself and stretched out beside him. Music wafting through the window from the courtyard lulled her to sleep.

Damian opened his eyes to the light of day, a loud pounding on the door and Sir Richard's voice calling to him. He jerked upright and was immediately sorry. Pain shot through him; he clenched his teeth until it became bearable. Moving slowly, he pulled the blanket over himself and Elissa and granted Sir Richard permission to enter.

Elissa awoke and sat up, clutching the blanket to her chest. "What is it, Damian?"

"Sir Richard has returned."

Dirt stained and disheveled, his eyes rimmed with fatigue, Sir Richard stepped into the chamber.

"Did you catch him, Dickon?"

"Nay. The bastard is canny as a fox. We found his stronghold, for all the good it did us. It was abandoned but for women and children. The men are tired and hungry. We'll continue the search after we've eaten and rested, if that meets with your approval." His gaze settled on the bandage Damian wore. "Are you all right, Damian?"

"I'm fine, Dickon. Get some rest, then we'll decide our next step."

Damian remained thoughtful after Dickon left. When he finally spoke, his voice was tense. "Are you sure Gordon doesn't know about the secret tunnel? Or where it exits in the forest?"

"He doesna know," Elissa persisted. " 'Tis a family secret."

Damian nodded. "I just wanted to be sure."

Their attention was again drawn to the door. This time it was Nan, asking for admittance. When permission was given, she bustled into the chamber with her medicine chest tucked under her arm. "I'll have a look at yer wound, me lord," she said.

" 'Tis fine, Nan."

Elissa slipped out of bed, pulling the top sheet with her. Nan took a stance beside the bed, waiting impatiently for him to turn around. It was obvious she wasn't going to leave until she'd had her way.

"You win, Nan," Damian grumbled, rolling over on his stomach.

Nan plucked the bandage away and clucked her tongue. "There's fresh blood on the bandage, but the stitches are still intact."

Damian glanced over his shoulder at Elissa and noticed that she had dressed and was preparing to leave the chamber. "Where are you going?"

"To fetch our breakfast." She opened the door and slipped away.

"Now that we're alone, me lord," Nan said in a hushed voice, "there is something I need to say to ye."

Damian sighed in resignation. "What is it, Nan? Have your voices spoken to you again?"

"Mock me if ye will, me lord, but listen well. Trouble is brewing and I donna like where 'tis heading."

Damian regarded Nan curiously, with a touch of apprehension. He knew better than to ignore the old crone. Her uncanny predictions often made sense. "What kind of trouble? Is this about Gordon?"

"Aye. Tavis Gordon is part of it, but 'tis more than that." She tied off the clean bandage and placed a hand on his head. "Yer fever is gone. My brew did its work but 'tis best ye stay in bed today."

Damian rolled over and sat up, wincing at the twinge of pain that shot through him. "Explain yourself, Nan, and start at the beginning."

"My 'voices' whisper of an enemy who speaks ill of ye." Her voice trembled. "I dinna want to believe it but they tell me Elissa will leave Misterly verra soon."

"Nonsense," Damian scoffed. "Elissa has no reason to leave me. She's my wife now."

"I dinna say the lass would leave willingly. All I know is that ye will soon be parted."

"Nan!" Elissa said, rushing into the chamber with

a tray balanced in her hands. "I heard what you told Damian. Donna plague him with your absurd predictions. 'Tis ridiculous to assume that Damian and I willna always be together."

She set the tray on the table and held the door open for Nan, inviting her to leave. Nan snatched up her medicine chest and scooted past Elissa. "Ye always were a stubborn lass," she tossed over her shoulder.

"Believe naught Nan said," Elissa advised as she removed dishes from the tray and arranged them on the table.

"Are you sure we should ignore her?" Damian asked.

"Donna give her another thought. Those 'voices' she keeps hearing come from her imagination. Come and eat before the food gets cold."

Damian rose naked from the bed and pulled a bench over to the table. "You must admit her predictions aren't always wrong. She has an uncanny ability to predict things that makes my blood run cold."

" 'Tis babbling, nothing more," Elissa dismissed as she spooned eggs and ham onto his plate. "Try a bannock. Winifred just took them from the oven."

Damian attacked the food hungrily; Elissa ate more daintily but with the same good appetite.

"You should go back to bed, Damian," Elissa suggested after they finished eating.

Damian rose and gathered up his clothing. "Don't coddle me, sweeting, I'm fine. In fact, I intend to join the search for Gordon this morning. Help me with my weapons."

"Is there nothing I can say to keep you in bed another day?"

"Nay. I want Gordon badly."

Elissa found Damian's sword and pistol and handed them to him. He buckled the sword around his waist, shoved the pistol into his belt, and placed primer, balls, and powder in his pouch.

"Kiss me good-bye, love."

Dutifully, Elissa lifted her face. "A real kiss," Damian said as he grasped her waist and lifted her into his crushing embrace. The kiss he gave her, and her heated response to it, nearly led them back to bed, but Damian steeled his resolve and reluctantly set her aside.

"Remember where we left off and we'll finish it tonight," he promised. Then he was gone.

Elissa helped the servants clean up the mess left by their wedding guests, then spent time with Lora, and later walked with her mother in the courtyard. Though she tried not to dwell on Nan's warning, her mind kept returning to her aged nurse's words.

Admittedly some of Nan's predictions in the past had come to pass, but Elissa had always assumed they were simply coincidences. Was her marriage to Damian really doomed? Elissa hadn't originally wanted this marriage, but now that she had finally accepted the fact that she loved an Englishman, she wanted their union to be a happy one. Damian had more honor in his little finger than Tavis Gordon had in his whole body.

Wedding Damian had finally put an end to all the years of hating Englishmen, of keeping the defeat at Culloden alive in her mind and heart years after the battle had been lost. It was time she laid the past to rest, admitted her love for Damian, and accepted her future as his wife.

Elissa wanted to believe Damian loved her but feared it was not true. She knew he cared for her on some level, for there was no other explanation for his stubborn insistence that she marry him. He had turned away Kimbra and the wealth she would bring to the marriage, and that had to mean something.

For whatever the reason, Damian had married her; they were now man and wife and she didn't care what Nan said; she wasn't going to be parted from him.

Damian returned to the keep exhausted and grim faced. Elissa had a bath prepared for him and helped him undress. His bandage was bloody and she removed it while the tub was being filled.

"You dinna find him, did you?"

"Not a trace," Damian replied. "We found only women, children, and graybeards at his stronghold. I don't make war on helpless people. We searched far afield but it was as if he had disappeared from the face of the earth. My gut tells me we haven't seen the last of the Gordons."

Sighing wearily, Damian sank down into the tub. Elissa knelt behind him and sponged his back. "Will you continue the search?"

" 'Tis pointless. Gordon can disappear at will in the mountains, or he might even leave the area. I've instructed the guards to be extra vigilant. Thank God Gordon doesn't know about the tunnel."

"The tunnel is a well-guarded secret," Elissa assured him. "One day we may have need of it." She poured water over Damian's head and rubbed soap into his scalp. "Would you like to eat in our chamber tonight? I can have a tray prepared."

Damian gave her a wicked grin. "I was just going

to suggest that. In days past a bride and groom closeted themselves and didn't come out for a week."

Elissa laughed. "Were they able to walk at the end of that week?"

"I don't know, but I'm willing to find out if you are."

Elissa fell back on her rump as Damian rose from the tub, splashing water on the floor. Before she had time to protest, he picked her up and carried her to the bed, tearing away her clothes in a fit of lustful fury.

She welcomed him with open arms and passionate kisses. Their loving became almost frantic as they both sought that high pinnacle where lovers dwelled. They loved, ate, and loved again. As Elissa fell asleep, she finally admitted to herself that she was happier than she had ever been in her life.

During the following weeks Damian gave Elissa no reason to alter her feelings for him. He pleased her in every way. Tavis Gordon remained at large but caused them no further trouble. Though Nan went about with a worried expression, Elissa chose to ignore her.

Elissa was so content that she gave scant heed to the arrival of a company of soldiers several weeks after her marriage. Her complacency was shattered, however, when she joined Damian at the front entrance to greet the new visitors.

"Welcome to Misterly," Damian said. "What brings you to the Highlands?"

Elissa heard the tension in his voice and noted his grim expression, and a frisson of fear snaked down her spine. Intuition warned her that this was not a friendly visit.

The captain of the guard dismounted, his gaze moving past Damian to Elissa.

"Are you Elissa Fraser?"

Warning bells went off in her head. "Aye."

Damian shoved her behind him. "What is this about?"

"Step aside, Lord Clarendon. We have orders to arrest Lady Elissa Fraser and escort her to London."

Chapter 17

❧

Fear coursed down Damian's spine. The soldiers were here to take Elissa away. "By whose order?" Damian asked, refusing to step aside.

"By order of the king," the captain answered.

Elissa grasped Damian's sleeve. "Damian, what do they mean?"

"Don't worry, love, I'll not let them take you."

"You have no say in the matter, my lord," the captain said.

"You don't understand, Captain," Damian tried to explain. "Lady Elissa is my wife."

That seemed to surprise the captain but did not sway him from his purpose. "My orders come directly from the king. We will rest here overnight and leave with our prisoner at dawn tomorrow. Unless you guarantee that the lady will not flee, I will be forced to place her under guard."

"I've done nothing!" Elissa cried.

"What are the charges?" Damian asked, struggling to keep the panic from his voice. He sensed Kimbra's fine hand in this.

"Conspiring to commit treason against the Crown," the captain replied.

Damian's heart seized. "The charges are not only false, but ridiculous."

" 'Tis not for me to decide," the captain replied. "Your hospitality is required for the night, my lord. Please make arrangements to feed and billet my men."

Damian had no recourse but to step aside and allow the captain and his men to enter the hall. Sir Brody appeared at his side to take charge of the soldiers. Damian ushered Elissa into the hall and the captain followed.

Damian seated Elissa at the table and invited the captain to sit down beside him. "Now, then, Captain . . ."

"Harding," the captain said.

"Shall we discuss the king's order more fully, Captain Harding? There must be some mistake. My wife is not a traitor."

"The king believes otherwise. My orders are to bring Lady Elissa to London to answer to the charges."

"If I cannot talk you out of this, then I shall accompany my wife to London and defend her innocence."

Captain Harding shook his head. "Nay, my lord. You are to remain at Misterly."

Damian bristled. "By whose order?"

"Once again, by the king's order."

"Please excuse me, Captain Harding, I wish to

speak to my wife in private. Sir Brody will show you to your chamber and inform you and your men when to return to the hall for the evening meal."

"Do I have your word that the lady will not leave the keep?" Harding said.

Though it nearly killed Damian to do so, he gave his word.

Taking Elissa's hand, he led her from the hall. Once they reached the privacy of their bedchamber, he took her into his arms.

"I can't stop him from taking you away, love, but I won't abandon you. I *will* do something about it, you can depend on it."

"What can you do?" Elissa asked in a quavering voice. "Why has the king done this? He could have ordered me to London long ago. Why now?"

"Kimbra," Damian hissed. "She must have filled the king's ear with poison."

"What about Mama and Lora? Will they suffer on my account?"

"Your mother and sister are safe here," Damian promised. " 'Tis doubtful Captain Harding even knows they exist!"

"Thank God," Elissa said on a sigh. "But how can you help me if the king has forbidden you to leave Misterly?"

"I'd defy the king for you," Damian murmured.

The strong emotions flaying Damian were so profound, the shock nearly sent him to his knees. Common sense told him he didn't merely lust after Elissa, for his feelings went far deeper. Was love the sentiment he was experiencing? What else could it be? He wanted Elissa in his life, in his bed, in his arms, and he wasn't going to allow the king to destroy what he'd found with her.

"If you disobey the Hanover you will forfeit Misterly," Elissa reminded him.

His eyes glittered with determination. "Do you think I value Misterly more than I do your life?"

Elissa's smile held a hint of regret. "You've given me sufficient reason to wonder."

"Wonder no longer, love. Why do you think I married you?"

"Because you needed my clansmen's cooperation."

"Nay. Your clansmen didn't enter into my decision. Misterly was mine whether or not I gained their loyalty. I wed you for myself, because I wanted you for my wife. I knew what I was risking and it mattered not."

Elissa melted against him, her eyes misty. "I love you, Damian, and I always will. No matter what happens to us."

Damian opened his mouth to speak but the words froze in his throat. He'd never verbally expressed love for a woman and wasn't sure he was capable of admitting to so tender an emotion. What if it came out wrong? This was all so new to him. Instead, he kissed her with all the feelings that were in his heart, filling her with his breath, his unspoken love, passion, hoping they sufficed until he found the words to convey his true sentiments.

Elissa tasted love in his kiss . . . and something else: the gnawing tang of desperation. Fear clenched her gut. Despite his brave words, Damian was as worried as she. They both knew there was little he could do to change the king's mind. She'd be punished for conspiring with Tavis Gordon even though she'd committed no treasonous act.

"Make love to me, Damian," Elissa pleaded. "This could be the last time we'll be together."

"Gladly, but it won't be the last time, sweeting." He grasped her shoulders. "Listen to me, Elissa. We'll be together again. Do you trust me?"

"Aye, but it will take more than trust to save me. Nan predicted we would be parted. We should have listened to her."

"To what purpose? Neither of us knew King George would order you to London, and Nan offered naught but an obscure warning."

"We have what's left of today and tonight," Elissa murmured. "I donna want to waste it talking."

She pulled his head down, rose on tiptoe, and kissed him with all the passion and love within her heart. He groaned. She trapped it in her mouth and returned it on a breathless sigh. Wrapping his arms around her, he held her tightly, as if he never wanted to let her go. But before she could satisfy herself with the taste of him, he drew back and began kissing her throat as his hands released the hooks on the back of her gown. She felt the neckline sag, felt his lips following the curve of her breasts. Then her gown pooled at her feet. His eyes glowed like silver coins as he dragged her shift over her head and tossed it aside.

"I want to make love to you," Elissa murmured against his lips.

She retreated a step, her smile seductive as she began to undress him. When he tried to help, she shoved his hands aside. "Nay, let me do it."

She slid his jacket down his arms and unbuttoned

his shirt. She stared at his bare chest, her eyes glittering. Then she dropped to her knees, placed her mouth on his nipple, and pulled on it.

"You'll kill me if you continue," he moaned.

She grinned up at him, then ran her tongue along the furrow of dark hair on his chest. But she wasn't through with him yet. She pushed the shirt down his arms and off. Her tongue delved into his navel; she felt him shudder as he grasped her head and buried his fingers in her hair to hold her in place. Her smile rippled against the taut planes of his belly as her fingers began working loose the buttons of his trousers. In moments she had them free, tugging them down, freeing his swollen manhood.

She stared for a breathless eternity at the turgid head and the pearly drop clinging to its tip, then feathered her tongue across the silken surface.

"Bloody hell!"

Damian tried to lift Elissa to her feet but she wouldn't budge. She gazed up at him, her eyes luminous, watching his face as she took him into her mouth. His expression was everything she could have asked for. Tormented, stricken, passion glazed. She tasted his pleasure and the scent of hot excitement on his skin.

"Enough!" he cried.

Before she knew it, Elissa found herself sitting at the edge of the bed, her legs spread wide and Damian kneeling between them. His wicked grin warned her he would allow no quarter as he buried his head in the vee between her legs and proceeded to pleasure her in the same way she had pleasured him, his mouth and tongue moving intimately over her slick, swollen flesh. There was no denying him.

Elissa clutched a fistful of bedclothes in both hands and succumbed to mindless abandonment.

Her climax was still thrumming through her when he pushed her flat on the bed and thrust inside her, deep, so very deep she had to bite her tongue to keep from shrieking aloud as her pleasure intensified. She held him against her, savoring the hot, wet thrusting of his shaft inside her, the luscious heat of their bodies clinging as they rode the peak together. She felt herself ascending to a new level of excitement, her passion rising once again to meet his demands.

With every muscle locked so tight she was shivering, Elissa shattered. In the dim recesses of her mind she heard Damian shout her name and felt his wet heat filling her. They rested, then loved again. Nothing mattered . . . not Captain Harding nor those below in the hall waiting for them to appear for the evening meal; their time together was too short and the thought of parting too painful.

Elissa couldn't hold back the dawn, no matter how desperately she wished to. She arose at daybreak and packed clothing for her journey in a small satchel. She was startled when Damian leaped from bed, grasped her shoulders, and said, "We could leave by way of the secret tunnel and board a ship for France. I could have my men create a disturbance, drawing attention away from the hidden door while we make good our escape."

Elissa gave him a sad smile. "Nay. I wouldna ask that of you and I canna leave Mama and Lora behind. There's virtually no hope of getting us all out together. Dragging Mama and Lora about the countryside with winter coming on would harm their health. Besides, you gave your word that I wouldn't try to escape, and I know how you value your honor."

Damian's shoulders slumped. "I do value my honor, but this is different! This is your life we're talking about."

"I have to believe the king will show mercy."

"It depends on how far Kimbra stretched the truth."

"Do I have time to bid my mother and sister goodbye?" Elissa asked.

"If you hurry. Captain Harding is probably eager to leave. I'm surprised he didn't come up here last night to check on us when we didn't appear for the evening meal."

As if to reinforce his words, Captain Harding pounded on the door. "Lord Damian, 'tis time to leave. Send out the woman."

"We'll be down directly, Captain," Damian answered.

"Now," Harding demanded.

"My wife isn't ready yet."

"Damian, what about Mama and Lora?" Elissa whispered. "Do you think the captain will let me see them?"

"I'm assuming Captain Harding doesn't know about them. Calling attention to them now would be unwise. I'm sorry, sweeting."

"I understand," Elissa said, swallowing her disappointment. "I'd never forgive myself if I placed them in danger. Tell them I love them and explain what happened." She squared her shoulders. "Open the door. I'm ready."

"Just remember," Damian said, "I won't abandon you."

Elissa threw her arms around his neck and choked back a sob. There was so much she wanted to say and so little time. They were able to share one final kiss before Damian opened the door to Captain Harding's persistent pounding. But it was a kiss Elissa would remember till the end of her days. Sweetly passionate, agonizingly tender, and filled with promise, it was if they had renewed their wedding vows with that one kiss.

"It's about time," Harding grumbled, shuffling impatiently on the landing. He grasped Elissa's arm but Damian retrieved it, placing it beneath his own.

"I'll escort my wife to the hall," he said in a voice that brooked no argument.

Arm in arm they descended the staircase. Harding followed close on their heels, carrying Elissa's satchel that Damian had thrust into his hands.

"Damian, look," Elissa cried when they entered the hall.

Damian halted. It appeared as if every Fraser from miles around had gathered in the hall. They stood together in small groups, speaking in hushed tones and glaring defiantly at the king's soldiers.

Sir Richard pushed his way through the crowd. "Our men are poised to fight," he whispered in a voice that only Damian and Elissa could hear. "You have but to give the word. And from the way the wind is blowing, the Frasers appear ready to join in the fray. They want to protect their lady, just as we do."

Before Damian could reply, Elissa clutched his arm. "Nay! No one must die on my behalf. Donna give the order to fight, Damian, please."

Damian summed up the situation in one sweeping glance. Captain Harding had joined his soldiers, prepared to give the order to retaliate should anyone attempt to interfere with their duty to king and country. Should a battle ensue, it would be a costly one.

"Nay, Dickon, there must be no bloodshed."

Dickon blinked. "You would let them take your wife away without a fight?"

Elissa touched Dickon's arm. "Damian has made the right choice, Sir Richard. I *must* go."

"Surely you know I will not let the king get away with this travesty, Dickon," Damian said earnestly. "I will do whatever necessary to set Elissa free. I have a plan, but I cannot act hastily. Know this, however— I'm going to go to London and petition the king on Elissa's behalf."

"If Damian says he will free you, my lady, then count on it. You can trust him with your life."

"I do trust Damian," Elissa replied. "If there is a way to help me, he will find it." She tucked her arms through Damian's. "You may escort me to Captain Harding now, my love."

Damian's footsteps faltered, but Elissa held him on course. Damian thought her more courageous than any woman he'd ever known. Most women in Elissa's situation would be weeping hysterically, but not his wife. Her faith in him humbled him. She trusted him to rescue her, and so he would.

Watching Elissa mount her mare and ride away was the most difficult thing Damian had ever done. Though she looked calm, Damian could tell she was frightened. When she'd turned to look at him over her shoulder as she rode off, her face had already begun to crumble.

Damian wasn't surprised to hear Elissa's kinsmen openly weeping, for he felt like crying himself. But

he wasn't allowed that luxury, for only he could re-
assure them. He turned and reentered the hall. He
waited until everyone had gathered around him before speaking. Dozens of faces turned to him expectantly, some furious, some sad, and some dismayed.

"I know you are all upset about what just happened," Damian began, "and you expected me to in-
tervene. But this wasn't the time to defy the king or
challenge his soldiers. Neither Elissa nor I wanted
bloodshed, and that's what would have happened
had I ordered my men to draw their weapons."

"What do ye intend to do?" Dermot demanded.
"Our lass is gone. She is yer wife; 'tis up to you to
protect her."

"I will protect Elissa with my life," Damian assured him, "and I'll move heaven and earth to return
her to Misterly where she belongs."

"Talk is cheap," Lachlan spat.

Damian faced the angry clansman, his determination clearly defined in the harsh slant of his jaw. "As
God is my witness, I will not rest until the Maiden of
Misterly is back home no matter what the cost to me
personally. I'm going to London to bargain with the
king for Elissa's freedom."

"When?" Dermot asked.

"The king has forbidden me to leave Misterly and
I don't want Captain Harding to know I'm following, so I'll give them two days head start. 'Tis best I
arrive in London without fanfare so I'm taking but
three men with me. The rest will remain behind to
protect Misterly."

His words appeared to placate the clansmen and
they began dispersing to return to their homes. Suddenly Lora came hurtling at Damian and began

pounding on him with her tiny fists. Damian snatched her up and held her close.

"Why did you let those bad men take Lissa away?" she cried between sobs. "I hate you! I hate you!"

"Lora, listen to me, sweeting. I had to let your sister go. We were in no position to stop those men. Trust me, little one. I won't let anything happen to your sister."

His pledge made little impact upon the distraught child as she continued to cry and flail at him. Damian suffered the weight of her condemnation with a heavy heart. Lora believed he had betrayed Elissa, and in a way he had. Had he accepted Kimbra as his bride and not wed Elissa, none of this would have happened.

But selfishly he had wanted Elissa for his own. Wanted her in his bed and in his life forever. Like a fool who would not be thwarted, he had turned Kimbra away and wed Elissa, endangering her life in the bargain. That Elissa loved him was a miracle. She had every right to hate him, just as Lora did.

"Lora, calm down, sweeting. Didn't I just promise that nothing would happen to your sister?"

"Why dinna Lissa tell us good-bye? Mama wouldna let me come down to the hall. She said there were bad men in the keep."

"Elissa wanted to see you before she left but there was no time. I'll explain what happened to your mother." He spotted Maggie hovering nearby and beckoned to her. "Take Lora to the kitchen and see if Winifred has a piece of warm gingerbread for her."

He set Lora on her feet. Still sniffling, Lora took Maggie's hand and followed her into the kitchen.

Damian was about to mount the solar staircase when Dermot hailed him.

"Did you wish to speak to me, Dermot?"

"Aye, me lord. My clansmen wanted me to tell ye that they wish ye well. Bring our lass home to us."

Unable to speak past the lump in his throat, Damian squeezed Dermot's shoulder. He dared not fail with so many people counting on him. Sometime during the past months he had become one of them. He felt as if he had always belonged to Misterly, and it to him. He would never be able to face Elissa's clansmen if he disappointed them. His mouth flattened into a determined line as he mounted the stairs and rapped on Marianne's door.

Nan opened the door to him. Damian regarded her through narrowed lids. Why hadn't Nan warned them? Where were her so-called voices when he needed them?

Damian stepped into the chamber, praying for the right words to tell Lady Marianne why he had let Elissa leave without fighting for her freedom. He spied Marianne standing by the window, a beam of sunlight bathing her pale face.

Marianne turned to face him. Damian saw her tears and his heart sank.

"She mourns her daughter," Nan said. "I explained what happened after the soldiers arrived and advised her and Lora to keep to their chambers. If it eases ye, she knows ye couldna have stopped what happened. She grieves for her daughter, aye, but I told her she shouldna weep for something that was meant to be."

Anger suffused Damian's words. "Didn't your

voices warn you that Elissa was in danger? Why were you not present to comfort her when she was taken away?"

"I canna make me voices speak when they donna wish to," Nan defended. "If ye recall, I told ye that danger approached, that ye and Elissa would be parted, but ye chose to ignore me warning."

Shaking with fury, Damian grasped the old woman's narrow shoulders. He would have shaken her had Marianne not rushed to Nan's defense.

"Release her, my lord. Nan is an old woman; she means no harm."

"Forgive me," Damian said sheepishly as he released Nan. "I am overset with worry. I would appreciate any news you can tell me, Nan. Have your voices told you anything regarding Elissa?"

"Donna badger her, my lord," Marianne gently admonished. "Nan can only repeat what her voices tell her."

" 'Tis true, me lord, I can tell ye naught else except . . ."

"Except what?" Damian asked impatiently.

"The king willna be kind to our lass. All may appear to be lost, but donna despair, 'tis only the beginning."

"That's it?" Damian all but shouted. "You've told me nothing!"

"I've told ye a great deal. Ye must prepare for yer journey, me lord. Yer stay in London willna be a short one."

Damian felt his control slipping. One more vague prediction from Nan, and he feared he'd wring her scrawny neck.

"Bring my daughter back to me, Lord Damian," Marianne implored. "I know in my heart that you love her."

"You are right, my lady," Damian admitted. "I've not regretted wedding Elissa. No matter what it costs me personally, I promise to return Elissa to you."

The following two days were hectic as Damian prepared for his journey to London. He chose carefully the three men who would accompany him and informed Sir Richard of his decision to leave him behind. At first Richard balked, demanding that he be allowed to accompany Damian, but he soon saw reason and agreed to remain behind to defend Misterly.

"We've heard nothing of Tavis Gordon but I don't think we've seen the last of him," Damian explained. "I'm depending on you to keep Misterly safe."

"You can count on me, Damian," Sir Richard maintained. "I hope Gordon doesn't take it into his head to storm the keep while you're away. It would be just like him to take advantage of your absence."

"If something unforeseen occurs, send word to me in London."

Damian left Misterly on a cold day that promised rain. Bad luck struck almost immediately. A day's journey from Misterly, his horse threw a shoe. The nearest village was several leagues away, forcing him to make an unscheduled detour. Then the rain. It poured down in icy sheets for three days straight, turning the road into a sea of mud that literally slowed their progress to a crawl.

Instead of reaching London two days behind Elissa, as originally planned, the bedraggled party entered the city on the eve of the seventh day.

Chapter 18

Elissa stood before the king, shivering beneath her wet cloak. Rain had fallen steadily during the past several days, leaving her damp and uncomfortable. The journey to London hadn't been a pleasant one, even though Captain Harding had treated her with grudging respect. She had been put up at inns when possible and had slept in a tent when no accommodations were available. After they'd left Misterly, the weather had turned dreary and cold. Then a chilling rain had begun to fall; Elissa couldn't recall when she had ever been so miserable.

Adding to her misery, she was taken before the king immediately after her arrival instead of being allowed to change her wet clothing and refresh herself with food and drink. Her knees were shaking as the stout monarch's disdainful gaze swept over her with what could only be described as curiosity. Lord Pelham, the Prime Minister, stood beside the king's chair, regarding her with frosty contempt.

"Is this the woman?" King George asked in German accented English so thick that Elissa could barely understand him.

"So it appears, Your Majesty," Lord Pelham replied.

"Does she know why she is here?"

"She's been told."

Elissa blinked. Why were they talking as if she wasn't there?

"Send for Lady Kimbra," the king ordered.

Lord Pelham spoke to a footman standing nearby, who left immediately, and Elissa prepared herself to confront her nemesis.

"Elissa Fraser," the king said, addressing her directly for the first time. "Lord Pelham will explain the charges brought against you while we are waiting for Lady Kimbra to arrive."

Elissa sorted through his words and finally understood what he had just said. "I am guilty of no crime, Your Majesty."

The king glared at her.

"You were not invited to speak, mistress," Lord Pelham reprimanded. "Listen carefully while I outline the charges against you."

He read from a scroll he held in his hand. "You plotted treason with the outlaw Tavis Gordon. You lured Lord Clarendon to your bed and convinced him to keep you with him at Misterly despite His Majesty's orders. You convinced him to send away Lady Kimbra, the lady he was to wed, causing her untold anguish and embarrassment."

Elissa squared her shoulders. "May I answer to the charges, Your Majesty?"

King George nodded curtly.

"I planned no treason. I was going to wed Tavis Gordon because my father arranged it when I was a child—long before Culloden.

"To the second charge, I can say only that I dinna lure Lord Clarendon to my bed. To the last charge, I assure you 'twas Lord Clarendon's decision to send Lady Kimbra back to London, not mine. I had naught to do with it. It was also his decision that I wed him."

The king rose from his chair. "You wed Lord Clarendon? You *wed* Lord Clarendon? Treason! Treason! He did not have our permission. We sent him a suitable wife and he rejected her."

Lady Kimbra entered the Reception Chamber while the king was still ranting. She must have heard the exchange, for she charged forward as if propelled. "Did I hear right, Your Majesty? Did you say that Lord Damian wed the Jacobite sympathizer? 'Tis an abomination. A harsh punishment is called for, Your Majesty."

"Please sit down, Sire," Lord Pelham urged. "You must not excite yourself so."

"May I speak, Your Majesty?" Kimbra asked sweetly.

The king gave permission with a wave of his hand.

"Elissa Fraser poisoned Lord Damian's mind against me. She wasn't satisfied until she had him in her bed. Then she cozened him into sending me away."

"Nay, she lies!" Elissa denied.

"Before I left Misterly, she tried to run off to join her lover, Tavis Gordon. She was caught and brought back. Once I was gone, she must have beguiled Lord Damian into marrying her. The Jacobite deserves to be punished, Your Majesty. Elissa Fraser committed treason and should be put to death."

Fear coiled in Elissa's chest. She was as good as dead, for she had no way to disprove Kimbra's lies. She had hoped for lenience, but that expectation died the moment she heard the venomous words spill from Kimbra's mouth.

"Death might be a little harsh, Sire," Lord Pelham said in an aside to the king.

"We will make that decision as we see fit," the king said. "Summon the scribe. The unsanctioned marriage between Lord Clarendon and Elissa Fraser must be ended. We will annul it forthwith."

Elissa felt Kimbra's eyes on her and intercepted a look of vindication, which quickly turned to unrelenting hatred. Then the scribe entered the Reception Chamber, and Elissa returned her attention to the king.

The scribe sketched a bow. "You summoned me, Sire?"

"Indeed. We require a writ of annulment prepared and presented for my signature immediately. We wish to annul the marriage between Damian Stratton, Lord Clarendon, and Elissa Fraser. We will require two copies—one for our records and the second for Lord Clarendon."

"Aye, Sire," the scribe said, bowing again.

The king waved him away.

Lord Pelham cleared his throat. "What are your wishes regarding Elissa Fraser, Sire?"

"We will think on it. Until we have reached a decision, lock her in the Tower." His gaze swept over her bedraggled form. "If she has not brought a change of clothing, see that she is provided with something dry to wear."

"You are too lenient, Sire," Kimbra complained.

"We will consider your recommendation, Lady Kimbra. The charges brought against Mistress Elissa are grave indeed; therefore we shall mete out punishment accordingly. If death is warranted, we shall do our duty."

Elissa blanched. "I demand a trial, Sire."

King George scowled. "You are in no position to demand anything, mistress. No trial is necessary. I will act as both judge and jury." He waved a lace handkerchief languidly back and forth in front of his face. "Leave me, I am weary."

Kimbra fell into a deep curtsy. Elissa's curtsy was neither grand nor respectful. Her fate was in the hands of a man who had dealt cruelly with Highlanders after Culloden. She could expect little mercy from the Hanover.

"Follow me, mistress," Lord Pelham said, shattering her dismal thoughts.

Elissa followed Lord Pelham from the chamber. She'd heard horror stories from people who had been incarcerated in the Tower and knew to expect no special treatment. Lord Pelham led her through a maze of hallways and then a door which led into a small courtyard. To her surprise, she found Captain Harding waiting.

"Captain Harding was instructed to wait for you," Pelham explained. "He will escort you and whatever personal belongings you brought with you to the Tower."

"Let me assist you," Harding said, as he helped

Elissa to mount one of the horses he'd brought with him.

"Inform Lieutenant Belton that Mistress Elissa will be his guest in the Tower until His Majesty decides her fate, Captain," Pelham said as he turned away.

Captain Harding mounted his own horse, grasped Elissa's leading reins, and guided them both through the arched gateway into a narrow street crowded with men and women who stared at her with open curiosity. Hawkers, beggars, pickpockets, and men of means blended together in a cacophony of sights and sounds that Elissa found confusing after living in near isolation at Misterly. Never had she seen so many people gathered in one place.

Someone from above shouted a warning and she ducked in time to avoid the stinking contents of a chamber pot. She wrinkled her nose in disgust when she saw raw sewage running down the gutters on both sides of the narrow street. Not for the first time she wished herself back at Misterly, where the air was pure and sweet with the scent of flowers.

When they reached Tower Street, Elissa stared in abject horror at the platform and gallows atop what she assumed was Tower Hill, where countless Highlanders, some of her own clansmen included, had lost their lives. They crossed the Thames over a stone causeway and then a wooden bridge that spanned a moat, entering the complex through the raised portcullis of Middle Gate. Captain Harding reined in before a heavy oak door studded with iron rivets and helped Elissa to dismount. He thrust her satchel at her, pushed the door open, and ushered her inside. Elissa stepped into a dark anteroom and came to an abrupt halt.

"Up the staircase, my lady," Harding urged.

Elissa's legs turned to butter as she stared at the damp stone walls and narrow winding staircase leading to Lord only knew where. Was this to be her tomb? she wondered dismally. Would she swing from the gallows on Tower Hill?

Harding poked her in the back and she moved woodenly toward the staircase. She shivered uncontrollably as an icy chill seeped through her damp clothing, chilling her bones.

Damian, my love, I need you, her heart cried out in mute appeal. *Will I ever be warm and safe in your arms again?*

She reached the top landing and waited for Captain Harding to direct her.

"Veer left," Harding said.

Elissa turned down a dank, smoky passageway lit by torches placed in sconces along the wall. It looked like something out of the Dark Ages. Her teeth chattered and she hugged herself, but found no warmth in her arms.

"Stop."

Elissa halted before a closed door. Harding knocked and opened the door when bidden to enter. He held open the panel and gestured for Elissa to enter ahead of him.

"Your new prisoner has arrived, Lieutenant Belton."

Elissa regarded the man sitting behind the desk with curiosity as well as a healthy dose of fear. He was a big man, with a ruddy complexion and large nose. His sausage-like body was encased in a uniform that strained at the seams. Rising from behind his desk, he studied Elissa with rapt interest.

"Who is she? What has she done?" Belton asked.

"Her name is Elissa Fraser; she's a Jacobite sympathizer."

Belton moved from behind the desk, his gaze fixed on Elissa's face. She shrank back when he extended a hand and pushed a damp curl from her forehead.

"I like red hair," Belton said, grinning. "Is she bound for the gallows?"

"The king hasn't decide the lady's fate. And make no mistake, Belton, she *is* a lady," Harding warned, surprising Elissa. "Treat her like one."

Belton shrugged. "She has nothing to fear from me. My wife doesn't allow it. But I can't speak for the warders, they're a rough lot, as you well know."

Harding sent Elissa a pitying look, then left her in Belton's care. Elissa trembled as she waited for Belton to tell her what came next in this nightmare into which she'd been cast.

"I'll show you to your chamber so you can get settled in," Belton said. "A warder will bring food and water to you later. Meals aren't as grand as you're accustomed to, but they should be sufficient for a little thing like you. Come along, mistress."

Gathering her courage, Elissa said, "I am a lady. You may address me by my proper title."

"You are a bloody nobody here, mistress. Follow me."

Clutching her satchel with nerveless fingers, Elissa felt her bravado falter as she followed him down the narrow corridor and up another flight of stairs. Finally Lieutenant Belton halted before a sturdy oak door. He fumbled with the ring of keys dangling from his belt, selected one, and turned it in the lock. Then he shoved the door open and pushed her inside.

Elissa set down her satchel and looked around her with growing apprehension. The chamber smelled of dampness and rot. She felt a cold draft and glanced at the small barred window across the room, shivering as another blast of chilling air wafted through. Forcing her gaze from the window, she saw a narrow cot covered with dingy sheets and a single blanket, and prayed they weren't infested with vermin. An empty candleholder resting on a small table and a low stool were the only furnishings besides the cot. There was no source of heat that she could see, and she didn't even want to think about the slop bucket sitting in a dark corner.

The foul odor arising from the bucket rocked Elissa back on her heels. Appalled, she returned her gaze to Belton, her brows raised, silently questioning his judgment in placing her in such wretched surroundings.

"Make yourself comfortable," Belton advised. "You'll grow used to it in time."

Her heart thumping wildly against her chest, Elissa knew she'd never grow accustomed to such depressing accommodations.

"A warder will bring food and a candle. Use the candle sparingly, for it is replaced only every third day. The slop bucket will be emptied each morning and you will be provided with two meals daily. Breakfast, and another later in the day. The warder will see to your needs as he deems necessary. If you have blunt, or can get your hands on some, give it to him and he will provide you with small comforts you wouldn't otherwise have."

"Small comforts?" Elissa asked. "I donna understand."

"Things like a warmer blanket, or a piece of meat in your soup. Perhaps a brazier to keep you warm."

"I have no money and know no one in London."

"Ah, well, too bad. Good day, then, mistress."

He let himself out the door and locked it behind him, cutting Elissa off from the world. Never had she felt so abandoned or been so frightened—it was as if her life were slowly slipping away.

Elissa sank down on the cot, too dejected and dull witted to think straight. Straw crunched beneath her and a moldy odor wafted up from the lumpy surface. Then a curious rat appeared from beneath the cot and scampered under her damp skirt. A scream froze in her throat as she leapt to her feet and scrambled atop the stool. The rat raised up on its hind legs and gazed at her through bright, beady eyes. It was a standoff of sorts, until the rat finally became bored and scampered off.

Frantic with despair, Elissa feared she would never survive the Tower. It suddenly occurred to her that maybe she wasn't supposed to survive, that the king meant for her to die here. Where was Damian? Had his promises been hollow ones?

She stepped down from the stool, gathered her skirts about her, and sat down on its hard surface. She remained there for what seemed like an eternity, shivering, yet lacking even the energy to change into dry clothing. The shadows had lengthened considerably when she heard the key turning in the lock.

A man entered the chamber. "I be the warder, mistress. I brung ye something to eat," he said as he slammed the door shut with his bootheel. Some of the contents of the bowl splashed out as he placed it, a hunk of moldy dark bread, and a spoon on the table. When she looked up into the man's face, her spirits ebbed to its lowest point, for he was leering at her through mean little eyes.

Placing his face close to hers, he said, "Well, mistress, are ye settling in?"

His breath was so revolting that Elissa reared backward to escape the stench. " 'Tis a terrible place," she said with a shiver.

He cackled, revealing a mouthful of rotted teeth. "Me name is Dooley. Yer better off here than at Old Bailey or Fleet Prison." He rummaged in his coat pocket and brought out a stubby candle and a few sulfur matches. He placed the candle in the holder and set the matches on the table beside it.

Elissa glanced into the bowl and recoiled in revulsion. "What is this?"

Dooley gave her an exasperated look. "Cabbage soup. Are ye blind?"

Elissa continued to stare at it. It looked like nothing edible she'd ever seen.

"Ain't it to yer liking, mistress?"

Elissa pushed it aside. "I'm . . . not hungry."

Dooley gave her a sly look. "I can get ye something more to yer liking if ye got blunt to pay for it. I can bring ye a brazier, too, and mayhap another blanket."

"I have no money."

"Then I reckon ye'll learn to like the food and endure the cold, won't ye?"

"I'd like some water, please."

"Bossy little thing, ain't ye? I'll go fetch ye some water."

He left and returned moments later with a bucket of water and a tin cup. "If ye want me for anything," he said suggestively, "bang on the door with yer cup. If ye change yer mind about those extra comforts I mentioned, there is more than one way to pay for them, if ye get my meaning."

"I don't need anything from you," Elissa bit out.

"Suit yerself, mistress," Dooley said. "Enjoy yer stay with us." The door closed behind him.

Elissa hissed out a grateful sigh after Dooley left. She had finally roused herself to the fact that she was freezing and needed to change her clothes before she became ill. A brazier would have been a welcome luxury, but she would happily freeze to death before selling her body to Dooley.

Retreating to a dark corner, Elissa removed dry clothing from her satchel and exchanged the damp clothes she wore for dry ones. Then she laid out her wet things over the table and stool to dry. Steeped in misery, she sat on the edge of the bed, pulled the blanket around her shoulders, and surrendered to despair. Tears began to flow when rats came out from their hiding places and sniffed around the bowl of cabbage soup she had sat on the floor when she'd spread her clothes out to dry.

Elissa allowed herself a few minutes of self-pity, then squared her shoulders and dashed her tears away. Succumbing to despair was not going to help her. She had to think positively if she hoped to survive. She had to believe Damian would come for her. If she lost hope she would lose herself, and she couldn't . . . wouldn't let that happen. Nor would she let those disgusting rats frighten her. She was bigger than they were, wasn't she? She didn't move from the cot, however, until necessity forced her to relieve herself in the nasty slop bucket. The rats finally scattered and she got up and dipped the cup in the water bucket. After drinking deeply, she dipped it in the water again and used it to wash her hands and face.

She sat in the dark a long time before finally dozing off. When she opened her eyes hours later, a square of murky daylight was seeping through the window. She greeted the dismal morning with diminishing hope and wavering spirits. Her legs were stiff and her hands cold as she moved off the bed, carefully folded the clothes that had dried overnight, placed them in the satchel, and removed her brush. She was trying to tame her tangled hair when Dooley arrived with breakfast. She glanced at the watery gruel and hunk of hard bread and promptly lost her appetite.

"Did ye sleep well?" Dooley taunted.

Elissa ignored him.

"Haughty little bitch, ain't ye? I can make things better for ye."

"I told you, I have no money."

He stared at her breasts. "Be good to me and I'll forget about the blunt." He touched her hair. "I'll bet yer a wild 'un between the sheets."

Shaking with indignation, Elissa slapped his hand away. "Donna touch me!"

Dooley glared at her. "Ye ain't in no position to give me orders, missy. Ye'll change yer mind, I'll warrant, when yer cold enough and hungry enough. Eat yer gruel. 'Tis all ye'll get till dinner." He picked up the slop bucket and headed for the door, leaving Elissa to her morbid thoughts.

* * *

Elissa languished in abysmal circumstances for more days than she wished to acknowledge. The offensive odor of the food she was offered made her gag and push it aside, and when hunger forced her to eat, she lost it more often than not to the slop bucket. She was cold, hungry, exhausted, and utterly miserable. Dooley's vicious taunting only added to her woes. He delighted in describing in detail the favors he expected from her in exchange for better food and physical comforts.

As the days passed, Elissa began to fear that the king had forgotten her and that Damian had abandoned her.

Covered with mud and sprouting a healthy growth of bristle on his chin, Damian reached London a full week behind Elissa. Though mindless with worry over Elissa's fate, he saw to his men's board and secured lodgings for himself above a tavern not far from Whitehall. Owing to the lateness of his arrival, it wasn't feasible to seek an interview with the king, so he ordered a bath and some food and rehearsed the plea he hoped to present to the king on Elissa's behalf the following morning.

What had happened to Elissa? he wondered. Was she still alive? He had stopped to question a hawker on his way through town and had been relieved to learn that no hanging had been held during the past week. That meant there was a chance Elissa was still alive. But in what condition?

After bathing and eating, Damian roamed the streets in search of information. A few people remembered seeing soldiers escorting a young woman through the streets of London, but no one seemed to know what had happened to her. Disheartened, he returned to his room and tried to sleep. He needed to be at his best tomorrow. Too many people depended on him to bring Elissa back to Misterly. Returning alone was not an option. Spending the rest of his life without Elissa was even less palatable.

The sun had barely risen when Damian entered Whitehall the following morning. He was forced to cool his heels in an anteroom until other petitioners began to gather. A short time later a scribe arrived to interview those who sought an audience with the king. When his turn came, Damian gave his name and stated his purpose for requesting an audience. The scribe wrote something down in a book and told Damian to wait for the king's summons.

Damian waited in the anteroom for hours while others were escorted into the reception hall. The day was half gone when the scribe announced that the king had retired to his Privy Chamber to rest and the audiences were over for the day. The remaining petitioners were invited to return the next day.

Damian was so furious he felt like throwing caution to the winds and pushing his way inside the king's Privy Chamber, demanding to be heard. Prudence prevailed, however, and he left without making a scene.

Damian returned the following day, and the day after that, growing angrier by the minute as his request for an audience was blatantly ignored. When he was finally summoned into the reception hall by Lord Pelham on the third day, his patience was all but shattered and his hope hung by a slim thread.

"Thank you for granting me an audience, Sire," Damian said in a voice fraught with impatience.

"What are you doing in London, Lord Clarendon? You were instructed to remain at Misterly, were you not?"

It took a long moment for Damian to sort through the guttural accent with any kind of understanding. At length, he said, "Aye, Sire, but I was anxious about my wife. Perhaps you'd be good enough to tell me what has become of her."

A feminine voice accosted him from the doorway. "I heard you were seeking an audience with the king, Damian. Hasn't His Majesty told you that you have no wife and never did?"

Kimbra moved toward him like a ship at full mast. "Lady Kimbra," Damian said, politely bowing over her outstretched hand. "I beg to differ with you. Elissa and I were married by Father Hugh after you left Misterly."

"Shall I tell him, or will you, Your Majesty?" Kimbra asked sweetly.

Her pleasant manner did not fool Damian. A sickness built in the pit of his stomach.

Lord Pelham undertook the explanation. "Had you remained at Misterly, Lord Clarendon, you would have received a notice of the annulment of your marriage. Since you weren't given permission to wed, His Majesty declared your marriage illegal. If you recall, the British Marriage Act forbids unauthorized weddings."

The color drained from Damian's face. "You cannot do that."

"Oh, but he can," Kimbra smirked. "Consider yourself fortunate to be free of the Jacobite."

"Sire, what have you done with Elissa?" Damian demanded to know.

"Nothing . . . yet," the king answered. "We have placed her in the Tower while we decide her fate. She is still there, is she not, Lord Pelham?"

"Indeed she is, Sire."

The blood froze in Damian's veins. The Tower! He had visited the Tower upon occasion and was familiar with the cold, dank chambers. He wouldn't wish his worst enemy there. "I want to see her."

Kimbra stepped forward, her expression almost feral. "Do not allow it, I beg you, Sire. The woman caused me a great deal of pain and embarrassment."

Damian struggled to contain his temper. "Elissa did nothing to you. You hated her on sight and made free with your insults. Nothing about Misterly pleased you. Your unreasonable demands made enemies of the very people whose loyalty I've been courting."

"He lies!" Kimbra hissed. "The Jacobite bewitched him. Lord Damian was remiss in his duty to you. He should have sent the woman to the convent as you instructed."

"You're bitter because I preferred Elissa," Damian charged.

The king raised his hand for silence. "We have heard enough," he said. "Lady Kimbra has told us all we need to know. Tell him of our decision, Lord Pelham, for English words do not come easily to us."

Lord Pelham cleared his throat. " 'Tis as His Majesty says. You disobeyed his orders and entered into a fraudulent marriage with a woman who conspired with an outlaw to commit treason."

A hard knot formed in Damian's gut. "Elissa did not conspire with Gordon." He glared at Kimbra. "She has been falsely accused."

Pelham made an impatient gesture. "Return to Misterly, Clarendon. There is nothing more you can do here."

"What is to become of Elissa?"

"Treason is a serious charge, punishable by death."

Gorge rose in Damian's throat. He would not allow such a travesty. "I beg you, take Misterly from me, strip away my title, do with me as you will, but spare Elissa."

"Perhaps there is a way," Lord Pelham said, stroking his chin as he exchanged a sly smile with Kimbra.

"Anything! Name it," Damian replied, his spirit soaring on a slender thread of hope.

" 'Tis a simple thing, really," Lord Pelham said. "His Majesty still feels that you are the best man for Misterly, and he wishes you to keep your title, with certain stipulations, of course."

"Of course," Damian said dryly. He expected no less.

"His Majesty wants your marriage to Lady Kimbra to go forward. I have spoken to Lady Kimbra and she is willing to put the past behind her and bow to the king's wishes."

"You want me to wed Lady Kimbra?" Damian repeated numbly.

" 'Tis a good match, my lord," Kimbra interjected.

"Will Elissa be spared if I wed Lady Kimbra?"

"Aye, Clarendon, 'tis just as I said. Is that not so, Your Majesty?"

King George nodded in acknowledgment and motioned for Lord Pelham to continue.

"It is His Majesty's wish that you and Lady Kim-

bra wed in his Privy Chambers ten days hence. Lady
Kimbra asked His Majesty that he postpone your return to Misterly until the end of the current Season
and His Majesty has graciously acquiesced. Is that
agreeable to you, Lord Clarendon?"

"That depends," Damian said slowly, "on your
plans for Elissa."

"Were you not listening?" Lord Pelham chided.
"The woman's life will be spared."

"Will she be free to return to Misterly?"

"Really, Lord Damian," Kimbra admonished,
"how can you ask such a thing? I do not want that
woman in my home. She'll live, let that suffice."

" 'Tis not acceptable. Elissa cannot survive if she's
to remain in the Tower."

"How dare you question His Majesty's generosity," Lord Pelham charged. "The alternative to the
Tower is death, if you recall."

"Your Majesty," Damian said, appealing directly
to the king. "Let me remind you that no one can defend Misterly as well as I. The Frasers have begun to
trust me. They rejected Tavis Gordon and his rebellious clansmen in my favor. If Misterly is given to another, there's bound to be trouble at a time when you
can ill afford it."

"Nevertheless," Lord Pelham said haughtily,
"you have not the right to demand anything from
your king."

King George cleared his throat and motioned for
silence. "We will listen to what Lord Clarendon has
to say. What will it take to gain your cooperation?"

Damian spoke firmly and without a hint of the
fear battering him. Elissa could die in the Tower if
his words failed to sway the monarch.

"I will wed Lady Kimbra, honor her as my wife, and protect Misterly with my life, but only if Elissa is released from the Tower. I will even agree to spend the Season in London to please Lady Kimbra, though it does not please me to do so. What say you, Sire?"

Damian's hopes soared as King George conferred with Lord Pelham in low whispers and exaggerated gesturing. Damian waited in gut-clenching anxiety for the king's answer. There was nothing more he could say. He prayed it would be enough.

"So, you really do love the Jacobite," Kimbra said in an aside while they waited on the king and Pelham. "How droll."

"You wouldn't understand, Kimbra. I'll never have with you what I had with Elissa."

Kimbra shrugged. "It matters not. I never asked for love. Your body will satisfy me."

"I promised the king I would do my duty by you, and so I shall," Damian said grimly.

Kimbra gave him a sultry look beneath fluttering lashes. " 'Tis all I want, Damian," Kimbra said.

The conference between the king and Pelham ended. Damian snapped to attention. He had spoken so boldly it wasn't unreasonable to think he'd end up in the Tower with Elissa.

"Lord Clarendon," Pelham began, "His Majesty acknowledges your courageous defense of king and country and wishes you to remain Lord of Misterly. Therefore, he will grant your request. Mistress Fraser will be released from the Tower and escorted to the St. Mary by the Sea Convent, her original destination.

"If you agree to those terms, His Majesty and the queen will host a wedding reception for you and Lady Kimbra."

Elissa was to go to the convent. Though it was less than Damian had hoped for, it was far better than the Tower and certain death.

"You are more than generous," Damian allowed, choking on the words. "I will wed Lady Kimbra."

"Oh, Damian," Kimbra gushed. "I knew you'd come around. I can't wait to begin the Season as your wife."

"Leave me," King George said, waving them away. "We are exhausted."

Kimbra clung possessively to Damian's arm as he escorted her from the Privy Chamber. The planes of Damian's face turned stark as he considered the dim future stretching before him. The king could force him to wed Kimbra, but no one could make him love any woman but Elissa.

Chapter 19

Wrapped in her cloak, a blanket bundled around her shoulders for added warmth, Elissa huddled on the bed, listening to the wind howling through the window. She felt nothing, nothing at all. In order to survive, she had willed her body and mind into a state of numbness. Time had no meaning. Had she been residing in the Tower one week, or two? It felt like an eternity.

She watched the rats playing tag with scant interest, for she'd lost all fear of the odious creatures that had grown fat on her uneaten food. Their antics had been diversions that served to take her mind off her misery.

Inured to external disturbances, Elissa paid little heed when the door to her chamber opened. She knew without looking that the warder had arrived with a bowl of gruel, which the rats would doubtlessly enjoy after he left.

Not for the first time Elissa wished for something decent to eat, but she knew she was unlikely to get it. She could no longer deny what she'd suspected since leaving Misterly. The signs were unmistakable. She carried Damian's bairn and needed healthier food if her child was to survive.

Unless her circumstances changed, however, Elissa feared she wouldn't live long enough to bring her bairn into the world. She had no mirror, but she knew weight had melted off her body and her cheeks were hollow, her eyes lusterless. Could death be far away?

Why had Damian abandoned her? Had everything he'd told her been a lie? Her head drooped against her chest. She was hurt, disillusioned, and devoid of all hope. Justice was not only blind; in her case it was completely lacking.

"Mistress, are you unwell?"

Elissa's head shot up. The voice didn't belong to the warder.

"Did you hear me, mistress?"

Lieutenant Belton. "Aye, I heard. What do you want?"

"You're to come with me. The king wishes to see you."

The dullness faded from Elissa's eyes, slowly replaced by wary comprehension. "The king wants to see me? Has he condemned me to death?"

"I know not. Once you leave here, you are no longer my responsibility."

Elissa rose unsteadily, a remnant of innate pride reasserting itself. "I canna appear before the king like this. I stink. I've not had a decent bath in more days than I care to recount, and my clothing reeks."

Belton approached Elissa, his nose wrinkling as

he cautiously sniffed the air. "Aye, mistress, there is indeed a rank odor about you."

"Well," Elissa demanded with a hint of her old pluck, "what do you intend to do about it?" Asserting herself again made her feel so good she automatically assumed the posture to accompany her attitude.

"Follow me. There's a bathing room near my quarters. You may use it."

"What about clothing? I refuse to appear before the king dressed like a pauper."

"I'll see if my wife has something suitable for you to wear. Come along."

Elissa picked up her satchel and followed Belton along twisting passageways to the bathing chamber in his private quarters. Excitement raced through Elissa when she spied the large wooden tub that sat in the center of the tiny room.

Belton summoned a servant and ordered hot water for the tub. "Don't tarry," he warned. "The king doesn't like to be kept waiting."

A half-hour later, wearing a drab, but clean, twill dress Belton's wife had generously provided, Elissa was ready to learn her fate. That kind lady had even brought a bar of sweet-smelling soap and a towel, and had wished her well.

Elissa had just finished running a brush through her wet hair when Belton returned.

"Time to leave, mistress. Your escort awaits you," Belton said.

Elissa followed Belton through dank corridors and down a narrow staircase to ground level. When he opened the door, unaccustomed light stabbed against her eyelids and she closed her eyes against the glare. When she opened them, she was surprised and somewhat heartened to find Captain Harding waiting for her. He was, after all, a recognizable face.

"Have you been ill, my lady?" Harding asked with concern. "You look peaked."

Elissa stifled a humorless laugh. Saying she didn't look well was a gross understatement. "A stay in the Tower isna conducive to good health," she stated dryly.

Harding merely nodded as he helped her to mount, attached her satchel to the saddle, and guided their horses through the gate and across the bridge into London's teeming streets. After being confined for so long, Elissa watched the people go about their business with rapt attention. Though she had little liking for London, she thought it an interesting city with its diverse population.

They reached Whitehall sooner than Elissa would have liked. She wasn't eager to hear the fate the English king had decided for her. Captain Harding handed her down, retrieved her satchel, and ushered her directly to the king's Privy Chamber and left her.

"God be with you, my lady," Harding said as a palace guard opened the door to admit her.

Elissa froze, her fingers curled around the handle of her satchel as if it were her lifeline to sanity. The king beckoned to her but she couldn't move. Facing her own mortality took tremendous courage, a commodity she was currently lacking.

"You may approach us, mistress," the king ordered. When Elissa failed to respond, he said in an aside to Lord Pelham, "You tell her, perhaps she didn't understand us."

"Did you not hear His Majesty?" Pelham asked

impatiently. "You may approach. Don't forget to make your curtsy."

Suddenly realizing she was making a spectacle of herself before the men and women attending the king, Elissa squared her shoulders and walked forward with all the aplomb she could muster. She performed her curtsy without appearing to grovel and waited for the hammer known as English justice to descend.

She heard a strangled sound coming from someone standing nearby but paid it scant heed, until she recognized the sound as her name. She turned her head, surveying the faces staring at her with avid curiosity. Her gaze swept past Damian, then snapped back to him. He wasn't alone. Kimbra was with him, pressed close to his side. Rigid with disbelief, she blinked, but they were still there when she opened her eyes. Pain squeezed her heart. She needed no further proof that the man she loved had abandoned her.

How could she have been such a fool? Elissa wondered. Damian hadn't wanted her, he wanted Misterly and would do anything to keep from losing his prize. Exactly how far would he go to that end?

"Mistress, are you attending us?"

Elissa forced her attention back to the king. "I'm sorry, Sire, my thoughts were elsewhere."

"Did you hear nothing we said?"

"I'm sorry," she repeated.

The king snorted his disapproval. "Tell her of our decision, Lord Pelham."

"What His Majesty was trying to tell you," Pelham repeated with waning patience, "is that he is releasing you from the Tower."

Elissa went still. "Releasing me? I'm free to leave?"

"Not exactly. His Majesty is aware of your Catholic

faith, and he hopes you will appreciate his generosity. An escort will take you to St. Mary by the Sea Convent, where you will devote the remainder of your life to prayer and good deeds. Should you leave the convent without permission, the Mother Superior will notify us. You will be declared an outlaw and put to death when you're apprehended."

Elissa gasped. She was to be sent to St. Mary by the Sea. The convent was but a day's journey from Misterly. Since few convents still existed in Protestant England, she supposed that sending her to Scotland was more expedient than banishing her to a convent in France or Spain. Secretly she rejoiced. Though a convent was restrictive, she preferred it to the Tower.

"A word of caution," Pelham continued. "The convent and its inhabitants are beholden to His Majesty for their very existence, so don't try to leave without permission or expect special treatment."

Elissa considered Lord Pelham's words and decided she would leave the convent despite the warning. Becoming an outlaw didn't frighten her, for she would be free. After she left the convent, she knew it would take weeks for word to reach London. It would be enough time to collect her mother and sister and take them to Glenmoor. The only problem was that it had to be accomplished before Damian returned to Misterly.

Elissa's silent rumination abruptly ceased when Damain approached the throne and asked the king if he might have a word with her. After a moment's hesitation, the king gave his grudging consent. Elissa could tell Kimbra wasn't pleased, for she snarled something to Damian that made him frown and remove her hand from his arm.

Damian turned to face Elissa and stared directly into her eyes, as if trying to convey a message. "I but wanted to wish Lady Elissa a safe journey," he said earnestly. "And to tell her that Lady Kimbra and I are to be wed."

Elissa reeled as if struck. She should have expected it, but it still hurt unbearably.

Damian looked like he wanted to reach out to her but Elissa knew she was imagining it. "Were you aware that our marriage was declared illegal?" Damian asked in a gentle voice that confused her.

Was he deliberately trying to hurt her? "Aye. I knew. Will you and your bride return to Misterly immediately following the wedding?"

"Nay, Lady Kimbra wishes to enjoy the London Season first," Damian replied.

The agony of Damian's betrayal was nearly unbearable, but she'd be damned if she'd let his callous words destroy her. Besides, if her plan to get her mother and sister out of Misterly was to work, it was best that Damian wasn't there to stop her. For all she cared, he could indulge his new bride all he wished, for it suited Elissa's plans perfectly.

"When is the wedding?" she asked with little enthusiasm.

Damian opened his mouth to answer, but Lord Pelham forestalled him. "The wedding is to take place in His Majesty's Privy Chamber in ten days. That's all you need to know. You will be escorted to the convent immediately."

Elissa wasn't surprised at this abrupt dismissal. She knew she was as welcome as the plague. Neither the king nor Damian could stand the sight of her. The sooner she was gotten rid of, the better. She was puzzled, however, by the Crown's decision to place her in the convent instead of executing her. Had someone petitioned the king for her life?

Elissa's thoughts skidded to a halt when the chamber door opened, admitting Captain Harding . . . her escort, she supposed. She caught a glimpse of Damian's face as she dropped into an awkward curtsy. His expression shocked her. Pain, pity, anger, anxiety, and something else. Love? Surely not. The love she thought had existed between them was a myth. Damian had everything he'd ever desired now, while she, she had nothing but the bairn he had put in her belly.

"I am ready, Captain," she said as Harding grasped her arm to escort her away.

Damian watched Elissa walk away, head held high, her spine stiff. Never had he been so proud of her. It nearly killed him to stand by and watch the love of his life walk out of it. Never again would he hold her in his arms, or make love to her, or tell her he loved her.

He had saved Elissa from certain death, but at what price? Though Misterly was still his, he'd happily relinquish it for just one more kiss from Elissa's sweet lips. Kimbra was no substitute for the wife he'd just lost, and God knows he'd have to force himself to bed her. And each time he bedded Kimbra it would be Elissa's face he'd see, Elissa's lips he'd kiss, Elissa's body he'd love.

A slow smile curved his lips. It suddenly occurred to him how he could see Elissa and tell her the truth about Kimbra. Could he make it work? A hasty plan formed in his mind as he escorted Kimbra to her bedchamber.

"That went well," Kimbra said smugly. "The Jacobite is out of our lives for good. Will you escort me to the Cavandish musicale tonight? It will be the perfect occasion to announce our upcoming nuptials."

"I have other plans," Damian said.

"Can't they wait?" She placed a hand on his chest. "I need you," she purred seductively. "We are betrothed. I want you in my bed tonight."

The harshness of Damian's expression should have warned Kimbra, but she appeared too absorbed in her own needs to notice as her hand strayed from his chest, moving boldly downward to his flaccid sex.

"I can make that hard for you, Damian."

Damian seized her hand and flung it away. "Ours is not a love match, Kimbra. We both know I'm wedding you to save Elissa's life. I'll do my duty, but not until I have to."

Turning on his heel, he left Kimbra without a backward glance.

Despite the cold, misty drizzle, Elissa easily kept pace with her escort as they journeyed north from London.

"We'll stop at coaching inns as we find them," Captain Harding informed her as he fell in beside her. "And seek shelter at private homes when no inns are available. We've also brought along a tent for your comfort." He searched her face. "You appear excessively wan, and far thinner than when last I saw you, so I'll try to make this journey as easy as possible for you."

"I appreciate your concern, Captain," Elissa said warmly. "The Tower isna a healthy place. Fresh air will do wonders for me, though I could do without this rain."

As if to mock her words, the skies opened up and rain poured down on them. Elissa pulled her hood over her head and shivered beneath her cloak. She was surprised when Captain Harding removed his own cloak and placed it around her shoulders. Compassion still existed in this harsh world, she thought, as she smiled her thanks.

She was only a little damp when they rode into the yard of the Royal George Inn. A lad ran up to take charge of the horses as Captain Harding hastened with her into the inn. Elissa went directly to the common room to warm herself before the hearth while Harding arranged for rooms and food. No one noticed the hooded man who entered the inn a short time later and sat at a table in a dark corner obscured by shadows.

Elissa dined on savory meat pie, creamy yellow cheese, and soft white bread, washing it down with hot tea. She even found room for a generous slice of apple cobbler.

After she finished eating, she rose and requested permission to leave. "May I retire now?"

"I will escort you, my lady," Captain Harding said.

"Thank you, Captain. You are kind."

"Not a bit, my lady. The king has dealt harshly with you when there was no need. In my opinion, you have done him no harm. Losing your husband had to have been distressing for you, and your stay in the Tower completely demoralizing, but at least you have your life."

"Aye," Elissa agreed softly. *And the life of my bairn,*

she thought, placing a hand over her stomach as she turned away.

Elissa's chamber was on the second floor. Harding wished her good night and locked the door behind her. She walked to the window, staring at the ground through the pelting rain. Thoughtfully she contemplated the thick oak tree that grew beside the building, and the leafless branches lashing the window. Only a fool would attempt such a climb. She had another life to protect besides her own, and anything that dangerous wasn't worth the risk.

Sighing despondently, she closed the shutters and retrieved her nightgown from her satchel. She undressed quickly and pulled it over her head, settling it around her hips. Then she blew out the lamp and crawled into bed, pulling the quilt up to her chin. She hadn't enjoyed such luxury in weeks. A full stomach, a comfortable bed; it was pure bliss. The only thing missing was Damian to keep her warm.

Elissa slept, but apparently not deeply enough, for she heard a noise and felt a rush of cold air. She tried to dismiss it as imagination until she felt something brush across her cheek. Still groggy from sleep, she tried to sweep it away, startled when her hand came into contact with warm skin stretched over bone. A scream gathered in her throat. A hard hand covered her mouth and the sound died for lack of air.

"Quiet," a voice close to her ear warned. "I'll remove my hand if you promise not to scream." Elissa nodded and the hand slid away.

"Damian!" Elissa whispered on a shaky breath. His face was obscured by shadows, except for his eyes, which gleamed like silver coins in the darkness.

The last vestiges of sleep fell away. "What are you doing here? Why aren't you with your bride-to-be?"

Damian perched on the edge of the bed and gently caressed her cheek. His touch, the tenseness of his body, everything about him conveyed sadness and pain.

"I followed you here," he whispered. "It wasn't difficult. I arrived shortly after you did and sat in a dark corner of the common room while you and Captain Harding dined. When you left to come up to your room, I was faced with a dilemma. I had no idea which room was yours." He smiled. "The innkeeper was very accommodating when I greased his palm with a coin.

"I still wasn't sure how I'd get inside your room so I went outside to study the lay of the building. Then I saw you standing at the window. The tree was a bonus I hadn't expected."

"You climbed the tree?"

"Aye. If the tree hadn't been handy, I would have found another way. I had to explain so you wouldn't hate me."

"Hate is too mild a word. You abandoned me. Wealth and possessions mean more to you than my love. Go away, I donna need you."

"Nay, you're going to listen to me. If I hadn't agreed to wed Kimbra, you would have been put to death. I pleaded for your life but the king refused to listen. He even forbade me to visit you in the Tower. I was frantic to see you.

"When the king promised to spare your life if I wedded Kimbra, I had no choice but to agree. Even if I never saw you again, you'd still have your life. And resourceful as you are, I knew the convent wouldn't hold you for long."

Elissa listened to Damian's words with open skepticism. She wanted desperately to believe him, and his explanation did make sense, but the pain of his rejection was difficult to dispel.

"Why should I trust you?" she asked softly.

"Because I'm telling the truth. Would I come all this way to lie? I didn't want you to believe I had abandoned you. I would have sacrificed everything for you. Someday, somehow, we *will* be together again."

She believed him. Blessed Mother, she believed him. She didn't have to see his face to know he spoke from the heart. But it was too late for them. Their marriage and their life together had been severed as neatly as if a knife had split them apart.

Needing desperately to touch him, she rested her hand on his chest. The heat of him flowed into her palm and rushed to her pounding heart. He reacted spontaneously. Groaning, he reached for her, fitting her against him. Then he kissed her with a tenderness that rocked her. He tasted of rain and musk and desperation.

The threat of permanent separation gave a frantic edge to their clandestine tryst. Drunk with the taste of her lips, Damian kissed her again and again, binding them together from hips to chest. If this was the last time they would love, Damian wanted to savor it. Aware, however, that being found with Elissa could prove disastrous for both of them, he reluctantly broke off the kiss.

"I want to love you, sweeting. Give me this memory to take with me when we part."

"Aye, Damian, I want that, too. I love you so much. No matter where you are or where I am, we will still be one in mind and soul."

Expressing emotion was difficult for Damian, especially when he was mired in hopelessness, surrounded by it, consumed in it. But he put every part of himself, heart, body, and soul, into his kiss. She tasted like ecstasy and felt like bliss. When her hands tugged at his clothing, he quickly shed them, breaking contact with her lips only when he bent to remove his boots and trousers.

"I've missed you," Damian whispered as he wrapped his arms tightly about her.

His hands slid over her bottom, gripping the rounded flesh beneath her nightdress, fitting her against him, his erection pressing hard against her lower belly. Dipping his head, he took one turgid nipple into his mouth, then the other, suckling each in turn, causing her hips to jerk against his in wanton abandon.

Murmuring hotly against her breast, he spread her thighs and slipped a finger inside her. She arched against the pressure, driving his finger deeper. His mouth descended slowly, kissing a trail of fire from her breasts to her woman's cleft, nibbling gently on the peak hidden in the damp cluster of curls between her legs. Propelled by the earthy taste and scent of her, his tongue circled slowly around the sensitive nub, while his finger flexed deeper inside her.

Her fingers clutched frantically at the back of his neck. "Please. Now, Damian. I want you now."

"Yes, now," Damian muttered, as his tongue found her heated center and dipped inside. He lashed and taunted mercilessly, anchoring her hips as she bucked against him. He continued his loving torment until he felt her stiffen and shatter in his arms.

Once her tremors stopped, he rolled away and

pulled her over him, easing her legs on either side of his hips. He rubbed his erection against her center, her damp heat anointing him with her essence. He groaned his approval when Elissa reached between them and guided him into place. He entered her slowly, at the same time raising his head to nibble at her swaying breasts. Sweat beaded his forehead as she pressed down on him, rising and plunging with a rhythm that set them both afire. He let her lead the way until he felt her sheath contract around him and she began to tremble, then he indulged his own raging need. Gripping her buttocks in his hands, he surged wetly into her one last time, pouring his passion inside her.

Her breath fragmented, Elissa rested her head against his shoulder and caressed his face with gentle fingertips. When Damian finally found the strength, he lifted her away and settled her into the curve of his body.

"I don't want to leave you, sweeting."

"I wish we could stay like this forever," she said on a shaky sigh. "Do you think we'll ever be together again?"

"If there is a God, we will."

Elissa remained silent for a long time. When she spoke, he heard the note of anxiety and cursed Kimbra for doing this to them.

"What about Mother and Lora? They won't be safe in your household with Kimbra as your wife."

"Trust me to keep them safe. I won't let Kimbra rule my household no matter how hard she tries. Your family will have the choice of remaining at Misterly or joining you at the convent."

A tense silence followed his words. "Is something wrong, Elissa?"

"Everything is wrong. I canna bear the thought of you making love to Kimbra. What we have together is special and not to be shared with anyone else."

"On those rare occasions I'm forced to do my duty, it will not even come close to what I feel when I make love to you." His eyes narrowed thoughtfully. "Perhaps I'll not bed her at all."

"Oh, Damian, I canna ask that of you. Donna make me that promise."

"Elissa, I . . ."

She touched his lips. "Nay. Make love to me again. 'Tis all I ask of you."

They came together again; their bittersweet passion was so intense, neither spoke for a long time afterward. When fingers of light poked through an overcast sky the color of wood smoke, Damian kissed Elissa one last time and reached for his clothes.

He dressed quickly in the predawn light, then sat down on the edge of the bed and kissed her tears away. "Don't cry, love. Promise you'll take care of yourself until we can be together again. If . . . when you leave the convent, and I'm sure you will, try to let me know where you'll be so I can find you."

"There is only one place I can go," Elissa said. "To my cousin Christy Macdonald at Glenmoor. She's wed to an Englishman, but they've been estranged since their marriage many years ago. If you hear that I left the convent, look for me at Glenmoor."

" 'Tis time," Damian said regretfully.

Elissa rose and pulled on her nightdress. "Be careful." She followed him to the window. An icy blast buffeted her as he swung open the shutters and placed a leg over the sill. He gave her another quick kiss, then disappeared. Elissa watched with trepidation as he lunged for the tree, grabbed onto a branch, and scampered down the trunk. When he reached the ground, he glanced up and blew her a kiss. Then he was gone.

Dashing away her tears, Elissa closed the shutters and returned to bed. Damian's scent still clung to the bedclothes; she shut her eyes and imagined he was still beside her, comforted by his lingering aroma and surrounded by his love. She must have dozed, for when she opened her eyes, fingers of weak sunlight were filtering through the window.

Elissa left the bed and washed the traces of Damian from her body. She had just finished dressing when Captain Harding arrived to unlock the door and escort her to the common room to break her fast.

Harding sat opposite her, his brow furrowed with concern as he searched her face. "Did you sleep poorly? You look tired."

"I'm fine, Captain, thank you. That looks good," she said as a serving maid placed a plate of eggs, kidneys, and fried potatoes in front of her.

"Take your time," Harding advised. "The food here is good, you should take advantage of it while you can."

During the exhausting days that followed, Elissa had many occasions to be grateful for Captain Harding's kindness. Whenever he became aware of her exhaustion, he called a halt to allow her to rest. When the biting wind or chilling rain was at its worst, he found them shelter, be it an inn, a private home, a simple shepherd's shack, or a tent hastily erected for her comfort. She did her best to conceal her bouts of morning nausea, but she knew Captain Harding had been aware of those times her stomach rebelled against food.

One day toward the end of their journey, Captain Harding fell in beside Elissa. "I've noticed your recurring illness upon arising each morning," he ventured. "Please forgive me for being presumptuous, but are you increasing, Lady Elissa?"

Elissa flushed but did not evade the question. "You're assumption is correct, Captain," Elissa said softly.

"Are you carrying your former husband's child?"

Elissa stiffened with indignation. "Are you suggesting I betrayed my husband?"

Harding immediately sought to make amends. "Forgive me. I would never accuse you of infidelity. The king was wrong to declare your marriage illegal. Please accept my apology for being a part of your suffering. I was but following orders. I wish I could help."

"You are a good man, Captain. You've helped by making this journey as painless as possible."

He raised her hand to his lips and kissed it. "You are a true lady."

Two days later they arrived at St. Mary by the Sea Convent, a stately structure poised on a cliff above a roiling ocean. The stone wall surrounding the imposing structure was formidable, but Elissa considered it merely a stepping stone to freedom.

Chapter 20

❦

Damian sat in his rented room, staring gloomily at the rain lashing against the window. Tomorrow was his wedding day. How could he wed Kimbra when Elissa was still so very much a part of him? She occupied his heart, his mind, and his soul. He vividly recalled the scent of her, the look of her, every small gesture she'd made. He'd have told the king and Kimbra to go to hell if he could have been certain Elissa wouldn't have been punished for his disobedience.

Bloody hell. Was there no justice in the world?

The resounding knock at his door barely registered until the pounding became too loud and persistent to ignore. Spitting out an oath, he opened it, stunned to see Jem, one of the men-at-arms he'd left behind at Misterly.

"Jem! Good God, man, come in. How did you find me? What happened to bring you to London?"

"I've been searching for you since I arrived yesterday," Jem said. "Luck brought me to the taproom below, where I ran into the men who accompanied you to London. They directed me here. There's trouble at Misterly, my lord.

"Tavis Gordon and his Highland outlaws stormed the keep. They broke through our defenses and gained control. Sir Richard sent me to London to find you when he realized we couldn't hold the fortress against Gordon's superior forces. We were outnumbered three to one. I barely escaped with my life."

His expression grim, Damian swung his cloak over his shoulders and headed out the door. "Tell the men in the taproom what you've just told me," Damian called over his shoulder. "Tell them to fetch the horses and be ready to leave London when I return."

Damian stormed into the palace and demanded an immediate audience with the king. He must have sounded desperate, for he was kept waiting but a moment before Lord Pelham appeared.

"Lord Clarendon, what is it now? His Majesty isn't to be bothered unless it's important."

"My business is most urgent, my lord," Damian said. "I just received word that Misterly has fallen to Tavis Gordon. I must return immediately."

"But your wedding . . ."

"The hell with my wedding! What is more important, preserving Misterly for the Crown, or marrying a woman I can scarcely abide?"

"We can't spare men to aid you right now. There's trouble on the Welsh border and the army has been sent to quell the uprising. Furthermore, France is threatening war again. We cannot spare men to send to Scotland."

"I have no need of the army. I can regain control of Misterly without outside help if I leave immediately."

"Hmmm. I must confer with His Majesty and Parliament first."

"I can't wait for Parliament to convene. You and His Majesty must decide now."

"Wait here while I consult with His Majesty."

Lord Pelham exited through a door leading to the king's private bedchamber. He returned a few minutes later with King George in tow.

"What is so important that you must disturb our nap?" the king whined.

Damian explained again why he must leave immediately for Misterly.

King George retreated into a thoughtful silence. After a lengthy pause, he said, "We cannot afford to lose Misterly to rebel forces, but Lord Pelham has informed me that we do not have the manpower to wage another war in Scotland."

"I don't need your soldiers," Damian argued. "What I do need is to leave London now, today."

"Impossible. Tomorrow is your wedding day."

"Do you want Gordon to gain control of Misterly and rally other Highlanders to his cause?"

"Nay. We cannot allow that to happen. Misterly is important to us. Can you guarantee success without our help?"

"Have I ever let you down, Sire? I have but one request."

"You want a boon?"

"Aye, I suppose you could call it that."

"What is it? More land? A more prestigious title?"

"Nay, nothing like that. All I ask is that you find another husband for Lady Kimbra."

"Lady Kimbra is an heiress," Lord Pelham reminded him.

"I know, but she is not the woman I want. I beg of you to reinstate my marriage to Elissa Fraser. 'Tis the only reward I ask for my loyalty."

"The Fraser woman is a Jacobite sympathizer," the king said.

"She is a woman whose father and brothers were butchered at Culloden. 'Tis true she doesn't like Englishmen, but can you blame her? As my wife, she will pose no threat to the Crown. This I promise you."

A suspenseful silence ensued as the king mulled over Damian's proposal.

"What say you, Lord Pelham?" the king asked.

"As you well know, Your Majesty, Misterly is important to us. Lord Clarendon is a man we can trust. If he wants the Scottish lass, I say, let him have her."

"Very well, so it shall be. Have two writs prepared, Lord Pelham—one reinstating the marriage of Lord Clarendon and Elissa Fraser, and another authorizing the release of the lady from the convent. But hear this, Clarendon: if you fail, all is lost to you." He waved Damian off. "You may return for the documents in one hour."

"I understand, Your Majesty," Damian said, barely containing his elation, "and I will send word of my success."

Damian bowed himself out of the Privy Chamber with undue haste. As luck would have it, he encountered Lady Kimbra in the hallway.

"Damian! How fortunate that I've run into you. You've been neglecting me." She tucked her arm beneath his. "Tomorrow can't come soon enough for me."

Damian removed her arm and backed away. "We are no longer betrothed, Kimbra. The king validated my marriage to Elissa."

Kimbra exploded in fury. "What! You're lying. His Majesty wouldn't do such a thing to me. Nay, I refuse to believe it."

" 'Tis true. Ask His Majesty if you don't believe me. Good-bye, Lady Kimbra. I wish you long life and happiness."

"Damn you, Clarendon! May you rot in hell. How dare you put me in this position! Court gossip will ruin me. I won't be able to show my face."

She was still shrieking as Damian walked away.

Two hours later, the documents tucked away in his pocket, Damian rode north from London through the pounding rain.

Elissa had been at the convent nearly a fortnight before she figured out a way to leave without the Reverend Mother's knowledge. Elissa didn't blame the Reverend Mother for adhering to the king's wishes where she was concerned, for the convent owed its very existence to the Hanover.

It didn't take Elissa long to learn that an old man named Freddie was the only male allowed inside the convent walls, though he never ventured inside the convent itself. If Freddie had a last name, no one seemed to know it. He slept above the stables, maintained the grounds, and drove the wagon to a nearby farm once a week for fresh milk and eggs. The gatekeeper, Sister Elizabeth, opened the gate for him early each Monday morning, and Elissa used that knowledge to plan her escape.

On the following Monday, Elissa awakened early,

donned her warmest clothes, and slipped away to the stables before morning Mass. She hid behind a bale of hay until Freddie arrived to hitch the horse to the wagon for his trip to town. She watched with bated breath as he went into the tack room for the harness. Once he was inside, she slammed the door shut and flung home the bolt.

"Sorry, Freddie," she called through the door. "I need the wagon more than you do."

"Is that you, Lady Elissa?" Freddie asked in a muffled voice.

"Aye, Freddie," Elissa said, reaching for Freddie's cloak and hat hanging on a nearby hook. "Tell the Mother Superior I'm sorry."

"Why don't you tell the Mother Superior yourself?" The feminine voice came from behind her and Elissa whirled, dismayed to find the Mother Superior standing behind her.

"Mother Superior! How did you know?"

"I didn't. I saw you leave the building and decided to follow. I suspected you'd attempt something like this one day." Her face softened. "Don't let me stop you."

Elissa went very still. "I donna understand."

"I don't suppose you do. England's king is not God. He may threaten, but in the end 'tis God's word we follow. I have prayed over your situation and searched my heart for an answer. You are not meant to take the veil." She peered closely at Elissa, her kindly eyes dropping to Elissa's stomach. "Is there something you wish to tell me, child?"

Elissa blanched. "How did you know that I'm carrying a bairn?"

"I merely suspected but was not sure. I also suspect God has something special in mind for you. Go with my blessing, my child. You need not fear the English monarch, for he will never be told that you no longer reside with us."

"How can I ever thank you?"

"By raising your child to love God," Mother Superior replied. "Now, quickly, pull on Freddie's cloak and hat and hunch your shoulders when you ride through the gate. I promise your absence will never be mentioned nor discussed by anyone dwelling within these walls."

Unable to believe her good fortune, Elissa quickly finished hitching the horse to the wagon, donned her disguise, and climbed onto the driver's bench. "I'll make sure the wagon is returned as soon as possible. I know how much you depend on it."

"Thank you," the Mother Superior said. "Go now, child, Sister Elizabeth is waiting to open the gate. May God protect you."

Elissa slapped the reins against the horse's rump and the animal plodded off. Once out of sight of the convent, she set a course for Misterly.

Darkness had descended when Elissa spied Misterly through a snowy mist that swirled down from a cloud-laden sky. Shivering, she pulled Freddie's woolen cloak closer about her, anxious now to see her mother and sister and bask before a warm fire while dining on Winifred's fine cooking.

Squinting through a curtain of snowflakes, Elissa made out the figures of the night patrol high up on the parapet and breathed a sigh of relief. Nothing appeared amiss. She thought it unlikely that anyone at Misterly had received word of Damian's marriage to Kimbra or her own banishment to the convent and she intended for everyone to know of the sacrifice Damian had made on her behalf. Then she would take her mother and sister to Glenmoor before Damian returned with his bride.

Elissa halted the wagon before the gate, waiting for someone to come out of the gatehouse to identify her. As she peered through the iron bars, a frisson of alarm crawled up her spine. Instinct warned her that something was wrong, but she had no idea what it could be.

She was enormously relieved when someone hailed her from the keep. Sir Richard? She waved her hand in response and waited for him to open the gate.

"Elissa?" a gruff voice asked. "Where did you come from?"

Did she detect a Scottish burr? Aye, that voice definitely *wasn't* Sir Richard's. To her knowledge, none of the men Damian had left behind were Scotsmen. And it didn't sound like one of her kinsmen. *Flee,* her inner voice warned. Unfortunately, she couldn't turn the horse and wagon fast enough. When she heard the gate being cranked open, she panicked and scrambled down from the wagon to flee on foot. Three men seized her before she'd taken her first step. She recognized Tavis Gordon immediately.

"Tavis! What are you doing here? Where are Sir Richard and the others? What have you done with Mama and Lora?"

"Bring her inside," Tavis ordered, ignoring her questions.

Elissa offered no resistance as she was hustled inside the keep, anxious to learn the fate of her family and the men Damian had left behind.

The great hall teemed with Gordons, and Elissa

feared the worst when she noted the absence of Damian's men. She brightened considerably when she saw Maggie racing toward her.

"Sweet Mother, you've returned," Maggie cried, hugging Elissa fiercely.

"What happened, Maggie?"

"The Gordons, that's what," Maggie hissed. "There were too many of them. Lord Damian's men were no match for the sheer numbers that scaled the walls and overran the keep. It happened shortly after Lord Damian left for London. What happened to ye? Where is Lord Damian?"

"Enough!" Tavis shouted. "Bring Elissa food and drink." Grasping Elissa's arm, he seated her at a table close to the hearth. "Sit down and warm yourself."

"What have you done with Damian's men?" Elissa demanded. "If you've harmed Mama or Lora, I'll never forgive you."

"Your family is fine," Tavis allowed. "I havena hurt them. As for the Demon Knight's men, they've been locked in the storeroom off the armory for the time being. 'Tis but the beginning, Elissa. I've rallied enough men to strike at the English garrison at Inverness. More displaced Highlanders will join us once they become aware of what I've accomplished. We will unite to bring the rightful ruler back from France and free Scotland from English oppression."

"Instigating another rebellion is sheer madness," Elissa warned. "Scotland is soaked with the blood of our clansmen; donna add to it."

"The time is ripe," Tavis raged. "Welshmen are occupying the English army along the border, and France is threatening war again. We'll succeed this time."

"Listen to me, Tavis. You'll lead your men to certain death."

Tavis glared at her. "What has happened to you, Elissa? Before the Demon Knight arrived, you lusted for English blood. What has he done to you?"

"I still donna like Englishmen, but I never lusted for blood. I lost too many loved ones to wish for another bloodbath. 'Tis over, Tavis. Leave Misterly before Damian learns what happened here. You know he'll return to reclaim what is his. You canna win. You're an outlaw with a price on your head."

"I know what I'm doing, lass. Tell me what happened to you after the soldiers took you to London."

"How did you know about that?"

"I had spies watching the fortress. Did you think I wouldna know what was happening here? Misterly should have been mine by right of marriage, and I'm not going to give it up."

"So you took advantage of Damian's absence and attacked."

"That I did," he boasted, "but you're evading the subject. How did you persuade the Hanover to let you return to Misterly?"

"I dinna," Elissa whispered, recalling with dread those horrible days in the Tower. "The king sent me to the Tower. I would have died there had Damian not pleaded for my life. He convinced the king to send me to the convent. I remained there but a fortnight before the opportunity to leave arose."

"Why did you come here? Not that I'm complaining," Tavis added. "You've always been mine, lass."

"I'm still Damian's wife. Where else would I go?" Telling Tavis that her marriage had been declared illegal served no purpose, Elissa decided.

"You're mine," Tavis snarled.

Maggie appeared with a plate of food, and Elissa began to eat while Tavis paced back and forth before the hearth. When she'd eaten her fill, she pushed away from the table. "Please excuse me, I'm exhausted."

Tavis gave her a leering smile that froze the blood in her veins. "Go find your bed, lass. I'll be up to join you later."

"You'll find my door locked," Elissa said with cool disdain. "Attempt to touch me and you'll lose whatever small control you have over my kinsmen. Burning their village was an act of cowardice and they donna trust you. The Frasers are not powerless. We have allies. You'll likely find yourself in the middle of a clan war if you violate me."

Elissa could see rage building inside Tavis and decided a hasty exit was wise. She saw Maggie hovering nearby and held out her hand. "Come, Maggie. Help ready me for bed."

Hand in hand they ascended the narrow staircase to the solar. "Have you seen Sir Richard?" Elissa whispered.

"Nay. I've been forbidden to visit the prisoners."

"Are they being given food and water?"

"Aye, just barely enough to keep them alive. What are we to do, Elissa?" Maggie asked worriedly.

"Donna fear, I have a plan. But I'll need the help of everyone loyal to me. Where is Nan?"

"She spoke out against Tavis and he banished her from the keep. He was afraid she'd put a spell on him. I heard she is living in that old hut in the forest."

Elissa knew exactly where to find the hut. It had been built above the exit to the secret tunnel. "Thank

God she's safe," Elissa said. "How are Mama and Lora?"

"Fine, though Lady Marianne is worried about Sir Brody. I wish we could help them."

"I donna think 'tis possible. What I hope to do is get Mama, Lora, and you, if you wish it, safely out of the fortress. Are either Dermot or Lachlan inside the keep?"

"Only Dermot. Lachlan is with his family in the village. The gate is kept closed. Tavis willna allow anyone to leave or enter without his permission."

"I hope Mama is still awake," Elissa said when they reached Marianne's chamber. Maggie opened the door and Elissa stepped inside. Marianne was sitting in a chair by the fire. She saw Elissa, gave a cry of gladness, and opened her arms to her daughter.

With tears streaming down her cheeks, Elissa fell to her knees and greeted her mother with kisses and hugs.

"What happened?" Marianne asked, dabbing her tears with a dainty handkerchief. "Did Damian convince the king to release you? Are you well? You look peaked. Where is Damian?"

Elissa took a deep breath and began to recount her tale, leaving out nothing but the depravations she'd suffered while imprisoned in the Tower. She didn't want to distress her mother now that her ordeal was over. Marianne interrupted at that point.

"Damian must have convinced the king to release you. I knew he would. He was that determined to gain your freedom. Where is he? I dinna hear sounds of battle below. He has retaken the keep, has he not? I've been so worried about Sir Brody."

"That's not exactly what happened, Mama," Elissa

explained. "The king refused Damian's plea on my behalf." She paused to dash away the tears spilling from her eyes. "Then the Hanover changed his mind and said he'd spare my life if Damian wed Lady Kimbra. The king had already declared our marriage illegal, so Damian agreed. But instead of letting me return home, the king sent me to St. Mary by the Sea Convent."

"Even I know those walls couldna hold you. I wish things could be different," she lamented. "Tavis Gordon controls the keep and we are his prisoners."

Elissa lowered her voice. "We're going to leave Misterly, Mama."

Marianne grew excited. "Can we do it? We'll need to be very careful. I wish Nan were here."

"Dermot is here, we can depend upon him to help. Tavis has informed me that he intends to share my bed, so we must leave before he grows impatient and breaks into my chamber."

"What about Sir Richard, Sir Brody, and the others?" Marianne asked.

"I'm sorry, Mama, but there is naught we can do for them without placing ourselves in danger. I know Damian will retaliate when he learns Tavis has gained control of the keep. We must trust him to find a way to free his men when he returns."

"Oh, Elissa," Maggie commiserated. "How sad for ye to lose Damian to Lady Kimbra. He must hate it as much as ye."

"Damian willna wed Lady Kimbra." Elissa whirled, surprised to find Lora standing in the doorway.

"I thought you were sleeping," Marianne said.

"I was, but something awakened me." She smiled

at Elissa. "I'm glad you're home, Lissa." She ran to Elissa and gave her a fierce hug. "I heard what Maggie said about Damian and Lady Kimbra, but it's not true. Nan said you and Damian would be together always, and that you would have his bairn."

Marianne's eyes widened. "Is it true, daughter? Are you carrying Damian's bairn?"

"Aye, but he doesna know yet."

"You must take good care of yourself, daughter," Marianne cautioned. "I understand why you are anxious to leave. Tavis is an angry man; one never knows when he'll explode or upon whom he will vent his rage."

"I canna go with you," Maggie maintained. "I'm sorry, Elissa, but I willna abandon Sir Richard. I'll leave you now, before you reveal your plan."

"Are you sure, Maggie?"

"Verra sure, Elissa. Take Dermot with ye."

"You must love Sir Richard very much," Elissa observed.

"Aye, 'tis why I canna bear to leave without him. How soon before ye go?"

"As soon as possible."

"May God go with ye, Elissa."

Damian reached Misterly on a frigid, windswept night. Though he shivered beneath his woolen cloak, he thanked God for the bitterly cold weather that kept his enemy safely tucked in their warm beds. Damian's horse danced beneath him as Jem rode up beside him.

"What are your instructions, my lord?"

"There's an underground tunnel leading from the keep to an outside exit concealed inside a hut in the forest. I'm going to enter the keep through the tunnel and assess the situation," Damian explained. "You and the other three men can follow after a short interval."

Damian led the way to a small dilapidated hut deep in the forest. Hidden by gorse and brush, it was old and looked as if it had been neglected for many years. When Damian had explored the tunnel after Elissa's escape, he had found the exit.

Damian dismounted a short distance from the hut and approached warily, surprised to see a light shining through slits in the boarded up window. He drew his pistol and reached for the door handle. The door opened abruptly. Damian tensed, then relaxed when he recognized the bent figure standing in a pool of lamplight.

"Nan! Bloody hell, woman! What are you doing here?"

"Waiting for ye," Nan said. "Ye must rescue our lass and rid the keep of Gordons."

Damian gave her a strange look. "Elissa is at the convent, not inside the keep."

"Believe me, me lord, Elissa is inside the keep," Nan maintained. "She dinna know Tavis had control of Misterly until she was inside."

"What are you doing here?"

"I was turned out of the keep with naught but the clothes on me back. Tavis fears me, as well he should, and I've been living here ever since. 'Tisn't so bad. The villagers provide me with everything I need. But ye must hurry," she warned, "while darkness is yer ally."

Damian entered the hut, went straightaway to the cot sitting in a corner, and moved it so he could get to

the trap door concealed in the floor beneath. He
brushed away the coating of dirt and lifted the door
by its metal ring.

"Ye'll need a light," Nan said, handing him the
lantern.

Damian accepted the lantern, nodded his thanks,
and lowered himself through the opening. His feet
found the ladder and he descended to the tunnel
floor, cautiously making his way along the narrow
passage. He had reached a sharp curve at the
halfway mark when he heard the sound of voices
echoing through the tunnel. Someone was ahead of
him, coming his way! More than one, he guessed
from the hushed whispers. He doused the lantern
and flattened himself against the wall, tense, waiting. Had Gordon found the tunnel?

A circle of light advanced toward him, widening
as it drew closer. He heard disembodied voices
speaking in hushed tones and squinted through the
murky darkness, trying to identify the approaching
figures. Sweat popped up on his forehead as he tried
to decide whether or not to retreat before he was discovered. Then a face suddenly appeared in the glow
of light and Damian nearly collapsed with relief.
Dermot was slowly advancing down the passageway, followed closely by Lady Marianne, Lora, and
Elissa. A smile stretched his lips. He should have
known his resourceful Elissa would find a way out
of a dangerous situation on her own.

Damian stepped into the circle of light. "Good
evening. 'Tis a perfect night for a stroll."

"Damian!" Elissa stumbled forward, one hand
clutching her throat, her eyes wide with disbelief. "Is
that you?"

"Aye, love, who else would crawl beneath the earth to save his beloved and discover she has rescued herself?"

"How did you know I was at Misterly? Where is Kimbra?"

"Kimbra is out of our lives for good. I'll explain everything later. Nan was at the hut when I arrived. She told me you were inside the keep."

"I left the convent with the Reverend Mother's help and returned to Misterly for Mama and Lora," Elissa said, "but I had no idea Tavis had gained control of the keep. He wanted me to stay and share his bed but I dinna want that. I knew I couldna hold him off for long, so I enlisted Dermot's help and made plans to leave through the tunnel. We chose tonight because the bitter cold weather made everyone eager to seek the warmth of their beds instead of lingering in the hall."

Damian's heart swelled with pride. No one but Elissa could manage such a brave feat. "You are a wonder, love. Thank God for your courage. Are my men still alive?"

"Aye, they're alive."

"Where are they?"

"I know where they are, yer lordship," Dermot spoke up. "Send the womenfolk on their way and I'll show ye. Are ye alone?"

"Nay. The men who accompanied me to London will follow shortly."

"Let me come with you," Elissa pleaded. "I can help."

"Take your mother and sister to safety, love," Damian said. "Wait inside the hut with Nan until I send for you."

"Who will protect your back?" Elissa asked. "You are outnumbered. You need me."

"Surprise is on our side. Gordon doesn't know about the tunnel and won't be looking for an attack on a night such as this."

"Damian, let me . . ."

"Elissa, obey me in this. I won't be able to concentrate knowing you're inside the keep. Don't you know I love you?"

"You love me?"

"More than my life. I've known it for a long time but couldn't find the words to express what's in my heart. The thought of losing you gave me the courage to unburden my soul."

"Oh, Damian, I love you, too, but feared you dinna return my feelings."

"I'm sorry it took so long. Please keep yourself safe for me, love. Please go now, and take your mother and sister with you."

"You'll let me know when I can return?"

"The very moment." She nodded and took the lantern from Dermot. Damian touched her shoulder and turned her toward him. "Elissa, I love you," he declared, then kissed her.

Chapter 21

❦❦❦

"**W**e're nearly at the end of the tunnel," Dermot said. "Sir Richard and the others are confined in the storeroom off the armory."

"I know the room," Damian replied. " 'Tis a large, windowless chamber that the previous lord of Misterly used as a temporary jail. If I recall correctly, it has a wooden bar that slides into place on the outside. Is the chamber guarded?"

"Aye, but the cell was rarely used by Lord Alpin. There is a guard, but he'll likely be asleep. Here we are, me lord," Dermot hissed as he doused the lantern and eased the door open.

Damian stepped past Dermot and glanced into the hall. He saw nothing but flames dancing in the hearth and an empty chamber filled with shadows. He stepped out of the tunnel but remained concealed beneath the staircase until Dermot joined him.

"Wait here for Jem and the others," Damian ordered. "I'm going to free Sir Richard and the rest of my men. I won't be long."

Damian crept through the hall to the narrow stone steps leading down to the armory. Flattening himself against the wall, he slowly descended the stairs. When he reached the bottom, he peered around the corner into the chamber used to store ancient armor and more modern weapons used by the fortress guards. A lantern hanging from the ceiling revealed a man stretched out on a bench, apparently sound asleep. Moving stealthily, Damian rendered him unconscious with a quick rap on the head with his pistol butt.

Then he turned his attention to the storeroom where his men were confined. It took but a moment to lift the bar and throw the door wide.

"You're free. Come out," Damian called through the opening.

Sir Richard stepped out, squinting against the sudden glare of light. "Is that you, Damian? Bloody hell, man, you're the last person I expected to see. How did you get into the keep?"

A stream of men surged out of the storeroom. "I'll explain later. Is everyone all right?"

"More or less," Richard allowed. "Thank God you came when you did. We're ready and eager to reclaim the keep."

"Arm yourselves first," Damian said as he chose a sword for himself. "Select your weapons from the armory and do it quietly, lest we rouse the Gordons from their sleep."

One man dragged the limp guard into the storeroom and secured the door while the others chose the weapons that suited them best.

"We're ready," Sir Richard said.

Sir Brody fell into step beside Damian. "I'm worried about Lady Marianne and Lora. They could be in danger."

"They're no longer in the keep," Damian replied. "Elissa took them to safety."

"Elissa was here?" Sir Richard said. "I had no idea. What about Maggie? Did she follow Elissa and the others to safety?"

"I didn't see Maggie, Dickon. She wasn't with Elissa."

Damian reached the top landing and led his men into the deserted hall. Dermot stepped from the shadows. Then Jem and the men who had followed Damian through the tunnel revealed themselves.

"Ye met with success," Dermot greeted. "I hope yer men fared well."

"Aye. They are all accounted for. Gather close for your orders. Jem, take two men up to the parapets and disable the guards. No killing unless it's absolutely necessary."

"Aye, my lord," Jem said, as he and two men broke away from the group and melted into the shadows.

"Sir Brody, I assume there are guards in the courtyard as well as in the gatehouse," Damian continued. "Take two men with you. You know what to do."

"Aye, my lord," Brody acknowledged.

"Dickon, I'm assigning you the most dangerous job of all. How many Gordons are there in the keep?"

"At least fifty men," Dickon recalled. "But I overheard two guards talking, and one remarked that half of them returned to their homes and families. Those who remained are billeted in the barracks."

Damian digested this information. "Take the remaining men to the barracks, Dickon. You're to subdue the enemy and confine them in the storeroom until I can deal with them. Remember what I said about bloodshed. Avoid it if you can."

"Consider it done, Damian. I assume you're going after the Gordon chieftain yourself."

"Aye." He turned to Dermot. "Where will I find the bastard?"

"He's taken yer chamber for himself," Dermot replied. "I'll go with ye."

"Nay. Find Maggie. Make sure she stays in the solar." Damian wanted neither the old man nor Maggie hurt.

"Thank you for thinking of Maggie," Dickon whispered as he moved off toward the barracks.

Grim-faced with determination, Damian crossed the hall and ascended the stairs to the tower. He paused before the chamber door, withdrew his sword with one hand, turned the knob with the other, and pushed the door open. The whisper of sound was barely audible but it evoked an immediate response from Tavis Gordon. He leaped from the bed, his naked form lithe and nimble in the glow of firelight as he reached for his sword resting against the wall.

"How did you get in here?" Gordon roared.

"I sprouted wings and flew," Damian taunted. "Surrender, Gordon. My men have gained control of the keep."

"I donna believe you," Gordon spat, thrusting his sword at Damian.

Damian easily evaded the sharp point and brought up his own sword to defend himself. "Even as we speak my men are rounding up your clansmen and locking them away for safekeeping. You're on your own, Gordon, I strongly advise you to lay down your sword."

"Never!" Gordon rasped. "You stole my woman. Both Elissa and Misterly should be mine. Alpin Fraser promised them to me. I'll kill you!"

Raising the sword in both hands, Gordon slashed viciously at Damian, unaware that he lacked Damian's skill as a swordsman. Damian laughed at Gordon's clumsy efforts and easily deflected the blade. Then he went on the offensive, feinting and thrusting until Gordon was backed into a corner. Gordon hacked furiously at Damian, but he must have realized defeat was at hand, for he began screaming, "A Gordon! A Gordon!"

"No one will come to your aid, Gordon. Toss down your sword before I'm forced to kill you."

"Not if I kill you first, Englishman!"

Damian thrust and feinted as he dodged and pirouetted to avoid the bite of Gordon's sword. Metal clashed against metal again and again as the blades met in a duel of strength. Gordon's naked body was streaked with blood, and a lucky thrust had nicked Damian's shoulder, but neither man acknowledged his wounds. Tiring of the game, Damian deftly brought the swordplay to its inevitable end.

Damian's next move came so fast Gordon failed to react quickly enough. Gordon's sword flew out of his hand at the same time the tip of Damian's blade pressed against a vulnerable spot on Gordon's neck.

"Go ahead, bastard, kill me!" Gordon challenged.

"That would be too easy," Damian bit out. "Get dressed."

A noise at the door distracted Damian and he turned slightly, spitting out a curse when he saw Elissa standing in the opening. "What in bloody hell are you doing here?"

"I had to come. I couldn't bear not knowing what was going on. What if you were hurt?"

The brief distraction gave Gordon a window of opportunity. He picked up his sword and flung it at Damian. Instinctively, Damian ducked as the blade whizzed over his head. Elissa screamed as the tip of the sword pierced through her sleeve and lodged in the doorjamb. His heart pounding with dread, Damian rushed to her side, fearing that she'd been seriously wounded.

Suddenly he was pushed aside and nearly trampled upon as Gordon fled past him and out the door. Concerned about Elissa, Damian made no move to stop him. Grasping the hilt of Gordon's sword, he pulled it out of the doorjamb and tossed it aside, relieved when no blood stained the blade.

"Are you hurt, love?" he asked, pulling her into his arms.

"Nay, the blade dinna touch my flesh."

He grasped her shoulders and pulled her against him. "Thank God. I ought to give you a good thrashing for disobeying me, but I'd much rather kiss you." Reluctantly he released her. "But it will have to wait. I have unfinished business with Gordon. Stay here. This time do as I say."

Just as he turned away, an ungodly shriek resonated up the staircase, raising the hair on the back of his neck. Motioning for Elissa to remain behind, he sped along the passageway and down the treacherous stone steps. When he reached the bottom landing, he saw Dermot bending over a figure sprawled limply at their feet.

"Gordon?" he asked, kneeling to examine the body.

"Aye," Dermot said. "Broke his neck. Are ye and Elissa all right? I saw her follow ye up to the tower."

"I'm fine," Elissa said from behind Damian.

Damian swiveled around and glared at her. "I thought I told you to stay where you were."

"Whenever did I do what you asked?" she said pertly. "Is that Tavis? Is he dead?"

"Aye to both questions. I'm sorry, love, I never intended to kill him."

"Don't be sorry, Damian. Tavis lost my respect long ago. Mama was against the marriage from the beginning; it was Papa who wanted it. Tavis and I both hated the English, but we differed in that I wanted no more bloodshed. There has been enough to last a lifetime. What Tavis planned could have destroyed us."

"His days of planning treason are over," Damian said, rising when he saw Jem striding toward him.

"The guards on the parapet are no longer a threat to us," Jem reported.

Before Damian could answer, Sir Richard and Sir Brody returned from their missions.

"Gordon's men have been rounded up and confined in the storeroom," Sir Richard said.

"Did they put up much of a fight?"

"Nay. It was a bloodless coup. They surrendered without a struggle when we awakened them."

"The guards in the courtyard threw down their arms when they saw us, and we had to awaken the gatekeeper so he could surrender," Sir Brody reported.

"Is that the Gordon chieftain?" Richard asked, prodding Gordon's lifeless body with his toe. "Is he dead?"

"Aye," Damian said. "He fell down the stairs and broke his neck."

"Good riddance," Richard said. "It looks as if Misterly is yours again. Have you seen Maggie?"

"I left Maggie in the solar," Dermot said.

"I'll fetch Lady Marianne and Lora if you tell me where to find them," Sir Brody offered.

"I'll show him the way," Dermot said. Damian nodded and the two men departed.

"What shall we do with Gordon?" Sir Richard asked.

"Take his body to the tool shed for now. The rest of you are free to seek your beds. I expect no further trouble."

"Is it really over, Damian?" Elissa asked. "Has the king truly given his blessing to our marriage?"

" 'Tis over, sweeting." He held out his hand. "Shall we go to bed?"

Hand in hand they climbed the stairs to Elissa's bedchamber. It was nearly dawn; the eastern sky was turning from black to gray as Damian helped Elissa undress. Then he swept her into his arms, carried her to their bed, and tucked her beneath the quilt. He felt her gaze following him as he stripped off his clothes and washed the blood from his body.

"You're hurt!" Elissa exclaimed.

" 'Tis just a nick."

"Let me bandage it."

"No need. It's already stopped bleeding."

Sighing with pleasure, he joined her in bed and gathered her in his embrace.

Elissa snuggled against him. "I feared we'd never be together like this again."

"So did I, my love."

"Make love to me, Damian."

"Are you sure? You must be exhausted."

"Not too exhausted to make love with my husband."

With mouth, hands and tongue, he kissed, caressed, and stroked her to unbridled passion, until her body became a living flame in his arms. They loved, rested, loved again, then finally settled down to sleep.

Suddenly Elissa reared up on her elbow.

"Damian! Wake up!"

"I don't think I can rise to the occasion again for at least an hour," Damian murmured sleepily.

"Please, Damian. This is important."

"Can't it wait? We're both exhausted."

"I suppose, but I thought you'd want to know that I'm carrying your bairn."

"Hmmm, that's nice."

Disappointed by Damian's reaction, Elissa sighed and lay back down. Suddenly he jolted upright. "What did you say?"

"I'm going to have your bairn."

"Why didn't you say so?"

"I just did. You're right, go to sleep. This can wait for another time."

"Like hell! How long have you known?"

"I suspected before I was arrested and taken to London."

His arms came around her and she felt him shaking as he held her against him. " 'Tis a miracle you didn't lose the babe, after what you've been through."

"Are you pleased?"

"Ecstatic. We'll found a dynasty for Misterly." He grew thoughtful. "Nan was right, wasn't she?"

"Aye, but I dinna want to believe her. She said we'd have a son."

"Son or daughter, it makes little difference. I'm sure this won't be the last child we make together. I love you, Elissa. I was a fool not to realize it. Can you forgive me for treating you the way I did?"

"Aye, my love. I wasn't exactly reticent in voicing my hatred for Englishmen. Who would have thought the Demon Knight had a soft heart?"

"I didn't know it myself until a Highland lass came into my life. You found something inside me I had no idea existed."

Elissa sighed dreamily. "And I found my one true love."

They slept through most of the day, finally emerging from their chamber to partake of the evening meal. Their appearance was cause for celebration, and everyone lifted their cups to them in salute. Marianne and Lora's greeting was no less exuberant. Everyone began to talk at once as the meal was served and consumed with gusto. After he had eaten his fill, Damian asked Sir Richard to bring the prisoners to the hall.

"What are you going to do with them?" Elissa asked.

"Send them to London, I suppose."

"Must you? Without Tavis stirring up trouble, the Gordons will present no further danger to England."

Damian stared at her. "Are you suggesting that I release them?"

"Aye. Most of the men have families to support and it hasn't been easy for them. Most of them live in caves or crude huts unfit for habitation. Ask the men to swear fealty to you and release them."

Damian grew thoughtful. "You ask too much of me, Elissa."

"Please, just talk to them. If they prove difficult, send them to London, but give them a chance to redeem themselves."

"You are very forgiving, my love."

"Please, Damian, try to make peace with the Gordons for my sake. They've lost their chieftain, the rebellion has been nipped in the bud."

Sir Richard returned with the prisoners before Damian could reply to Elissa's plea.

"You have been declared outlaws," Damian told the sullen prisoners. "If I send you to London, 'tis likely you'll be sent to the gallows. Have you anything to say for yourselves?"

The Gordon men shifted uncomfortably, then one man stepped forward. "We throw ourselves on yer mercy, my lord. Our chieftain is dead; there is none among us who wishes to carry on what he began. We all have families to feed and clothe. There is never enough food to go around and our children are starving."

Damian listened intently. Then he turned to Elissa. "What say you, wife?"

Elissa's heart leaped with joy. Was Damian really going to let her decide these men's fates? "I'm inclined toward leniency," she said, "but that is for my husband to decide. How many of you would be willing to swear fealty to the Lord of Misterly?"

A long pause ensued, then one by one, each man

dropped to his knee before Damian. Damian rose, spread his arms wide, and said, "So be it. It would please my wife if you brought your wives and children down from the mountains and made your homes in the village. Misterly's lands are vast. There is always need for shepherds and farmers. I will provide the building materials for cottages to shelter your families."

A hush fell over the assembly. Then the cheering began. Damian raised his hand for silence. "You have my permission to take Tavis Gordon's body to his family for burial and to return to Misterly with your kin. Jem, see to the arrangements."

"Thank you, Damian," Elissa whispered. "I know you won't be sorry."

After the Gordons filed out, Sir Richard stepped forward and cleared his throat. "Damian, may I have a word with you?"

"Certainly, Dickon, what is it?"

"Well, I've been thinking about this for some time." His gaze found Maggie and he held out his hand. Smiling, she walked to him and placed her hand in his. "Maggie and I would like your permission to wed."

Elissa jumped to her feet. "Oh, Maggie, I'm so happy for you. I know how much you love Sir Richard."

"Am I to assume this is a love match?" Damian drawled.

Sir Richard smiled at a blushing Maggie. "I never thought it would happen, but aye, 'tis a love match."

"Then you have my approval," Damian beamed. "When shall we hold the wedding?"

"As soon as . . ."

"Wait," Sir Brody interrupted, sending Marianne a tender look. "Lady Marianne and I would like to make it a double wedding."

A startled look crossed Damian's face. "Lady Marianne, do you wish to wed Sir Brody?"

Lady Marianne smiled shyly. "If it's all right with you and my daughter, my lord."

"Mama! I had no idea you were contemplating marriage," Elissa cried. "Of course it's all right, and I'm sure Damian agrees."

"We'll make it a grand celebration," Damian said. " 'Tis just what we need to bring the clans together again in peaceful coexistence."

"What about me?" Lora asked plaintively.

Damian laughed. "You're too young to wed, but I promise you'll have the finest husband in the land when you're ready."

"You can help me plan the weddings," Elissa offered.

That seemed to placate Lora, for she threw her arms around Elissa and gave her a fierce hug.

"We're a family now, aren't we, Damian?" she asked shyly.

Damian planted a kiss on her forehead. "Aye, little one. We are indeed a family."

Suddenly Nan stood and raised her cup in a toast. "Drink up, all ye braw laddies and bonny lassies. Drink to the new Lord of Misterly and his lady. Drink to the heir our lass carries, and to the peace and prosperity his birth will bring."

"Amen," Damian said, raising his cup and drinking deeply.

Everyone stood and saluted the Lord and Lady of Misterly.

Damian grinned at Elissa, then pulled her into his lap and kissed her soundly, passionately. Everyone laughed and cheered as Damian swept her up and carried her away. But the lovers heard nothing but the pounding of their hearts and saw nothing but the love shining in each other's eyes.

"I love you, my glorious Highland lassie," he whispered as he held her close to his heart.

"And I love you, my fierce Demon Knight."

~ *Coming next month . . .* ~

Avon Romantic Treasure
Claiming the Highlander by Kinley MacGregor

To end a long-running feud proud Maggie convinces her clan's women to deny their men *everything*. But warrior Braden MacAllister might get her to change her stubborn mind . . .

Avon Contemporary Romance
The Dixie Belle's Guide to Love by Luanne Jones

What's an ex-beauty princess to do when she suddenly finds herself without a man? Why, eat all the cookies she can and loll about the house in a comfy pair of sweatpants . . . until the sexiest man in town comes knocking at her door.

Avon Romance
The MacKenzies: Jared by Ana Leigh

The MacKenzies are a proud breed of men and women—as wild and untamed as the land they call home. Now, meet Jared, the sexiest, strongest of them all . . .

The Lily and the Sword by Sara Bennett

Lily finds herself married to her mortal enemy, Radulf, the King's Sword, never dreaming that she could fall in love with such a man . . .